FLAME GAME . . .

Nothing prepared me for the sight that met me when I rushed into the hall. Men ran in every direction, their shouts inaudible against the force of the prodigious wind blasting down the chimney and pouring out of the hearth, bearing a huge plume of flames before it. This terrible mass of fire shot straight to the count's great curtained bed and encircled it in an impenetrable whirlwind of flames.

As I stared in horror, a black form appeared within the terrible whirlwind of fire and lurched halfway out of the flames, then fell to the floor. It was Bruno. "I couldn't—get—to the Count," he gasped through blackened lips. "They've got to—save him."

Men staggered in carrying a huge tub of water, which they emptied into the flames around Count Galoran's burning bed. But the water vanished into steam without the slightest effect. I concentrated with my inner eye. Yes, there could be no doubt. The wall of flames vibrated with magic.

There was but one thing to be done, and it must be done instantly....

BAEN BOOKS by C. DALE BRITTAIN

Wizard of Yurt Novels
A Bad Spell in Yurt
The Wood Nymph and the Cranky Saint
Mage Quest
The Witch and the Cathedral
Daughter of Magic

Voima

Count Scar
(with Robert A. Bouchard)

C. DALE BRITTAIN

Count Scar

ROBERT A. BOUCHARD

COUNT SCAR

Copyright © 1997 by C. Dale Brittain & Robert A. Bouchard

A Baen Books Original

Baen Publishing Enterprises
P.O. Box 1403
Riverdale, NY 10471

ISBN: 0-671-87801-8

Cover art by Darrell K. Sweet

First printing, September 1997

Distributed by Simon & Schuster
1230 Avenue of the Americas
New York, NY 10020

Printed in the United States of America

Chapter One ~ Galoran

1

Snow had fallen steadily all day, muffling the sounds of hooves. As we sat around a blazing hearth, celebrating New Year's, we did not even realize anyone had arrived until the guards brought them into the hall: the messengers come to tell me I was going to be count.

Everything was as abruptly transformed as if the wintry night had been ripped away to reveal the summer sun. A few minutes ago I had been staring unseeing into my wine glass, thinking that the purposeless and fruitless year just over was about to be replaced by another equally purposeless, but now in an instant possibilities and opportunities waited on every hand. I was too startled at first to show any emotion at all.

My nephews were the most excited. "A count! With your own county! Can we come visit you, Uncle? Is it as good as being emperor?"

My older brother the archduke, far more exalted than any count, tried his best not to seem patronizing. "A place of your own at last, Galoran!" he said, resting his elbows benevolently on the trestle table before him. Was there the slightest emphasis on "at last"? "Well, after all your service to the emperor and to me, God knows you deserve it."

His wife, my sister-in-law, was less successful in the sincerity of her congratulations. "Isn't that the little county up in the mountains your grandfather came from originally?

1

I understand he was delighted to be able to come north and become an archduke." She paused to finish delicately biting the flesh from a roasted bird's wing. "I'm sure you'll be glad to be down there, however, where you won't always have to wonder if you're in our way."

The messengers had pulled off their travel cloaks and stamped the snow from their boots and now warmed their hands by the fire. Their skin was darker than anyone's around here, and their eyes black and shadowed. They watched me as though intensely interested, although I had the least to say of anybody. The bouteillier brought them hot mulled wine, and they continued to observe me as they sipped it.

My niece had retreated shyly behind her mother when they first came in, but now she darted across the rush-strewn floor and threw herself into my lap. "Are you really going away, Uncle Galoran?"

There were tears at the corners of her eyes, but as I bounced her on my knee I felt a wash of pure joy pour over me. A county of my own, land and income of my own, a castle and knights to direct as I pleased. No more sharp comments from a sister-in-law who would clearly have preferred that I never existed, no more landless service to an older brother whose constant and rather forced good-humor toward me seemed intended to make it seem that he had forgotten what neither he nor I could ever forget.

And maybe as a count in the south, something more than a scarred and landless man, I would find women, well-bred and elegant women, who would tolerate my attentions. After all, I tried to persuade myself, plenty of men came back from the wars every year with much more disfiguring scars than mine.

"I'll miss you, Gertrude," I told my niece, meaning it but unable to keep from smiling. Her blond braids had worked out from under her little bonnet as I bounced her. "Yes, I shall have to go away."

She reached up then and touched the left side of my face, the large reddish patch whose texture was more like leather than human skin, where the beard would never grow. Gertrude's brothers had each in turn asked about my face when they had first reached the age of wondering about the adults around them, rather than simply accepting whatever they had found in the world when they came into it. Gertrude had never asked, but then she was still very young.

"If you're leaving, Uncle Galoran, I want to ask you something first. Why does your face look like this? And," turning in the circle of the arm that held her, "your hand?"

"It's an old burn," I said easily, as I had said before to my nephews. "From a fire a long time ago, when I wasn't much more than a boy. Did you know you're named for someone who used to live here in this castle," I added as though irrelevantly, "someone also named Gertrude? Your parents will tell you about her some time when you're older."

For a second my brother Guibert looked toward me, but he cast his eyes down before they met mine.

"Does it hurt?" asked Gertrude with grave concern.

"Not now. It hurt horribly once, of course—and watch how you stand on my legs, or you will hurt me even more!" I laughed as I seated her again on my lap. "It's never kept your old uncle from being a good fighting man, as my years in the emperor's service proved."

"You're not so *very* old, Uncle," she protested.

But one of the messengers interrupted before I could answer. "You are the emperor's sworn man?"

"Of course," I said, surprised at the note in his voice. "I fought up and down the Empire for five years as his liege man."

The messengers conferred for a moment in lowered voices. I had already noticed that they had a trace of an accent, and what they spoke now did not sound like any language I knew. I felt a brief moment of doubt. In spite of the great fire on the hearth, in spite of the warm lump of Gertrude—shy again—on my lap, my brother's hall was chill on this cold night, and drafts found their way through the carpeting covering the narrow windows. Would the men who were going to be under my command even understand the orders I gave them?

"You see, my lord," said a messenger, and it took me a second to realize that he was addressing me and not my brother, "Duke Argave expects all the counts of the region to swear liege homage to *him*. His honor demands it. But down in the south the Empire is distant enough that it may not matter that you once took an oath to someone else."

And the emperor was unlikely ever to hear about it, or care if he did. Five years in his service was all he wanted before taking on a fresh crop of noble fighting men to captain his soldiers.

"Duke Argave?" I repeated aloud. I realized I knew virtually nothing about the county which I had just inherited. My grandfather, himself a younger brother, had come from there originally, but he had already been old when I knew him, and I had had scarce time as a boy for an old man's stories. That had been, of course, before the fire.

"We are the duke's men. Did you not hear us say so? It was he who chose you."

I almost expected my brother to make some jovial comment about he and Duke Argave being fellow dukes, but for once Guibert was silent. They might once have met at the royal court, however; when I had him alone I would have to ask.

"There was a choice?" I asked the messengers slowly. "I was not the only possible heir?"

"The countess's death being so sudden, of course, and with some saying—" The messengers had been suave and assured, but now their assurance cracked. "But here," pressing a sealed letter into my hand. "You can read about it yourself."

I sent Gertrude back to her mother. My sister-in-law had started laughing and talking to her boys again as they ate, as though uninterested in my county. Guibert, however, was not even pretending not to listen.

The parchment roll was sealed with red wax, impressed with the image of a man on horseback. Around the image, very tiny, were the words, *Argavius dux.* I broke the seal with my thumb and unrolled it slowly.

My new liege lord the duke might have men who spoke a language I couldn't understand, but his chancellor wrote a fair hand. The letter started with flowery invocations of the triune God, told me that it was an honor to be the first to address me by my new title of Count, and then got down to the hard details.

"The countess's sudden death left the county without a head at the worst possible time," Duke Argave told me, "just when there are rumblings from those despicable fools over the border, and rumors that the heretics may be spreading their spew again, not just back in the mountains but in the towns themselves." I had no idea what he was talking about. "And a second death so soon after the first makes it even worse. Her husband, of course, acts as though it has never occurred to him that doubt might fall upon him, and was outraged when he learned I would not accept him as successor. When you have met him, I would like to learn your opinion of him. I think you can guess mine."

I looked toward the fire, not seeing it. There were suspicious circumstances, then, surrounding the death of my predecessor the countess, my own second cousin, a woman I had never even met. And not all of my new subjects might welcome me gladly since there was apparently another claimant to the county. Visions of lying back in the warm, soft grass under the olive trees, several silk-robed maidens arrayed around me, faded before I could even begin to enjoy them. I knew how to talk to children and how to talk to soldiers, not to politicians and learned men of law. I took a deep breath. It appeared I would be learning soon. "You can't be harder to face than the emperor's enemies—or for that matter the emperor himself," I muttered to the distant duke and turned back to his letter.

"My messengers will escort you to your new home," Duke Argave concluded. "Make whatever preparations you may need and come as quickly as you may. I shall expect you each day I do not see you." He had drawn a monogram for his signature, a tall "A" with the other letters dangling off it, in a heavy hand that left a wider line from the quill than his chancellor's.

I leaned back, slowly starting to smile again. The duke with his insinuations might have meant a dozen things, but by the time I had learned what he really believed I would be lord of my own castle.

The snow fell heavily that night and kept the roads closed for the best part of a week, and I spent the time making my preparations, but I could have done them all in a single day. For thirty years I had been a son of this castle, and yet how little effort there seemed now in preparing to leave it behind me.

When I had first gone off to the imperial court, as a little boy who had scarcely begun to trace his letters on a wax tablet, I remembered my mother and her ladies spending frantic weeks in the preparation of my clothes and supplies. When I had gone again to the emperor's court, this time as a young man sworn to fight in his service, there had been months spent in readying the armor, the weapons, and the warhorses, not just for me but for the knights who would follow my banner. Both my parents had been gone by then to the convent in the next valley— my father to the mausoleum, my mother to pray among the nuns for another two years yet—but my brother Guibert had followed all my preparations closely, grudging, I knew, everything I spent because it all came from his budget, but refusing to say that he begrudged it.

Now there was little to do but pack a few warm clothes for the journey—I would buy new in the south, where I had heard they had recently started wearing shoes with long pointed toes—polish my armor, and sharpen the excellent sword I had received from the emperor's hands. The messengers had brought spare horses with them, distrusting northern steeds, and everything else could wait until I reached my county. I would take nothing this time from Guibert. It was easy now to leave the castle because it was no longer my home. It was his alone and his sharp-voiced wife's.

Only one person from here would accompany me, Bruno, the old soldier who had fought under me and who had asked the emperor to release him to follow me home when I left imperial service. Too stiff in the joints to be much of a warrior any more, he liked to think of himself as my bodyguard, but I thought of him as my friend.

"No more biting winter winds, Captain," he said with relish, "once we live among the olive trees down in the south."

Guibert took me aside the evening we finally decided that the weather had cleared enough to start in the morning. For a moment I wondered if he was going to talk at last about Gertrude, but of course he did not. "For your journey," he said gruffly, pushing a small jingling pouch into my hand.

I accepted it with a nod and without counting it. The money the emperor had given me when I left his service was long gone, and while I trusted the duke's messengers would have enough for the journey, something extra was never amiss.

"I met this Duke Argave once," Guibert said, "when we were both at the royal court at the same time." Over at this edge of the kingdom we served the emperor more than the king, but my brother was liege man of both—something he had never told either one, though they doubtless knew and didn't care, as long as the peace held between them. "The duke asked quite a bit about our grandfather," he continued, "how he had come to marry an heiress and become an archduke. He seemed better informed on our grandfather's ancestry than I am myself."

"What is this Duke Argave himself like?" I asked.

"Dangerous." Guibert let the word hang for a moment. I had never credited my brother with much imagination, but perhaps I had underestimated him. "Watch yourself around him, Galoran. There are always rumors of intrigue from the south, and at least one new count riding up every year to swear fidelity to the king after unfortunate accidents to their predecessors, but Argave has so far survived them all, for far longer than either you or I have lived."

I would have to become the king's man as well as Duke Argave's, then. Someone, I hoped, would understand all my new responsibilities and deign to share the information with me. But any trips back to the north, I resolved, could wait until summer.

"Argave," added Guibert slowly, "has, how shall I express this, the manners of a dancing master, including both the elegance of style and the love of intrigue, but the soul of an assassin."

2

The trip south took close to a month, over roads either deep in snow or, as we began approaching my new county, thick with mud. The inns were crowded and fetid; the monastery guest-houses were cleaner but the food there worse. Once among sullen gray hills we fought off an ambush, and another time we outran a pack of twenty bandits. Bruno's horse broke a leg, and we were out-bargained on the price in buying a new one. Four times we became seriously lost, and once we had to swim the horses across an icy river when the duke's messengers could not find the ford they insisted had been there when they came north.

Although I tried questioning them about my county, they resisted both open and subtle questions. The closest I got to interesting information was one beginning to tell me that my new castle had long been rumored to have hidden passages, maybe even lost treasures, but the other silenced him. They did, however, know a number of delightful southern songs, some bawdy, some sweetly sentimental, which they were happy to teach Bruno and me. We sang the bawdier ones in the evening at the inns and the more sentimental ones at the monastery guest-houses.

As we continued south, even through treacherous countryside, I could feel dropping away behind me all the oppressive weight of living on the charity of my brother. It was as though the scar itself was peeling away from my face, though I could still see it there in the polished metal of my mirror. And if the thought of leaving Guibert's castle further behind with every step was not always enough to push me forward, then I could always imagine the county waiting for me.

The vision of the sun dappling the soft grass through the olive branches kept me going as we left the snows behind for sleet and cold rain and started at last into the southern mountains, with their steep uphill climbs and jaw-dropping descents. The vision lasted until, after a long day's ride up an increasingly rocky incline through barren fields, the messengers pulled up their horses to point.

"There's your castle. There's Peyrefixade."

My mouth fell open. Bruno at my shoulder muttered, "It's like somebody wanted to stick a thumb in the eye of God."

Thrust up from a knife-ridge of rock far above us, the dark red castle was the best positioned for defense I had ever seen. The faint track of the road before us twisted back and forth, back and forth, in its slow ascent. As we watched, a dark rain cloud came down the ridge and obscured the castle from sight. Night reached us at the

same time. I sighed, knowing in my thoroughly chilled
bones that while dragging all the stones for the castle up
to that peak no one had thought to install a modern
fireplace.

That evening I was too tired to inspect my new castle
properly. The castle seneschal greeted me and formally
passed the huge iron key of the front gate into my keeping.
He appeared gaunt, the skin on his neck and arms slack
as though he had recently lost weight rapidly, but I was
too exhausted to wonder about his troubles. I received
the bows and murmured welcomes of the knights and
servants, more obsequious than anything I had ever
received in my life. The bouteillier, dressed like a nobleman
and with a nobleman's manners and bearing but the most
deferential of all, brought me wine and a slab of cold meat,
which I ate and went straight to bed.

The hearth, as I had feared, was built in the old-
fashioned way in the middle of the hall, but while it made
the room very smoky it also kept it warm. My entire adult
life I had preferred fire safely housed in a fireplace, but
I thought tiredly that I could deal with this—at least until
next week when I would order the masons in.

The great curtained bed, at one end of the great hall
in which everyone in the castle ate and slept, was doubtless
the same one, I thought, that the former countess had
died in. At least she seemed to have insisted on a goose-
feather mattress on the rope-strung frame and warm wool
stuffing in the brocade coverlets. I just hoped someone
had thought to change the sheets after her death.

But I awoke with my mood much improved as dawn
broke over the ridge, lighting up the greased parchment
stretched over the windows. I threw on my clothes and
stepped over still snoring men to go out and survey my
county by daylight. Bruno was among the sleepers, his
face in respose showing the lines of age and exhaustion
he tried to deny during the day. Him I smiled at indulgently,

but a little discipline, I could see, would be needed among the rest.

Yet faint clanking and rattling sounds elsewhere in the castle indicated that I was not the only one awake. I could recall seeing no priest among the staff last night, but I would have to get one and start them all off right with the divine office every morning. I went out into the courtyard adjoining the great hall, where the cold morning air carried the scent of distant snow as well as of mud, then followed an unroofed passage to the base of the great tower I had seen from below and began to climb.

Stairs winding upwards within the walls led me to the top. From there, as I had hoped, I could survey this whole region of the mountains. The view was spectacular and the drop stunning. On all sides were further peaks. To the south, I must be looking miles into the next kingdom. Perhaps the duke had heard I was a good fighting man, I thought, able to defend Peyrefixade against the political ambitions of enemies not far away.

As I gazed downward through oceans of air I realized it would be a sheer fall from a dozen different points on this castle to the valleys on either side of the ridge, and the people living in those valleys would never forget the presence of the castle above them.

Fields that had appeared desolate the night before now had a faint green cast, of early grass breaking through, and far below I spotted what were doubtless flocks of sheep. On one hillside I could see a large vineyard, still in winter dormancy, though nothing I could recognize as olive trees. So far below it could have been a toy, such as I had sometimes made for little Gertrude, was a tile-roofed village, smoke rising lazily from the rooftops in the still air. I leaned on the battlements, well wrapped in my cloak, letting it sink in that this was really mine, and trying to remember all the words of one of the bawdier songs.

A little terrace opened out a storey below me, and as I looked around two of the servants came out onto it, beer mugs and pieces of bread in their hands. Neither looked up. "So," said one, "what do you think of our new master?"

An accent like the duke's messengers' but perfectly intelligible. I leaned forward, intensely interested and scarcely breathing.

"It's a southern name, Galoran, for all that he talks like a northerner," commented the other around a mouthful of breakfast. "I understand he's a cousin or something of our late Countess Aenor."

"I gather he's not married. Maybe he's holy or something."

This "or something" seemed to give the other pause, because he was silent for a moment before saying, a bit too loudly, "They don't have heretics up in the north."

"Or maybe he's one who likes the boys better," the first servant suggested. "Or maybe no lady would have him."

The second laughed. "Once they learn he's Count of Peyrefixade they'll come flocking around. He'll have plenty to choose from then, will our Count Scar."

Count Scar. My own servants were calling me Count Scar.

I had scarcely gotten used to the sound of Count Galoran, to the image of the wise, severe but just lord from the north, and already it was being altered out of recognition. I waited in silence until my servants—I didn't even know their names, but I marked them as best I could from above—had finished eating and gone back inside, then went in search of breakfast of my own.

At least they had seemed to think that I would have plenty of ladies to choose from.

The first order of business when I finished my beer and barley bread was to start acquainting myself with my castle. It had clearly been built and rebuilt over several generations, with an effort in manpower getting the stones up here which I couldn't even imagine. Maybe their efforts had been assisted by magic, which I understood was much more widely used in the south. But I dismissed the thought.

The castle was smaller than my brother the archduke's, but to me it felt like a kingdom. It had a formidable keep, many unexpected passages and rooms, a gracefully proportioned chapel leaning far out over the precipice, and plenty of places where the unwary foot could have slid with fatal results. My initial exploration revealed no secret tunnels, but if they had been easy to find they would not have been secret.

"I heard one of the stable boys refer to you as Count Scar," Bruno shuffled up to tell me triumphantly. "But after a good thumping he agreed to use your rightful name from now on."

Though I now felt that everyone in the castle was looking at and wondering at the dark red disfigurement of my face, the feeling did little to dampen my good mood. After all, I was long accustomed to that. No matter what they said behind my back, they were still mine to command— as soon as I knew what commands to give them.

By now all the men were busy about their day's tasks, the knights tending their gear or practicing their swordwork, the staff cooking, cleaning, making barrels, attending to the horses, renewing the slates on a bit of roof line, hammering away in the forge, and a dozen other chores. It was somewhat disconcerting to realize how well the castle was already functioning without me and my discipline. There were no women at all in sight; the few ladies who had lived there had doubtless left at once when the countess died.

But I missed them almost immediately. The chief cook spotted me when I looked into the kitchens around noon to check on dinner's progress. He hurried over, full of deep bows and apologies, to acquaint me with the state of the spice chest. "For you see, my lord, these two months gone I have not been able to buy, and this time of year the prices are always scandalous, yet we are shockingly low on pepper and dangerously low on cinnamon."

I wondered briefly if irrelevantly on the dangers the

lack of cinnamon posed to Peyrefixade, then realized with a cold thud what he was asking: he wanted money, and all I had was the pitiful sum left in the bottom of the pouch my brother had given me. This county must produce an income for its count, but how was I to gain access to it? Surely there was a bailiff or stewart somewhere who saw to the rents and tolls coming in, but I could not recall meeting any such person last night. The seneschal must not have the money himself or he would have been able to supply it to the cook.

And why was the cook bothering *me* about the spices anyway? I knew nothing of these things. At home first my mother and then my sister-in-law had always supervised the kitchen provisions. The ladies who flocked around Count Scar had better be well trained in castle management.

We were interrupted before I could ask how many peppercorns he could get for the few solidi I still had. A clear note of a horn sounded through the castle, then again and a third time.

"That's the signal that someone's coming up the road, my lord," said the cook helpfully. "It was blown last evening when you were spotted, though of course we didn't realize at first it was you."

"Of course," I said briskly. With a castle like this, someone could roll out of bed with nothing on but his shirt and still defend it, but it was good to know that a certain discipline was already established even without me. Soldiers I could always talk to; I should start with the guards once I had dealt with whoever was now making the climb up my mountain.

Bruno met me outside the kitchen, and the castle seneschal silently fell into step at my shoulder as I hurried toward the front gate. The latter looked just as gaunt this morning as he had last night, but lugubrious rather than ill, I judged. He had murmured something then about the great sorrow of the countess's death: an old family retainer, I thought, but he was not really so old.

The duke's messengers who had brought me south joined us at the gate. "It is Duke Argave," one informed me. "We sent a message from that inn three days ago, and it is good to see he received it."

A small group of horsemen labored up the last climb, led by one carrying an enormous black banner. Behind him on a powerful stallion rode a man who could only be the duke, clean-shaven, with dark eyes that seemed even at a distance to be looking into mine. Dangerous, my brother had termed him. He was tall and heavily built, graying but still graceful in the saddle, wearing a red silk tabard over his armor.

"He said in the letter he sent me," I muttered to Bruno, "that he wanted me to start south at once, and he is certainly wasting no time making my acquaintance."

"Halt, in the name of Galoran, Count of Peyrefixade!" shouted my guards to my surprised delight, as they leaped out in front of the gate and stood with crossed halberds.

The duke stopped twenty yards below them, before the final loop of the road. "Tell your master that Duke Argave requests permission to enter the castle which he has vouchsafed him." He must know who I was but was not looking at me now.

I stepped forward. "Enter my castle, esteemed lord, for I would gladly greet you and bow the knee to you." They might pride themselves on their dancing-master manners here in the south, but I was sure that none of them had experienced anything like the ceremony of the imperial court on a high holy day.

Argave gave a sudden smile and kicked his lathered horse for the final assent.

It was quite clear that I would never have inherited this castle were it not for the duke, so there was no use in holding back. When he reached the gates I was already down on one knee, reaching for his stirrup to hold it as he descended.

He nodded in satisfaction but said, "Rise, Galoran. You

will come to my court at Ferignan for formal investment next week, and until then you need not bend the knee to me." He gave only the slightest flick of his eyelids at the sight of my scarred face. I came to my feet slowly but maintained my grip on his stirrup until he had dismounted. He took a heavy, linen-wrapped box from the back of his saddle, then the grooms appeared to lead the horse away.

His messengers immediately burst into a flow of words that I could not understand. The duke looked at me over their heads and smiled as though enjoying my discomfort. But he said in a friendly enough tone, "You do not understand our region's language? Come, lads, let us not appear to be discussing secrets before Count Galoran. You can tell me all these things later if they have any import."

"I speak the Royal Tongue," I said stiffly, "and Allemann of course, from my years in the imperial court." Let him learn about that from me and not from his messengers.

"Auccitan, our region's language, is in your blood," he replied good-naturedly. "You should quickly pick it up, as it is not so different from the Royal Tongue."

And if they persisted in speaking a language I did not understand, I thought, then Bruno and I would converse before them in Allemann.

"I knew, of course, of your service to the emperor," the duke continued, just when I thought he would not deign to mention it at all. "And how you left that service two years ago." Duke Argave, I thought, had good information—perhaps from my brother, perhaps from other sources—but did not always care to share that information with those under him.

"Here in your own court," he added thoughtfully, "you may hear nothing but your own Royal Tongue. After Countess Aenor came back from offering her obeiance to the king, she ordered that none but his language be spoken here, and she was obeyed. Of course," he put in almost as an aside, "she did not live a year after that, so the lesson may not have taken thoroughly."

The countess had died within a year of taking office herself? Clearly there was a great deal that the messengers had deliberately kept from me. I led Duke Argave into the great hall, though he doubtless knew the way better than I did.

Here, with a flourish, he whipped the linen away from the box and handed it to me. It was even heavier than I had expected from the way he carried it, and I came close to dropping it. It was made of age-darkened chestnut, bound with bands of iron, and locked with a massive lock. But the duke produced a key, and under his gaze I slowly opened it.

It was, as I suspected, the treasury of the county of Peyrefixade. The cook would be able to buy more peppercorns after all, I thought, hefting the leather bags within. I didn't want to count my money with Duke Argave looking on, but then I suspected he had long since counted it himself. The bags seemed somehow less full than I had hoped, though I tried to reassure myself that most of the money would be in gold. There was no use whatsoever in suspecting the duke of having improved the condition of his own spice chests while guarding my treasury for me.

The bouteillier hurried in with flagons of wine. He said something in rapid Auccitan to Duke Argave as he served us, but the duke did not answer. This southern wine was better than anything my brother had in *his* castle, I thought as we sipped.

"The spring rents come due next month," said the duke. Everything he said had a slightly amused, ironic undertone, but that seemed only his way of speaking, not a comment on my rents—I hoped. "Your seneschal can inform you about your rent collectors. He's a good man, devoted to your family."

I nodded, noticing a sheaf of parchment in the bottom of the treasury box. A quick glance showed that a few were property deeds or judicial records, but most were chirographic records of transfers of property *away* from the county patrimony. The ones I leafed through all represented gifts to a religious house dedicated to the Three Kings.

"How did the countess come to die so suddenly," I asked without looking up, "having held the office such a short time? Was it the perils of childbirth?"

Duke Argave chuckled, and then I did meet his eyes. They were dark and piercing, with very little real humor in them. "You should know better than that, Galoran. If she had had a child, there would have been no need to summon you all the way from the north!" He wore a large emerald ring, doubtless worth many times the contents of my treasury box, and he turned it thoughtfully as he spoke. "Her grandfather, old Count Bernhard, had outlived his son by many years and died beloved and venerable last winter. His granddaughter, the heiress, would doubtless have been loved just as much—eventually—if it had not been for her accident."

So there had been some sort of trouble during her short reign. "Accident?" I repeated.

"Late fall, the time of fogs and mists. She must have decided to walk on the ramparts by herself in the evening. No one knew she had even left her chamber until they heard the scream. . . . It was not until the next morning that they found her body."

"So she fell to her death." I stirred uneasily in the great carved chair in which I sat. She had presumably known the castle all her life; I would have to watch my own step very carefully.

"Or was pushed."

The duke's words seemed to echo through the empty hall. "But who would have pushed her?" I asked, horrified.

"Not her husband," he answered with assurance, "as he was never out of the sight of at least a dozen witnesses that evening, at least one of whom I trust completely. And there was scant reason for him to want her dead just yet, even had he despised her, which he did not. For without a child of his body to inherit, he had no further legal claim to be Count of Peyrefixade. He tried to argue it with me, of course, even hired some men of law to make his case, but I could tell his heart was never in it. Without his wife Lord Thierri is just one more dependent at my court again. That's the real reason I haven't brought him to the ordeal."

This was what the duke had hinted at in his letter to me. I felt a cold suspicion that there was still much more to this than he had said. He could certainly have accepted the countess's consort as the new count if he had wanted, without fearing anyone would dare oppose him. But for some reason, without even having met me, he had decided he wanted me instead.

"But who do you suspect, then?" I asked. "Surely by now you must have charged someone with this hideous crime."

"No witnesses to her fall," said the duke regretfully, "and those who might seem to have the most to gain are all beyond suspicion. Oh there was *one* witness, too terrified to come forward the night she died, one of the staff here who spoke of apparitions and horrors. But it was clear nonsense, illusions of the mist to wine-blurred eyes."

He rose briskly, his cloak swirling around him, and I stood up too. "No, I will not stay for dinner. I shall leave you now to learn more of your own castle and will take my lads with me. But you shall attend my high court next week and make your oaths before all my other men. You are also sworn to the king through your oaths to me, so there will be no need to go north to the royal court before midsummer—I hear the roads can be poor this time of year."

"I noticed," I said dryly.

"And you shall make the acquaintance of my daughter Arsendis, a charming young woman who has expressed great interest in the new northern count." I suddenly found myself smiling hugely. Apparently, even with the scar, I would not be too horrifying to a maiden's sensibilities. The duke handed me a small square of parchment. "You might enjoy this miniature of her."

It was a woman's portrait, done very small, showing someone black-haired smiling over her shoulder at me. Her dark eyes tilted up at the corners and gave the impression she was enjoying a private joke. The picture was startlingly realistic; I had never seen a portrait look so much like a living, breathing person. I rubbed at it with my thumb, vaguely suspecting magic.

"Keep it for now," said Duke Argave with a wave of his hand. "You can return it to Arsendis when you meet her at my high court next week. Oh, and before then, your *capellanus* will arrive."

"My *Kapelanner*?" I said, so surprised that I used the Allemannic word. "A spiritual advisor? I have one?"

He was already heading out toward the courtyard. "I requested him particularly. A bright young man who is wasting his considerable talents holed up in the religious house of the Three Kings."

There were too many pieces for me even to start putting them together yet. "Isn't that the house," I asked, hurrying to keep up with the duke, "to which old Count Bernhard, my predecessor, was so generous?"

Argave turned toward me suddenly and smiled. "So you have learned that already, have you? I knew I need not fear someone of your family would be slow-witted." Out in the courtyard the winter sun was shining, but the stone passage in which we stood was shadowed and chill. "But did you know they are the Order that practices magic?"

"Magic!" It seemed I was repeating about half of what the duke said, but he had surprised me again. "I knew all priests study a little magic," I sputtered, trying not to be scandalized, "as they learn all branches of knowledge and science. I knew that the most pious men of God may peruse some pagan learning, even read the love poems of antiquity while learning antiquity's language. But a whole Order devoted to it! I would have thought that heretical."

The duke's whole manner changed abruptly. He had seemed detached and amused all during our conversation, but at the mention of heresy he became deadly serious. He turned to face me, speaking with quiet intensity. "Well, some of the heretics back in the mountain valleys—the Perfected, as they like to call themselves, if you can imagine such hypocrisy!—certainly practice dark magic. In the terrible wars of my boyhood, they wielded almost unimaginable magical powers, and hundreds, even thousands were slain on both sides. It is not however the magic that separates the heretics from the True Faith. It is their perverted belief that this world is not God's creation but the devil's, and that by cleansing themselves, freeing themselves from the taint of earth, they can become totally pure through their own efforts. They *say* that they are so Perfect that they do not need God's mercy and atonement, thus misleading many pious souls into damnation—especially as I hear they often reward themselves for fasts and flagellations by afterwards indulging in gross orgies. That is why God-fearing sons of the True Faith need to oppose them with their own weapons. *And* that is why," with a slight flaring of his nostrils, "not long after the war against the heretics, I helped the old count, your great-uncle, establish the Magian Order. I was then a very young man, and it was one of my first acts on inheriting the duchy."

I immediately bit back all the issues I had been about to raise questioning the wisdom of learning more than the slightest bit of magic. "The path of wisdom," I said heartily, trying not to meet his eyes. "So my new *capellanus* will be a Magian?"

"His name," said the duke, "is Melchior."

Chapter Two ~ Melchior

1

"His name is Galoran."

I had been startled at first when a novice had interrupted my afternoon period of study to summon me to the office of the provost, then filled with deep apprehension that the day I had begun to hope might never arrive was upon me at last. Had someone denounced me? Was I to be banished despite all my labors, despite a spotless record of devotion to the Order and the True Faith from my first days as a novice? As I hurried past the chapter house, the terror that I might never again be allowed to enter that octagonal chamber and participate in the business of the Order as a full brother had been truly terrible.

Arriving before Provost Balaam filled with such doubts and fears, I had been surprised and confused to have him launch into an apparently conversational account concerning the arrival of a new count at the castle of Peyrefixade, a good day and a half away. Now I raised my eyes from his narrow face to the wall behind him, studying the ivory madonna and the fine wooden sculpture of our Order's namesakes, the Three Magi, that hung there, while I tried to decipher the meaning of this conversation. After a moment I ventured, "A southerner's name: interesting for a northern count."

"It was the name of his great-grandfather, who was count at Peyrefixade before the time of our Order." The Provost paused to shift one of the innumerable scraps of scribbled parchment that littered the desk in front of him. It was a standard trick of his when collecting his thoughts—or when preparing to impart some uncomfortable news, for despite his dry manner he was not an unkind man. "That old Count Galoran had two sons. The elder, who succeeded him, was our own great patron Bernhard. The younger eventually married the heiress to a holding on the northern marches; he was the grandfather of this Galoran."

I began to relax, thinking perhaps the provost had merely felt like talking of this novelty—though why he should have selected me for a listener seemed a mystery. "I had never even heard our patron had a brother, let alone that such a brother had given rise to a lineage of his own up in the grim border lands adjoining the Empire."

"Few did. No one in this region has had any cause to think or speak of our late patron's brother for over forty years. But our esteemed duke—" Provost Balaam smiled without mirth "—clearly knew all about it. He makes it his life's business to know of such things, as one never knows when one of them might be turned to advantage."

My mind was racing now. It was evident that I was expected to understand something from this recitation, but what? I had never enjoyed gossip concerning the maneuverings of the world's mighty, even during the three years I had been compelled to spend among them away from our mother house. If I had, why would I have chosen to seek a life of quiet contemplation devoted to prayer and the study of the magic arts in the cloisters of the Order, over the chance to be named heir to my uncle's modest lands and castle when I was but fourteen? But now it appeared I must again aspire at competency at this skill for which I felt such scant inclination. Well, I certainly knew something of the duke and his ways. After a moment's consideration, I ventured, "So, our duke finds something to his advantage in suddenly producing this unknown but quite legitimate heir."

"Good, you are perspicacious. The question for us is

whether the arrival of this Count Galoran will also be to the advantage of our Order, or otherwise. It is in this regard that I summoned you."

"Your servant stands ready to serve in whatever way the Order may require," I declared automatically, casting my eyes humbly downward and stretching forth my hands in an effort to retain my calm and patient expression despite my dawning understanding that all this talk of count and duke actually might have some direct bearing upon me.

"I presume you are aware that our Order has always furnished a *capellanus* to the castle of Peyrefixade, to serve both as an aide and a spiritual advisor to the reigning count. Our revered father Abbot Caspar has requested me to ask that you take up this post in the service of this new count."

"I—see." As soon as he'd spoken, I'd realized my foolishness in not having guessed for myself. My heart felt like a stone in my breast while all of my long and carefully cultivated detachment seemed to leave me in an instant. "The reverend abbot—does me great honor. But is this not an assignment for a more—a more seasoned brother?"

"Some argued so. But the—the abbot thought otherwise, and so do I. You are about the same age as this new count. He will be coming into his situation feeling himself a stranger to everyone, so this fact may help you in winning his confidence. Moreover, there is reason to believe that the priest of our Order assigned to Peyrefixade should be an expert in the magic of divination, and I happen to know that subject has been one of your particular studies. It's a taxing branch of magic, one that requires a young healthy Magian like yourself. Moreover, the duke himself specifically requested you." The Provost gave his mirthless smile once more. "You must have made a surprisingly strong impression upon him during the period you served in his city a few years ago."

Well that's done it, I told myself. Until Provost Balaam's

last statement I had hoped I might yet persuade him to return to the abbot and the officers of the Order with my carefully reasoned arguments as to why I would be so much less suitable for this task than several other brothers whom I could readily name. But that was out of the question now. Our Order of the Three Kings had attained whatever small security and prosperity it now enjoyed thanks principally to two great patrons: the late old Count of Peyrefixade and the duke himself.

The good old count had supported us out of a genuine interest and belief in the possibilities of magic as a force for good, so long as its study and practice was conducted by men also sworn to holiness and living under the well-understood discipline of the cloister. But as for the duke, his reasons for doing anything were seldom either so single or so simple, and our Order had consequently found it well always to give the most serious consideration to any request from him—and indeed, to comply—unless some highly compelling spiritual objection could be produced. What conceivable action or virtue of mine the duke might have witnessed during my periodic attendance at his court, in an *extremely* junior capacity, to make him think of placing me at Peyrefixade was completely obscure to me. But it made no difference. Bowing my head and folding my hands in the posture proper to an obedient junior canon, I produced the only possible response, the one I'd so often heard given by many a greater figure than myself: "Then of course it must be as our lord duke wishes."

"Exactly," said old Balaam, and I almost thought I glimpsed the hint of a smile tugging for a moment at the corner of his flat mouth. "Mark well that you take care always to give such politic answers once you have taken up your new duties."

"And when am I expected to go take up those duties, my father?"

"Why, tomorrow, of course!" Provost Balaam declared, looking as if my question was the most surprising thing he'd heard in the last twelvemonth. "The weather augeries look excellent for the next three days, so there is nothing to delay you. Moreover, it would be best if you were with this new Count Galoran as quickly as possible."

He turned his head at the sound of the bells announcing nones. "We must be off to the holy office now. As soon as that's over, go pack your belongings and other things and make the preparations for your journey. Come see me again tomorrow morning before you depart and I shall advise you concerning a few practical matters you will need to know." He rose briskly and stepped over to his little stand to wash the inevitable ink stains from his long wiry fingers, nodding in dismissal. I started to go out, but the sight of the crucifix that hung above his wash stand, or perhaps a glimpse he caught of something in my face, caused him to call after me. "Oh, and Brother Melchior—?"

"Yes, my father?" I said, turning back.

"The Order asks that you assume this service for its welfare, but also because it truly believes it will aid your own, your spiritual welfare. And also your progress as a member of the Order. You know, younger Brother, one may master the technical knowledge necessary to do powerful magic far younger than one can acquire the wisdom needed to decide when and how to use that power. The latter comes with time and experience, experience that can only be gained by taking what you have learned out into the world of the men and women we serve. And remember, though you leave our walls and our company, you are never alone while you have the disciplines of self-examination and prayer you have learned among us to guide you. I suggest that once you've collected your things, you go pray in one of the chapels. Or better yet, take a walk in the cloister until it's time for vespers. Listen to the stones, let them remind you what is the purpose of our Order and why you became one of us. It will do you good, believe me. Even today, our Revered and Glorious

Master never fails to go and walk there whenever he comes on one of his visits."

It might have been only illusion, but his expression looked almost kindly as I shut the door behind me.

By the time I'd stood through the singing of nones, then gone to my cell and packed up my few personal items and the books and tools of such magic arts as I had managed to master in some fifteen years of diligent study, the brief February afternoon was already moving swiftly on towards nightfall. Feeling low and also obstinant, I slipped away for a walk outside the walls instead of going to the cloister. The air was still and warm for the season, with even a trace of the scent of spring. I walked from the gates as far as the little porter's lodge and stood for a while, looking down the steep, narrow road up which I and everything else that had ever come to our Order's house—including its very stones—had traveled. And down which I'd be going come morning. The lodge and the road itself, at least as far as my vision reached along its winding course down the mountain, were deserted and still.

I turned and looked back toward the spire, walls and buildings of the Order's house outlined against the fading sky, and a sense of deep woe swept over me. Within the House's calm daily round of prayer and magical studies, I had felt I was making real progress at last. Despite the provost's words, I didn't see how I could continue to move ahead amid all the distractions and demands that would come in serving as spiritual counsellor and Magian in a great castle under a steel-hearted northern count—for such the man must be, or our hard Duke Argave would never have decided to set him there.

And yet, it suddenly struck me, these very thoughts might themselves be temptations, born of hidden pride. After all, how much better this was than the true banishment I had so often dreaded! What good was my oath of faithfulness and obedience to the Order if it brought only an outward concurrence that concealed a rebellious heart? I bowed my head and prayed earnestly, trying to bring myself to accept and embrace this new charge.

After a while a chill wind began to rise out of the deep valley. I shivered and turned back inside the walls. As I passed the corridor leading to the cloister, my footsteps lagged, then turned. A moment later I had covered the dozen paces to the low archway and stepped through, fully obedient now.

I walked slowly along, gazing out between the columns of the arcade to where the central fountain of the cloister sent its peaceful sound echoing through the little garden. The air was calm and almost warm in this sheltered place, and I began to feel its peace stealing into my heart.

At the southwest corner of the arcade, I paused to study our finest carved capital, which depicted Simon the Magician slinking shamefacedly away after having been denied in his attempt to augment his own magical powers by purchasing a share of the immeasurably greater spiritual powers of Our Lord. The magician had been carved with a face in which lines indicating considerable wisdom had become coarsened, with keen eyes that now appeared bitter. He clutched a sack of money in one clawlike hand, and was surrounded by sculpted street urchins who pointed at him, jeering and laughing. Around on the opposite face of the capital a crowd of rapt listeners was ignoring him entirely as they gazed up toward a high place where the unseen Master had resumed his preaching. A cautionary tale for any in our Order who might chance to fall into the error of supposing even briefly that his modest command of mere earthly magical capacities could make him in any way close to being the equal of those whose powers came from a far higher source.

As I stepped away from the carved scene a faint sound filtered to my ears through the rush of the fountain: a low tapping, which came in short bursts interrupted by periods of silence. It seemed to be coming from the opposite corner of the cloister. I walked quickly up the west arcade, past columns whose capitals mostly bore only symbols of the planets and the zodiac, or else twined acanthus leaves or simple faces, then along the north side of the cloister.

Reaching the northeast corner of the arcade, the only unfinished section, I came upon old Brother Quercus chiseling away in the shadows, finishing the capital that one day soon would crown this corner of the cloister. He was seated with his back almost against the wall, working in nearly complete darkness, but that was unlikely to bother him: he was blind.

Or at least blind as most of us account such things. Brother Quercus had been one of the first to join our dear and glorious Father back in the earliest days of the Order. Time had long since stripped his wavering old eyes of the power to detect light, just as it had stripped the untonsured parts of his head of every hair except for the dense eyebrows that hung down over his sightless eyes like old thatching on a ruined cottage. He had to be assisted in the morning to his carving bench by two novices these days, but his old arms and hands were still strong as oak when he deftly plied his hammer and chisels. He had carved every column and every capital in the main church building well before I'd joined the Order, then turned to the work of decorating this cloister at an age when most canons were content merely to sit in the sun by summer or near the fire by winter, until someone comes to lead them off for meals or prayers or bed. For Brother Quercus had turned his magical studies to mastering the second vision as his own sight had departed, and the undiminished vigor and power of his carving attested to his success. Indeed, it was he who taught the basics of second vision and hearing to the novices. Rumor among them whispered that he had now gone even beyond the second vision in his own studies, delving deep into the third vision that can see across time and space. As I drew close, he lay

down his heavy hammer and turned his ancient head in
my direction. "Good evening, Brother Melchior," he
croaked with complete assurance as to who was before
him.

"Yes, it is I, elder Brother."

"Have a look here, then; see what you think."

I bent to peer at the nearly finished capital. It depicted
a knight in armor—no, there was a crown on his mailed
head: a king. He stood alone in a wild place among rocks,
facing an ancient woman with a pinched face both
cunning and fearful. The hag was crouched like a spider,
all drawn up except for one long arm flung out with
pointing finger to indicate something around the corner
of the capital. I leaned over and saw a bearded figure
with a wrathful face, who appeared to be rising up out
of the earth amid billowing fog. Looking at the king again,
I realized that despite his tall person and massive limbs
he was cowering away from both the hag and the
apparition. "Ah, it is Saul and the Witch of Endor, with
the ghost of Samuel!"

"Good, good! Just about done; it's nice to find that
someone with decent scriptural knowledge can recognize
it straight away. Looks all right to you, then?"

"It is magnificent, elder Brother." But in fact something
about the king's pose struck me as odd. Stooping over, I
saw that one of his legs was bent in a manner that defied
normal anatomy very slightly. It also greatly increased the
effect of a normally strong man reduced to shrinking terror,
however, so I supposed it must have been an artistic
decision by Brother Quercus.

"You're looking at that leg, aren't you?" he creaked as
if reading my thoughts—was he, perhaps? "Thinking I
did it that way for the effect. Well, look a little closer."

I obeyed, and after a moment I saw a little flaw in the
limestone: a bit of quartz crystal, just at the place where
King Saul's leg should have bent if it had been carved
naturalistically. "A happy accident, then," I said.

"It's a scar, a scar in the stone." Brother Quercus abruptly laid down his tools and thrust out his hands in my direction. After an instant's confusion, I understood that he was requesting me to help him rise. "Getting chilled; that's enough work for one day. Take me along to my cell, Brother Melchior. I'd like to rest and pray for a little while until it's time for the evening offices and meal. The boy will fetch in the tools from the damp when he comes."

We walked slowly, as I carefully matched my pace to his. He didn't speak again until we were turning down the corridor that led to his cell. But then, "Funny things, scars, on stones or on men. You have to work around them, you know."

"So you couldn't carve across the 'scar,' then."

"Funny things. Stuff's often the strongest right around them. But you can't strike right onto them, or something may crack. What shows on the surface is only part, you see. Scars always go down deeper than you can see. They can be the key to the whole fabric, even in the strongest block." We had reached the door of his cell, but as he was about to enter, he turned sharply about, his face directly toward me though his yellow old eyes were rolled sightlessly upward beneath his bushy brows. "You hear all that, Brother Melchior? You hear what I just said?"

"About scars in stone? Yes, Brother Quercus."

"Stones *and* men, Brother Melchior, stones and men. Just you remember that; you may find it of use before you expect. Scars can be important things, in stones or men. Other men—or yourself."

As soon as he made this pronouncement all the oaken hardness seemed to go out of him, and I found myself only looking at a blind, weary old man. He turned and shuffled into his little cell, and I set off for mine, puzzling as I went over the question of whether I had just listened to something extremely vital or merely the random vaporings of a holy but crumbling old mind.

2

I arose after fitful slumber an hour before the singing
of matins the next morning and took a last walk inside
and outside every part of the Order's buildings. After the
singing of the first office, while the eastern sky was still
just reddening with the coming dawn, I went along to
see Provost Balaam once more. I found him already at
his desk, writing by the light of a candle. "Ah, good
morning, Brother Melchior. Are you ready to be on your
way?"

"One of the novices is loading my baggage onto a
packhorse, my father. I shall depart as soon as our interview
is over."

"Excellent; then I shall endeavor to be brief. There
are just one or two matters you should be acquainted with
before you leave." He looked at me for a minute with
the same expression he habitually wore when perusing a
questionable bill from one of the tradesmen who supplied
our house with necessities from the village down in the
valley. "You passed your first fourteen years in a mountain
holding, so I presume you gained at least some knowledge
of the *Im*-Perfected, did you not?"

I stared at him in deep dismay, wondering what might
be hidden behind this question. Could this be a trap; had
the provost somehow discovered what I had thought was
known only to the old Master and Abbot Caspar? Yet his
face did not look suspicious. Summoning courage, I
managed to answer in a normal tone, "Yes, like anyone
who grew up in these mountains I have some knowledge
of the Perfected Ones. But I—I hope no person has found
any reason to voice doubt concerning *my* commitment
to the True Faith."

"No, not at all. It is merely that Peyrefixade was originally
built by those who styled themselves the Perfected, as
one of their castles. It was the seat of one of their own
greatest Magians at the time of the great war against them.

The possibility exists that it may still harbor certain—ah—
manifestations even after so many years, things that a
trustworthy son of the True Faith thoroughly trained in
the arts of divination, particularly one with at least some
knowledge of the so-called Perfected, might perhaps be
able to uncover. I simply wished to make it clear that you
should be alert for any hint of magical forces lingering
anywhere about your new station, whether old or recent.
It is a matter of some importance for the Order."

I began to relax again, and realized that my hands, hidden
within my sleeves, had clenched with his first mention
of the Perfected into fists so tight that my nails had bitten
into my palms. "Then I shall strive to be alert. But it would
be easier if I could know a bit more."

"I suppose so." He paused, looking as if he would rather
not go on. Controlling and doling out information as
well as money is the life of every provost, and like most
of the rest, ours was always chary of parting with either.
A sigh. "You will recall that Peyrefixade passed from the
hands of our late beloved patron Count Bernhard to his
granddaughter about a year ago, and fell vacant again
just in November when the countess met with an—
accident." As he said this, he reached over to the box
where he kept his inks, took out a little spill, and scattered
a dusting of soot over the piece of fine parchment spread
on the desk before him. He closed his eyes in deepest
concentration, then passed his hand across the parchment
and began to speak in a low voice. I had never gone far
in this magic art, and I forgot all my questions and
concerns while I focused all my attention on the beautiful
patterns of magic that were forming on the parchment.
The soot sifted about like fine sand in a breeze until
the face of a woman not much above my own age, adorned
with a fine silk headdress and a necklace, formed itself
upon the white surface. I had seen the late countess on
one or two occasions among other great ladies, when
the region's high nobility had gathered for some great

occasion at the duke's court, and was stunned by the excellence of the likeness.

"Of course. The tale of her having fallen while walking alone upon the ramparts was everywhere at the time."

"But are you not also aware that her untimely death, though most regrettable, was not entirely a bad thing for our Order?"

It was now my turn to think it might be better if Provost Balaam did not disclose too much information to me. "Well, of course I knew there had been some misunderstanding between our Order and the countess, my father. The novices, and even some of the more senior brothers, were always gossiping about it. There was even talk of a possible case at law. I tried to pay as little attention as possible to such idle gossip; I wanted no idle distractions from my studies and devotions." Which was perfectly true—in fact I had simply walked away from several discussions when they had turned to this subject. I only wished I could do so now, but having once made a beginning, Provost Balaam evidently meant to go on.

"The matter begins even before you returned from our priory in the duke's city of Ferignan to join us here at the Mother House. Not long before his death, full of years and virtue, our esteemed patron the old count had been contemplating a final gift to us, one more munificent even than the one in which he joined the duke when founding this house of ours. Just two months before his end he visited our dear and glorious Master at his place of retirement to discuss the matter. Abbot Caspar, the dean, myself, and several other senior officers joined them there one day and heard all about it. The gift was to establish a memorial for the souls of his dead wife and son, as well as his own, and would have been generous enough to establish an entire new daughter house! But the good old Count Bernhard died suddenly before the firm arrangements for the larger part of this gift could be completed, though title to certain very seemly lands had already passed to us. After a decent interval, our man who was then serving as *capellanus* at Peyrefixade approached our patron's granddaughter, the new countess, to see if she intended to carry through what her grandfather had proposed to undertake. She demurred, though she did go so far then as to make a modestly handsome gift of her own in order to establish anniversaries for her grandfather and the others I have mentioned.

"A few months later, however, her seneschal called upon our father the dean to inform him apologetically that half the annual profits from the mill at Riveau-Noir, which the old count had long remitted to our Order in their entirety, would no longer be coming to us." Provost Balaam took up a feather and swept it lightly over the countess's image, murmuring once more. Her image vanished, and the deeply lined face of a man of about fifty, with intelligent, sad eyes, slowly replaced it. "Several such visits and announcements followed over the succeeding months. Soon it became evident to the brother then serving as *capellanus* to the countess's court that her consort, Lord Thierri, was prevailing upon her to look on our Order with far less favor than her family had formerly shown."

He passed the feather across the parchment once more and the seneschal's image also dissolved, as the elegant magic patterns shifted the soot to form the face of a courtier in a velvet hat, a fine-boned man with a subtle expression. "Such situations are not uncommon from time to time between an established house and the new heir belonging to a family whose heads have traditionally been patrons, as you know. But it was nonetheless highly distressing. We reasoned with the countess, of course, and for a time we thought the matter had been amicably settled. Then in the autumn we learned to our distress that the countess and her consort were now contemplating bringing a formal dispute before the duke—and if that did not answer, the king!"

"Yes, even I heard those rumors. But no one in the

cloister knew any particulars, so it was hard to be sure how much was real."

"Oh, it was real enough. They intended to contest all the lands and other properties that the good old count had managed to convey to us just before his death, and even some of his previous patronage as well. Nothing formal had been done in the case at that point, but we received positive information that the entire matter would be placed openly before the duke when the countess and her consort attended his winter court. But the countess, heaven rest her, died first."

"Heaven rest her indeed." One must say this, or be thought to have presumptuously assumed that the hand of God had intervened in our behalf. "But aside from the fortuitous aspect of the misfortune occurring just at the time, how is our Order's interest affected now?"

"It is affected because there is a rumor that some form of Magic Arts may have been employed to cause the accident. And *that* has caused whisperings, and sometimes more than whisperings, in circles where anything to our discredit would be far from unwelcome."

"But surely the brother who was on the scene at the time must have investigated at once, if magic appeared to be involved! What did he find?"

"He was given little chance to discover anything. The countess's consort sent him away from Peyrefixade the very morning after the accident and summoned a parish priest from the local village to perform the offices for his wife instead. Brother Nuage did manage to get close very briefly to the place from which she fell, just after her body had been discovered, and believes he did detect a hint of recent magic there. The late countess's consort did not permit any member of our Order to enter Peyrefixade after that, so there could be no confirmation. But now, with the arrival of this new Count Galoran and your entry into his service, you shall have ample opportunity to investigate the matter on the spot. Of course it is far too late to find any trace of magical activities where the countess fell, but you can be alert for any sign that someone may be working magic now."

He paused to open a box and took out a little sheaf of parchment scraps bound together with an old bit of thong. When he handed them to me, I saw that they were pages salvaged from old books and scraped free of the original writing, standard material for recording informal notes. "Brother Nuage has been staying at our priory in the duke's city ever since he left Peyrefixade. This is the account he wrote concerning everything he saw or surmised during the last part of his time at the castle. It may aid you. Remember, however, your first order of business must be to impress this Count Galoran with your diligence and loyalty as his priest and advisor. His arrival represents a new chance for our Order to regain the good-will and patronage of Peyrefixade. It will be up to you to guide his thoughts in that direction—and to defend him from any magical attacks such as the one that may have killed the countess."

My spirits were low once more as I left Provost Balaam's office. I was not merely being sent forth from my peaceful life of prayer and my magic studies in the House of the Order to take up once again a post out in the world I had rejected, this time in the service of some hardened northern soldier I had never met. I was also charged with looking into a matter that might involve the most sinister sort of magic—with nothing to guide my efforts but months'-old rumors and a few impressions of the brother who had been the last *capellanus* at Peyrefixade. I would be responsible for the well-being of all the souls at the castle too, including this Count Galoran's—and in addition to his soul's safety, that of his physical person. Stepping into the courtyard, I waved to the novice holding the reins of my packhorse and of my mount to wait a little longer. Then I turned and went into the church to offer a final prayer for strength and resolution.

Chapter Three ~ Galoran

1

Two days after the duke's visit, the triple note of the horn again announced someone riding up from the valley. Busy with the cook and his accounts, I sent Bruno, who shuffled back a minute later to tell me a priest on horseback was coming up the steep road.

"I had better go meet him myself, but I'll be back," I told the cook. "This will be the *Kapelanner* the duke promised to send us." As Bruno and I headed toward the gate I said, for his ear alone, "Probably the duke expects him to spy on us for him. And he as good as told me he has another spy in the castle already, someone he 'trusts completely.' Maybe they're to spy on each other as well." I chuckled. "This is as good as being back in the imperial court."

I was very interested in meeting this magic-working member of the Order of the Three Kings. Nothing beyond faint rumor of such a thing had ever made it north; I gathered from what the duke had told me that the Order had been formed only after my own grandfather had left to marry my archduchess grandmother on the borders of the Empire. I persisted in thinking there must be something heretical about it, except that the duke clearly believed in this Order and just as clearly detested the heretical Perfected Ones.

The priest appeared perfectly ordinary as his mare and packhorse toiled up the final incline. No magical flying powers, then, or he certainly would have used them, and no particular desire to make himself appear a griffin or a cockatrice in order to impress me.

When my guards challenged him, he looked up calmly. "I am Brother Melchior, least of my Order, *capellanus* and spiritual advisor to Count Galoran if, God willing, he wishes to receive me."

One thing leading soldiers into battle quickly teaches is the ability to recognize reluctance. This priest, I realized with a start, was in spite of his calm words as reluctant to be at Peyrefixade as I was to have him. Yet there was a determination there too, something that would have been courage in a soldier: a readiness to press forward no matter what the opposition if the cause was right.

"Enter, then, Father Melchior," I said, stepping out from the shadow of the gate, watching for his reaction to my scar.

The duke had not deigned to notice it. Melchior's eyes went very wide for a second, then he dropped his head hurriedly to urge his steed up the final incline.

Surprise, I thought, a surprise that went well beyond seeing a man with an old burn. It was as though he had just made an unexpected connection with something else. Was there some prophecy in his Order about the Last Days arriving when a scarred count ruled at Peyrefixade?

Then I hope they don't arrive quite yet, I thought with an inner smile, before I had a chance to enjoy my castle properly.

"I am glad to have a priest here, Father," I said as he dismounted. "I'll want divine office sung in the chapel at dawn every morning."

"Of course. And I will start by conducting a service immediately. This has not been done here since the countess's death. And I wish to know at once if there are any sick or dying in the castle who wish to confess their sins, or any others who would profit from God's word."

Good man, I thought, one who knew his business and

went straight to it. I considered him critically a moment as he helped the grooms remove his luggage from the packhorse. With none of the urbanity or veneer of one who had spent his life in society, he had a face that was very easy to read. Yet I did not feel that I understood at all what was going on in his mind that gave rise to the expressions I recognized. His was not a soldier's face, but one with complicated thoughts beneath the surface, connected in ways I did not yet grasp. Clearly he would be worth closer study.

"I want to attend your first service," I said. "If you will wait for a few minutes while I finish some other business, we can go to the chapel together and also discuss your duties a little more." He nodded and trailed after Bruno and me as we returned to the kitchens, while the grooms took his baggage away.

"I like this priest more than I expected," I muttered to Bruno in Allemann. "The duke may have chosen himself a good spy."

I had spent much of the morning going through the cook's accounts with him, a process made much more complicated by the very elaborate tally system he had devised to keep track of what was on hand, what he had bought, and what he had used. The records for the spices alone comprised several sheets of parchment closely covered with lines, crosses, circles, and little wiggles. "I still don't see, my lord, how I could have used so much pepper the last few months," he said, looking up from the pages with a frown. "But we slaughtered the pigs almost immediately after the countess's death, and I was so distracted that I must have used most of it up in the processing without even noticing."

"All right," I said, wishing again for a lady to do this. My job should be the castle's defenses and the county's justice, not the staff's diet. "You say we have enough meat, enough flour, enough vegetables, and enough wine. The seneschal says we need candles and cloth and leather, so

I'll have him buy enough spices when he's in town to last us until the prices come down a bit in the spring."

I was distracted by the sight of someone wrapped in a cloak slipping quietly across the far end of the kitchens. Bruno saw him too and jumped for him. "What's this, lad?" he cried, seizing him by the shoulder. "Spying?"

The cook, startled, looked up to say, "That's no spy. That's my assistant." But then he added sharply, "Where do you think you're going? Don't you know we should be serving dinner before too long, and me too rattled by the accounts to have made much preparation?"

"But tha' knows tha' always leaves me go visit m' mother every week," mumbled the assistant, keeping his eyes down. Nervousness had strengthened his accent. His face was flushed, and he tried unsuccessfully to ease himself from Bruno's grip.

"That's right, lad, that's right," the cook started to say.

"I am count here," I barked. "No one leaves to visit anyone without my express permission." The cook started to object and thought better of it. His assistant's cloak had fallen back when Bruno took hold of him, and I could see now that he held some sort of pouch that he was unsuccessfully trying to pull the cloak back over. "And show me what you're carrying!"

"Nothing!" he protested. He was young, not much more than a boy, and genuinely terrified.

I took the pouch from him and opened it. As I suspected, it was full of food: several loaves of bread, a ham shank, some turnips, and, in the bottom, a cloth bag the size of my fist full of peppercorns.

"This explains your disappearing spices," I told the cook, handing it to him.

"But Cook ha' tol' me 'twas all right to take a little something to m' old mother—" the boy said desperately.

"But not to take and sell the single most valuable item in the kitchen," I replied grimly. The scar on my cheek felt as though it was pounding with anger. "How long have you been doing this? Were you cheating the countess too, or did you start after her death?"

He was down on his knees now, trying not to cry. "I'm sorry, m'lord Compte! Forgive me! I ne'er did it before! I'll ne'er do it again! 'Twas just this winter when m' old mother—"

"I don't need to hear about your old mother," I retorted, drumming my fingers on the hilt of my sword. "I only want to hear what choice you make. Your options are the following. You can leave my service immediately, with nothing but the clothes on your back, not even taking enough time between here and the gate to scratch a flea on your butt. Or else I shall accuse you formally of gross theft, put you to the ordeal before the knights, and have you horse-whipped when I adjudge you guilty. After that, and assuming you live, you will be told to leave with the same haste with which I am telling you to leave now."

But he was gone before I finished speaking, leaping up from his knees to sprint toward the gate. "Tell the guards, Bruno," I said, "that he is not to be admitted again under any circumstances. And tell them why." He grinned as he hurried off.

"There should be enough pepper here for a few days at least," I told the cook, "until the seneschal makes his trip to town. You did not, by any chance," looking at him sternly from under my eyebrows, "know what he was taking on these little visits to his mother?"

His protests were nervous but sincere. "You were right to dismiss him, my lord," he said timidly, "but without my assistant I'm afraid dinner will be late today." I nodded briskly and turned to find Brother Melchior staring at me.

Disapproval, I thought. Well, he was a priest. Probably in his Order erring brothers were given a chance to fall on their knees and attain forgiveness. I shrugged. If this had happened six months from now, I might have forgiven the boy myself. But if I failed to act decisively in the very first instance I discovered someone trying to cheat me, I would not have a castle to call my own in six months. The lessons from leading soldiers were clear: discipline first, mercy after discipline had been well established.

But the priest surprised me as we walked toward the chapel. "Do you suspect others of stealing from you?" he asked. "If you are planning to horse-whip all the thieves, you might prefer to have certain knowledge that your suspicions are accurate. And there— Well, magic can help."

We stopped while I looked at him more thoroughly. About my age and about my height, with the air of assurance that all priests have that they are doing precisely the right thing at all times, but with an intelligence and an intensity behind it that I had not seen in many priests. "Divination," I asked slowly, "isn't that what they call it? The power to see what is hidden?"

"That is correct."

"So are you going to tell me the boy *hadn't* been robbing me?"

"Oh, no." He turned to continue again toward the chapel. "I practiced no magic here. Some of the older masters of our Order can practice their particular art wherever they are, but I need my vials and powders and my books even to begin. In this case— When you had his confession, divination seemed scarcely necessary. I hope to begin unpacking immediately after divine service so that I may continue my studies while here."

"You might try to find out," I suggested, "why the late countess fell off a rampart she should have known as well as she knew her own image in the mirror."

His eyes met mine for a second, his expression a mix of intensity and of the curious reluctance I had seen before. "The provost of my Order," he said slowly, "suggested the same thing."

In the next few days the castle began settling into a comfortable routine. Brother Melchior sang the divine office in the chapel each morning as yellow dawn broke over the mountain peaks, and I saw to it that no one overslept more than once. Leading a castle, I decided, was no harder than leading men into battle—easier, because I didn't have to deal with raw terror, either theirs or mine.

"I wish there was some sort of map or plan of Peyrefixade," I said to Seneschal Guilhem on the second day. "I think I know where all the principal chambers are now, but I'm still not sure of the extent of the store rooms, and that old part of the castle around to the back is very confusing."

Guilhem gave me the lugubrious look that seemed customary with him. "You might ask the bouteillier. He was making a map."

Surprised, I sent for Bouteillier Raymbaud. The seneschal's responsibilities were the castle itself and its income, and I would have thought the bouteillier had plenty to do supervising the staff and the wine cellars. Maybe, I thought with an inner smile, he had his eye on the seneschal's position if Guilhem became too ill to continue his duties.

"Raymbaud's only been here since shortly before the countess took over," Bruno informed me while we waited for him. He seemed to be seeking out information about Peyrefixade as assiduously as I was, and it helped that his information was different. "The duke recommended him when she and Lord Thierri were married, but the rest of the knights and the staff have all been here since the days when old Count Bernhard still ruled."

Raymbaud was a young man with a courtier's grace but a heavy accent in speaking the Royal Tongue. Or not a heavy accent, I corrected myself, because he didn't sound anything like the cook's fool assistant, but his intonation differed from that of the rest of the staff in ways my northern ear could not yet clearly identify.

"Of course, my lord, I would be delighted to show you

my map," he said with a dip of the head. "During the empty and sorrowful days this winter after the countess's tragic death, when we did not even know yet that the duke had sent for you, I was able to keep my mind focused by mapping every room, every corridor, every stone."

I had expected some rough sketch and was stunned when he produced what appeared to be a completely realistic image of the castle, such as an eagle might see in flying over it. It was not even a single sheet of parchment but an intricate series of flaps and folds, which one could open to see each of the storeys within each part of the castle. I unfolded them gingerly, almost expecting to see a tiny image of myself in the middle of my great hall. "You did not do this with brush alone," I declared.

"No, my lord, I do have some small skill in magic," Raymbaud said with a rather self-satisfied smile. "And if you will follow me, I can show you that my map represents Peyrefixade quite accurately."

Bruno and I spent much of the rest of the day with Raymbaud as he led us around, showing us each feature of my castle as proudly as though it were his own. I forced myself to put aside my immediate and unreasoned thought that there must be something sinister about a man, not even a priest, who had studied the rudiments of magic; clearly my northern expectations had no place here.

I already was familiar with the courtyard, entered by the great gates opposite the keep, with the stables on one side and the kitchens opening off the other. The keep, with the great hall on the main floor and chambers above, I also knew, but I hadn't realized how extensive were the store rooms underneath. Raymbaud led me around behind the keep, circling the tower where I had stood on my first morning in Peyrefixade, to a little terrace from which a steep stair led down to the postern gate, the private way in or out of the castle. Bruno and I took a torch to follow the long, long spiral of stairs down and back. Then, with the magic map in hand, I was finally able to make sense of the tangle of passages and stairways at the back of the castle, an area now apparently little used except for a small practice yard, shadowed by a squat square tower that stared away across the mountains.

Several knights were practicing their sword-fighting there, and I joined them, both to assure myself that my skills had not become rusty during the long trip down here and to assure them that a scarred count could fight as well as anyone. Raymbaud also joined us and showed himself a polished if rather cautious swordsman.

"You were clearly brought up as a knight," I said to him when we stopped to mop our brows. "You know fighting as well as you do your wine barrels. A younger son?" An archduke's younger son, I thought, at least had the opportunity to fight for the emperor. The landless younger son of a manorial lord would be lucky to find himself a service position at court that was not too degrading.

"That's right, my lord," he said with an accommodating smile and another dip of the head. "And I count it my good fortune that I have been able to serve both in Duke Argave's court and more recently here in Peyrefixade. My goal is always to provide service of the level that I would want were I lord here myself."

"He must be the duke's spy here," I said in private to Bruno later that evening. "Our duke seems to have a taste for Magians. Say nothing to Raymbaud to let him know we've guessed his secret. Even aside from his abilities in castle management, which the next man the duke tried to plant on me might not have, a known spy can be dealt with as long as he does not realize he has been recognized."

Once I had learned the names of the rest of the staff and had stood watching them at work long enough that I had a good idea of their functions and abilities—and they had come to the realization that I would be no slipshod master—I turned my attention to the documents in the bottom of the treasure chest. The old count, my great-uncle, had kept very good records. Most people who give property to the Church trust the monks or canons to keep the records of the transfers themselves, but he had had his own scribe draw up the charters and make chirographic duplicates of all of them. The two identical accounts had been written on a single piece of parchment, side-by-side, with the word CHIROGRAPHUM written vertically between them, and then the two had been cut apart through the letters of that word, so the two halves could be fitted back together if there were any question of their authenticity.

"The religious house our *capellanus* comes from was built on what was once Peyrefixade land," I told Bruno, leafing through the records while seated with my feet up in a window seat in the great hall. If I turned my head I could look out the narrow window at clouds scudding across the ridges, first obscuring and then revealing distant peaks much taller than mine. "And the brothers pasture their sheep on more land that the countess's grandfather gave them, and grind their grain in a mill theirs by his gift."

"So is that why his Order wants him here?" suggested Bruno. He sat on the floor beside me, sharpening his knife. "Keep an eye on you, make sure the new count doesn't try to claim it back?"

"That would make sense from the canons' point of view," I said with a frown, "but it doesn't explain the duke. Sending Brother Melchior here seems to have been our duke's idea—certainly not Melchior's own. But the county of Peyrefixade must be, at least potentially, the most troublesome in his duchy. If, for example, I decided to defy him or to make an alliance with the princes south of the border, he would have real trouble rousting me out. Perhaps he's hoping that a priest from the Order of the Three Kings will encourage me to make even *more* gifts to his Order, thus ensuring that I never have a strong material base from which to threaten him."

Inwardly I wondered, as I had several times before, if the duke's hints about his daughter were also part of a plan to keep me even from thinking of challenging him.

The emperor had confidently assumed that his sworn liege men would never turn on him, and I would be sworn to Duke Argave at the end of the week, but perhaps here in the south they anticipated that men would break their word.

"I don't understand about that priest," said Bruno with a quick look around and a lowered voice, though there was no one nearby. "He's supposed to be a Magian, but I haven't seen him do any magic yet. Even the bouteillier can do better tricks than he can. And if the priest's whole Order is made up of conjurers, why can't they just conjure food and clothing out of the air rather than having to make it like everybody else?"

"You'll have to ask Melchior that yourself," I said, returning to the charters. "It looks as though the late Countess Aenor tried to take back some of her grandfather's pious gifts after she inherited."

"Did the canons use magic to stop her?" asked Bruno, interested.

"I don't know. All I have is the record of the agreement when the quarrel ended." I skimmed through the document, puzzling over some of the words in the antique language still used for formal charters. "This suggests, without actually saying so, that they threatened to stop praying for her grandfather and for her own parents, who had died earlier. They all seem to be buried at their religious house."

"Well, they couldn't be buried here on the mountain," said Bruno reasonably. "No soil to speak of—certainly not six feet of it."

"Earlier counts must have had a mausoleum," I said absently. "Maybe that's what those rumors I've heard about secret passages here were all about—though Raymbaud's map didn't show any mausoleum."

"There weren't earlier counts," said Bruno unexpectedly. He held up his knife to the light, squinting to judge the sharpness of the blade. "Your great-grandfather was the first count at Peyrefixade. The castle was built by the heretics, those people who call themselves the Perfected."

"How did you learn that?" I demanded, swinging my feet to the floor. "There are no charters in here more than forty years old." This was *my* castle and should not have such dark secrets in its past, certainly not secrets I didn't even know.

Bruno grinned. "Talking to some of the servants. You can learn a lot that way. Men will tell things to another servant they'd never tell a master."

"And that's why I put up with having you around," I said good-naturedly, leaning back again. "But tell me about these heretics. I thought my own grandfather was from a count's family."

"Your great-grandfather led the war that drove the filthy heretics back," said Bruno in a storyteller's voice, enjoying this, "though his two sons were the actual field commanders. It was a great and terrible war, with thousands killed on both sides, but the followers of the True Faith won at last and drove the devil's spawn to that little strip of land they still control in the high mountains along the border. Your great-grandfather was named Galoran, too—did you know that? After the war he was rewarded with the title of Count of Peyrefixade, the first count of your line. A little later when he died, his younger son, your grandfather, went north, but his older son, Bernhard, held the county for a great many years, until he finally died a year ago and his granddaughter started raising trouble with the Magians."

"I've heard mention of that war, of course," I said thoughtfully, looking out the window again. I could see, half way up my mountain, a single rider. "They must indeed have had God on their side to be able to capture this castle. My family surely hated the heretics as much as the duke does."

"Maybe the secret passages were hidden by heretic magic when they fled from here," Bruno suggested.

But he was interrupted by the triple note of the horn.

The person I had seen approaching had not looked particularly important, so I waited for him to come to me rather than going out to the gate. I returned the parchments to the treasury box along with the remains of the countess's money. Less of it was gold than I had hoped, but there was still enough for supplies until the March rents—assuming the seneschal's figures were accurate, for he, unlike the cook, seemed to keep everything in his mournful head.

In a minute a somewhat bedraggled knight entered, escorted by my guards. His cloak was torn and stained and the hauberk under it rusty. He went down on his knees before me, with only the slightest encouraging push from the guards, and offered me his sword, hilt first. "I'm sorry I didn't get here right away, my lord," he mumbled, "but I was busy."

"No one should be so busy that he cannot greet his new lord," I said sternly, deliberately turning the scarred side of my face toward him. As I spoke I wondered who he could be. Another member of my staff who had been on one too many little visits to his old mother? Not a dependent castellan, because the seneschal had told me Peyrefixade was the only castle in the county; I wouldn't be like my brother the archduke, with scores of castellans to oversee. Perhaps a village mayor with delusions of grandeur?

It was the latter. I accepted his sword and held it by the hilt, making no motion for him to rise, while he explained why he had finally decided to come up the mountain. "And so it was a clear case of adultery," he said, finishing the complicated details of an affair that must have entertained and scandalized his village for months. "I've ruled them guilty, but because it's a capital case you have to seal my justice-roll. For the duke," he added as I frowned.

"If this is a case of high justice," I said slowly, "then only I, as count, can adjudicate."

"Well, yes," he said, hesitating now, "but Countess Aenor always told me to go ahead myself. She trusted me and sealed the roll."

"But I am not the countess." I thrust his sword back at him. "If you're my man, you have to do things my way." I had no desire at all to ride down the mountain and hear a bunch of villagers scream at each other, but it appeared I had no choice. Delegating authority in capital cases was the easiest way to lose prestige among underlings and to encourage abuse of power. That was one thing even my brother had known well. "You haven't put any of them to death *yet,* have you?" I asked in some trepidation.

"Well, no," he said, trying to justify himself. "Sealed ruling first, execution afterwards."

"I seal no decision of high justice," I said, reaching for my cloak, "until I hear it myself." Bruno resignedly stood up, and I motioned to two knights to accompany us as I strode through the courtyard on the way to the stable. Further perusal of parchments—or search for secret passages—would have to wait.

2

I had never seen anything like Duke Argave's court.

It was located in the wealthy market town of Ferignan, in a broad river valley where several streams came together, including one that flowed from the base of Peyrefixade and one that, according to Brother Melchior, flowed from the peak where his Order's principal religious house was located. The hills surrounding the town were planted with the olive trees Bruno and I had missed in Peyrefixade, although this time of year their branches were sere and gray.

The duke's castle was located on a slight rise above the guild halls and merchants' houses that provided supplies for my castle and probably half the other villages and castles in the duchy. I thought it showed Argave's ancestors' supreme confidence in their own power that they had not sought out an inaccessible peak like Peyrefixade. Even in the cold wind of a late winter afternoon a few beggars clustered at the duke's gates, and I threw them a handful of coppers. The castle's outer walls were pierced with arrow slits and had grim towers commanding every corner, but within was a softness and luxury I had never seen, even at the imperial court.

The duke's guards met us at the gates while I stood staring in at the fountains and arbors of the courtyard. "All swords and knives to be surrendered," they told us briskly. "The duke keeps the peace within his walls."

The half dozen knights I had brought along did not seem surprised and indeed started unbuckling their sword belts immediately, but Bruno and I looked at each other in amazement. I had never been unarmed in a public place since I was a boy. Well, the emperor did practice something similar on his high feast days, but as a member of his trusted guard I had always been one of those few who *retained* his weapons.

"Knives, too," a guard insisted as I reluctantly handed over my sword. The guards were giving out velvet gloves in return, in a variety of different colors and embroidery patterns that I presumed would help them identify our particular swords later. But I would feel very foolish in the meantime trying to defend my life or honor with a velvet glove.

"Without my knife, how am I supposed to cut my meat?" I demanded.

"Dinner knives will be provided."

Brother Melchior handed over his knife; he of course did not wear a sword. I was interested to note that he thrust the crimson velvet glove he received in return deep in a pocket of his cassock, as though embarrassed to be seen holding anything so gaudy.

The duke himself came across the courtyard to meet me as soon as we were through the gates. Not all the fountains were running this time of year, but there was a constant background sound of tinkling showers and a hint of sandalwood essence in the air, masking the cold, dry scents of February. Faint but lively music played somewhere in the distance. The paths between the shrubbery of the courtyard were not gravel but slabs of marble.

The duke was resplendent in silk and velvet, the pointed toes on his shoes twice as long as the ones the seneschal had hastily bought for me here in town the other day. Around his neck he wore a wide, tightly pleated ruff; no one had told me anything about the fashion in ruffs. "My dear Galoran!" he cried, clasping my arm. "How delighted it makes me that today you shall become my man!"

Since the price of Peyrefixade seemed to be swearing myself to a duke I didn't quite trust, I pulled back my lips in an accommodating smile. I noted that Argave himself was wearing a sword.

"I shall introduce you to some of the others before the ceremony," he said, leading me into his hall. Bruno, Melchior, and the knights came behind. Here, too, marble had been used enthusiastically, pink marble for the floors, with just a slightly rough texture, and green marble for the walls—wherever the walls showed amidst the hanging tapestries—polished until the stone seemed covered with a layer of glass. Here I spotted the source of the music, a little group of men playing on lute, recorder, and krumhorn. Out-of-season flowering plants stood on small tables throughout the room, and braziers tucked discreetly into corners warmed and softly perfumed the air. Men and women in brightly colored clothing stood in groups around the room. Most of the men, I noticed, had velvet gloves thrust in their belts. Light came from glittering candelabra suspended from the high ceiling.

The duke introduced me to a half dozen young women, all of whom wore silk dresses cut much closer to the body and *much* lower over the bust than anything my sister-

in-law had ever worn. Without my sword I felt awkward
and half naked myself. Their smooth white necks were
encircled with strands of gold and pearl. All smiled to
meet the new master of Peyrefixade and averted their
eyes politely from my scar, but they gave no immediate
sign of "flocking around," as my servants seemed to expect
they would. None of them were the duke's daughter
Arsendis.

And then I saw her on the far side of the room,
recognizable at once from her portrait. She was fully grown,
perhaps a year or two older, I would have thought, than
the age at which a duke would normally marry off his
daughter. Rather than having her curly black hair decently
covered—as even the ladies I had just met did—she wore
it loose around her shoulders, covered only by a thin gold
net set with tiny pearls.

She was deeply absorbed in conversation with a middle-
aged lord, smiling up at him, keeping her dark uptilted
eyes intently on his face. A few yards away, looking at
the man just as intently but scowling instead of smiling,
was a knight about my age. Arsendis ignored him pointedly.
Jealousy, I thought. It looked as though the duke's daughter
already had two suitors even without me.

Brother Melchior, at my elbow, surprised me by
whispering, "The young *ducissa* refused the count whom
her father chose for her two years ago. Three men so far
have been killed in duels over her."

She left the current suitors readily enough, however,
when her father called her, and crossed toward us with a
swirl of blue silk, giving a saucy smile over her shoulder
to the knight she had been ignoring.

"My daughter Arsendis, Count Galoran," said the duke
formally. "I trust you will welcome him warmly for my
sake, my dear."

I went down on one knee—careful not to trip myself
on my new shoes' long toes—to kiss her hand gallantly,
as Bruno had informed me he had heard southern men

used to do when visiting the countess at Peyrefixade. This put my eyes level with her breasts, very full for a woman so slim, and apparently on the verge of breaking out through the low neck of her dress. Flustered, I scrambled back to my feet and fixed my eyes on her face.

A definite look of mischief lurked at the corner of her red-painted mouth. Back in the north, only the loose women who welcomed merchant travelers to town or who followed the armies painted their lips. Amusement glinted in her dark eyes, as though she understood very well why I was flustered.

It did not help that she pressed herself briefly against me, standing on tiptoe to plant a *kiss* on my right cheek—the cheek without the scar. "Welcome to our home, Count Galoran of Peyrefixade. We are very glad to have your addition grace our company," she murmured, the polite hostess, then glided away without giving me a chance to answer, to speak again with her middle-aged lord.

For a second I stood stock still, expecting the duke to challenge me for daring such intimacy with his daughter. Bruno would back me up, but I wasn't sure I could count on my knights in a situation like this, and Bruno and I would not get far opposing steel with velvet.

But Duke Argave only smiled. Perhaps that was how young ladies normally greeted special visitors here in the south. I shook my shoulders, thinking I could get used to this *quite* easily. My sister-in-law, I was sure, had never kissed a special visitor in her life. A laugh I had to suppress fought upwards as I wondered just how many times she had even kissed Guibert.

"And I wish you to meet Lord Thierri, husband of the late Countess of Peyrefixade." The duke spoke perfectly easily, but his eyes met mine for a second, narrow with a warning to remember all he had told me of this man.

"I would be in all ways delighted," I said, trying for the same courtly tone but having it come out more awkwardly than I intended. The duke steered me across the room with a hand on my sleeve, the hand with the emerald ring. Around us I could catch scraps of conversation in what sounded like the local Auccitan tongue. I really was going to have to learn it.

Thierri, no longer Count of Peyrefixade, turned toward us, and the duke performed the introductions. In a court in which almost everyone was dark complexioned, Thierri had hair red as a fox and sharp green eyes. His neck ruff was as wide and as elaborately pleated as the duke's.

"Really, the new count?" he said with a hint of a drawl as he looked me up and down. "What a fine jest, my lord Duke! I confess you completely took me in. I had thought this one of the beggars from the gate dressed up in silks to entertain us, so what a surprise to discover he is instead a scarred soldier fresh from the uncivilized backwaters of the north. Fell in the fire when he'd drunk too much for his weak head, I'll venture. Is this what you chose to sleep in my bed at Peyrefixade, Argave?"

All conversation around us came to an abrupt halt, though the musicians kept on playing. I closed my fists slowly, looking at the duke from the corner of my eye. If someone in the emperor's court had insulted me like this, I would have drawn my sword at once—or, if it was someone the emperor didn't want dead, have knocked him down and sat on his chest to pummel him until he begged for mercy. Both of those alternatives seemed out of the question in this elegant hall.

But he had insulted the duke as well as me, and Argave was waiting to see what I would do. I deliberately pulled out the ridiculous velvet glove I carried instead of my sword and slapped Thierri across the face with it. The music stopped short, and everyone in the hall seemed to draw a sharp breath together. Thierri winced at the blow but did not retaliate—I was almost sorry he didn't. "Outside, in the courtyard," I said between my teeth. "There I shall give you one opportunity to withdraw those words."

Duke Argave stepped briskly between us. "First the ceremony, and then dinner," he said loudly. Everyone else in the room was staring at us. But after only a second the musicians found their place and began again. "I cannot risk losing my new count even before he gives his oaths! But then, if you two hotheads still insist on imperiling the ducal peace of my court, you can walk in the chill of the outside air until your tempers have cooled." But he gave me a quick sideways look, lifting his eyebrows and the corner of his mouth as though very well pleased.

The ceremony of my allegiance to Duke Argave went smoothly. The duke's *capellanus* hovered in the background—his cassock was cut just like Brother Melchior's, though of finer material, and I guessed that he too was of the Order of the Three Kings—but Melchior himself presented me the relics on which I swore. Bruno and the knights who had been mine for only a week all went on their knees at my back as I put my hands in the duke's and promised to be his liege man, giving him good counsel and good aid, thwarting his enemies and never turning against him, forsaking the allegiance of all other lords.

He drew me up then and kissed me on both cheeks, not flinching from the scar. "Thierri's a coward at heart," he murmured in my ear as he turned me around to present me formally to all his other sworn men.

A separate dining chamber, adjacent to the great hall, had already been prepared, and we all proceeded in. White candles flickered, sending light dancing across silver serving platters. The duke's chamberlain moved unobtrusively among us, directing each toward the tables chosen for us. I ended up at the high table with the duke and his daughter Arsendis.

Brother Melchior brushed against my elbow again. He seemed able to move quickly and quietly even in a crowd. "I shall not stay for dinner," he said in a low voice. "I have had more than enough of the duke's court over the years and shall spend the night at the little priory my Order

maintains outside the castle walls." I glanced up and saw
the duke's own *capellanus* at the door, apparently also
ready to leave. Melchior started to turn away but then
turned back. "Thierri is deliberately trying to provoke you.
Do not give him the satisfaction of it, but turn the other
cheek."

Though I was pleased at his concern for me, I was not
worried about Thierri. We would both be weaponless out
in the duke's courtyard, but I was, I judged, much stronger
than he. Instead I turned my attention to the duke's
excellent dinner.

There were as many courses as at any dinner I had
ever eaten at the emperor's court, beginning with roast
geese, their feathers reassembled around them to make
them appear lifelike on the platter, and proceeding through
fried eggs, baked garlic and leeks, lemon sherbet, boiled
beef with turnips, roast pork—the meat again reassembled
into the body's original shape, a glaze of honey and bits
of lemon peel providing the appearance of skin and bristle
and the boar's head itself glaring at us from the end of
the platter—milk pudding, spiced honey cakes, and
chestnuts.

Arsendis, seated at my elbow, entertained me while we
ate with highly moral tales from antiquity, similar to the
stories taught me as a boy in the emperor's court, and
inquired graciously how I was finding life at Peyrefixade.
Although she was attentive, there was none of the warmth
in her manner I thought I had seen her show to the older
lord, but then he was seated just a short distance away
and watching us.

The duke had indeed provided his guests with dinner
knives—sharpened only along one side—and even with
dinner forks, small versions of serving forks such I had
never seen used before, but which enabled one to
immobilize the meat while cutting it, far more gracefully
than using one's fingers. The tiny dish from which Arsendis
and I dipped salt with our littlest fingers was plated with

gold. There were no dogs under the table or even rushes on the floor, but by watching the duke I discovered that one of the plates was specifically meant for the bones and gristle, removed regularly by the servants. With each course came glasses of wine, both white and red. By the time the servants were gathering up the chestnut shells and bringing us basins of warm water in which to wash our fingers, I was full and a little drunk and had almost forgotten Thierri.

But he had not forgotten me. The musicians began playing again out in the great hall as the duke rose to his feet. Several couples hurried at once to begin dancing among the flowering plants. But Thierri sauntered up to me, his green eyes glittering, and asked, "Are you still interested in accompanying me on a little promenade in the courtyard, Count Scar? Or has this excellent meal slaked your need to avenge your honor?"

I located Bruno and the knights, standing up from a table at the far end of the room and looking as well satisfied as I felt, and gathered them up with a jerk of my chin. If Thierri had knights of his own with whom he hoped to overpower me, my men and I would be prepared to wrestle.

But no one accompanied him as he led me through the doors from the great hall into the courtyard. A number of people observed us go, but none moved to follow. The cold air hit us at once. Night had fallen, but the marble paths among the arbors and shrubbery were lit by flambeaux, and a nearly full moon gave fitful light when not obscured by fast-moving clouds.

Thierri's manner changed at once. "Good to get out of that overheated atmosphere," he said companionably, taking deep breaths of the cool wind. His voice was crisp and sober; he must have drunk much less than I had. "A soldier like you surely feels as restricted by all that womanly delicacy as I do, and I have to live here all the time now!"

I considered him thoughtfully, wishing my head did

not feel so thick. "You're a courtier among the courtiers, but want to appear a simple knight of the military camp to me? I would be more impressed if I had spent less time in military camps—or in the emperor's court."

"Insulting you before everyone," he said with a chuckle that sounded just a bit forced, "was the only way I could think of to get you out here for a private conversation. And let me say right away, Count, how *sincerely* sorry I am to have said those things to you!" He bared his teeth in an insincere smile. "None of what I said then reflects my true respect for you and your position, but I felt it was my only chance. Merely asking you to talk with me would have made everyone suspicious, but this way they'll leave us alone for at least half an hour. You won't need your knights," motioning toward Bruno and the others, who stood waiting for my orders. These knights had, I reminded myself, obeyed Thierri until two months ago.

"What sort of private conversation did you want?" I asked cautiously, not at all sure whether to accept such a lame apology. The wind made the flambeaux smoke, and their flames cast alternating light and shadow across his face.

He dropped his voice and leaned toward me. His red hair had been turned dark by the night. "About Peyrefixade. I need to reassure you about my wife's death."

"I was very sorry to learn of your loss," I said, stiffly and belatedly.

"And to warn you of what's happening there."

He certainly had my attention, but that didn't mean I trusted him in the slightest. "Suppose I break your nose before we have this conversation," I suggested. "That way we'll allay everyone's suspicions that we've been discussing secrets."

He chuckled again, sounding even more forced. He had, I decided, absolutely no resources other than his tongue and sheer bluff. Perhaps he really had insulted me for the purpose of getting me out here for a conversation, but he had certainly meant it as an insult as well—and a chance to remind the rest of the court to beware of his tongue. Back among all the other members of the duke's court after less than two years at Peyrefixade, he had been cut off from ready income, his own knights, or even the respect of his fellows. Even if not formally accused of his wife's death, he must be a suspect in many people's eyes.

Pity pushed aside my anger with him. He was even worse off than I had been in my brother's castle. Breaking his nose could wait for another occasion. We turned and strolled slowly among the fountains and shrubs, leaving the knights by the hall door.

The cool air, if not reminding me of the plains of battle, did at least sober me up a bit. "You were about to assure me," I said when he was silent, "that you know absolutely nothing about your wife's tragic accident."

"But I do," he said quietly, looking up at the moon and not at me. "I had no hand in her death myself, of course. I was always within sight of a dozen people, not even counting my own servants, the night she fell and died. Even Duke Argave admits that. But what he will not admit or even consider—and I know the real reason he would not accept me as the new count to succeed my wife—was that she was killed by the priests of the Order of the Three Kings."

I was so startled that I could not immediately answer.

But he did not wait for an answer. "They always hated me, the whole time I was at Peyrefixade. My wife's grandfather was a pious old fool in his dotage, giving away half the county patrimony to those self-styled holy men. Greedy hypocrites if you ask me. The spiritual advisor he'd brought to his court claimed to be a Magian, but I couldn't even get the man to work a few magic tricks to entertain my guests. Anyway, as soon as my wife inherited she and I started trying to recover some of what the old man had let slip into the Order's fingers."

When he paused I put in, "She became penitent,

however, when the Order threatened to stop praying for
her parents and grandparents."

The torchlight flashed on the whites of Thierri's eyes
as he looked quickly toward me, then away. "Your priest
tell you that? Yes, it's true, she did weaken at one point.
Having to hire men of law to argue that the old man was
incompetent in his final years started to seem a little sordid
to her, even disrespectful. She needed reminding of the
final goal."

As Thierri himself seemed more than a little sordid
and disrespectful to me, I remained silent.

Appearing to take my silence for doubt, he hurried on,
"And there's more to my certainty of their guilt in her death
than the fact that the Order had a good motive. They were
seen. One of my servants had gone to look for her, because
normally she joined us in the hall when I was entertaining.
And he says that for a second the ramparts appeared very
different than they ever had before, as though there was a
room or terrace where none had ever been— It was a foggy
night, so at first it was hard to be sure. But he realized
that it had all been a magical illusion, designed to make
her step out into the air, when he heard her scream."

Here he paused, as though recalling that he was
describing not just any strange event but the tragic details
of his wife's death. "It must have been very terrible for
you," I said sympathetically, wanting to keep him talking.
My head had started aching now. Sounds of music and
laughter drifted out from the duke's hall.

"Oh, yes," he said without any particular force. "As you
can imagine, I dismissed our charlatan spiritual advisor,
Nuage his name was, that very night. Priest or not, he'd
have been put to the ordeal two months ago if the duke
hadn't refused to hear anything against the Order of the
Three Kings. But I see he's already saddled you with a
new *capellanus* from their number!"

"The duke seems very sympathetic to the Order," I
agreed. If any of what Thierri was saying was true, and

Brother Melchior's Order had used magic to rid themselves of a troublesome countess, then I would have to be especially alert around him. But then I was not at all certain that anything Thierri said was true.

"Argave *says* that the Order is the best bulwark against the evil magic-workers whom the heretics employ," he continued. "He hates the heretics so much that it blinds him to everything else."

"And why does he hate the heretics so much?" Even if I did not trust his answers, they continued to raise intriguing possibilities. First I had thought Melchior a spy for the duke, but now he might be an agent for his Order with a hidden mission.

But I was not prepared for Thierri's answer. "I thought everyone knew. Argave's own son Gavain was lured away by the Perfected."

"And they killed him?" I said, shocked.

"Even worse. He joined them."

We strolled on slowly for a moment, the soft sounds of our shoes on marble almost lost amidst the murmur of the fountains and the rustle of the wind in the shrubbery. "The duke has hated them all his life. That may be why his son and heir—rebellious and troublesome as all boys are, as I'm sure you were yourself!—joined them five years ago. Since then, anyone who opposes the Perfected can do no wrong in Argave's eyes."

We were near the back wall of the garden now, at the furthest point from the hall doors. "By the way, Thierri," I said casually, "why are you telling me all this?"

"To see justice done. To bring the evil murderers of my wife before the tribunal and to see them hang."

"There's more," I said slowly. "If you only wanted vengeance for the death of your wife, you wouldn't need me."

"I want to warn you, of course," he answered heartily. "I don't want to see the same thing happen to you as happened to her!"

"Why not? I would think my sudden death an excellent opportunity for you. The duke has to have *someone* at Peyrefixade, and if I were gone he might settle on you after all."

He shook his head, a faint motion in the darkness here away from the flambeaux. "If you were gone, Galoran, he'd simply choose someone else from your family. Don't you have some brothers or nephews back north? Because the Order's complained to Argave about me, he'd just send off again for your replacement."

"But suppose I was frightened away?" I persisted. "If I fled home in terror, none of my relatives would be likely to listen to the duke's messengers again."

Thierri never had a chance to answer. Out of the shadows a dark form sprang toward me. The flambeaux behind us glinted on the steel of his knife.

Instinct saved me, born of years on the battlefield. I dropped and rolled, coming up behind him while he was still striking at the spot where a second ago I had stood. But then I lost valuable time groping for where my sword should be before I remembered and dodged just out of the way of another slashing blow. Wine had slowed my reflexes. There was a tug at my sleeve and a ripping sound as the assailant's blade momentarily caught in the fabric before he jerked it free.

The toes of my new shoes caught as I spun around. But I kicked upward as I fell, feeling a foot land satisfactorily in the assailant's gut. I sprang upwards, head into his chin, and heard the knife clatter free against the paving.

For a second we rolled, grappling for each other's throats. I still had not seen his face. Then there was another shadow over us, a sharp blow of a fist, and my assailant went momentarily limp.

I struggled free of his grip and grabbed his arms to pin them, though after a second he began struggling again. At the same moment torchlight flashed anew on the steel of the blade. Thierri had picked up the knife. While I was still pulling the man's arms behind him, Thierri jerked back his head by the hair and slit his throat.

I let him go and pushed myself slowly to my feet, my new finery ruined by the rush of blood. My arm stung where the sleeve was ripped—he must have nicked me after all. My chest rose and fell in great gasps, and, now that it was safely over, the fear I had not had the opportunity to feel in the few seconds of the fight all caught up with me.

"Well, Count Scar," said Thierri triumphantly. His back was to the flambeaux and his face invisible in shadow. "I've just saved your life. Do you still think I'm trying to get rid of you?"

My knights were suddenly all around us. "I could have told you not to go off walking alone with this one," muttered Bruno. We dragged the assailant's body back toward the torchlight. His blood left dark streaks on the marble.

"Is this anyone you know?" I asked them all.

No one claimed to recognize him. His features distorted, his hair thick with his own blood, he might have been hard to recognize even in daylight, but he certainly did not look like anyone I had ever met. "Probably someone hired by the Magians," muttered Thierri.

The duke's guards had appeared by now, expressing horror and dismay that the ducal peace had been broken by such an incident. "You might want to pay more attention to the walls at the far side of the garden," said Thierri pointedly. "It looks to me as though someone scaled them when you weren't paying attention, someone who hated our new Count Galoran."

But I pulled him aside. He was almost as bloody as I was, though I thought it all the assassin's blood. "Are you *quite* certain," I asked, low and intense, "that this was not an assassin you hired yourself?"

"To kill you? My dear Galoran," with a remarkably convincing attempt at a chuckle, "your imagination has run away with itself. Why would I save you from my own assassin?" He tried without success to extricate his arm from my grip.

The duke had been summoned and was rapidly approaching, his sword drawn. Inside the music had stopped, and the other courtiers and guests clustered in the doorway.

"You killed him so that he could not accuse you," I told Thierri, speaking fast. "When you realized he would not succeed in murdering me, you had to make sure no one would ever mention *your* role in hiring him."

"But I had his knife. It would have been easy enough to kill you myself if that had been my plan! Because I suspected this was a magic-worker—either a heretic or another Magian of the sort we've just been discussing— I had to kill him before he blasted us with an evil spell."

Duke Argave stood over the body, talking rapidly with my knights and members of his own guard. Men raced off in all directions to search the shrubbery for lurkers. I turned toward the duke, but just before I did I added in a whisper to Thierri, "I think that blow of yours, before you cut his throat, was meant for *me*, not him. You were slow enough to come to my rescue and only did so when you realized your plan had failed."

I whirled away from him then, not waiting for his answer. It was such an appealing explanation that I only wished I could believe it.

Chapter Four ~ Melchior

1

Arriving once more within the familiar walls of the priory after several years' absence, I was surprised to find my spirits rising almost as if I'd come home. I, who had been so eager to leave this place, that seemed too much within the worldly influence of Duke Argave's nearby court, for isolation and study at the Mother House! I was, however, disappointed to discover upon asking that Brother Nuage was no longer to be found there. His notes had been of little help so far, and I'd been hoping to talk with him.

"No, he left over a week ago for our new daughter house up toward Haulbé," Prior Belthesar told me. "They've been growing quite a bit of late and wanted someone to teach divination to the novices. If you'd still been with us, I'd have recommended you! He was happy to go; said he would be glad of something new to do in a different place."

The bell rang for the office then, and the evening meal followed. Afterwards, Prior Belthesar asked me and a few of the brothers I'd known best during my earlier time in the priory to come sit with him a while and take a little wine.

"So, Brother Melchior, you have left the Mother House now and are out with us serving in the world once more," said one of them, a fat worldly brother I'd always rather disliked. "*Capellanus* to a count, forsooth! How does your new place of service suit you? Are you able to keep up your magical studies amidst all the demands of life at a court? I know you are very much devoted to them."

"I am finding some time for those, Brother," I told him. "Count Galoran does not keep a 'court' in anything like the style our lord the duke does. You will find no velvet gloves or crystal fountains at Peyrefixade. Stone and cold steel is more to his liking."

"He was formerly a soldier to the emperor of the Allemanns, I believe." Trust Prior Belthesar to possess good information; he'd likely had this from the duke himself. "Is he a hard sort of man?"

"He can be. I saw him dismiss a thieving servant to certain poverty and degradation the first day I was in his house, then he rode down into the village two days later and hanged an adulterous couple. He ate a hearty supper in the hall both those nights."

"Like our lord duke then, but without the polish," laughed the fat brother. "Poor Brother Melchior! This doesn't sound the sort of man in whose service *you'll* be very comfortable."

"Are you in fact finding this service difficult for your strength to bear, my son?" Prior Belthesar asked me.

"Any service to which one is called should not be too much for one's strength, my father." I saw the fat brother looking at me with open skepticism and felt I must say more. "I begin to discover that Count Galoran is an interesting man, a man of some character. I do not believe he wholly trusts either me or our Order, for instance, yet he seems to approve of how I am going about my duties as his *capellanus*. I think he is willing to suspend final judgment until he sees what we are for himself. He is fiercely determined to discharge his office as count properly, and all his actions are bent toward that single goal. But he is not stupid in his singlemindedness. Also, I am finding many opportunities to improve my own spiritual discipline at Peyrefixade. Being solely responsible for the religious welfare of an entire castle and all its people, conducting the divine offices entirely by myself every day at dawn, have been good." I paused in surprise; I hadn't realized all of this myself until I heard myself say it.

"Excellent, my son." Prior Belthesar gave a slow smile over his wine cup. "Our Order's mission is to be active in the world for human good as priests and magic workers as much as to deepen knowledge of the magic arts and pursue religious devotions within the cloister. You have just spent a considerable period in withdrawal and study. It is well that you are now out in the world again to put all you have learned to use among ordinary men and women. I felt sure you would be—goodness, what can be the cause of this commotion? Brother Melchior, it sounds to me very much as if someone is calling your name."

At a nod from the prior, the brother nearest the door slipped out to see what was happening. He returned at once, accompanied by a pair of the duke's armed guardsmen, a scandalous sight in the prior's private parlor. But more shocking still was the news they brought.

"My God: Count Galoran attacked!" I blurted. "Lord Thierri must have been behind this!"

"No, Father, they are saying Lord Thierri saved him."

I shook my head; nothing in this seemed to make sense. But my duty at the moment was clear. "Is the count seriously injured, does he require extreme unction?"

"No, but our master the duke thought it proper that you be informed at once."

"The assassin is dead, you say. But do they have his weapon?" Prior Belthesar asked the men.

"Yes, my lord Prior."

His shrewd eyes went to me, and I knew at once what he was thinking. "I—I shall need the appropriate materials, my father. My own are at Peyrefixade. Lodestone, and powdered copper, and—"

"I hope I still know what is required for such a problem, even if I have never mastered that particular branch of magic to the same extent as yourself," he replied. The fat brother was sent off, huffing noisily, to return with a fine ivory chest in his hands. Prior Belthesar took it and presented it to me. "This is the very diviner's box with which you perfected your own studies during your time here, if I am not mistaken. Now let's be off."

"You are coming too, my father?"

"This involves Duke Argave as well as your count, my son. Lest you forget, I serve as *his capellanus*, and his chief Magian as well."

The shrubbery of the duke's garden appeared almost black in the flaring light of the flambeaux as we hurried out along the marble paths toward the crowd of elegant people gathered near the back wall. They parted before us, and I saw the duke and the captain of his guard standing over a contorted body. Another guard stood by, quietly holding Lord Thierri by his fashionably broad sleeve. Then my eye found Count Galoran. He was standing by the wall with the scarred side of his face turned away from the light, the fine clothes that had earlier looked so strange on his hard soldier's body covered in blood. A shock went through me when I saw that his man Bruno was binding a bandage around one of his arms.

"Just a little nick in the meat, Father Melchior; I've had scores worse from friends on the practice ground," he muttered as I reached him. "I didn't even notice it until the excitement was past."

Without pausing to reply, I snatched the diviner's box from the guardsman who had been carrying it for me. Bruno and Count Galoran stared as I took out the large opal and the silver speculum that had been stowed, *Deo gratias,* exactly where they were supposed to be by whichever student or instructor had last used the box. I placed the opal upon the area of the wound and positioned the speculum close above it, then called to one of the guards to bring a torch and hold it close. I had to shut my eyes for a moment, but then the words and phrases to form the linkages came. When I looked again I sagged in relief to see the opal and the silver mirror both shining as clear as before. "Hmm, good," said Prior Belthesar, who had stepped up beside me unnoticed. "And quickly done, too, my son."

"It is not unheard of for the daggers of assassins to be poisoned in these parts, Count Galoran," I heard him explaining a moment later, as if at a distance. I had been forced to put out my hand and lean against the wall momentarily; doing the magic so rapidly had left me feeling dizzy and sick. "But there's no poison here."

Bruno was staring at the opal and mirror with wide eyes, while the count looked interested but also skeptical. But there would be no time to explain the art of detecting poisons now. The captain of the duke's guard had stepped up next to Prior Belthesar, holding out a cloth. Upon it was a dagger that still bore a few traces of blood. One of Duke Argave's servants appeared next to him, holding out a goblet of honeyed wine. I drank it gratefully; I was going to need strength.

I had performed the difficult bit of grammery now required many times in practice, first with teachers and more recently on my own. But tonight would be the first time to do it in earnest before an important audience. Composing my features to a look of professional calm, I motioned for the captain to lay the blade on the marble path, then turned my face away while I softly murmured the appropriate prayers. For this to work, my mind must be wholly composed and my spirit motivated only to seek pure truth rather than being bent on any malice or revenge. When I looked again Prior Belthesar had taken the articles I required from the box: a piece of lodestone, a phial of powdered copper, a bunch of dried mistletoe, and a length of strong silk thread. He left the kit's own finding knife in its satin niche; for the present task the weapon that had actually been used in the attempt would be far more efficacious as a tracer.

I could see both Count Galoran and the duke watching closely as I knelt and laid these items on a cloth beside the dagger, so I began to speak while I worked, describing each step in the procedure as if I were instructing a class of novices. "First we must find the balance point of this blade," I said, holding it on my palm, then across two fingers, and finally balanced on just one. "Now I bind the thread around both dagger and mistletoe—" I made a loop and slipped it around the spot "—so that the knife hangs flat in the air, free to swing and twist. Next I stroke the blade with the lodestone seven times toward the point as I speak these words:

> *'Armum ferri audi me*
> *Auxilium fer nobis*
> *Ostend locum originis celeriter*
> *Rogamus te ut ducas.'*

"Last, I shake a little of the copper dust into the mistletoe, hold the blade suspended in the air, and concentrate all my attention on it." The knife twisted back and forth a number of times, so many I began to feel sick discouragement. But then I detected the lines of the magic forming themselves, becoming ordered. The knife came to a stop, pointing toward a spot further along the wall. A fine line of copper dust slid down the blade and flew from its point, glinting in the light of the flambeaux. "There," I declared. "The assassin came over the wall there."

"That's right, sir, we found marks on the wall, and some of the vines are torn free just at that spot," the captain told Duke Argave. Prior Belthesar asked some of the guards to fetch flambeaux and hold them high by the wall so we would see their light when we came to the same spot outside. A moment later I found myself leading a grim party back through the courtyard and around into the street outside. Along with the prior, our group included Count Galoran, Bruno, the duke and his captain, and several guards with torches. The duke had evidently decided Lord Thierri should also accompany us, for he walked between two guards with a far from eager expression. As we reached the gate, several waiting attendants handed Count Galoran and his men their swords.

The path outside was dark and quite deserted. When we reached the spot where the light of several flames flared above the wall, I stopped our group with a sharp gesture. My mind was now fully locked into the lines of the magic, and it seemed not at all strange to command both a count and a duke. I stepped forward to cast a little of the copper dust on the ground, passed the knife over it three times, then called one of the guards to bring a torch. Outlined in gleaming powder we could see two sets of footprints of very different sizes coming to the spot, but only one—the larger set—leading away.

"So, he had help getting over my wall," said the duke.

"Yes." Count Galoran bent over the tracks. "You can see right here where big-foot stood to boost smaller-feet. This path is hard, but this one set of big-foot's prints has actually sunk into the ground. We'd never have seen the others without this magic of Brother Melchior's, though. Look, you can see how big-feet stood shuffling about for a while, then ran with long strides back the way they'd come, probably as soon as he was sure his friend had failed and would not be returning." He looked at me with that quirked smile I'd seen a few times since joining his retinue, which looked pleasant on the unmarked half of his face and bitter on the scarred side. "I can see I've neglected to utilize some of the talents you could put at my command, Father Melchior. That shall be remedied."

"That would be wise, Count," said the duke. "But now I should like to know how the bigger man managed to stand here undisturbed for so long without my sentry finding him. Brother Melchior, can you use your dagger and bright dust to trace these two footpads back to where they came from?"

"I won't need to use the copper anymore." I held the knife out on the silk thread, absolutely confident now. The blade swung twice, then pointed along the lines of footprints as steadily as if I were gripping it tightly in my hand. "This blade knows the way by which it came. It will lead us."

We had scarcely made twenty paces when we came upon a dark form near the path. The captain shoved past me with a curse, then muttered, "Sorry, Father." The torchlight revealed a man wearing the duke's livery, his throat cut, the moonlight reflecting in his sightless eyes. Prior and I crossed ourselves and murmured a quick prayer for the dead as the captain bent over the body, then turned to the duke. "It's Pierrou all right, my lord. The poor bast—fellow!"

The duke's expression was angry, but he spoke with his normal ironic tone. "Ah, well, he was done in any event. If we'd found him alive, I'd have presumed he'd been bought and hanged him as a traitor. Lead on, Brother Melchior."

At the end of the wall the path descended a short distance to where it connected with the street. The knife swung to the right at once, and I could feel the lines of magic vibrate up the silken cord as we followed the direction indicated. At first we found ourselves hurrying along broad ways among the fine town-houses of wealthy courtiers. Then we passed through the gate marking the boundary of the duke's quarter and into streets lined with mansions belonging to merchant families grown rich supplying the court and town. A few late strollers stared as we hurried past, bowing low when they saw Argave. Another gate brought us into a quarter of narrower streets lined with the shuttered houses and shops of artisans, tradespeople, and money changers: virtuous working folk now mostly abed. At the far end of their commune, we entered the poor section of town.

We had gone quickly until now, with only a few corners

where I must halt us until the knife found its bearing. But here the streets were mere alleys, cramped and twisted as the veins in a cheese, and smelling just as ripe. Tottering houses leaned against each other like drunkards, and real drunkards staggered in and out of the taverns that sheltered in the ground floors of more than a few of them. God's wayward children were here in force: idle footsoldiers mustered out with the current peace, fat ox-drovers, runaway peasants, dissolute apprentices, and the bawds who waited to relieve any or all of them of whatever coins the taverns didn't take. Those men or women we encountered upon the streets slunk quickly up alleys or faded into doorways when they realized who they'd met. But we could hear raucous laughter, curses, and snatches of lewd songs from nearby houses every time we stopped to wait for the dagger to show the way, and such halts became frequent in these twisting streets.

At last the knife pointed up a black alley between two tottering houses that had leaned in toward one another until someone had felt it advisable to brace thick oak beams between them several stories up. We edged around a pile of rotting cabbages halfway along, then the knife swung to guide us into the inner courtyard of the house on our left. The captain stepped up to a weathered but quite solid-looking door and hammered upon it with his mailed fist, bellowing, "Open in the name of Duke Argave!"

The woman who eventually answered was a surprise. Her gown, though old and worn, was satin, her bearing queenly, and her hard face had once been beautiful and was still striking. She swept dark eyes over us, then bowed low and spoke in phrases as well turned as any court lady's. "Greetings my lord Duke, good Magian fathers, gentlemen all. My pardon for your having to wait; we fastened this door for the night some moments ago. You do too much honor to my poor house."

The duke, to my interest, looked momentarily nonplused at the sight of her. Then he shrugged and replied in the same fashion, "I fear we have not come on a social visit, madame. It appears that your house has recently harbored assassins and may hold one still."

"Indeed." Her black eyes shifted from him to me, and then to the dagger quivering on its line below my outstretched hand. "Then you had best enter at once and seek him out. I want no such miscreants within my walls."

The cramped corridor passed a locked door through which low voices and the click of dice could be heard. But the knife led us on without a quiver to a steep narrow stair that wound upward at the very back of the house. I could feel the lines of the magic grow stronger and stronger as we climbed. We heard a woman's high laughter as we passed one landing and a man cursing at the next. Then, on the fifth landing, the knife jerked at its cord like a hooked fish. The ancient wood floor of the gloomy hallway was creaky and uneven, while beams leaned unexpectedly out of the walls or pressed down from the ceiling. I heard both the captain and Bruno bump their heads and curse ripely behind me. When I reached the third chamber the knife actually pulled the cord from my grasp and went clattering to the threshold. Duke Argave growled a command, and a bulky guardsman stepped forward and smashed the flimsy door in with one blow of his thick shoulder.

The big man lying in the garret room beyond made no objection. He would never object to anything again.

"It's big-foot all right." Count Galoran said as he stood up from examining the dead man's feet. "The size is right, and you can see the same worn spot in his right shoe that showed in the tracks."

"Madame, is this fellow one of your household?" the duke asked the dark lady, who was standing in the doorway looking with pitiless interest at the dagger in the dead man's chest and his staring eyes.

"Of course not, my lord Duke. I let the chambers on this floor out to any who can pay. This man and another fellow simply appeared two days ago and hired a room. They paid through tomorrow."

"His friend was a smaller man?"

"Yes, and with just a hint of the gentleman about him which this poor fellow definitely lacked. They kept entirely to the house until tonight, then suddenly appeared downstairs, took a couple of quick drinks with the gamblers, and left. I didn't even know this one had returned until now."

"And can you tell us their names or anything else about them, madame?"

She gave a short laugh. "If a man *should* ever happen to give a name here, the one thing of which I would be quite certain was that it was not his own, my lord Duke! I *can* tell you that they had one visitor: today. He came and went wrapped to his eyes in a long cloak. But I knew from his voice and manner that he was a courtly gentleman."

"Might he have been this lord?" asked Argave, motioning the guards to nudge Thierri forward. She shook her head.

"No chance of it, my lord Duke. I'd certainly have remembered that red hair! This lordling was taller and had dark brows. Besides, he spoke with a touch of the Nabarrese in his tongue."

"Ah—so Alfonso is behind this!" cried the captain, and the duke nodded thoughtfully. "It could well be so."

"I know nothing of that, my lord Duke," the lady said. She pointed to the dagger in the dead man's chest, then at the one on my cord. "But those are both Nabarrese daggers. I saw the smaller man slip one into his sleeve as he and this fellow were leaving tonight, though he'd carried only a soldier's dirk before. It may well be their visitor presented it to him earlier." An ironic smile pulled the corners of her bitter mouth. "Then he came back tonight, met this fellow upon his return, and remedied an earlier oversight by giving him one also."

Prior Belthesar put his arm under mine as we followed the others down the steep stairs and back out to the street, murmuring, "That work was well done, my son." I was grateful for the aid, as my body had been seized with the quivering weakness that inevitably follows any major piece of magic-working. But after we'd gone a little way I summoned enough energy to whisper, "A question, my father."

"Yes, my son?"

"Duke Argave treated the keeper of that house with a great deal more forbearance than I would have expected, and spoke to her as if to a lady of rank. Does he know her?"

The prior gave a low chuckle and checked to make sure the duke was walking well ahead of us before answering. "Ah, yes, that would have been a good ten years or more ago, long before the period when you were attached to our priory. Yes, that fine lady was a glittering ornament in the duke's assemblies at one time. A great courtesan, and for several years Argave's principal mistress."

2

"Tell me something, Father Melchior," Count Galoran said, turning in his saddle to face me. "Was all that business with the copper and the cord and the canting in the ancient language necessary for what you did, or is it just for show, like the passes of a street conjurer?"

We'd remained in the city through the day after the attempt on his life. This had been a good thing for me, as I would have found it difficult indeed to ride any distance immediately after doing so much magic. I'd spent the whole of the time at the priory either resting, eating, or praying, awakening this second morning refreshed and ready if not wholly eager for the journey back to Peyrefixade.

"May I assume you don't think what you saw was mere illusion such as a street conjurer's tricks?"

"Oh no, I'm convinced enough that you Magians can

do real magic now! But if I'm to have you as my *capellanus*, and especially if I'm to continue my family's patronage of your Order, I should also like to know a bit more."

I put up a hand as if to adjust my hood in order to hide a smile. This northern count might play the straightforward soldier to the world, but he had his subtleties when he cared to exercise them, just as I'd told them at the priory. He'd clearly divined the Order's interest in placing me in his service. "The exact answer to the question you pose has been much debated, Count. Some argue that all the materials and charms are but aids to focus the mind of the trained magic-worker, but that the mind alone does the real business. Others maintain that the natural properties of certain objects, such as the power of lodestone to make iron seek and point, renders those objects essential to the doing of specific types of magic except for the most skilled. As to the charm and spells, they have come down to us from magic-workers of centuries and even ages past, some even from long before the time of the great Urbs itself. We study magic, like all other learning, in the language of antiquity, and at least most of us find we need that language to summon it up."

"Interesting. You must show me some more of your magic when we are home at Peyrefixade again." We rode in silence for a while. Peasants out pulling a few last turnips from the fields or gathering brush from along the road for their fires looked up, to see the count passing with his retinue of knights and his priest, and bowed briefly before turning back to their work. Then he said, "Tell me something more of this Prince Alfonso."

"I do not know that I can add much to what Duke Argave must already have told you, Count."

"What Argave tells one is colored by Argave's eye. I want the view through yours."

I turned my gaze toward the south for a moment, where the border mountains loomed beyond the hills that enclose the long valley up which we were riding. "Prince Alfonso inherited very young, much younger than yourself, Count. Indeed, he is not much older than you even now. His principality, Nabarra, is as you must know the first region one reaches when traveling south out of our own kingdom. I saw a good deal of him once, when he made a visit to our duke's court during my time with the priory. He came to settle with the duke over some land up in the mountains to which both had laid claim and stayed a whole fortnight. He is proud and easily angered; he struck a page who spilled wine on his sleeve so hard the poor boy lost several teeth and almost lost his eye. He is also reputed to be ruthless in dealing with enemies—and those who merely might be enemies."

"I have some reason to believe that is true." He laughed grimly. "According to Duke Argave, this Alfonso would be happiest to control Peyrefixade himself. Failing that, he would prefer it be in the hands of someone who would offer little resistance if he should decide to war openly upon the duke one of these days. Apparently having a man seasoned in Emperor Friedrich's service holding Peyrefixade is not to his taste."

"That is not unlikely. Former princes of Nabarra warred often with our duke's ancestors. Alfonso's house has long believed it has a rightful claim to this side of the mountains. Peyrefixade commands the key invasion route used in those past wars."

"And does this Alfonso obtain magical assistance from these heretics I hear of, as the duke and the counts of Peyrefixade do from your Order?"

"Oh no, Count. Alfonso and Argave may agree on little else, but their minds are alike here. The prince's father was another matter; he died excommunicate for making the Perfected too welcome in his domains after the war. There are supposedly many of them there still, passing now as followers of the True Faith. But the prince is reckoned a faithful son of the Church, and is if anything an even fiercer persecutor of the Perfected than the duke himself."

"And how do these heretics, these 'Perfected,' manage to pass themselves off as honest folk?" the count continued. Something in the way he asked made me think he had already heard much of their ways but again wanted my own opinion. "Don't the heretics need to assemble to perform their devilish rites? Don't people notice when they sacrifice babies and animals to their idols?"

I felt my face burn and could not hold my tongue. "Those are lies, Count! The Perfected read the same Bible as ourselves. They have no idols, and they certainly never sacrifice babies, or even chickens. They believe, however, that it is possible to attain salvation through human effort alone, without either grace or the sacraments. They hold that one must overcome the body and its appetites and strive until one lives quite without sin. A person who has become thus perfected is in fact saved while yet on earth."

"Ah, hence the name 'Perfected'! I must say, this all sounds a good deal less vicious and heretical than I had been led to suppose. Did not some of the early fathers of the True Faith, the ones who withdrew into the desert to live away from worldly temptations, preach something similar?"

"In certain respects," I answered, speaking more calmly now. "But the True Faith teaches that those men were seeking merely to be worthy to receive grace if the Lord so willed, not trying to win it by their own human power. The True Faith also tells us the Lord sent his only Son to bring us grace through His earthly sacrifice. But the Perfected believe the Lord had *two* sons, and that the elder was Lucifer. He rebelled against his Father, was cast out, and then created this flawed physical world to affront his Father and entrap humans, who were originally the entirely spiritual creations of the Lord. They also believe that the Lord later sent his *second* son to teach

us all how to overcome Lucifer's false creation by our
own efforts and reattain the higher realm that is human-
kind's rightful home."

"Most interesting. It sounds in this story as though the
Lord's younger son did better for himself than I ever have,
but then my older brother was anything but rebellious!
Clearly there is more to this heretical doctrine than we
have ever heard in the north. You must tell me more of
these Perfected one day soon. I see that I shall need to
understand them better in case there may be some lurking
within my own domains."

The sun was setting far up the valley by the time we
came clattering up the last steep track toward Peyrefixade.
As we drew near the gates, I saw one of the knights who
had been left on duty trying to shoo away two ragged
figures: a youth and a bent old woman. It was the cook's
dismissed assistant and his mother.

As soon as they saw us they came running and threw
themselves on their faces right in front of Count Galoran's
horse, so close he had to make it rear to avoid trampling
both of them. "Mercy, m'lord Compte, mercy!" the old
woman cried in the Royal Tongue, with a Auccitan accent
even thicker than her son's. Bruno pushed his horse forward
to whip them out of the way, but the count stopped him.

"On what account do you ask for mercy from me, old
woman?" he asked quietly. "Your son was caught at open
theft in my house. You are quite lucky I did not hang
him."

"I know, m'lord Compte, what 'a did was very wrong.
But he's all I ha' lef', and he's ne'er been aught but a
servant here i' the castle. Our food's run out and it's long
yet 'til there'll be work i' the fields. We'll starve, m'lord
Compte!"

I cringed inside my cassock, peering covertly at Galoran's
grim scarred face. The knights and even the servants along
the wall were all watching now, and I expected the Count
would feel it necessary to have these two whipped away,

if he didn't merely ride them down. Instead he paused for a long moment's thought, then reached down to his belt, took a small purse, and tossed it to the old woman.

"This is for you," he growled. "I give it assuming you were quite innocent in this matter. If you freely choose to spend some of these coins to feed your miserable son as well as yourself, that is your own affair. Now be gone, and don't come here again."

She tried to seize his knee, crying, "Oh bless you, m'lord Compte!" Without looking down again he pushed her away with his boot, not roughly, then jerked his head and led us on into the courtyard.

When I came down from the chapel the following morning, after performing divine service, washing the holy chalice, and returning everything to the altar, I stumbled hard over a great heap of stones near the side entrance to the great hall. I'd forgotten overnight how the place had been torn up by the masons the seneschal had brought in during our absence. A servant ran to help me, but I waved him off with thanks and went to collect my breakfast. Then I took my bread and beer over to see how work on the new hearth was coming.

The progress was impressive, considering they'd only been at work three days. A great opening had been made in the cut-stone wall at the end of the hall behind Count Galoran's huge curtained bed, exposing the rubble fill between the inner and outer walls of worked stones. A scaffold of timbers had been erected within this hole, and wiry men in rough blue smocks were already at work inside, rapidly making the cavity bigger. Some stood up on the scaffold, heaving with bars and chisels as they pried chunks of rubble out of the fill. Others seized stones as fast as they came free and passed them quickly down to muscular apprentices, who dragged them off on pallets to add them to the pile.

The seneschal stood at one side talking with the chief

mason, while Bruno, Bouteillier Raymbaud, and several of the castle knights looked on. The seneschal seemed to be making his whole breakfast on a crust and a cup of water, but the bouteillier and most of the knights held rough loaves with a smear of olive oil and tankards like mine. I decided to stand with them while I ate so I could watch and listen. I needed to put more effort into getting acquainted with all of the souls under my care, and that included the masons as long as they were in Peyrefixade.

"It'll take at leas' four more days to tunnel clear up thro' this wall to the top, sir," the chief mason was telling the seneschal, showing a decent command of the Royal Tongue. "Wonderful well built, these castles from the time o' the great war. It's easier goin' here than in some I've worked on, for there's been stones shifted within this wall before, but that must ha' been long ago and the fill has settled firm since. And the lads ha' to go more and more careful the higher they get i' the rubble. Shouldna' want a collapse, with good lads killed or hurt and twice the work after putting it all right again after."

"The count understands that," said Seneschal Guilhem in his dull voice. "Just see the work is done well and he won't mind the cost."

"Oh, it will be, sir! Once we've cut a shaft to the top o' the wall, we'll line the whole flue very pretty wi' a sill inside to make her draw smooth as butter and put in a hearth here at bottom broad enough to roast an ox in't. Then we'll fit up the opening here with a grander carved fireplace than even a man such as the count what's served wi' the Allemann emperor has ever seen."

"Sounds like we're to have a bit more real style in our hall when this is done," one of the young knights said. "Maybe Duke Argave's pretty boys won't look down their long noses at us so much then."

"Style is never amiss in a nobleman," agreed Raymbaud.

"Maybe," muttered an older knight. "But by my spurs, I can't fathom why Count Sc—Count Galoran wants to piss away his money having a fireplace put in his very first month in possession."

"Oh, you'd like to know that, would you?" said Bruno, turning to him. "Well then, I'll tell you. Captain Galoran—Count Galoran, I mean—is as brave a fellow as I ever knew in almost everything you could name. I don't know that he'd fear to face any man living. But he does have a powerful dislike of fire. The Allemann winter is no soft season such as you boys have hereabouts. But I've seen him stand shivering in his cloak in camp after a day's march because he didn't like to get as close to the watchfire as the rest of us. He was burned terrible bad in a fire as a boy, you see; that's how he came by those scars. Why, I once saw him ride straight into a breech to fight three men when everyone else was minded to retreat—rallied the assault and saved the day, was commended and rewarded by the emperor himself—and afterwards he confessed to me private-like that he'd ten times rather go forward against such odds than try to ride back over the mess of blazing oil the defenders had thrown down behind us from the battlements! He'll sleep a sight better once the fire burns in this nice hearth instead of out in the middle of the hall, my boys, believe me."

"Well, you can't blame a burned man for not liking fire," said the older knight with a slow nod. "I'd rather an honest sword cut any day myself than a burn. I was in a siege once myself, a little walled heretic settlement that turned up back in the foothills, and—"

But I heard no more. My attention had been drawn by something imperceptible to everyone else in the hall but like a thunderclap to me: the unmistakable resonance of magic nearby. Not magic being worked, but latent magic, lines of it embedded in some object. I felt the hairs stand up on the back of my neck at its power. I'd tried several divinations during my first days in the castle but without success, scarcely surprising considering I'd had nothing to use as an indicator to seek out long-latent magic. But even latent magic will resonate when suddenly disturbed, and a novice in his first year would have detected this! Then I heard rubble falling and the workmen talking excitedly in Auccitan. *"In there—a cavity—something in a box!"*

Striding to the base of the scaffold, I called to them in the same language, *"What is it? What have you found?"*

The chief mason had already climbed up there. He spoke down at me over one shoulder. *"We're not sure, Father. The lads will have it out in a moment—there. Here it is, Father."*

I seized the lead box he passed down to me with shaking fingers. It was gray, misshapen, and covered with grit, but I could feel waves of magic emanating from inside as I pried at the lid. Suddenly the box popped open and a surge of power came out that staggered me. Inside lay a golden medallion: old, over four inches across, on a massive chain. The medallion was extremely plain with only a single device worked in its exact center. It was a circle—the symbol of Perfection. And the gold of the pendant resonated powerfully with the unmistakable vibrations of old, potent magic: complex lines and knotted patterns as beautiful and frightening as the diamond eye of a serpent, laid into it by a truly formidable Magian long ago.

"And what have you there, Father?" came Count Galoran's voice just behind me.

I froze, my fingers clenching tightly about the medallion without conscious thought. I felt a brief impulse to run, to try and get away with the thing somehow, anyhow. Then my mind cleared again, and I recalled I was both a sworn canon of the Order and the count's own *capellanus*. I turned and handed the amulet to him.

"I am not sure, Count Galoran. It is something that was hidden here long ago. I think it once belonged to a Magian. Not of my Order, or even of the True Faith, but one of the Perfected."

Chapter Five ~ Galoran

1

"I have an aunt?" I was so surprised I almost dropped my mug of morning beer.

In an effort to learn Auccitan, I had been practicing it with Brother Melchior for the last week, every morning after divine service. It was close enough to the Royal Tongue that, once I got used to the differences in how words were pronounced, I could almost follow a conversation in it—or at least grasp the gist of what the masons were yelling at each other. Producing the words and syntax myself was harder. I had just tried to say, "I wish I knew more about the history of this county," though it came out more like, *"Me want county many know."*

And the priest had answered, in the fluent Auccitan he told me he had learned in the cradle, *"Why don't you ask your great-aunt?"*

Now, as we stood together on the little terrace outside the great tower, he looked at me quizzically over the rim of his mug and asked in the Royal Tongue, "You mean you don't know your Great-aunt Richildis? The abbess of the convent of the Holy Family?"

"No, I don't," I said in exasperation. This was supposed to be *my* castle and *my* county, and it kept seeming as though everyone else knew much more about it than I did, but neglected to tell me. "I never heard more than a few stories about this region from my grandfather before he died, and my own father and older brother were even less interested than I was—then."

"She was the younger sister of old Count Bernhard and of your own grandfather," said Melchior. "She must be very old by now, but I hear she still carries out the governance of her convent herself." He paused, frowning. "I wonder if you ought to make a gift to the house of the Holy Family for the soul of the late countess, your cousin."

I shrugged, again in exasperation. "Probably." As I moved I could feel the medallion, hung around my neck under my shirt.

At first, when the masons had found it in the wall and the priest had given it to me, I had locked it up in the treasure chest under the bed, along with my money and the records of my predecessors' pious generosity. An artifact of the Perfected, Melchior had called it, and therefore I thought something that should not be left out in the open. Perhaps I would turn it over to the duke, I decided vaguely, or possibly the Mother House of Melchior's Order.

But over the next few days I had found my thoughts drawn to the medallion again and again, and several times at night I had awakened in my great canopied bed, seeing the faint light from the fire in the middle of the room through the curtains and hearing the snores of the men all around me, and almost wondered if I also heard the medallion's voice. Something that once belonged to a Magian, Melchior had said, but as I was no magic-worker I told myself that no magic that might still linger in it could possibly affect me. Then one day I had slipped it on under my shirt, for no particular reason, and had not taken it off since.

"I had been going to visit the convent of the Holy Family anyway," I continued. The sun was well up now, shining on hills that seemed greener every day. The high mountains beyond them, however, were still white with snow. "Did you know that half of the rents from one of my villages go to the nuns? The nuns' own bailiffs collect all the money, and according to the seneschal he has to go every year to collect the count's share from the convent."

"Doubtless that dates from Richildis's entry into the convent as a girl," suggested Melchior.

"Well, the seneschal didn't explain why, or even tell me the nuns were headed by my own aunt. There are no records of an entry gift for the Holy Family that I've seen, but then the old count doesn't seem to have kept the records from before he moved here to Peyrefixade. And the seneschal doesn't say a lot about anything. At first I thought he was ill, because he always looks so terrible, but I think it must instead be sorrow for the death of the countess. I said something about her one day when we were going over the accounts, and he was so overcome he had to excuse himself. He certainly seems to miss her more than that husband of hers does."

I watched Melchior for a reaction as I spoke. Since his excellent work tracking the assassin to a literal dead end at that disreputable inn in the duke's city, I had gained a new respect for his abilities. It was disconcerting to have a priest who could learn by magic those things which everyone else thought hidden, but a good captain should be able to put to use any ability of the men in his service. Even if the priest was spying on me for the duke or plotting against my best interests for the benefit of his Order, he was an intelligent man, and I liked trying out ideas on him, some that I would not even have tried on Bruno.

"I have not pressed Seneschal Guilhem to open his heart to me," Melchior said contritely. "Perhaps I should—he would learn that God will wipe away the tears even of the most sorrowful."

Well, I should have expected that reaction from a priest, but it wasn't my concern. "Ill or mournful," I grumbled, "I'm worried that if he dies or retires he'll leave us no record whatsoever of what my rents ought to be. That's part of the reason I need to go around to all the villages

now, *before* the rents come due: both to make a display
with my knights to discourage any peasant who might
have been planning to use the succession as an excuse to
'forget' what he owes, and also to get proper rent rolls
down on parchment. God knows what a mess it would
be if the seneschal really did take ill, leaving me to deal
with incompetent and probably corrupt mayors in sorting
out what I'm owed."

The cold weight of the medallion shifted again against
my chest. Sometimes I had the feeling that while I was
wearing it my thoughts were more focused and concentrated, but not at the moment. I drained the last of my
beer. "I'm going to go see how those masons are coming
on my fireplace."

I had not let the masons sleep in the castle. Their
foreman grumbled about it at some length until Bruno
stopped him—doubtless using persuasions that it was good
I didn't know about—but if someone was trying to
assassinate me I didn't want strangers in the castle after
dark. The guards who spent the night in turns watching
at the gates would keep out external enemies but would
never have a chance against enemies within. And I certainly
wasn't going to be like the emperor and have a trusted
guardsman stand watch, awake by his master's bed, all
night—I myself had been that guardsman several times
too many. My knights and servants here in Peyrefixade I
thought I could trust, because the attack had come at
the duke's court, not in the castle where an attacker would
have had much more opportunity, but the masons I
considered suspect. The seneschal had found tents for
them in the storeroom, which they pitched below the gates,
but they ate well enough with the staff and certainly worked
hard for the money I was paying them.

The fireplace was now virtually completed. They had
also put in a hearth in the chamber one storey up, and
when finished it should all be very warm and cozy. The

seneschal, supposedly supervising, leaned against a wall, his mouth drawn down and his eyes looking far away. It would be good, I thought, for him to get out of the castle on my tour of my property—a tour, it now seemed, that would include a visit to my Great-aunt Richildis.

Chilly as it was in the hall, the masons had already peeled off their blue smocks, and sweat stood out on their muscular backs as they heaved cut stone into place: red sandstone newly quarried, dragged up to the gates by oxen and then inside by the men themselves, and costing me a larger proportion of the amount left in the treasure chest than I liked to recall. Trained fighter though I was, none of the masons would have needed a weapon beyond his powerful hands if he wanted to kill me.

"Prince Alfonso wanting me dead I think I can understand," I muttered to Melchior as we watched the masons work. The prince's lands, according to the duke, lay just south of mine, and if Peyrefixade was long without a count it would be an excellent opportunity for him to claim the county for his own. "But if any of these lads were in Prince Alfonso's pay, they would have struck by now." I didn't have nearly the ear yet to distinguish between an Auccitan and a Nabarrese accent, especially since I wasn't sure I had ever heard the latter—the grunts from the assailant while he and I were trying to strangle each other hardly counted. A number of people had tried to kill me over the years, but it had always been in battle or else, twice, in a drunken brawl, never by stealth. Most of the time I tried not to dwell on my present danger, but sometimes, unaccountably, I felt my ears begin to tingle and the hair stand up on my neck, though when I turned there was never anyone there.

I didn't tell Melchior that my imagination kept providing me other alternatives I liked even less: the duke, the priests of the Order of the Three Kings, or Lord Thierri. Since Thierri had killed the would-be assassin, it was much more difficult to suspect him than I preferred, and even harder to suspect Duke Argave, who might be capable of a subtle and complex game, but hardly one that involved sending for someone from the distant north just to assassinate him. A priest-assassin I would have dismissed—even if a suspicious mind might have suggested that Melchior had had excellent first-hand information to help him follow the trail of dead men—except for what Thierri had told me, of a spell that so confused the countess she fell from her own ramparts.

2

We passed the spot where they had found her body as we rode out a few days later, the priest, the seneschal, Bruno, half a dozen knights, and me. We followed a track down the opposite side of the ridge from the road where people normally came and went, toward a village tucked into a fold of the mountain, only a few miles from the castle but almost into the next kingdom—Alfonso's territory. Melchior pulled up at the fatal spot, directly below the ramparts though the ride to reach there had been well over a mile. He seemed for a moment lost in thought, but produced none of his powders and mistletoe. The rest of us continued, and in a moment his horse came hurrying up behind.

I wanted to know if his powers of divination had discovered anything, but that could wait for a more private conversation. He had already told me that he had written to the priest who had served in Peyrefixade before the countess's death, but had been able to get no information beyond what we already knew. "So tell me what they owe us in this next village," I said instead to Seneschal Guilhem.

The seneschal came back abruptly from a reverie of his own and began running down lists of payments in coin and produce. No labor dues, as I had already learned: all had long since been commuted into monetary payments. Perched high on its knife-edge of rock, the castle didn't even try to have fields of its own. Some lords, I had heard, were so determined that their peasant tenants work for them that they created tasks: dragging building stone into place or grinding wheat into flour in handmills. I myself preferred to have my grain ground efficiently at a watermill and my stonework done by professionals.

"It's a good fireplace," I said to Bruno. "I heard a few of the men grumbling last night that they weren't as warm as they had been with the blaze in the middle of the room, but they'll soon grow accustomed to it."

"Now we just have to hope," he said darkly, "that none of those masons were spying out the castle for whoever hired the footpads in Ferignan."

I didn't answer. We were now at the village—walled, though the gates were open—and everyone turned out to stare at us. The fields surrounding the village were small and stony; I guessed the villagers lived mostly from their flocks. The women, as I expected, were the most frightened, the men the most sulky, the little children the most interested.

"As I'm sure you've all heard," I said loudly, "I am your new lord, Count Galoran." The horse shifted under me and I stilled it with a hand on the reins, turning my head so they could all get a good look at the scar if they wanted one. "I am here surveying my property, so that we are all agreed on what is owed when the March rents come due, thus avoiding any unpleasantness."

There was a voice beside me, and I realized in surprise that Melchior was translating what I said into Auccitan. This close to the castle, I thought—if I had turned around I would have seen it looming behind us—and they couldn't be counted on to understand me. Well, better a translation than having them all double up with laughter over my mispronunciations.

We started through the village. The mayor, who appeared somewhat tardily wearing a black velvet cape that looked like something old Count Bernhard might have discarded years ago, led the way. At each cottage he, the seneschal, and the householder had a short but complicated discussion, and Brother Melchior finished by writing something down. The knights sat their horses ostentatiously, looking around haughtily and playing with their knives, but I dismounted to listen and to frown when frowning seemed called for.

Last year my brother had had to go around to several of his villages to sort out the rents, and I had been one of the knights conveying an unspoken threat. Tedious as this whole process was, it was still vastly improved by having it *my* rents under discussion.

At the third cottage a little boy crept up beside me. He was younger than my nephews and had dark eyes and a disarming smile. *"Are you the great and terrible count?"* he asked in Auccitan.

Two weeks of practice with Melchior wasn't a lot, but it would get me started. *"Yes,"* I said with a grin to match his own, *"I terrible. Eat boys."*

He clearly didn't believe a word of this, but as he laughed he gave a quick look around—perhaps for the mother or older sister who did. I picked him up to have him at eye-level and bared my teeth at him, which set him laughing again. Enough of this, I thought, preparing to set him down, or the villagers would all decide that the great and terrible Count Galoran was harmless and try to persuade the seneschal that they owed me no more than a single chicken a year. And I really didn't want to have to set the knights on them.

And then the boy touched the left side of my face, no longer laughing. *"How did you get this ___?"*

I didn't recognize the word, but the meaning was clear enough. *"Fire,"* I said simply. *"Long ago."*

During the next week we proceeded through all the villages and hamlets of my county, until Brother Melchior's parchment rolls were dense with figures and annotations.

It was still too early in the year for the men to have taken the flocks to the high pastures, so almost everyone was home—and in the few cases where the householder was unaccountably missing, and I barked out an order doubling his rents, he always fortuitously reappeared before we left the village.

Sometimes the sun shone, promising that green and bursting spring must arrive very soon, but more often fast-flying clouds came up over the mountains, dragging curtains of rain to drench us and turn everything around us a cold gray. At night we lay under the tents, which still smelled a little of the masons' sweat, listening to rain on the canvas. Here I did have a knight awake all night to guard me, though if an assassin was trying to track us stealthily through these mountains and this weather I had to admire his resolution.

Not everyone in the county, of course, owed me rent. Probably in most of the villages, especially those furthest from the castle, fewer than half the inhabitants did, and that didn't even count the entire villages where no one paid rent to Peyrefixade at all. These included the ones which old Count Bernhard had given to the house of the Three Kings, some others that owed their rents to other landlords, even to the duke, but also a large number that had apparently—or so the villagers claimed—always been free of dues, since their intrepid and resourceful ancestors had come with their families and their sheep to settle in high valleys that nobody else wanted, centuries ago. At every village, including these, we stopped long enough at least for a chat with the mayor, to remind him that even if I was not everyone's landlord I *was* everyone's judicial lord, and that justice and law came ultimately from me.

One thing surprised me a little: no sign of heretics. If Melchior was right, and they were able to pass as followers of the True Faith, I might have talked to many of them and not even known it, but I would have expected someone at least to mention it. But most of these villages were too small and isolated to have a church or priest of any kind; maybe no one had ever bothered to check into their religious beliefs.

But as we approached the final village down at the base of the mountains, the village where half the rents went to the Holy Family, we saw some sort of commotion before the gates and heard shouting and screaming.

We kicked our horses forward. Now we could see a stake erected outside the gates, a whole mob of people swirling around it. "Looks like another mayor has forgotten to talk to the count before hanging the local criminals," suggested Bruno.

But this wasn't gibbets. That was a stake for burning heretics.

Brother Melchior realized it at the same time as I did. He clutched so hard at the reins that his horse pulled up abruptly, then shook the reins violently and kicked the beast hard. "Stop them!" he cried as his horse shot past mine. His face had gone dead white. "Stop them, in the name of God!"

I was right behind him. If the archbishop from over in Haulbé had found some people guilty of heresy, there was nothing I could do about that decision, or even want to. But when it came to the actual burning, *no* one was going to be put to death in my county except by me.

They already had the heretics, two men and a woman, tied to the stake when we thundered through the crowd. I didn't hesitate. Years of leading men into battle had taught me that rapid decision and rapid action were always best. Bruno, at my shouted order, snatched a burning brand right from the hand of a wizened little priest in brown. "Stop!" I yelled as the crowd surged forward. My horse reared, sending the first row of people pushing back against those behind them. "As your count, I command you to stop!"

The shouting continued, but my knights all had their

swords out, and the crowd was now surging back instead of forward. Men, women, even children like the boy I had pretended to threaten up in the shadow of Peyrefixade, glared and snarled at me like scavengers cheated of their prey.

But all I had attention for was the heretics, dressed in white shifts and tied to the stake, their eyes glazed as though they hadn't even noticed me. Drugged, I thought. "Free them," I snapped at Bruno. He handed the burning brand to a knight and swung down to cut the ropes. No one came forward to catch the heretics as they sagged forward—no one dared show himself as their friend.

"And put that fire out!" I yelled at the knight who now held the torch. The woman heretic, her pulled-back hair streaked with gray, was much too old to be my little sister. But for a second I saw Gertrude.

The wizened priest pushed his way forward, trembling with fury. "I will have you know I condemned these heretics to death by the authority of the Apostolic Curia itself!"

"And I free them," I said, trying hard to keep my own voice from trembling, "by the authority of Count Galoran, myself."

"Inquisition," muttered one of the knights next to me. There was an unmistakable note of fear in his voice.

Brother Melchior was off his horse, helping the heretics away from the stake since no one else seemed about to, lowering them to the ground and murmuring prayers. *He* at any rate did not seem terrified. When the knight standing with the torch in his hand seemed paralyzed, Melchior took it from him and ground the flame out in the dirt, sending up a smudge of dark smoke.

I took a deep breath as the priest of the Inquisition continued to glare at me. After the great war against the Perfected, I seemed to recall, the bishops of the region, urged by the distant Apostolic Curia, had set up the Inquisition to uncover any of the damnable enemies of the True Faith who had gone into hiding to save their

skins. The last thing I wanted was to appear to give support
to any such demon-worshipers, especially in my own
county, or to risk the fury of the Church.

But no one was going to be put to death here—most
especially by fire—if I wasn't consulted. "I commend you,
Father," I said in a somewhat more conciliatory tone,
dismounting to be able to speak to the priest more easily,
"for hunting out this spawn of Satan. Were they brought
before the archbishop in council? Were they given every
opportunity to repent of their error when it was pointed
out to them, so that they could be welcomed back into
the fold and their miserable souls might still be saved?"

The emperor didn't have heretics like this in his domains,
but over on his eastern borders there were plenty of people
who still clung to the old pagan practices, and I knew
how all such enemies of the Faith were to be treated.
Cut them out if you had to, before they became a cancer
eating away at the body of the faithful, but first give them
every chance to repent.

The little brown priest shot me a look full of venom.
Small and vicious like a viper, I thought. His voice was
low and intense. "When I discovered their heresy, there
was no time to wait for a council, no leisure to let them
infect others with their noxious beliefs! You are new here,
I understand, the new count from the north, so you don't
know how slippery these people can be. Now step aside,
step aside before anyone suspects you of sympathy with
them, and let God's will be done!"

My knights were wavering, not exactly abandoning me,
not exactly standing firm in my support. The Inquisition
must have an even more formidable reputation here in
the land where it began than up in the north, where we
only heard of it as something distant and ominous.

Melchior unexpectedly strode over to stand beside me.
"I hope you recognize me from my habit, Father," he
said quietly. "I am of the Order of the Three Kings,
dedicated to the pursuit of knowledge of magic for God's

pure purpose and to the overcoming of all heretical beliefs and practices. I stand with you on the necessity of rooting up Perfected depravity before the tares overwhelm God's good seed. But you cannot have forgotten our oaths as priests. You and I can shed no blood—and cause no skin and flesh to shrivel and crack with fire."

The priest of the Inquisition looked back and forth between us, then over at the three heretics, who were sitting up on their own now, looking dazed and incomprehending. His lips pulled back from his teeth in what might have been a smile. "Your point is good. I was perhaps precipitate in putting these people to the torch myself, because as you rightly remind me, Brother, we priests ask the secular arm only for mercy, not for death. But there were no representatives of secular power here. Now that the count has arrived," with a nod toward me, "he can return them to the stake and light the flames himself."

There were a number of things that I could have done— and indeed *had* done in my years serving the emperor— some distasteful and unpleasant, some bitterly cruel, some that made me wake up in a drenching sweat in the middle of the night thinking about them. But lighting the faggots at someone's feet, even a heretic's feet, was not among them.

"I'm afraid you misunderstand," I said, loudly enough that those nearby could overhear. The crowd's mood had changed from avid hunger to something of an air of uncertainty, and I thought I could see the back rows slipping quietly away. My scar throbbed, and I was intensely aware of the medallion lying against my chest. "I do not merely object to your forgetting that it is the secular power, and the secular power alone, that can put a man to death. I remind you of something you said yourself: I am the *new* count, and the Church has no agreement with me!"

I had no idea what the agreement had been between old Count Bernhard and the archbishop of Haulbé over the treatment of heretics—doubtless followed by the countess—but they must have reached some sort of understanding when Bernhard took over the former Perfected stronghold of Peyrefixade. But I could make up legal precedent faster than some wizened little brown priest who had let raw power carry him beyond his capabilities.

"The reverend archbishop will need to come himself to visit me at my castle," I continued sternly. I had never been to Haulbé, I wasn't even entirely sure in what direction it lay, and I had not the slightest idea of the archbishop's name. "Tell him I will welcome him at Peyrefixade whenever he desires to come. Until then, I give him—and you—no permission whatsoever to judge heretics in my county. The Church's jurisdiction touches only members of the clergy, *not* laymen."

"We have the right to discover and judge the Imperfected!"

"Only at my predecessor's good will. He is dead now, and so is his agreement. I seek the end of heresy as heartily as you do. But it must be achieved through the proper legal forms."

"You will not find the archbishop at the gates of your castle," the priest said between his teeth, "but the Inquisition!"

I managed a laugh. "That castle was taken from the heretics by my grandfather's family. This time it won't be a group of ragtag wild-eyed herdsmen from the high valleys trying unsuccessfully to hold it against my relatives. It will be you and other priests, men who bear no weapons, trying to take it from *me!*"

"We shall complain to the duke," he said then, switching tactics, but I didn't give him a chance to finish. A switch at this point meant he felt the legal basis for his authority slipping away.

"And *I* shall complain to Duke Argave as well, that the judicial authority over laymen in my county, which I received from the duke's own hand, is being snatched from me! But come, Father. We need not be enemies.

Our goals are the same. Tell the archbishop I am eager to welcome him at Peyrefixade, so we can decide together how the Perfected are to be discovered and judged— and, if necessary, executed."

He hesitated, and in that hesitation I knew I had him. It was not until I found myself letting out all my breath at once that I realized how close it had been. Without Melchior's help at a few key points, it might well have gone otherwise. My *capellanus* was definitely proving himself useful.

"In the meantime," the inquisitor said, looking at me from under his eyebrows, "what do you expect me to do with these heretics?"

"Set them free."

"Set them free! But they will run away!"

I nodded impassively. "Let them take their heretical spew high up into the mountains, where they cannot infect the God-fearing." Up among the peaks somewhere, I thought, where the duke's son and heir was in hiding with them. "When the archbishop and I have reached an agreement, it will be simple enough to capture them again if we wish."

Without giving him a chance to contradict this extremely unlikely statement, I whirled on my knights. "You, you, and you! Take these heretics up to the mountains and let them go. The archbishop and the Inquisition cannot judge laymen in my county until our agreement is renewed, and my own authority does not touch issues of the faith, so no one can legally hold them prisoner. Now!" I shouted, when for a second, just a second, the knights hesitated. "I shall see you tomorrow, back at Peyrefixade."

I swung back up on my horse and nodded for the rest of the knights to do the same. The crowd by now was melting away, giving us a wide berth. I galloped away from the village with my cloak flying behind me, feeling no further chat with the local mayor was necessary about the extent of the count's jurisdiction.

Bruno pulled up beside me when, after a mile, I slowed my horse to a fast walk. "Are you really going to make the archbishop climb up to Peyrefixade to see you, Captain?" he asked in admiration.

I smiled. "Of course not," I said in a low voice, for his ear alone. "The archbishop will send me a very firm letter, and I will send him back a letter all conciliation and apologies for some simple misunderstanding, and then I will go to Haulbé myself to work out the arrangement by which the Inquisition may function in my county. I'll tell you this, though, Bruno: every heretic will get a chance to face his accusers and to repent."

"I hear in the castle," he said darkly, "that those so-called Perfected don't ever repent. It's like they *want* to die."

"Then I will confirm the sentence of death and have them hanged."

"But heretics have to be burned!" he said, shocked, but I turned away as though not hearing.

We were now in sight of a tall church steeple and began passing between plowed fields. The convent of the Holy Family must lie just ahead. I looked around at my men, trying to put the recent incident from my mind to be able to concentrate on the meeting with my Great-aunt Richildis.

The seneschal, I noticed, looked drained and deathly pale, as though scarcely able to stay on his horse. This must have been an exhausting week for him, I thought, the constant travel when he was already weak, on top of the stress of trying always to be scrupulously fair while constantly feeling my eye on him. It was a good thing this was the end of the tour of my property—and a good thing it was all recorded on the parchment in Brother Melchior's saddlebags.

The latter rode stiffly, without seeming to see any of the rest of us. His willingness to help the heretics away from the stake seemed curious in a man dedicated to the

True Faith, now that I thought about it, and he had been quick enough to come to the Perfected's defense when I had earlier asked about their child sacrifices. I shook my shoulders. Almost being assassinated had made me overly suspicious. It was highly improbable, I told myself, that Melchior was spying on me for the heretics as *well* as for the duke and for his Order.

But I nudged my horse next to his just before we reached the gates of the convent complex. He turned toward me with a start, as though having forgotten me. "You must have seen heretics before," I said conversationally, "even tucked safely away with your books and prayers at the House of the Three Kings. Tell me: have you ever personally known anyone who turned heretic?"

He turned his face away, and for a minute I thought he wasn't going to answer. Then he spoke so quietly I could just hear him over the sound of hooves on the flagstone paving of the nuns' outer courtyard. "My grandfather. He clung to their false faith to the end and was burned at the stake."

Seneschal Guilhem roused himself enough to discuss rents with the convent's seneschal. The two of them sat in the visitors' courtyard, with Brother Melchior scribbling details. A few fruit trees in a sheltered corner were putting out their first leaves, and somewhere a bird sang. High in the tower a bell's mellow note vibrated. There was no sign of any of the nuns, and I wondered if the abbess would even want to see me.

But we had only been sitting a few minutes when a young woman in the white habit of a novice came out. She blinked at my scar but dipped her head to me shyly and said, "The Reverend Mother will see you in her parlor, Count," then scampered away, leaving me to follow as best I could.

The abbess's parlor was a wide, dim room with a stone floor and no furniture beyond two chairs. There was a fireplace, but the hearth was cold on this late winter afternoon. The Abbess Richildis, severe in a black habit, turned at my step. I had a quick impression of a serene face with a large nose in the center, a nose just like my grandfather's. She looked as though she had once been very tall, but she now sat stooped in one chair, supporting herself on a cane. The novice hovered at her elbow.

I unbuckled my sword belt to leave it at the door and went down on one knee before her, hands upraised and head lowered. "Reverend Mother, I am Count Galoran of Peyrefixade, and, I believe, your own nephew."

"Greetings, in God's name," she said. There was no quaver in her voice; it could have been the voice of a woman twenty years younger. The touch of an Auccitan accent, I abruptly realized, was the same accent my grandfather had had, which I had only thought of as his way of talking and never identified as coming from the south. "I know very well who you are, Count Galoran, grandson of my own brother. Come sit beside me. You may leave us, my dear," to the novice, "for the space of a half hour."

The girl curtsied and retreated. The Abbess Richildis turned her eyes toward me, bright even in this dim room. They, too, though set beneath thin white eyebrows, were not the eyes of an old woman, and they looked calmly into mine as though staring straight through my flesh, including the scar, down to my soul.

"I am very sorry to say, Reverend Mother," I said somewhat nervously as I seated myself in the other chair, "that I only learned extremely recently that I even had an aunt. I have been trying without success to remember my grandfather speaking of you, but he died while I was still a boy myself."

"There may have been no reason for him to mention me," she answered. Her tone was resonant with a great serenity, born of decades of prayer and contemplation, but I thought I sensed in it something else as well, a curiosity and an enjoyment of experience that had not been superseded by the religious life but which she had incorporated into it. If she saw into my inner heart, apparently she did not object to what she saw there.

"I became a novice here at the age of six," she continued, "and died to the world. And my two brothers, Bernhard and Galoran, were much too busy with boys' affairs to concern themselves about a little sister. But you don't want to hear about me. I want to hear about *you*. When I learned that the duke had brought back a great-nephew of mine to rule at Peyrefixade, I very much hoped that you would come to see me. Otherwise, in a little while, I might have had to send a message to you, and very strange I'm sure you would have found it to be summoned by the abbess of the Holy Family, as though you were a recalcitrant neighbor who had begun fencing in the convent's pasturelands! So tell me first, did my brother Galoran succeed in taming that wild northern archduchy after he married the heiress?"

I found myself after only a few minutes talking easily and comfortably to the abbess. I thought of telling her not to believe anything the Inquisition might relay about me, but decided it was better not to mention the incident at all. She would certainly hear of it, but by then I hoped the archbishop and I would be well on our way to a cordial understanding. Perhaps standing up to the wizened little priest the way I had was not entirely the way of wisdom, but if the other choice had been to light the fire myself then I had had no choice.

"So you too were from a family of two brothers and a sister?" the abbess asked.

I nodded. "My brother Guibert inherited the archduchy, I've now become count here, and our sister Gertrude— she died as a girl."

She nodded. "I received one or two messages from up north over the years, but a nun does not exchange letters with her relatives as though she were a young woman making a visit to the royal court! It is curious, Nephew Galoran, but I was elected abbess as a reward for years of faithful prayer and unworldly thoughts, and now as abbess I have very little time for my private devotions and have had to become aware of the world's affairs as I was not for fifty years."

"You must have been in contact in recent years with your brother Bernhard," I said. At least I might be able to learn something more about Peyrefixade, and the close relationship that had apparently been maintained between the old count and the Order of the Three Kings—the close relationship that Thierri had wanted to break.

"Contact beyond the semiannual disposition of rents?" she said with a small smile. "Our parents were generous when they offered me to the Holy Family." So Melchior had been right, I thought. "That, of course, was before the great war against the Imperfected, so I never saw the heretic castle which my father and then my brother made their own."

I should have realized that, I thought. No chance then of learning anything firsthand from her about my castle.

"I did see my brother Bernhard occasionally," she continued, "perhaps every two or three years for a brief visit even while I was a nun, more frequently in recent years once I became abbess. He sometimes came himself to collect the rents rather than sending his seneschal. And that is why," her voice suddenly dropped, and she leaned forward so sharply in her chair that for a moment I was afraid she was going to fall, "I would like to ask for your help." She lifted her eyebrows apologetically. "He and his granddaughter, of course, were not truly my family, because I have belonged since I was six to the Holy Family. But humor an old woman's whim. I do not seek revenge, only knowledge. Help me find out why they died."

I cocked my head, surprised. "There's no secret about it. The countess died a few months ago from a fall from the castle ramparts. No one saw the accident, though there are plenty of rumors." Would I have to offer lands and rents for my cousin's soul, I wondered, or would some new altar vessels and cloth for the nuns' habits do as well? "As to her grandfather, the old count— I never heard anything specific, but I assume he died from old age."

"I do not mean the method of their deaths," she said quietly. "That of course I know perfectly well. Indeed, although ultimately my brother's death *was* from old age, the precise cause was a broken hip. He was riding with some of his knights and Lord Thierri, his granddaughter's husband. His horse became spooked somehow and threw him, and he declined rapidly and was gone within a month. No, I mean something more, Nephew Galoran. I want to know *why* both of them died within a year. Was it merely a coincidence, or the devil jealous of their good works in the world? Or was there a human agent, perhaps one who preferred someone else at Peyrefixade?"

She was touching on something I wanted to know myself. "The duke chose me to become count at Peyrefixade," I stammered, "but I scarcely suspect him of getting rid of the old count and the countess in order to bring in a man he'd never met!"

Inwardly I was thinking that people who got too close to Thierri seemed strangely inclined to die: first his wife's grandfather, although I had not heard before the faintest rumor that Thierri might have hastened the old man's death, convenient as it may have been for him, and then Countess Aenor herself. Nothing Thierri had told me, including his suspicions that the Order of the Three Kings was responsible for her death, could be given any credence.

Abbess Richildis gave a small smile. "The duke I might suspect of many things, if it were not inappropriate in a nun to have such thoughts, but pushing my niece from the castle ramparts is not among them. I hope you realize, however, Nephew Galoran, that he may possibly be making plans for *you*."

The room had become darker while we spoke, though

I could still see the brightness in the old abbess's eyes. "Is this a veiled warning," I hazarded, "about his daughter Arsendis?"

"Then you have met the young lady!" the abbess said, pleased. "I am sure you have been told that she rejected the match her father had made for her, even though it was an excellent one as the world reckons these matters. Ever since the duke's son left his court—I will not recount that story, as it is very painful to contemplate—Argave has had to treat his two daughters as his heirs." She paused for an embarrassed titter, surprising in one so serene. "You see how my duties have forced me to be aware of the world's rumors! The oldest daughter obediently married a count from some distance east of here five years ago, and the duke feels it imperative that young Arsendis also marry well, though he will not force his choice upon her. It is possible, Nephew, that Duke Argave may be considering your potential as a son-in-law— especially if he fears the alternative is Prince Alfonso."

"Prince Alfonso!"

"The prince has repeatedly proposed the union to Duke Argave in the strongest possible terms. He even came here once himself, promising a rich gift to the nuns if I would second his cause with the duke." The abbess shook her head. "You see how much the world distracts me!" But the Abbess Richildis, I guessed, had not acceded to Alfonso's request.

I smiled. "I myself seek only a gently-born lady who would have me as I am, and I do not flatter myself that Arsendis is that lady."

Before the abbess could add anything more to this intriguing discussion, the young novice returned. "It has been a half hour, Reverend Mother."

"Of course, my dear. Help me rise." I hurried to assist the old abbess with a hand under her elbow as she levered herself to her feet, supporting her weight on the cane and the novice's arm. She might once have been as tall as I, but was now so stooped she came no higher than my chest. "Bless you, Nephew Galoran," she said, turning up her face toward mine, "and thank you for visiting me." This close I could see all the wrinkles that age had left, but none of them threatened either her serenity or the spark in her eyes. "If you learn anything about that of which we spoke, come visit me again."

It was not until she disappeared through an inner door, and I had retrieved my sword and gone back out to see how the rent rolls were coming, that I realized that I had never discussed with her my gift for the countess's soul.

It was good to be home in Peyrefixade. As I settled down in my own bed again—I had long since stopped thinking of it as the countess's bed—I felt secure as I had not for a week. Just seeing the dark red tower from the valley below had made my spirits lift. Now that I had seen my whole county, I knew that being the scarred Count of Peyrefixade was better than being the unscarred Lord Galoran of anywhere else. The duke might be developing elaborate plots in which I played a major role, plots that could take a distinct turn for the worse once he discovered I had defied the Inquisition; Lord Thierri might be thinking up ways that he could replace me here; Prince Alfonso might be planning to eliminate me to make easier his access to my county, not to mention to the duke's daughter; the heretics might want their castle back; and the Inquisition might feel that I was behaving entirely inappropriately for a son of the True Faith; but none of them could touch me here.

I sighted contentedly, looking through the bed curtains to the soft glow from the fine new fireplace. All around me I could hear the men settling down to sleep and even the first snores. The muscles that had been gripping a horse all up and down my county slowly relaxed, and I dozed off.

When I opened my eyes again in a short time, rolling

over to go from dozing to deep sleep, I could still see the fire's warm glow, but it seemed somehow brighter than I expected. The bed had gone from comfortably warm to unpleasantly hot, and a loud crackling surrounded me. I sat up abruptly, my heart racing in panic as I tried desperately to determine what was dream and what was reality.

The reality was worse than any dream. The bed curtains were on fire.

Chapter Six ~ Melchior

1

Count Galoran and the others might be happy to be home, but I had returned to Peyrefixade sore in body and troubled in soul. I had been a sworn canon of the Order more than half my life and a priest since I was twenty. I held myself to be a faithful son of the True Faith. Yet all my confidence, my painfully constructed fortress of detachment, had crumbled into nothing when I saw those three poor souls about to be consigned to the flames, just as Grandfather and his companions had been on that terrible day when I was still just a boy. As soon as the hall settled down for sleep, I rose quietly from my pallet and slipped up the stairs to the chapel, to spend the hours until it was time to sing the night office in deep examination of my heart and earnest prayer.

I was kneeling on the cold stones, staring into a book depicting the stations of the Cross and repeating its familiar phrases for the third time, when I realized that a confused clamor of sound had been echoing along the corridor for several moments. Flickering orange lights and leaping shadows appeared as I hurried down the spiral staircase toward the noise, but nothing prepared me for the sight that met me when I rushed into the hall.

Men ran in every direction, shouting and gesturing, but their words were inaudible against the force of a great roaring sound that seemed to vibrate the very stones. It came from a prodigious wind blasting down the fine new chimney and pouring out of the hearth, bearing a huge plume of flames before it. As if from the bellows of a giant forge, this terrible mass of fire shot straight to the count's great curtained bed and encircled it within an impenetrable whirlwind of flames that towered up high into the vaulting. The rushes on the floor all around were burning fiercely. As I stared in horror, a black form appeared within the terrible whirlwind of fire, twitching and jerking like one of the big insects that sometimes fly into the tapers upon the altar in midsummer. Suddenly the figure lurched halfway out of the flames and crashed to the floor. By the time I reached the spot the seneschal and some of the knights had managed to drag the burning man clear. Raymbaud and two of the men hurriedly muffled the flames on him with blankets while the rest beat at spots of fire on their own clothing. But it was not the count; it was Bruno.

"I couldn't get—to him—Father," he gasped through blackened lips. "They've got to—save him."

"Water! Where's the barrel of water?" I screamed into a knight's face, pointing toward the entrance of the hall where a huge cask was always kept brim-full in case of need.

"Empty, Father!" the seneschal shouted. "Someone bored a hole in the back side and let it all run out! Here they come with some from the kitchen cisterns."

I whirled to look and saw the cook and two men stagger in from the kitchen carrying a huge tub, which they emptied into the flames around Count Galoran's burning bed. But the water vanished into steam like a single drop on hot iron, without the slightest effect. This could not be an ordinary fire! I covered my ears against the tumult and concentrated my attention upon my inner eye. Yes, there could be no doubt. The wind blasting from the hearth, the great plume of fire, the wall of flames around the count's bed: all vibrated with magic. And all were being interwoven into a powerful vortex of magic, terrible in its furious beauty, emanating from within the burning curtains of the bed itself.

There was but one thing to be done, and it must be done instantly, for even those thick winter curtains of wool would fly up into ash in another moment. I groped within my cassock until my hand found the cool carved stick of old ivory given to me long ago by my first tutor in magic, the man who had scorned to employ its aid himself at the last. Drawing it forth, I held it before me, so that the image and symbols of Aquarius faced the flames, and walked toward the hearth. Waves of heat beat into my face, and my robes began to smoke. Standing as close as my weak flesh would allow, I called out the words I had learned so long ago from a well-loved Auccitan-accented voice.

> *"Flamma impero tibi*
> *Ut nihil fias*
> *Hoc est hora."*

Within the ivory in my hand, I felt a stirring of long-latent power as the lines of magic I'd laid down within it through many days of difficult incantations awoke all together to sudden life. I strained my mind to its utmost and directed that flow of power straight into the fireplace. With a surge that staggered me, a full third of the stored-up magic poured itself out through the mouth of the little jar held by the carved Aquarius and into the heart of the inferno upon the hearth. The huge wind ceased instantly, as if a giant lid had been clapped over the chimney high above. Within the fireplace itself, the monstrous flames leaped high, then collapsed into a little heap of glowing coals, all that remained of the pile of thick logs that would have sustained any natural hearth-fire throughout the entire night. I spun about, to see the whirling pillar of fire around the count's bed begin to waver and grow thinner. But then the lines of magic from the hearth reached out to the vortex of magic within those curtains, and the flames reared high once more. Stretching out the ivory rod again and focusing my attention now upon that nexus of magic, I again spoke the activating incantation. In another instant every trace of flame and magic had vanished from both bed and hall.

The cook and his scullions had been standing transfixed in the doorway with another huge tub, watching all this. Now they hurried forward and doused the smoldering rushes and bed curtains with water. The curtains, reduced to ash, dissolved and collapsed like sodden cobwebs, and the count staggered out into the room wearing nothing but his long shirt. I started toward the bed, then sank to my knees, weak as a baby from channeling so much magic so swiftly. As a knight bent to help me, his face wavered and dimmed before my eyes while a roaring filled my ears, and all went dark.

My next sensation was of lying on my back with my eyes closed. When I opened them, the faces of Count Galoran and the seneschal loomed over me. The scar on the count's grim visage looked red and angry but he himself appeared unhurt. He was dressed now in the usual rough soldier's jerkin and hose he favored at home.

"So, Father Melchior, I learn I have you to thank for saving my life," he said. "You shall find me appreciative, but those masons may think more ill of you for doing so when I catch up with them."

"The masons are not to blame—at least not the whole crew of them." Weak as I felt, my mind seemed startlingly clear and the thoughts within it quite complete. It was as if I had been pondering deeply the whole time I had been unconscious.

"What do you mean, Father?"

"That was no mishap due to faulty construction. It was a magical attack upon you."

I saw him shoot a look at the seneschal, who dropped his sad eyes. "So, I actually suspected as much. It was well I had a magic-worker of my own at hand, it seems. As it is I'm likely to lose a good man."

The memory of Bruno enveloped in the whirl of flames leaped up before me and I struggled to rise. "Where is he? Take me to him! I must confess him at once."

"You should rest, Father; it is still the middle of the night. We are going to send for the priest from the village," the seneschal told me, trying to make me lie down again. But the count waved him away. He took my arm and helped me to my feet with what looked like a grim smile of approval.

"He's right across the room, Father Melchior. We set up a little infirmary for the two of you here in the great guest chamber."

I had to lean on his hard arm just to get across the room to the other bed, where a serving boy with a frightened face stood watch. The scorched clothing had been cut away from Bruno's body, and he'd been wrapped in a clean length of white linen, but I could see enough to know that he was burned everywhere. As I knelt by the bed, I saw the count beside me press his lips together and turn his face away.

The old soldier's eyes flew open as soon as I spoke his name and called upon him to confess his sins and be absolved. But when he spoke, his urgent words were unintelligible.

"He's talking border Allemann," Count Galoran told me, taking up a cup and pitcher from the stand. "The tongue of his boyhood. He is asking for some water, and then to be shriven. Will it do, Father, if I translate between the two of you?"

"That will be perfectly all right," I told the count as he cradled Bruno like a baby while the old soldier drank through blistered lips. "The Lord knows all the tongues of women and men, and in the end cares only for what they have within their hearts."

By the time I'd heard the aged knight's translated

confession and repeated the old comforting formulas and prayers over him, I felt slightly stronger. The count started to lead me back to my own bed, but I stopped him. "No, take me down to the hall. I must examine the hearth at once."

We got there just in time to forestall the servants upon the point of kindling a new fire. I had them lever the big logs back out onto the hearth-stones. Even the slight magical effort required to peer into the ashes with my second eye made me dizzy once more. The count called for a stool to be brought, and I sank down onto it. Fortunately, I found what I was seeking almost at once, wedged firmly into a gap between two stones behind the iron at the back of the hearth.

"It is a *telesma*," I said once a servant had worked the object free with his knife and placed it in the count's hand. "An object gradually charged with great magical force sometime in the past and capable of releasing that force whenever it is given a specific incantation, or else exposed to a specific situation." I pulled forth my carved ivory rod. "I used a telesma of my own to extinguish the fire."

Count Galoran stared at the telesma from the hearth, then put it hastily in my hand. "Do you think this thing could kindle another such fire?" he asked.

I took a deep breath to gather strength and examined the telesma with both my fleshly and second eyes. It was nothing more than a small piece of ceramic tile that had been stamped with alchemical symbols, then glazed and fired. Traces of the magical lines that had been laid into it were still discernible, but it now felt as light and empty of magical substance as a plant husk. "No, it seems quite spent," I said, then slumped as a great tiredness swept through me.

The count barked out a command and Raymbaud himself fetched a glass of wine, which I drank gratefully. "You'd better go back to your bed now, Father Melchior,"

Count Galoran said. "I am only beginning to understand how much this magic-working can take out of a man."

A huge heaviness seemed to drag at my limbs, and my eyelids kept sinking shut as I answered, "I believe—you are right."

2

I awoke in the great guest bed to cold morning light. My body felt as if it had been beaten all over with heavy sticks, a sure indication of having wrought too much magic far too rapidly. The ache brought recollections of the night flooding back, and I realized immediately what it was that had been nagging at the edge of my attention from the moment I had begun using my second vision in the hall. I raised myself up to call for the count—and found him already sitting at my bedside. His features were stamped with a bitter weariness and set like stone. I knew even before I looked past him what I would find. The form lying upon the other bed was now swathed completely in white linen, and tall candles burned at both head and feet.

"He is dead."

"Yes." When Count Galoran turned his eyes toward me his face seemed to be all scar. "My only friend here, my only tie to my old life: my good, hard, simple soldier's life. Loyal as an old dog, Bruno. He'd have followed me anywhere. He knew I would never be able to make myself come out through that wall of flames, so he went in after me even though he had to know it was hopeless."

"I shall sing the office of the dead for him today, as soon as I feel a little stronger. But we must now speak of something else."

"Indeed we must. But you shall eat first." He helped me from the bed and led me into the adjacent small guest chamber, where a loaf and beer had been set out on a table flanked by two chairs. A good fire had been laid to warm the chamber, and a log split with a blaze of sparks just as we passed the hearth. I felt Count Galoran's rocklike forearm flinch under mine as his whole body tensed, but neither of us said anything as he helped me to my seat.

As soon as I saw the food I became ravenous. As I began to eat, trying not to cram down the bread and guzzle the beer, the count continued, "You said this attack upon me was magical, and I certainly do not doubt you. It missed me, thanks to your quick work, but it killed a man I do not intend to leave unavenged. The learning of a castle's *capellanus* is supposed to be at the disposal of its lord, and you have the magical learning that shall be needed for the matter at hand. You are going to help me catch the man responsible for this, Father Melchior."

"The man responsible, and the one behind that man: yes." I nodded my head, a rash act that sent a blinding stab of pain through my head. I sat very still until it passed, then took another long drink and continued more carefully, "I shall of course do everything I can. Even if we set aside my present position in your service, my oath to my Order requires that I do all in my power to check any misuse of magic. But there is something else we must discuss now. Last night's attack upon you was performed by means of a telesma. Under your shirt—upon your breast—hangs another type of telesma. I now realize that it can be highly dangerous. It should be sealed away at once, under proper magical locks, until I can take it to the best masters of my Order for examination."

The count looked at me with no expression on his closed face for half a minute, then his hand went to the opening at the throat of his shirt. He took hold of a cord and pulled forth the medallion with its simple circle, asking, "And why should I agree to this?"

"I did not recognize it before because it is a type of telesma I have heard and read of but never seen for myself. It is called a *conviare*. An ordinary telesma is as I described, an object that has previously been charged with a store of magic that can be released all at once or in set portions when the proper incantation or conditions occur. But a conviare is imbued with the capacity to channel and direct magic forces coming from outside itself, without depleting its own potency. It is a sort of speculum or lens for magic, like the ones for light made by the greatest glass artisans. When the attack began last night, this conviare drew the magical wind and fire to you far more powerfully than would have occurred had you not been wearing it, and also greatly enhanced their strength."

Count Galoran had drawn his knife from his belt before I was finished speaking. With a single motion he slashed the cord and thrust the conviare into my hand. The corner of his eye twitched as he muttered, "Then take the damned thing and seal it away in whatever fashion will best secure us against its power. I want no more devil's fires here! Indeed, would it not be best to have the blacksmith simply melt this deadly weapon down at once and be done with it?"

"I think we should keep it, Count Galoran. It is not dangerous in itself, only when dangerous power is directed toward it. It was not necessarily even fashioned to be a weapon. Your attacker simply took advantage of its capacities."

His chest rose and fell rapidly, then more slowly, and when he finally spoke he was able to make his voice at least sound level and calm. "Which leads straight back to my first question: who might that attacker have been? And how do we go about finding him?"

"It will not be easy. Almost anyone could have inserted the tile telesma into the gap between the stones any time from when work was finished on the lower fireplace to the day the chimney was completed. The person need not even have known the nature of the object he was placing. It may have been one of the masons, of course. But the man could just as well have belonged to the castle."

"That hadn't escaped my notice." The count paced quickly to the window and stared down into the yard, where Raymbaud and some of the knights were practicing with their swords. I could see the tension in his shoulders easing as he watched the men going about their soldiers' tasks. After a minute he continued, "But it is hard to see why. I know the duke has a spy in the castle, but there is no reason Argave should have put himself to the trouble of bringing me all the way down from the northern marches and setting me here, merely to have me killed shortly afterwards. It's clear I have some enemies about, considering what almost happened at the duke's court, but no one new has joined us here at Peyrefixade. I don't see how an enemy could have subverted a member of my household so quickly." He stiffened, then slowly turned to face me. "However . . . Perhaps I'm unwise to ask you, since you are a priest yourself, but I conclude from your behavior when you helped stop the burning of those poor wretches that you have no great love for the Inquisition. Do you suppose they might be behind this?"

I felt an immediate shiver go through my own body, but relaxed when I thought on this a little further. "I think not, Count. The same argument applies to them as to any other enemy of yours: they've not had time to subvert any member of the household. Of course, it is entirely possible *they* may have had a man placed here for years, but it is unlikely they would use such a spy in a covert attack like this. They employ spies and agents of all sorts to gain information, but their true power derives from destroying whatever enemies they uncover in the most public fashion possible, not by stealth."

"That's true enough. But what you say raises something I had not properly considered before. The attacker may have been someone who was in the castle long before I myself came here, but one who has nothing to do with either Duke Argave or the Inquisition." He went back to the window and stared down with a grim expression at the knights practicing below, jerking his knife halfway out of its sheath and jamming it back repeatedly while he considered this. "An enemy of my whole family and house, not merely of myself."

I paused to swallow the last of my bread and drink, giving me time to decide I must tell him the rest. "Yes, there may indeed be such an enemy here. The masters of my Order believe that the death of your predecessor the countess was caused by someone using magic."

Count Galoran glanced sidelong at me from his place before the window. From my angle only his unmarred side was visible. With some surprise, I found myself looking at the profile of a thoughtful but firm-looking man, with rather handsome features. That profiled face was stamped with sadness at the present moment, but also with determination—and surprisingly, a certain detached interest, even some ironic amusement as he willed himself to become calm again. I had thought of him as pure steel when I'd first met him. Now, once again, came a hint that perhaps there might be more to the man.

"I have heard rumors suggesting something like that myself, Father Melchior," he said dryly. "Well, if the countess's killer and my own attacker are the same man, then he's still here in the castle and may well try for me again. But he will not find the way so easy now that we have been alerted to the danger. I think I and my knights can handle any attacker bearing weapons of steel. May I rely upon you to defend us against any further magical assaults?"

I surprised myself with how readily the answer came to my lips, "For as long as you may keep me in your service, you may."

We buried old Bruno later that day in the cemetery down at the village, the nearest place with soil deep enough for graves. I had recovered enough strength to sing the office of the dead acceptably in the chapel, but was very glad to ride rather than walk when we followed the rough coffin down the steep winding road. The sexton of the village church, alerted that morning, had already prepared the grave by the time we arrived. We performed the interment quickly, for this would be only a temporary tomb for Bruno. Count Galoran had decided that the old soldier's final resting place would be at my own House of the Three Kings. Indeed, it appeared ironically that I had done much toward mending the Order's standing with his family simply by doing what both instinct and duty had demanded the night before, for the count had told me as we rode that he intended to make a gift sufficient to establish anniversary observances with singing of the high office for Bruno as well as for his predecessor the countess. Now the count, a somber Raymbaud, the gloomy seneschal, the knights, and a few of the villagers standing to one side bowed their heads as Bruno's coffin went down. As we remounted, I saw Count Galoran look back at the little mound, just once. Then he set his face toward the castle and led us home.

I was in my little study off the chapel toward evening a few days later, doing the first of the several cycles of incantation that would be required to replenish the magic store of my ivory telesma, when I heard a diffident knock. It had been very pleasant to feel up to undertaking some real magic, without feeling exhausted, for the first time since the night of the fire, and I wanted to have this job done before we left to go down to the duke's spring court, to be held at the same time as the Paschal Feast. So I set the telesma aside with regret at the interruption and called out, "Enter!" To my surprise it was Seneschal Guilhem who appeared, asking if he might consult with me for a few minutes.

"It concerns the rent rolls and the other records of the count's property you prepared during our trip across his domains," he explained, holding out the bundle of documents with a deferential expression on his gloomy features. "I shall shortly be summoning the bailiffs to give them their instructions as to the actual collecting of the rents and dues. I wish to make absolutely certain beforehand that I have exactly the same understanding as to what those revenues should be as the count himself."

"Then I shall be happy to go over the records with you now, of course." As he sat down and began to spread the parchments out on the table an expression of relief passed momentarily over his face before it subsided back into its accustomed sadness. I felt more than a little sympathy for him. The seneschal had clearly realized that Count Galoran, while a fair and even generous master to those who served him diligently, was not the man to tolerate incompetence or failure from a subordinate.

It had become obvious during that week we'd ridden together over the lands of the county that the seneschal had always carried all of the records in his head up to now. As we went over my lists and notations, I confirmed something else I had also come to suspect. Like many of his profession, men who were generally drawn from the more intelligent younger sons of small landowners and who had received a decent education but could expect no inheritance, the seneschal could read but not write—at least nothing beyond the occasional single word, scrawled in what looked like a child's first letters, as a prompt to memory. Once I had convinced myself of this, I fetched an ink and pen from the other end of the table without making any show about it and commenced adding brief but full annotations to the margin each time we came to a place where the information I had noted down during our journey was unclear to the seneschal. It took surprisingly little time, as the fellow's memory was in truth phenomenal and the points to be clarified were therefore few.

When we had finished he gathered up the parchments with a murmur of thanks, but then hesitated near the door as if he had something else he was searching for a way to say. "Stay a moment more, Seneschal," I immediately said, seeing this as a providential opportunity. I'd been feeling guilty again about not having done more to seek out and talk with those in the count's household who might be in need of spiritual counsel, and this sad man certainly appeared to be one such. He resumed his seat and I said, "You seem greatly troubled at heart; would you like to speak of it?"

"Yes, Father Melchior, you are right. I bear a heavy burden of sadness." He spoke with downcast eyes. "The unexpected and so sudden death of our dear Countess Aenor, the horrible manner of it, they haunt me night and day."

"I have read my predecessor Brother Nuage's account of the event; it was indeed very terrible."

"Ah, he was a good man, Father Nuage. I was so very sorry when our countess's *consort*"—as the seneschal pronounced this word a passion and venom that burned like a sudden flame entered into his flat voice—"sent him away from us so abruptly right after the accident, voicing baseless slanders. I would have given much for his kind counsel in the awful days that followed. That vile man Thierri so suddenly master of this place, lording it over us all, hardly seeming to think of his lady so recently dead under the wall—and him no true part of the family, with no real claim. Oh, he went about in mourning with a long face, but he couldn't completely hide his delight in thinking his vile plans to become undisputed Count of Peyrefixade had come to fruition so much sooner than expected! What a pleasure it was to see him ride cursing from the gates after the duke's messenger came to tell him he must quit this place and return to court. Cast down to simple Lord Thierri once more, lord not of lands and men but only of mincing ways and sneaking schemes, of stratagems and spoils!"

He actually struck his fist upon the table as he spat out these final words, then fell silent, staring straight ahead with blazing eyes. I sat dumbfounded: this, from our sad, dour seneschal! Then a chill of suspicion went through me and I asked, "Do you mean by this to say that you believe Lord Thierri plotted his own wife's death?"

His eyes swung to meet mine with a glare that struck like a blow, then went suddenly dull. All the quivering intensity seemed to drain out of him as his body slumped in the chair. "No, not that, Father," he whispered, so low I could barely hear. "Swine though he is, Lord Thierri did not cause our sweet lady's death. I myself can attest that he was on his high seat in the hall swilling wine when the—the terrible event occurred." His eyes met mine once more, this time filled with what seemed all the sorrow in the world. "At least she has gone to a better place now, one where we can be sure *he* shall never go to join her."

Rather than go into the arcana of the doctrine of possible salvation for even the worst of us, with a man who was clearly not prepared to listen, I shifted back to the original subject. "I see that the countess's death has indeed affected you greatly. But you do right to hope that she has already gone to a better world, or soon shall do so."

"Oh, I am sure she already has, Father! So sweet and innocent a girl she was when young, and so good and virtuous a lady as she grew into womanhood! Always with a kind thought or word for all of us who served her, always thoughtful to ease our lot and make our tasks in her service as light as possible! She was never interested in rich clothes and show, or gluttonous for fine foods in the manner of so many great ladies, you know. And she loved simplicity in everything and was always so pious. Surely so pure a lady had nothing left to shed of earthly dross at the hour of her—her death."

Tears were coursing down his hollow cheeks. Though his account did not square perfectly with every particular I had heard of the late countess, nor with Brother Nuage's notes, I murmured, "You may well be right."

"Ah, if you had only known her, Father Melchior, then you could not doubt! I strive now to be pure, to shed all taint of desire or want and live only as a wholly virtuous person in the line of service to which I have been called, for so long as I must still travail within this flawed world, but I must advance far indeed before I attain even a fraction of the virtue she possessed of her very nature. And I have such sins from which to free myself! I study constantly for ways to give up all desires, to shed every calling of the dross flesh. But you are a man of Faith, Father Melchior, I need not speak of such matters to you. I should like to ask, however: do you not think that a person who has done a great wrong, but done it without intending to do so—can such a person not shed that stain?"

"Certainly we are taught that the gravity is much less for an unintended sin than one committed with active purpose." I repeated this standard bit of doctrine almost automatically, for my soul had been gripped by another dreadful suspicion. "But tell me something, friend seneschal. I have noticed that you eat and drink scarcely enough to sustain life. Do you practice the discipline of fasting?"

"Oh yes, Father, yes indeed! And I sleep directly upon the hard stones of the hall each night, putting down no bedding. You, who come from an Order dedicated to holiness: you can understand these things. You will know what it is to practice disciplines that purify. I strive constantly in my own poor way to do the same."

"Yes, yes, strive for purity by all means, Brother Seneschal. But remember that you also need to seek grace. If you have some sin that burdens you, you should confess it and seek absolution with a contrite heart." My own heart was beating fast as I spoke, hoping that he would unburden himself, hoping that the fears that had now sprung up within me were unfounded.

But his eyes had dropped again and were now veiled. "Perhaps I should do as you say, Father Melchior. But my way is uncertain, my heart confused. I need to consider carefully." He rose, swaying from what I now realized was the weakness of semistarvation while he gathered up his parchment rolls again. As he left I called after him,

"Remember that you can come to me at any time and I shall hear you without judging or condemning."

I sat with unseeing eyes for a long time after the door had shut itself behind him, my mind racing. The ideas he had expressed—the seeking of purification through self-deprivation, the contempt for the flesh and its needs as wholly evil, the suggestion that salvation could come strictly through personal virtue—these ideas were all deeply imbued with the doctrines of the Perfected.

Of course, it would have been hard to find any lay persons from the countryside hereabouts who didn't have at least some hint of this strain in their thinking. And the man was clearly laboring under a great burden of sadness; his mind might even be unhinged, at least to some degree. Nor had he ruled out coming back at some point to confess whatever this sin of his might be and seek grace as the True Faith directed, rather than trying to overcome his sins through his own unaided efforts.

Besides, I was no inquisitor; I was nothing like that desiccated fanatic Count Galoran had only barely managed to prevent from putting those poor villagers to the torch. I could let the matter rest for now, hoping and praying that the seneschal would find his way to the proper path and trying to guide and encourage him whenever the opportunity offered. Whatever his real or imagined crime might be, it clearly had nothing to do with the recent attack on the count. The seneschal's conviction that he must continue to do his best in the job to which he had been "called" for as long as he remained in this world would never have allowed him to place an object he would clearly have recognized as having dangerous significance anywhere in the count's castle without telling him of it. No, I would keep this matter to myself for now. Only if I found myself confronted with incontrovertible evidence would I even consider informing the count that the man he was trusting to discharge the office of his seneschal might have joined the enemies of the True Faith.

Chapter Seven ~ Galoran

1

During the days I kept hearing the sound of Bruno's voice in the distance, or catching his step as he came down the corridor. During the nights I kept hearing the crackle of mage-fire all around my bed, and in a dream my eyes would jerk open to see the curtains a pulsating red and the dark shape of Bruno trying to beat his way through to save me. When I opened my eyes in earnest, to find all dark around me except for the faint glow from the hearth, which I had reluctantly agreed to have kindled again when on the second day the men's grumbling about the cold had become pronounced, I would be bathed in sweat and shaking hard. Sometimes it took nearly until dawn to fall asleep again.

None of this, of course, did I hint at to anyone. Bruno was the only one of the knights whom I would have trusted with it. And Bruno was dead, his bones lying in the cold soil of the churchyard of the village where I had hung the adulterers, waiting to be moved to the House of the Three Kings. I would give the Order the rest of the rents, I decided, from the village that had already been half given to the nuns of the Holy Family two generations ago. Let my great-aunt's bailiffs divide the rents with the Order rather than with me. That was the village where the people had welcomed the Inquisition; I didn't want their money anyway.

From years of leading the emperor's soldiers I knew

much better than to let the men think their leader was afraid. Melchior might have guessed, but if so he had too much sense to ask if I required spiritual counsel and kept a prudent silence. The brave Count of Peyrefixade was not afraid of fire, not afraid of an assassin, not even afraid of the Inquisition, which might have been worrying my knights the worst of all.

And yet I wondered about the Inquisition during the two weeks that the bailiffs were collecting my rents. Seneschal Guilhem, Melchior, and I went over the accounts together as each bailiff brought in the proceeds: the sums that wouldn't add up on the abacus even though the individual figures all seemed right; the man who had inexplicably disappeared without paying; the coins that looked suspect or else were from a mint that the tenants had said gave them greater value than those from the Haulbé mint, and thus required fewer to meet their obligations; the one family who had decided to pay their rents entirely in baby chicks even though the seneschal assured me they had always before paid in cash. Once we decided that each bailiff had collected the money as fairly and completely as he could, and that there was no use sending him back to the village a second time—or perhaps a third—I paid him his fee myself and notched his wand of office to show that the accounts were accepted.

The archbishop of Haulbé was doubtless going over his own rent rolls with his own bailiffs, but I would still have expected a letter from him, if not indeed a self-righteous inquisitor speaking in the bishop's name. Melchior might also have been wondering what would happen there; several times I caught him looking very thoughtful, as though he was formulating some sort of suspicion or plan, although he did not share it with me.

Should I suspect *him* of heresy? My initial thought when I learned of an Order devoted to magic had been that this had seemed dangerously unorthodox. Although once I had gotten to know this intelligent and conscientious priest I had put aside these thoughts, I had been staggered by the appearance of the telesma in his hand, especially so shortly after he had demonstrated such sympathy toward the condemned Perfected.

Counting piles of coins, almost the last to come in, I gave a grim smile. It would be ironic for me to start suspecting evil of the man who had saved my life even if he couldn't save Bruno's, the one man in the castle I now felt I could trust at my back. A telesma that doused fires more effectively than any water barrel could be extremely useful. I was hundreds of miles from all members of my family except for the abbess, and had no friends I had known more than two months. A possibly heretical priest would have to do.

At least the accounts had kept my mind occupied, I thought, stretching. And there would be little opportunity to brood even now, for in a few days it would be time for the duke's Paschal Court. Perhaps it was surprising that I hadn't heard from Argave, either; someone as vehemently opposed to the Perfected as was the duke must be a great supporter of the Inquisition.

Or maybe, I thought, sweeping all the copper coins off the table and into a bag, no one had climbed up to Peyrefixade because they knew how difficult it would be to get in if I didn't choose to receive them. It was much easier to wait until I came out by myself.

2

No one, wild-eyed heretic, self-righteous inquisitor, or skulking Nabarrese, tried to attack us as we rode down to Duke Argave's Paschal Court. After forty days of nothing but bread, vegetables, a few eggs, and fish—and most of that salted—it would be good, I thought, to have another banquet such as the one Argave had served when I first arrived at Peyrefixade. I would, however, quite happily skip the incident with the assassin this time.

I left the seneschal in charge of the castle, taking only

the priest and a half dozen knights, the ones who had accompanied me around to my tenancies and whom I felt I knew now. That three of them had obeyed me in returning the condemned heretics to the mountains after I saved them from the stake—and I had questioned the knights closely on what the heretics had done when set free, to make sure they hadn't knifed them themselves— spoke well for their loyalty. The bouteillier Raymbaud had wanted to accompany me, speaking of buying new wine in Ferignan, but I quite deliberately refused his request. He had come originally from the ducal court, and I was still convinced he was the duke's eyes and ears in Peyrefixade—especially since I had gradually given up suspecting Melchior of being the duke's spy. If so, I wasn't going to make Raymbaud's conveying of his reports to his real master any easier.

"So here is the man who defies even the Inquisition!" said Duke Argave in greeting as we entered his courtyard, having once again yielded our weapons to his guards. A quick glance around showed men in livery posted all around the garden, including by the back wall. Spring was advancing rapidly; flower beds that had been sere two months ago were now dense with green. "I wanted a powerful count at Peyrefixade to form a barrier against Alfonso," the duke added, "and I may have gotten even more than I expected!"

He smiled as he spoke, but his eyes looked cautious and calculating. "I have no quarrel with those who seek out the heretical dogs of the mountains and their perfidious doctrine," I said smoothly, "only those whose precipitous judgment may undercut my authority, the authority I received from you, O Duke." I dropped to my knees and took his hand—the one with the big emerald ring—in both of mine. "After attending your court, I intend to make my way to Haulbé this week to assure the archbishop of my faithful adherence to the revealed Truth."

The duke's smile abruptly looked much more genuine.

"You shall have a chance to meet with him even earlier than that, Count, for Archbishop Amalric will be riding over here in a few days."

"Good," I said placidly. "Direct conversation on matters of importance is always better than messages and letters, where misunderstandings may inadvertently arise." I rose to my feet, dusting myself off with as much nonchalance as I could manage, aware that my knights were all watching closely and that Lord Thierri had emerged to hover in the background. The brave Count of Peyrefixade wasn't afraid of the archbishop either.

"In fact," said Argave for my ear alone as we walked together toward his hall, "it may be time that a few of the more fanatical members of the Inquisition were reminded that they are to cure men's souls but not rule their bodies." He lifted an eyebrow as I turned toward him, his lips curved in an ironic smile, but he did not elaborate.

He said nothing more of the Inquisition that evening. It was the last night of the period of penitence, and though there were no musicians playing, the ducal cook had produced an excellent fish chowder, better than anything my own cook's conscientious efforts had ever come up with. All the duke's castellans and manorial lords were there, most of whom I had met on my earlier visit, as well as a count new to me. He was Duke Argave's son-in-law, married to the duke's oldest daughter; they had come to the Paschal Court from their own county some distance to the east.

Come perhaps to learn about me? I wondered, as I found this count constantly at my elbow, asking about my family back north, about the new construction at Peyrefixade of which everyone seemed to have heard— he seemed disappointed when I told him it was nothing more than a new fireplace—and even trying to learn delicately how I had come by my scar.

"A fire a long time ago," I said shortly, irritated because

his presence on one side of me at the duke's high table kept me from paying more attention to the duke's younger daughter, Arsendis, who sat on my other side.

But maybe I was happy after all for the distraction. The memory of the conversation with my aunt the abbess came back vividly. Could Argave possibly be considering me as a prospective second son-in-law as well as a barrier between his duchy and Nabarra? And if so, what did his dark-haired and white-throated daughter think about it?

Whatever she thought, she seemed favorably enough inclined toward me to become my companion in hawking the next day. We had of course all been up before dawn and out in the duke's garden, to hear his own Magian priest and Father Melchior sing the divine office together, and ourselves to sing Halleluia to the risen Savior as the sun rose in a pale yellow sky. After the best breakfast in forty days, we prepared to ride out with the hawks.

"The cranes and storks are coming north," Argave explained to me, "and my gyrfalcon grows rusty with little sport. I have a goshawk that you may use."

And so not much more than an hour after sunrise our party rode out, the gyrfalcon hooded on the duke's gloved fist—a magnificent bird, almost pure white—and the rest of us carrying lesser but still excellent birds from his mews.

The Lady Arsendis positioned her palfrey next to mine. Today she wore a chaste white wimple over her hair, but a few dark curls had worked their way out by her cheek. "Let Father have the sport of the cranes," she told me, "and you and I, Lord Count, shall have twice the birds he does at the end of the day. I know where thrush and woodcock may be found in abundance."

The spring air was warm and softly scented with mud and growing things as the hunting party spread out across fields and hills. Arsendis's rich scarlet cloak floated behind her in the breeze. The ground was slightly damp under our horses' hooves, and trees and bushes on every hand were loud with birds' voices. "Not yet," said Arsendis when

I lifted my fist. The high and low bells on my goshawk's legs were tuned in harmony, as were the high and low bells on her sparrowhawk, but somehow their notes clashed with each other.

After a highly propitious start to the morning, everything quickly began to go wrong. As a commander I had always had to size up a situation rapidly, and the years had taught me to base my conclusions on the least optimistic estimates. One would have had to be unusually optimistic to find this morning going well.

First Thierri appeared unexpectedly just when I thought we had eluded him, gracefully sitting a horse both swifter and more light-footed than mine, his red hair shining like burnished copper in the morning sun. Arsendis insisted he ride with us for a mile or two, though telling him teasingly that he would have to leave again before she showed me the secret home of thrush and woodcock. Then she retold a long, complicated story she had from her sister the countess, about some quarrel her sister had had with her neighbors back home. Thierri seemed politely interested and chuckled appreciatively; I rode in stony silence.

After half an hour Thierri obediently rode off, laughing and saying, "I'll leave you alone with your *galant,* my lady." But by then an awkwardness seemed to have developed between us, so that she, who had been chattering away like a blackbird a minute before, now spoke in monosyllables, which I had to force myself to answer. I glanced toward her from the corner of my eye and found her staring at the side of my face. Though she immediately turned away, I knew all too well that she had been looking with revulsion at my scar.

"Your cloak is most attractive," I said, trying to be the flattering *galant* Thierri had mockingly called me. "The scarlet suits well your hair and eyes."

She gave a quick smile. "A gift from someone who said the same thing."

A suitor, then, I thought, doubtless someone she would have preferred to have accompany her rather than the scarred count to whom her father had said she had to be polite. "Lord Thierri has made no further insulting comments toward me—or your father for bringing me south," I said as lightly as I could, wondering if she would have preferred to have been hawking with him. "Perhaps the Paschal season has curbed his tongue."

"Or perhaps he has finally realized," she answered with a mischievous laugh, "that the reason my father sent all the way to the northern marches for a new Count of Peyrefixade was to make absolutely sure that Thierri could not possibly raise a legal claim himself to the county against the late countess's own cousin."

So was that all I was to the duke, someone whose bloodline assured him that he need not accept Thierri as count?

"But do not imagine, Count, that he was *quite* so desperate to find an alternative to Thierri that he would choose even a direct blood descendant of the first Count of Peyrefixade without the most careful inquiries as to the man."

I could not tell now whether she was mocking or complimenting me. Unable to find an appropriate answer, I lapsed into silence, even knowing that my silence itself must give Arsendis ennui.

"This meadow is always very productive of birds," she said at last in a small voice—regretting bitterly having no company but me, I thought. But she was right about the birds. As our horses walked through the long grass a covey of woodcock abruptly shot out from under their hooves with a boom of wings. We each pulled off the hoods and cast our hawks after them.

Both hawks were on their prey immediately, swooping down from above with a bite of taloned claws. The birds struggled to free themselves, but Arsendis dismounted at once, seizing and expeditiously dispatching the woodcocks with a knife while I held the hawks by their jesses. She cut each hawk a minuscule bite of flesh, then they were hooded again, and the dead woodcocks went into her game bag.

"A good start!" Arsendis said with a laugh, waving away my assistance as she remounted gracefully.

I began to hope that perhaps she was not regretting my company after all. However, the meadow seemed temporarily denuded of birds. We waited, sitting on our horses as they cropped the new grass, for the birds to return from wherever we had frightened them. After a minute in which the awkward silence started to reassert itself, I asked, "Are you acquainted with this Archbishop Amalric?"

Arsendis flashed me a quick look from dark eyes and pursed her red lips. "You mean you did not know?"

"Know what?" I said in irritation. If someone would just explain to me who all these people were among whom I now lived, and what quarrels and alliances they had developed in years of association with each other, life would become much easier.

"He is my uncle, my mother's brother."

"Dear God," I muttered. I stared at the ground, knowing I should have guessed something of the sort, or inquired more closely of my men at Peyrefixade. But without Bruno no one brought me random bits of information unless I knew to ask—not even Melchior, who kept on (and quite rightly, I had to admit) putting his responsibilities as spiritual advisor ahead of those as worldly informant. When I felt Arsendis's eyes on me, I added, not looking up, "I *thought* your father's reaction to my having defied the Inquisition was a little mild. Now I realize he was just waiting to give his brother-in-law free rein with me."

When I heard her laughing I did look up, both mortified and discouraged. "You think that because the mighty Duke Argave and the great Bishop Amalric are brothers-in-law, they are then dear friends and allies?" she asked with a teasing smile. "You should spend more time at our court, Lord Count, rather than hidden away at Peyrefixade."

She shook the reins on her palfrey, and we rode slowly through the meadow. No partridge or woodcock exploded from beneath our horses' hooves, but other birds seemed to be returning. "They have to be courteous with each other, of course," she continued thoughtfully, "and I am sure Uncle Amalric, back when he was still a cathedral canon at Haulbé, considered it a great victory when his sister married the young duke. But, as I'm sure you'll see, they don't agree on everything—he can scarcely have been happy when he realized that Father did not intend to give up his mistress."

I remembered the woman in the rooming house in the thoroughly disreputable part of town, the house where the search for whoever had wanted me assassinated had ended. "The archbishop could hardly approve of that, I'm sure," I said, putting indignation into my voice. Arsendis, I thought, must detest the women who had held a greater place than her own mother in her father's affections.

But Arsendis gave her tinkling laugh again. "Of course he couldn't. But that didn't keep some of the rest of us from approving. I only met my father's mistress a few times—he gave her up at last when I was still small—but I still liked her much better than my own mother. My brother, on the other hand—"

She went suddenly quiet. She had not meant, I was sure, to mention her brother, the one who had left home to follow the heretics. But I thought, looking at her profile, that even though she would not speak of him she had not yet cast him out of her heart. As for the duke, he detested the heretics because they had taken his heir from him—but did that mean he thoroughly approved of the Inquisition, or was he constantly in fear that they would find and burn his own son?

"Let's get some more birds!" Arsendis called in a bright voice that did not quite ring true. She jerked the hood from her hawk and cast him into the air, bells ringing, and I immediately followed suit.

Her sparrowhawk mounted higher and higher above us, then shot down toward an unwary thrush. A second later it had the bird in its talons. Arsendis whirled the lure and called, and after only a few seconds' reluctance the hawk returned to her fist, bringing the dead thrush with it.

"But where is your hawk?" she asked, slipping the bird into the game bag.

My goshawk was gone, whether pursuing some other prey or merely obeying the inherent perversity of all hawks. I swung the lure and shouted, the shout that always brought back my brother's hawks.

Then I realized Arsendis was laughing again. "Do your hawks in the barbarous north indeed respond to such a repellent call as that?" She called herself as she had called to her own hawk, and hers shifted on her gauntleted wrist, but my goshawk remained invisible. I whirled the lure harder, searching the wide sky desperately for the hawk's dark shape. I knew perfectly well that although we could not see it, it could see us with its far sharper eyesight, and was probably having a good laugh at my expense.

"Let's listen for the bells," Arsendis suggested. We went silent for a moment, straining for the sound, hearing nothing. How was I going to explain to Duke Argave that I had lost his hawk?

After a moment Arsendis shrugged. "That goshawk was always a bit difficult. I blame my father," with a pout of her pretty lips, "for sending you out with it. But do not worry. It's bound to become hungry and show up in someone's farmyard sooner or later. Everyone around here knows that a jessed hawk will bring a good reward from my father no matter whose it might be, so he should have it back in a day or two."

I could not be so sanguine. She flew her own hawk several more times while I tried not to appear surly, but found it increasingly difficult to find anything to say to fill the long silences. At least, I thought, the day could not go any worse than it already had.

Abruptly I heard a sound of bells from the far side of the meadow. I jerked upright and saw a goshawk perched in a tree, fluttering as though its jesses were tangled. "There it is!" I shouted, swinging the lure.

"Oh, I'm so pleased!" she cried, belying everything she had said about how recovering it would be no problem.

In a minute, when the hawk did not come, I realized it must be too tangled in the twigs to break free. "I'll have to climb up and get it," I said cheerfully. A simple problem like this, one I could solve with a little physical exertion, was welcome. "Wait for me."

I rode across the meadow and tethered my horse to the tree's lower branches, then cautiously started up. Arsendis rode after me but had the sense to stop a little distance back, silently watching. The hawk looked at me with deep suspicion, ringing its bells loudly as it struggled unsuccessfully to move out of reach.

Slowly, so as not to further frighten it, testing each brittle branch before I put my weight on it, I climbed upward. Twigs bit into my skin and caught my hair. I tried all the soothing things the master of my brother's mews said to his hawks, but the goshawk's yellow eye remained wild, and as I carefully reached up a gauntleted hand toward the trailing jesses it tried to strike at me.

"The Inquisition doesn't operate in my county without my permission," I told it firmly, "and no hawk evades me, either." It did not seem impressed.

I settled a shoulder against the tree trunk and reached up again, and this time was able to snatch the ends of the trailing jesses. But they were truly tangled, and though I tugged and the hawk beat its wings to get away, it remained trapped among the branches. The only solution was to use my other hand to work the jesses free.

This hand did not have the heavy gauntlet. I tried to

snap off the twigs that held the hawk imprisoned, not letting the hand get too close to the hawk's beak, as I balanced uncertainly on a branch fifteen feet above the ground. There, and there! Another sharp tug and the last imprisoning twig snapped free.

And the hawk dove at my unprotected hand.

I jerked it back out of reach just in time. But the sudden movement cost me my balance. The sole of one riding boot slipped on the hard bark of the branch. Trying to catch myself, I grabbed at the tree trunk, the jesses slipping through my fingers. The hawk shot up and away, ringing its bells jeeringly, as I crashed downward through the branches.

I hit the ground hard. For a minute I lay without moving, waiting to recover my breath, trying to decide what parts might be broken. The initial sensation was the stinging where twigs had cut at my face, but there was a throbbing pain building in one foot. Arsendis leaped from her palfrey and dropped to her knees beside me, which only made it worse. I had been going to show her my abilities, not complete the demonstration that the scarred count from the north was an utter fool.

Her hair had all come loose, and her face was white. "Galoran!" she cried. "Are you yet alive? Can you hear me?"

I choked back several irritable comments and reached out my arms to the side, flexing them one at a time. "Arms not broken," I said with a desperate attempt at good humor. "Now for the legs."

The knees functioned, but my left ankle gave a warning shot of pain when I turned it. Broken or just strained? I pushed myself up to a sitting position, tugged off the boot, and carefully felt the ankle, trying to rotate it. No bones poked through the skin, and I could turn the foot in all directions, even if I had to do so with my teeth set against the pain.

"Nothing broken here, either," I said, my voice coming

out too high. "But I'd better get some cold compresses on this as soon as I can." Bruno would know the best way to treat a strained ankle—but Bruno was dead. "I'm sorry I've ruined your hawking."

I tried to pull myself to a standing position, but black spots came before my eyes and I had to sit down again abruptly. "This is nothing for an old soldier," I tried to tell Arsendis, head between my knees.

"I shall ride back at once," she said in resolution, "and have a cart brought to fetch you. Try not to move while I'm gone."

But I grabbed her hand, then dropped it immediately. "A duke's daughter should not ride through the countryside alone," I said, appalled at the image of being brought back to the ducal court in a cart like some peasant—or a feeble old knight whose failing body no longer allowed him to mount a horse. "I'll be able to ride just fine, in just a minute."

I tried to put my boot back on, but the ankle had already swollen too much. With Arsendis's hand under my elbow and her breath on my cheek—it would have been a very pleasant sensation if it were not also so mortifying—I managed to stand up this time, and hobbled and hopped in my stockinged foot over to my horse.

Here another difficulty presented itself. I could put the left foot in the stirrup, but when I tried to put enough weight on it to mount the black spots returned and threatened to overwhelm me.

"See if mounting from this rock is easier," Arsendis suggested. She led my horse over to it, then again assisted me as I scrambled up one-footed. For an elegant lady she was surprisingly strong. I looked at her out of the corner of my eye and realized I had not heard her laugh once since I had fallen—probably saving it all up for when she related this to the other ladies back at court.

From the top of the rock I was able to throw myself across the saddle, then used my good leg to lever myself into position while Arsendis held the startled horse's head as capably as any groom. "This will be fine," I said through my teeth, trying not to sway. "Could you hand me my boot?"

It was now midday, the first really warm weather we had had this year. Rivulets of sweat ran down my face. "Would you like me to sing to distract you from the pain?" Arsendis asked solicitously as we started slowly back toward town.

"An old soldier like me doesn't mind pain," I tried again, feeling sure she would despise me for the slightest sign of weakness. The worst pain I had ever experienced was not from war but from fire. The physical pain from that had long ago dulled—leaving fully intact the horror and the failure. "But I would very much appreciate it if you could talk to me. I would like that even better than your singing."

"And what should I say?"

Not only did I want distraction from the pain, I wanted distraction from thoughts of my coming conversation with the bishop. I had been trying all morning, even before my fall, not to think about it. What could I say to him to persuade him that I was a follower of the True Faith, an obedient son of the Church, when I was also going to tell him that no one was ever going to be burned at the stake in my county again for any reason?

"Anything you like," I said. "Tell me about growing up at a ducal court. Tell me about your family."

Too late I realized that it sounded as though I were trying to learn more about her brother, a topic her father had clearly forbidden her to discuss with *anyone*. But trying to apologize at this point would only make things worse.

Arsendis gave me a quick, amused glance from her uptilted dark eyes. "I must say you are the first *galant* ever to inquire about my family. I would have thought everything was only too evident!"

"You don't need to tell me that you are the duke's

younger daughter," I persisted. At this point I had to say *something* quickly. "But what was it like to be a child here? What games did you play? Did you have a tutor?"

She wrinkled her brows in a becoming frown as though giving the inane question serious thought. "I understand you were an archduke's son, Count Galoran, but life in your court in the barbarous north must have been very different. Of course I had a tutor. He taught all three of us, my sister and brother and me, while we were all young together." I let the mention of her brother pass, hoping she would not notice herself that she had let it slip. "So I had a tutor to teach me letters and figuring each morning, and a music teacher to teach me the lyre and flute in the afternoon, and a dancing master when I grew a little older, and my mother taught me sewing and spinning and embroidery whenever she had a few minutes. This was, I should say, whenever she was not running through the halls with my sister and me at her heels, supervising all the life and business of the palace. That was before she died, of course."

"Then you've been trained well to be the lady of a great castle," I said, trying to make it into a graceful compliment and not having it come out right. Did she think I was commenting on her suitability to take up a position at Peyrefixade? I stared straight ahead, feeling myself grow red and hoping she would attribute it to pain.

But she laughed, for the first time in a long while. "It might have worked for my sister, but it didn't work for me. *She* was always my mother's favorite. When she married her count, she was ready to have the castle keys at her belt. But *I* never wanted to waste my time learning how many loaves of bread can be made from a bag of flour, or how many tunics from a bolt of cloth." A smile dimpled her cheek. "Whoever marries me had better hire good servants!"

So much for having my kitchen problems at Peyrefixade solved by marriage. I smiled at my own thoughts—little likelihood of having the Lady Arsendis there under any conditions.

Arsendis caught the smile. "You mock me, Count," she said, pouting, but not as though she meant it. "Do you think me nothing but a pretty ornament, a woman without brains or abilities beyond flying a hawk or dancing well? If I seem so," and suddenly she sounded more serious, "it is at least in part intentional."

I turned toward her, surprised, and because of my surprise spoke more directly than I intended. "Intentional? But why would anyone not wish to be prepared to have the governance of something of one's own?"

"Is Peyrefixade what you've always wanted, Count?" she asked, still serious.

"Of course!"

"Then you and I differ," she said decisively. "If they are breeding and training me—as though I were a blood mare or a fine gyrfalcon—then they have found me somewhat unruly. They can never be sure that *I* will not slip my jesses and fly away. When Mother died, I told my father I was too young to take over management of the court, and insisted that I need not have a tutor or learn spinning anymore." Her manner became teasing once again. "I already said I liked my father's mistress. Maybe I'll become some prince's mistress someday."

"Perhaps Prince Alfonso's?" I said without thinking. Immediately I bit my tongue. The midday sun, the pain, and the awkwardness of being alone for so long with a lovely young woman seemed to have destroyed whatever wit I might once have had.

But she laughed again. "You mock me still, Count! Do you misunderstand me so badly? Or are your women in the frozen northern wastes so different? I shall agree that he has a handsome form, curling hair, and a lively step in the dance, but he is too much in love with his own fine face and high position for ever a lady to need to love *him*."

"Then where will you find your prince?" I asked, trying

to adopt her own teasing tone. It was hard with my ankle hurting steadily worse, and the sight of the town spires slowly approaching, with the reminder that I would have to tell the duke I had lost his hawk.

"I'll keep on looking," she said and hummed a little. "Do not the men in the songs keep on looking until they find the perfect woman? Well, then, a woman can keep looking, too. So far my father has not forced me to marry someone I did not like." There was a brief pause. "So far."

The throbbing in my ankle and my whirling thoughts competed to keep me restless all night.

The duke's personal physician-surgeon had felt the ankle with long, cool fingers, pronounced it only strained, which I had already determined for myself, wrapped it in bandages and ice from the ducal ice house, and given me a musty smelling powder to swallow, which I surreptitiously scattered on the floor as soon as he turned his back.

Arsendis insisted on attending me—as would the lady of the castle, I thought, the lady that she did not want to be—but her manner combined such ostentatious concern for my well-being with so many teasing half smiles that I was sure she only wanted to humiliate me for cutting her hawking short.

The only person in this court, in this entire city, that I felt I could trust was Brother Melchior, and he was not even here, having gone again to stay at the Magian priory outside the duke's walls. Duke Argave had said casually that no more assassins would bother me in *his* court, and I had seen him talking not at all casually to members of his guard, but I still fidgeted at every creak or murmur of the wind or mournful call of a nightbird. After freeing the heretics I had boasted to Bruno—Bruno who was now dead—that I would be able to resolve all my problems with the Inquisition with a few letters or conversations with the bishop. I now wished I remembered what I had been going to tell him.

Archbishop Amalric of Haulbé arrived in the ducal city
at noon three days later, accompanied by several priests
and three dozen knights and men-at-arms. I had hobbled
up to the ramparts, with Arsendis's assistance, my
disposition not improved by having learned this morning
the duke had had to buy back his goshawk, for a stiff price,
from the peasants who had finally found it. Arsendis and
I spotted the archbishop's party coming through the streets
at a rapid trot, a white banner with the emblem of crossed
shepherd's croziers flying above them. People dived for
the sides of the street to get out of the way. Despite the
Paschal season, no one was scattering palm branches before
the procession of *this* holy man.

From our vantage point I could see the duke going
out into the courtyard to greet his brother-in-law, as the
archbishop's knights put up a perfunctory quarrel before
agreeing to yield their weapons. Archbishop Amalric's voice
floated up to where we stood. "Where is that count who
thinks he is more powerful than the Church?"

A bad beginning for a rational conversation, I thought.
Arsendis patted my arm and gave what was probably
supposed to be an encouraging smile before assisting me
back down the spiral stairs.

The duke motioned me into a little parlor off the great
hall where his brother-in-law was already waiting. The
room looked out into the spring garden through tall
windows and was decorated with hanging tapestries and
a silver candelabra: far more elegant, I thought, than the
parlor where I had spoken with my aunt the abbess at
the nunnery of the Holy Family. But I dragged my attention
from contemplation of the room to the man I had come
to face.

He sat in the duke's carved wooden armchair like a
field captain in his headquarters, his riding boots planted
solidly on the floor, white mantle thrown back from his
shoulders, sharp eyes watching me from either side of a
long hooked nose. I could see absolutely no resemblance

to his niece anywhere. If he noticed my scar he gave no sign—from his point of view, there was much worse with me than that. Archbishop Amalric had missed his calling, an irreverent voice commented in the back of my brain. He would be more at home commanding the emperor's armies than overseeing the spiritual well-being of people like my Aunt Richildis or Father Melchior.

But he was in essence both a military and a spiritual commander, I reminded myself, going down on my knees like an obedient son of the Church. A war had been fought here with the heretics within my aunt and the duke's memory and doubtless his as well. He wore a big onyx episcopal ring on his thumb, which I kissed reverently.

"Rise, my son," he said, in exactly the same tone of voice as if he had said, "Get up, soldier." I had become used to Argave and Arsendis's soft Auccitan accents, but the archbishop's was very pronounced. He pushed back his wind-tousled mane of white hair and glared at me as I rose, awkwardly because of the ankle, and seated myself across from him. "So what do you mean by ordering the Inquisition out of your county?"

"No disrespect to either you or the Church, Reverend Father," I said, as meekly and obediently as if I were receiving a dressing-down from the emperor himself. Having him get straight to the point certainly made it easier. "But the priest on the spot seemed to have temporarily forgotten that he could not himself order anyone executed, particularly when they had not been examined or allowed a chance to repent. Not wishing the common people to be led astray or to forget the lovingkindness of God's ministers, I thought it best to stop all executions, even of despicable heretics, until you and I had come to a full understanding on this important issue. But of course the March rents came due just then, which have unavoidably kept me occupied—as I am sure Your Reverence has been busy as well."

The archbishop gave a snort, certainly not as though he believed me, but not entirely as though he rejected my explanation. I wished I could tell Bruno all the details of this conversation later. Bruno would have enjoyed it. "You had your men set the heretics free," Archbishop Amalric said with a scowl. "You'll soon have people saying you're a heretic yourself, Count."

"A risk I am willing to bear for the good of the True Church," I said serenely. This was something I had learned from the men who had served under me. It is impossible to yell at someone properly if they meekly accept whatever you say—and it is an intensely irritating experience for the person trying to do the yelling. "The Church, even the Inquisition, needs to show its merciful face to the faithful, even while it is salutory that at least a few captured heretics escape to the hills to warn their benighted brethren what horrible punishments await them if they do not repent. And you could certainly not expect me to take heretics back to Peyrefixade, once the Perfected's own castle! Then there really *might* have been doubts about my orthodoxy."

And Peyrefixade might be harboring a heretic priest, I thought, but I wasn't going to mention this.

"Then if you want a 'full understanding,'" growled the bishop, "you and I shall have one."

"There is nothing that would please me better, Reverend Father."

It turned out, as I expected, that the archbishop and my cousin the countess had never had a formal agreement on the disposition of heretics in the county, although her grandfather had. While Archbishop Amalric did not actually say so, I had the impression that during her short rule the Inquisition had burned heretics itself, having her seal the orders eventually if someone remembered, just as the village mayors had started carrying out capital sentences with only perfunctory reference to the authority of Peyrefixade. I wondered briefly if there had been an increase in the number of burnings while the countess ruled there, and if the heretics had held her responsible and thus been involved in her death.

The bishop produced from a box by his hand the agreement sealed years before by the late Count Bernhard and a former archbishop of Haulbé, at the same time as the count took over at Peyrefixade. I looked it over, thankful as I had rarely been that my own tutor had been so assiduous in teaching my brother and me the language of antiquity. Burning was most definitely not set out specifically. Rather, the wording stated that the archbishop and the priests of the Inquisition would release heretics to me, once a council had examined their beliefs and given them a chance to repent if found to be in error. It would be entirely at my discretion what happened to them next, although the word "mercy" appeared several times.

"If your chancellor could produce a new charter on these specifications," I said with an ingratiating smile, "I would be happy to seal it, and observe it to the letter, just as I trust the Church will."

The archbishop glanced toward me suspiciously from under heavy eyebrows and scanned the parchment quickly himself, as though wondering if there was something in it that had escaped his attention. But then he nodded and reached again into his box. "As it happens, Count, I have already had such a charter drawn up."

The duke and several of his and the archbishop's attendants were called in as witnesses. The archbishop's chancellor read the agreement out, then both Amalric and I signed, using our monograms, and attached our seals. The archbishop had a signet he carried in a pouch, with both a seal for the front side of the blob of hot wax he hung from the bottom of the charter—a lozenge bearing a miniature portrait of a bishop, with the words *Amalricus archiepiscopus* around the edge—and a counterseal, a stag, for the back. I thought uncharitably that Amalric's portrait on his seal made him look like a large-nosed frog.

All I had for a signet was the ring the emperor had given me when I left his service, silver carved with the imperial crown, which I sought to apply to the wax as nonchalantly as though I sealed documents with it every day. The chancellor added the names of the witnesses to the bottom, below our monograms, and Duke Argave sealed as well. One more thing Peyrefixade needed, I thought, watching the duke return his signet to its pouch, was a seal for its new count.

"We shall hold a general council this summer," the archbishop told the duke and me. "Efforts against the heretics have become, shall I say, somewhat uncoordinated of late." He gave a mirthless smile. "The Inquisition may be under the command of the Apostolic Curia, but they need reminding that I am still the chief spiritual authority in my archdiocese. I shall summon all my metropolitan bishops and the secular lords of the archdiocese, which includes you two, the other counts and castellans of the region, and Prince Alfonso."

I frowned to cover my surprise. "I had not known Prince Alfonso's territory was within your archdiocese, Your Reverence."

"Nabarra is indeed under my spiritual guidance," said the bishop, and for a second an expression almost like a smile flitted across his stern features, the first sign of humor I had seen in him. "Alfonso is, if possible, even more stiff-necked than you are, Count. And despite his considerable efforts the heretics are becoming denser and more restless in his principality. Especially since the rumors started . . ."

"Rumors?" I asked, since he seemed to be hoping for a reaction.

"Have you not heard them? They have been reported to me by several members of the Inquisition." His voice dropped, and his eyes gleamed fiercely. "The Perfected are said to be searching for something powerful, something they lost a long time ago, something they believe that at last they may be close to finding again."

"Do you mean to say, Amalric," said Duke Argave, not even bothering with the bishop's honorific, "that they've found—"

The bishop shook his snowy mane. "Not *that*. That was only an old superstition anyway. The damnable Perfected could never have obtained the Grail. In the Paschal season it is error even to think such sacrilegious thoughts. But we need to attack them more vigorously as their activity becomes more threatening. I know our predecessors thought it made sense to leave them that little strip of land as part of the conditions of peace, after the horrors of war, but we might now reconsider. Two inquisitors in the past year have disappeared into the mountains of Nabarra and not been seen again."

Argave ducked his head, leaving me wondering what powerful object the Perfected could be seeking. Could all this possibly have anything to do with the telesma found buried in the wall at Peyrefixade, the conviare Father Melchior now carried in a leaden casket bound with magic seals?

After dinner that evening, I retired early to my chamber, feeling too sour to watch dancing in which I could not participate. Arsendis, I felt quite sure as I listened to distant snatches of music, was happily doing graceful figures with her middle-aged lord, or some other *galant* who had caught her fancy.

I slept and woke, dozed and slept and woke again. As I tossed back and forth, trying to ignore the pain in my foot and the headache building behind my eyes, there came a soft tap at the chamber door. I went still, waiting. The tap came again, and then the voice of the knight whom I had posted to guard me. "Are you awake, sir?"

I hobbled across the room to unlock the door. My knight and one of Argave's liveried servants, holding a candle, stood outside.

"I am very sorry to disturb you, sir," said the servant, "but there is a person here to see you."

"A person?"

"Whoever it is won't come in but is standing out in the street—saying only that it is very important."

Could it be Melchior? I wondered. But I could think of no reason why the priest would not come in. Or the man who had sent the assassin, back for another try?

I'd be ready for him this time, I thought, hopping as I pulled on my clothes. Ankle or not, I almost hoped it *was* another attempt on my life. A good fight would take the sour taste of humiliation from my mouth.

The night was well advanced, and the flambeaux in the courtyard had been extinguished. The music was over, and the windows into the duke's great hall were dark. My own knights and members of Argave's guard strode at my back and shoulders, our feet loud on the marble, as I crossed toward the gates.

In the guardhouse I insisted on having my sword back again before ordering the gates opened. Outside, as the servant had said, someone waited, someone well wrapped up in a cloak.

Sword in hand, I came through the gates slowly, forcing myself to put weight on my left foot so as not to advertise my weakness. The person turned at my step, someone smaller inside the cloak than I had looked for.

Unexpectedly, I heard a woman's voice. "Good, Count Galoran, I am delighted you were willing to come out. You will understand that I do not feel it appropriate now to enter the duke's court myself. But I have a message for you."

"A message?" I said stupidly, my heart still pounding from anticipation of a fight.

The woman's voice was strangely familiar. She came a step toward me, into the light of the guard's torches. "This message," she said, with a glance past my shoulder to the guards, "is for your ears alone."

And then I knew her: the woman at whose house the search for the assassin had ended, the woman who had once been the duke's mistress.

Chapter Eight ~ Melchior

1

"Well, Melchior, my son," said Prior Belthesar as soon as the doors to his private parlor had been sealed, "let us all see what you have brought us."

I unwrapped the leaden casket, set it on the table, then stepped back and spoke the words to dissolve the binding spells. At the prior's nod, the treasurer stepped forward with an ornate knife and pried off the physical seals of lead I had also set upon the little box. Aside from him, myself, and Prior Belthesar, only the cellarer, the other chief officer of the priory, was in the room.

When I had arrived late the previous evening and told the prior what I had brought, he had decided that an examination of the items by the chief officers of the house should be performed right after the office of prime the following morning. I could feel my hands trembling slightly under the eyes of these senior masters of my Order as I opened the little box. They crowded round, peering down at the two objects I laid on the table. One was the small tile telesma that had come out of the hearth, the other was the conviare.

"Perfected work, no doubt of it," declared the treasurer after peering at them through a lens. We all crossed ourselves. Prior Belthesar took up the telesma and closed his eyes while he ran his fingers over it, feeling below its smooth glazed surface with his second touch—a skill in which he excelled. He opened his eyes after a minute and set the tile down. "You were right, my son, this object is quite depleted. But powerful magic was laid into it by whoever made it!" Glancing at each of us with a small smile, he added, "I would not care to say this in front of the novices, but some of those Perfected Magians in the old days, especially the high ones they called Maguses, were skilled beyond anyone in our Order today, save, of course, for our revered Master."

"Hmm." The treasurer had taken the objects to the window to look at them again through his lens under better light, then ran his own fingers over them. "This tile is *not* an old telesma, Prior. The lines of magic in it were not laid down many years ago, perhaps not even many months ago. Moreover, these symbols were drawn on the clay by someone schooled in the modern bookhand, not the writing of fifty years ago. The *conviare*, on the other hand, looks like it could certainly have been the work of one of those great old heretic maguses. Its magic lines and knots are deep with time, and its visible design is not at all modern."

"The tile's not old, you say?" Prior Belthesar's face normally held the hint of a suppressed smile no matter what he was doing, but that was not the case now. "That means that even today, suppressed, hunted, and harried though they be, the Perfected yet number some highly skilled Magians among their ranks."

"Tell us in full about the attack upon your count using the telesma of fire, Brother Melchior," the cellarer demanded. They listened to my account without interrupting, but I saw the cellarer's eyes grow narrow when I described how I had extinguished the vortex of flame. "Just how did you happen to have a telesma of your own about your person, Brother Melchior?" he inquired as soon as I had ceased to speak. "Particularly one good against fire?"

"The Order was well aware Brother Melchior possessed this object at the time he was sent to take up his station at Peyrefixade," Prior Belthesar told him smoothly before I could formulate any answer of my own. "It was believed on good authority by Abbot Caspar himself that the castle might harbor interesting and potentially dangerous magical objects, so it was felt appropriate that Brother Melchior be equipped to deal with various contingencies. Would you take out your own telesma and show it to the cellarer now, my son?"

Trying not to appear nervous, I drew the old ivory rod forth from its place near my heart and laid it on the table. The cellarer and the treasurer bent close. "As you can see, brothers, it is a telesma of extinguishment," Prior Belthesar continued after touching it briefly, managing to convey the entirely false impression that he'd seen it many times before. "It is carved in the form of the water carrier to symbolize its function, which is to quench. That includes putting out fires, certainly, but it is also good against pain, thirst, or even hunger. Properly used, it can also nullify magic projected either by a person or another telesma. That is what happened in this case, I am certain. This telesma extinguished not only the physical flames about the count's bed, it also quenched the current of magic between the tile in the hearth and the conviare suspended around the count's neck. That is why the vortex was dissipated so abruptly and effectively."

The masters spent another ten minutes looking over the telesma and conviare. But they found nothing further, so I put the tile and the gold medallion back into the lead casket, and the treasurer and cellarer took them off to seal them away in the vault where the priory's own telesmae were stored. Once they were gone, I said, "Prior Belthesar, may I ask you something?"

"Of course, Brother Melchior. Just step over here." He led me to facing stone seats in the window that looked out into the priory's modest cloister—and which might conceivably have hidden a listener crouched beneath its sill, a possibility now eliminated. Reaching into a pouch at his belt, he removed a small telesma and set it on the window ledge. "That makes us secure against anyone trying to spy with second vision or hearing. Now, what is troubling you?"

"Did you truly know of my telesma before today?"

"Why, of course, my son!" His usual expression of just-suppressed good humor had returned. "Did you not confess to possessing that object to our revered Master himself while you were still completing your novitiate? Did you imagine he would not have informed me of this when you were sent here to serve under my authority five years ago? I had to know, just as Abbot Caspar had to know when you returned to serve under his authority at the Mother House. But that does not make it the business of the brothers in general, or even my esteemed treasurer and cellarer."

"And did he also inform you of how I came to possess it?"

"Certainly. He told me it had been given you by your grandfather, shortly before he was put to death as one of the Perfected." I must have looked stunned, because he laughed out loud. "My dear son, did you suppose that would upset me? It is the proper business of the head of any religious house to understand all he can about the souls entrusted to his authority. I need to know each brother's particular capacities and talents so that I may choose those assignments for him that he will best perform to the credit of the True Faith and our Order. I also need to know his weaknesses and flaws so that I do not put him in the way of things that would most encompass his peculiar temptations and thus endanger his soul. Occasionally, however, a brother may have some aspect about him that is at once both a possible strength and a potential source of danger. Your family background is such an aspect."

"If my background was a possible source of danger, why did the Order choose to send me forth again into the world rather than keep me at the Mother House?"

"Because it was equally a possible source of strength for your assignment! We have but few younger brothers nowadays who possess a personal history such as yours. But those of us who are older know how valuable intimate experience of Perfected magic and Perfected persons can be. Did not our revered Founder and Master himself come dangerously close to becoming one of them before God called him back to put the knowledge of magic he had learned among them at the service of the True Faith instead? Do you not understand that virtually all of us who are senior members of the Order were drawn at least to the *magic* of the Perfected when we were young, and that most of us at least briefly studied their doctrines as well? Whence come most of the magic books we have carefully copied for you youngsters to study, the magic objects that we use in teaching you? From where else but the Perfected! From its foundation, the whole business of our Order has ever been to salvage magic for the service of the True Faith. You and your grandfather's telesma represent one more victory in that long fight."

"And do you and the elder masters never worry that a telesma like mine—a telesma which was given me by a man who died as one of the Perfected—might not draw me or others into error?"

"My son, your telesma is a magical object, not a demonic one. Magic is but one more high and ancient branch of human knowledge, just like rhetoric or philosophy or history or poetry or art. Do not the orders who make it their business to study and preserve those branches of learning examine and revere the works of the best ancient authors or artists, though many of them were outright pagans? Why should we be any more hesitant to take whatever may be good from the best practitioners of our own branch of learning in all times, whether they may have been temple priests of the ancient Riverland or

Master Maguses of the Perfected? All knowledge issues ultimately from God. It will work either for good or evil depending on what lies in the heart and soul of the person who employs it, whatever proximate source it may have come from."

He smiled. "The Order has great confidence concerning what is in your heart and soul, Melchior my son, confidence that you are fit to deal with any temptations or other hazards to your soul that may beset you. I certainly do, or I would not have advanced your name so strongly for your present assignment, first with the Order, then with Duke Argave." As I stared at him, stunned by this news, he paused as if considering whether to say more, then spoke on. "It is time for you to understand, my son, that our Order often has to give difficult assignments to its most promising younger members in order to assess what will be the proper roles for each of them in the future. The great elders, the first generation who joined with our Master at the very start, are now old or gone to their rewards. My generation is still fairly hearty, but though laboring always in their shadows most of us have still never gained quite the mastery of magic you will find in the elders. We also lack the youthful strength, possessed by you younger men, for the hardest magic. We do, however, know you youngsters as the elders cannot. It is the task of each of us in authority to bring forward the best we find among our subordinates." He signaled for me to rise. "Now leave me. I know that you are very eager to consult the *Liber Telesmarum* and other pertinent books in our library, and also to refresh your spirit by hearing the offices sung by someone besides yourself! We shall talk further before you leave."

It was only later, walking in the cloister after a long and pleasant afternoon among the books as I waited for compline, that it occurred to me to wonder whether Prior Belthesar's statement of confidence might have been intended not so much to assure me that I was in fact already fit for my task and spiritually armored against every hazard but rather to inspire me to become fit and armor myself.

2

The next few days flew swiftly by. On the fourth morning after Paschal Sunday, I was sitting at a table in one of the *incantoria* carefully resetting some of the final lines of magic needed to fully replenish my telesma when the prior suddenly swept in. "No, no, Melchior, my son, don't bother to rise!" he commanded. "I only stopped in for a moment to inform you that Archbishop Amalric arrived at the duke's court yesterday. Duke Argave is giving a great banquet and entertainment in his brother-in-law's honor tonight, to which I shall of course be expected to bring a proper delegation representing our priory. Meet us in the courtyard at the third hour after midday office—wearing your best vestments, of course."

When I arrived at the appointed time, I discovered that this delegation comprised only Prior Belthesar, the cellarer, the treasurer, and myself. Despite what the prior had said and the clear-cut status lent me as the count's *capellanus*, it still felt strange to be ranked as an equal with these long-time superiors. Arriving at the duke's gates, we were immediately ushered through the elegant gardens and into the reception hall. The big room was already filling up with courtiers, ladies, canons from the city church, wealthy townsmen and their wives, who were dressed more richly, if less tastefully, than many of the ladies. There were also the members of the duke and the bishop's retinues of knights, who seemed to be vying as to who could appear more numerous and warlike despite the handicap of bearing only velvet gloves. We presented ourselves before the duke and the archbishop immediately, and were as immediately dismissed except for Prior Belthesar and the treasurer, whom Bishop Amalric led off into a side chamber for a private talk. The cellarer quickly located friends of comparable station among the city canons, and I found myself left on my own.

I looked about the hall for Count Galoran, but he didn't seem to be in sight. Seeing more finely dressed people out on the terrace, I walked out there but had no better luck. As I stood by a tall urn filled with flowers brought to bloom a month ahead of their time by the duke's skillful and costly gardeners, a musical voice suddenly spoke beside me. I turned to find myself facing the Lady Arsendis.

"Greetings, Brother Melchior," she said with a mischievous smile. "It has been long indeed since you have graced my father's court with your presence on a festive occasion such as this."

Long enough to be extremely rusty about my courtly manners when conversing with beautiful highborn ladies, I thought, feeling far from ready for one of those conversations where every phrase must be a studied turn in elegance and every reply of the lady must be carefully scrutinized for possible multiple meanings. But I managed a passable bow as I answered, "The loss has been entirely my own, my lady."

"You seemed to be searching diligently for someone; may I flatter myself it was I?"

"I would not so presume, my lady. I am seeking my master, Count Galoran."

"I am afraid you shall most likely have to wait until dinner time, Brother Melchior—and you may have to look quickly even then. The unfortunate count injured his ankle when we were out hawking the other day, and he has nursed the wounds to both his leg and dignity in his chamber as much as possible ever since, just as a hurt hound keeps to its kennel." She glanced into the hall, then stepped around the urn with a graceful swirl of silken skirts. I turned my head just in time to see an older lord whose name I could not recall appear in the archway. He passed his eyes vaguely over the elegant people scattered about on the terrace, then turned and walked back among the throng inside, peering from side to side.

"That poor gentleman really is becoming rather nearsighted; I fear he did not see me," Lady Arsendis laughed as she stepped away from the urn. "He provides me excellent protection from the unwanted attentions of others, but can grow tiresome himself at times. Now come, Brother Melchior. I wish to take a walk in my father's gardens while the light lasts, and should be very glad of your company."

The marble paths had been freshly swept, but few other than ourselves seemed to be enjoying them at the moment. It was too bad, for the duke's gardeners had performed extraordinary feats, of which the urn of flowers had been only a foretaste. Whole beds of spring blooms spread alongside the paths, where they had been forced in cold frames that had doubtless just been removed today. At one point we came upon a tree which actually appeared to be bearing fruit! But when the lady bit into one and then handed me another, they proved to be cunning confections.

"You are bold, Brother Melchior." She laughed. "The very first man to accept fruit from a lady's hand brought much trouble upon himself and all of us who have followed."

"If this fruit truly were forbidden, your father would have taken care that fact should be known to all, my lady." Now that I was into it, I found I was actually enjoying this chance to exchange well-turned phrases in good Auccitan with the lady; I had begun to feel quite stupid having to use the Royal Tongue week after week in the count's castle. "And I do not feel either much wiser or more sinful than before I ate of it."

"Yet there may be a serpent or two in this garden nevertheless, Brother Melchior." I followed her look and saw Lord Thierri lounging a little way back along the path, apparently examining a statue. "Let us go this way," she said, turning down a walkway that led to a small stone belvedere holding just two seats and overlooking a little pond.

Once we were seated, she smiled and declared, "There, now no one can approach near enough to hear us without obviously and rudely intruding. This is the only sort of private conversation possible for a woman in my situation on a public occasion, when gentlemen press about offering her their finest compliments and vying to prevent all the others from having the same chance: conducted in full view of everyone with a man of unquestionable virtue who is no possible competitor in matters of love. So, then, tell me your opinion of Count Galoran. He seems an interesting man."

"He is, my lady. I first thought him uncomplicated, but I now begin to see that he is a complex man bent on simple goals. He has been set as count at Peyrefixade, and he means to acquit himself well."

"Yet he is not always politic. He does such audacious things as publicly defy the Inquisition. How am I to understand him?"

"He is his own man. Do not misconstrue; I have no reason to suppose he would prove other than loyal to his lord your father in a crisis. But I believe Count Galoran decides what his conduct as count should be in important situations based on what he thinks himself, not what he believes the world expects."

"Goodness: 'His own man'—you are quite right to catch yourself up and add at once that he should nonetheless prove a loyal vassal! Though in truth I think Father was not unhappy to find Count Galoran capable of acting forcefully according to his own ideas of what is right. He certainly was not a bit sorry to hear that the count had checked the Inquisition in performing immediate and arbitrary executions of accused heretics."

"Yet your father is scarcely known as a friend to the Perfected."

"Nor to fine legalisms as a general principle, either; I

can say it if you will not, Brother Melchior. But we who are not schooled in deep philosophy as are you clerics tend to derive our overall rules of what ought to be done from those matters that touch us personally. To speak plainly, my father would be deeply anguished should he learn that one particular heretic had been caught and put to death without first being granted every possible opportunity to repent his errors, rejoin the community of the True Faith, and be restored to his former rank and station. Given this, he has no real choice but to hold that all heretics should be accorded the same rights he would want to see extended to his own son."

She fell silent for a moment, wrapping her scarlet cloak closer and gazing out at the water with a thoughtful, even sad, expression. This was not entirely the same Lady Arsendis I remembered from my earlier time at the duke's court.

"But if my good father remains capable of entertaining so tenuous a hope in his private moments, you well know that he is not the man to base any practical plan of action on such sand. He is bound to look about for something firmer." She looked past me, then made a little motion of her graceful chin toward the garden and whispered, "Tell me, Brother Melchior, what see you there?"

I turned my own head slowly, as if idly gazing about during a lull in conversation. "Why, it is your elder sister, my lady, walking with her husband."

"Quite, but what do you *not* see when you look at them, either now or at any other time?" Her eyes seemed to have regained some of their usual sauciness.

"I am poor at riddles, my lady."

"Fie, brother Melchior: this from the man I have very often heard Prior Belthesar assure my father had been the best young diviner who had ever served under his authority! But I suppose it is unjust of me to expect you to work without your powders and such. What you do not see with them is children. No sturdy little grandson,

or even so much as a sweet little granddaughter, to gladden
my father's heart and relieve him of his worries concerning
the succession."

"Ah, my lady, of course! It is now—what—more than
five years since the two of them were wed, is it not?"
Suddenly her gravity and her questions both made sense.
"So, your father is becoming anxious to see you married
where it will best assure the succession, and thinks Count
Galoran may be the man."

"Indeed. Especially since he seems recently to have
grown a little disillusioned with my sister's noble husband,
no longer sure he is quite the man to hold the duchy
securely should the need arise. So now Father casts his
net, fishing for a better man. Or perhaps I ought to say
he casts his line, for he certainly uses bait. Myself." Abruptly
she turned her dark eyes and lovely face full upon me.
"What do you think, Brother Melchior: is Count Galoran
likely to answer?"

"I—I cannot say, my lady," I stammered. "I have never
thought—"

"Oh, what poor simple creatures you men can be at
times! Always so caught up in worrying over what you
would call 'practical' matters that you fail to think about
what is directly in front of you. And what is more charming
still, Count Galoran seems uncertain about the matter
himself. He sees what is obvious to a soldier, of course.
He sees that the long narrow county of Peyrefixade points
out of the mountains like a dagger at the heart of the
duchy, and concludes, correctly, that my father wants a
resolute and reliable man there to form our first bulwark
against Nabarra and its prince. He also has noticed, as
he could scarcely have failed to do unless he'd been a
great dolt, that my father has presented me to his attention.
Yet despite everything, despite having received a good
deal more encouragement from my father than has led
certain lordlings in the past to think themselves virtually
the duke's sons-in-law, this Count Galoran still remains

hesitant! He likes it well enough that I am a duke's daughter, he likes the fact that I am not displeasing in face and form, yet this man who is so fearless a soldier is a timid lover! I could almost persuade myself he would like to win not only my hand and the added advantages and wealth that would bring but also my heart and my regard, and fears any false step might prove ruinous. He seems perfectly confident among the men. He treats my father with dignified subordination but no servility, and faced my formidable uncle the archbishop with perfect aplomb. So why, Brother Melchior, should he be so behindhand with a mere lady?"

I hesitated, transfixed by the dark beauty of her uptilted eyes, yet unsure whether I would be disloyal to share my private inferences concerning Count Galoran's character with a lady I had in the past seen to be quite mocking, even cruel, toward aspiring lovers. But that had been in the days when she was still in the first flower of her young womanhood, enjoying the power over men that her position and beauty brought her and giving scant thought to anything beyond the delights of being courted by every young nobleman in the duchy and playing them off against one another in various intrigues. This older Lady Arsendis seemed to have a more serious strain. Though she still put her questions and observations wittily, I did not think she was simply making fun of Count Galoran. "This would only be my own guess, lady, but I have seen that the count always watches to find how people will react to the fact that he bears a scar. He might well feel uneasy with a lady because of that."

"Ah, how like a man. Because you often look no further than to see whether a lady is beautiful, you assume we are the same. I of course except priests such as yourself, who look only at the beauty of the soul." She smiled mischievously as I blushed. "If the count only knew how many of my handsome suitors in the past have shown themselves to be but whited sepulchres, he might perhaps credit me with more depth in my assessments of men now." A chill breeze stirred the dark waters of the pond, and she drew her cloak closer. Without our noticing, the warmth of the afternoon had gone below the wall along with the sun. "Now, I think it is time for you to take me back inside. My aging *galant* will still be seeking me, and I shall want the protection of his presence until our friend the count at last deigns to appear for dinner."

As I took her graceful hand to assist her down the steps of the belvedere, she cocked her head and exclaimed, "Listen: it is a troubadour! Father hired several to entertain, but the wretches have all been keeping themselves inside until now."

The musician was strolling along the main path as we reached it, playing upon his lute. Spying us, or rather the Lady Arsendis, he bowed low and began a new song:

> *"Ah, Madame, do I waste my time?*
> *Is it your wish that I retire?*
> *Ah, Madame, do I waste my time?*
> *Or shall I have what I desire?"*

He went on to spin a series of well-turned verses describing the charms and high *valour* of the lady in question and the alternating exaltation and despair of her would-be lover, always returning to the first verse as a refrain. When the fellow had done, Lady Arsendis threw him a brilliant smile and a bright coin, and he bowed again and went on his way.

"Ah, that severely lightens my purse, I fear. But the pretty fellow put that question so much more gracefully than most of my genuine suitors. Especially as I have generally suspected they desired something in addition to my sweet favor and charming person. The troubadours sing of purest love, Brother Melchior, and courtly suitors know well enough how to dance to such measures. But when all's done, their love for a lady is like their love for a fine hawk or hound; they esteem each in exact proportion to what it can fetch for them. But I am not a hawk who would fly for any knight, nor the sort of hound who would course for any hunter. I shall make my own free choice, or—ah, good day, Uncle."

Archbishop Amalric and a lean priest had come suddenly into view where the path curved around a mass of shrubbery. Now they looked up from their conversation and returned Lady Arsendis's greeting. The bishop's wintery eye shifted to me, and he added, "And good day to you, Brother Melchior."

"I did not know you and my uncle were acquainted," said the lady as we walked on toward the terrace.

"Nor did I, my lady! I know *him*, of course, but I would never have expected him to recognize me."

"Indeed? Then you must be a rising man, despite your charming diffidence: marked out for great things by the powers of this earth! You and Count Galoran make a good pair. Let us hope neither of you makes a misstep and loses his chance."

We reached the terrace, which was now deserted, and walked to the archway leading into the hall. The lords and ladies had gathered down at the end of the big room, where troubadours were singing to entertain them, accompanied by others on various instruments. "Ah, it is the music of the great Machaut! A chaste priest like yourself, but nonetheless he wrote often of love. And look, there is our friend Count Galoran, standing with my father and some other gentlemen and looking around while he pretends to attend to their conversation. Notice how he gives no attention at all to trying to flatter my father, quite unlike the others."

As she finished this statement in an approving tone, I saw the count's eye fall upon us. His expression, which had been sour, changed at once, and he smiled and bowed. "He seems highly pleased to see you, Brother Melchior; let us go join him. And may I say you have done well, especially for one who has been seldom at court for several years. Your every speech has held just that right mixture of flattering attention and deference that a real gentleman's words to a lady ought, while never straying into anything that would be improper from a priest! So, thank you for your company. It is always worth while talking to an intelligent man."

As we rode along the track up the valley toward Peyrefixade the next afternoon, the knights were speaking among themselves of the duke's fine Paschal hospitality, of his excellent food, of his lavish entertainment. I also overheard (without giving any sign) more than one mention of visits to places of entertainment in the lower town, housing ladies whose virtue was negotiable. But the count rode at the head by himself, wrapped in silence. After a time I kicked my horse to move up closer to him. To my surprise, he was humming! After listening for a minute, I recognized a fine old tune of Machaut's we'd heard the night before, the one which begins, *"When I have returned once more/ Come from seeing my lady . . ."*

If my mission from the Lady Arsendis was to deliver a message of encouragement when needed, it seemed unnecessary to do so at this moment, so I slacked the reins and started to fall back. But the count spotted me from the corner of his eye and motioned for me to move my horse up and ride abreast with him. I expected him to speak of the lady, but he surprised me by instead asking, "So, Brother Melchior, tell me what you know of this Prince Alfonso of Nabarra."

"I believe that I have already given you a full account of my personal impressions, Count Galoran."

"Of the man himself, yes. But I need to hear about the prince. Is he a man of honor in his public dealings, whatever his personal character may be? Would he, for instance, invite a man to a parley with promises of safe conduct, only to seize or kill the fellow once he had him in his grasp?"

"And when and where is this parley to take place, Count?"

He smiled, a pleasant enough expression since I was riding next to his unmarred side. "Very good, Brother Melchior. Yes, the prince has asked me for a meeting. He suggests a spot in the mountains, up near the boundary where my county and his principality adjoin. It seems there is a stretch of land up there containing a village or two which have been in dispute for a long time. The prince claims he wishes to meet with me and make an amicable settlement of the matter once and for all. Hence my question."

"Ah." I thought for a moment. "Well, you are right to ask me to discuss the prince separate from the man, Count. Alfonso is a stranger to guilt in most matters, but he does possess a strong sense of shame. I should say he would never commit an act such as you describe not because it would stain his soul but because he could not bear the disgrace to his public honor should word of it ever get out, as it surely would."

"And are you confident enough of your opinion to accompany me when I ride to meet the prince? I am in need of a local man whose knowledge and intelligence I can trust."

"My Order has assigned me to serve as your spiritual advisor, Count Galoran, and you have accepted me into that office. Unless you should discover some flaw in me so grave that it warranted my dismissal, my place in any exigency is at your side."

"Meticulously put, as always." The count's voice sounded amused, and I felt myself blush. "You like studying things through, don't you Brother Melchior? You like to know exactly what you have to deal with, to be quite sure of your ground, before you speak or act."

"I have been trained so, Count, both practically and spiritually. A Magian must know exactly what he is doing before he begins if he's to succeed, and a priest must always strive to be sure of his moral ground."

"And perhaps a man is the more likely to be attracted to either or both of those stations if he is inclined that way to begin with?" He gave me a sidelong glance with one of those smiles that looked so pleasant on the unscarred side of his face. "Don't misunderstand me, Brother Melchior; I like this in you. It's a comfort to any commander to know he has a man by him who has put in the effort to be sure of his skills when called on, whether these be as a fighting man or as a Magian and counselor. So then, give me your most meticulous thinking on this question. Is it likely that the great Prince Alfonso has gone to all the trouble of sending a secret emissary to set up a meeting with a mere count simply to settle an old dispute over a few hardscrabble stony acres up in the hills? Or must he have some other purpose?"

I paused automatically to consider my answer, saw him smile behind his hand, and found myself laughing. "Ah, Count, how do you expect me to give your questions proper consideration if you make me self-conscious? But the answer to this one is simple. You have reasoned correctly: Prince Alfonso must indeed have some motive other than the one he has stated to seek a meeting with you."

"But if the prince's intent is not to lure me into an ambush for my destruction, what can it be? Does he perhaps hope to shift me from being the duke's man to his own? That seems the most likely possibility, though I find it more than a little insulting that he should imagine I could easily be turned into so ripe a traitor."

I paused before answering, quite deliberately stretching it out this time. "That, Count Galoran, is something we are not likely to discover until we are before the prince himself."

Chapter Nine ~ Galoran

1

The wind hit us as we came up onto the high ridge, snapping our cloaks behind us and whirling the horses' manes. The air was thin in the nostrils and cold with a bite of ice from the peaks above. I pushed the hair out of my eyes and looked for Prince Alfonso.

Half a mile ahead, across a dry and stony upland, waited a group of men and horses, gathered in front of yellow striped tents. Morning sun glinted on helmets and shields, and their cloaks and tunics were as brilliantly colored as our own. It looked as though Duke Argave's former mistress had transmitted Alfonso's message accurately. I glanced down at the blue-and-white velvet in which I was clad, thinking ruefully that the puffed sleeves and long-toed shoes would be a real hindrance if it came to a fight. But that was why I had my knights with me.

I kicked my weary horse into a canter, and after only a momentary hesitation Brother Melchior and the knights followed. We thundered up to the waiting group of men from Nabarra. I reined my horse in before them so hard that he reared, ten feet short of courtiers who scrambled to get out of the way. I leaped from the saddle and managed to land without stumbling in spite of the residual pain in my ankle. Prince Alfonso was going to be forced to discredit any rumors he might have heard that the scarred Count of Peyrefixade was also lame.

"*Greetings, Prince!*" I shouted in Auccitan. He was easy

to spot among his knights and courtiers, a man roughly my age, wearing a scarlet tunic worked with elaborate embroidery in gold thread, a thin gold circlet on the dark brown curls Arsendis had mentioned approvingly. I noted with satisfaction that although my own new velvet clothes were much simpler than his, he had a gravy stain on his chest.

"*Greetings, Count,*" he replied, or something close, although it did not sound like the Auccitan Melchior had been teaching me. Nabarrese, perhaps? I had the impression that Nabarrese was as different from Auccitan as the latter was from the Royal Tongue. The prince's next sentence might have been, "*I am glad you are not tardy to our meeting,*" but it was impossible to be sure.

My lips pulled back from my teeth in an attempt at a smile. If he wanted to confuse me by speaking a language I didn't understand, he was not going to have the satisfaction of succeeding. Standing here on a windy plateau, over the border into a kingdom where I didn't belong, surrounded by friends whom I had known only a few months, by armed enemies who might have reinforcements hidden beyond the next ridge, and God knew how many fanatical heretics lurking in ambush, I had to project confidence or I might as well offer my throat at once and get it over with.

The prince's mouth was twisted into a sneer, although looking at him it occurred to me that this might be his ordinary expression, not something put on just for me. In spite of his dark hair and complexion, his eyes were a startling pale blue, giving him, I thought uncharitably, something of the look of a piebald gelding. He made no attempt to conceal an open stare at my scar, and I turned the left side of my face toward him to allow him a good look.

"Your fair messenger did not tell me the true reason why you wished to meet with me, Prince," I said in the Royal Tongue. If he was not going to speak in the Auccitan

I had been practicing so assiduously with Melchior, I saw no reason why I should. Too bad I hadn't yet taught the priest any Allemann; we could have seen what the sneering prince had to say to *that*. "I am sure the question of who administers justice in the village of Three Cuckoos was just a pretext, since it could have been solved easily by our seneschals. But I am glad we are finally having this chance to meet face-to-face. It gives me the opportunity to ask why you've been trying to have me killed."

He followed what I had to say all right, keeping his pale eyes on my face and frowning with concentration. But he did not respond, only muttered something to the man next to him—chancellor, I decided, from the heavy chain of office around his neck.

I glanced over at Melchior. He had an intense expression and seemed to be following their low-pitched conversation—listening perhaps with second hearing? There might be even more advantages I had not yet appreciated in a magic-working priest.

The chancellor stepped toward us and spoke for his master, in an intelligible if heavily accented version of the Royal Tongue. "The prince comprehends not your talk of killing. He wishes only to talk of the village, of Duke Argave, and of heretics. Can you speak not Auccitan?"

"*Of course I speak Auccitan,*" I shot back in that language. The priest had been coaching me well. Two weeks ago I would have said, "*Me talk Auccitan good.*"

The chancellor made a quick gesture to a servant, who brought out and assembled several camp chairs. The prince and I looked at each other from under our brows for a moment, then both reached abruptly for the buckles on our sword belts, striving to be the first to prove his courage and his own good faith by disarming before the other. While I settled into my chair, with Brother Melchior at my elbow, I said under my breath to the priest, "I hope he realizes what he said to me a minute ago was not Auccitan."

Melchior glanced over at Prince Alfonso, who was arranging himself in his chair, with his chancellor's assistance, in a way that would not wrinkle his cloak, and made a low sound that I could almost have imagined was a chuckle. "There is one additional aspect of the prince's personality about which I might not have informed you fully. He is genuinely stupid."

Fortunately—or unfortunately—Prince Alfonso seemed to have decided I was as defective in language ability as he. He spoke his version of Auccitan slowly and distinctly, enunciating each word in a patronizing manner that made it easy to follow—that is, whenever he did not forget the word for something and insert the Nabarrese word instead, or give a perfectly innocuous Auccitan word a strange pronunciation. There was enough room between his sentences for Melchior to mutter a running translation—though more often into Auccitan than into the Royal Tongue.

The village of Three Cuckoos, having served its purpose in getting me here, seemed to have dropped immediately from Alfonso's attention. I was concentrating so hard on his words I almost forgot to pay attention to the meaning—until he got to his fourth sentence.

"It is good we are meeting at last, Count," the prince said, *"two lords whose territories run along the border between two kingdoms. I am true to my own king, as I am sure you are true to yours—"* Here he hesitated for a second as though about to depart from what was clearly a prepared speech but changed his mind. *"—but that does not mean that you and I might not have interests in common. If you listen to what I have to propose, you may find me a more useful ally even than Duke Argave. But first I need to warn you against the heretics who seek to kill you and seize Peyrefixade."*

"What heretics? What do you know?" I burst out as I realized what he was saying, then paused to repeat it in Auccitan. It would be deeply ironic if the heretics were trying to assassinate me at the same time as the Inquisition was feeling grave doubts whether I might not be a hidden friend to the heretics.

And *what* was happening back at Peyrefixade while the prince kept me out of the castle?

His smirked a little, pleased to have startled me. Melchior spoke before I had time to find the words I wanted. "*If you have information about the Perfected, then I order you as a son of the True Faith to tell us at once.*"

Prince Alfonso seemed to take in for the first time that the counselor at my elbow was a priest. "*If you want me as an ally,*" I said after only a brief pause to make sure I had the words right, "*prove it by telling me what danger awaits me, and how you know it!*"

Alfonso muttered to his chancellor a minute. He wanted to give his prepared speech at his own pace, I thought, and did not like Melchior and me interrupting with questions. The chancellor said as much, speaking for the prince: "*If you will but be patient, Count, my gracious lord will explain it to you in his good time.*" I nodded curtly and sat back, trying to appear relaxed although the nails bit into my palms.

"*The members of the Inquisition who operate in my principality,*" Alfonso continued, "*always consult me about anything they learn from the Perfected they question.*" The sneer was such a permanent part of his expression that it was impossible to tell if he had heard that the Inquisition had been operating in my county without any reference to my own judicial authority and was mocking me for it. "*And recently I have heard a tale that was recounted by several, my Count. It is a tale concerning Peyrefixade, their intention to recapture the castle that once was theirs—because they have learned that within the walls a powerful secret object is hidden.*"

The conviare, I wondered, which I had worn around my neck until it drew the magical fire to my bed? If so, the heretics would be gravely disappointed to dig into the wall by the new hearth and find nothing there at all.

"*And do you know what they seek?*" I asked casually. Could the heretics whom the archbishop said were looking for something long lost have decided it was in Peyrefixade? It sounded as if, in desiring my castle, the heretics planned far more than covert devilishness—they intended to retake the power and presence that had once been theirs. The sun climbed slowly higher in the sky, but the wind continued strong and chill.

Alfonso had clearly been enjoying the telling, but at my question he had to shake his head in disappointment. "*Even under the most refined tortures they would not, or could not, say what it might be. But two suggested separately that there might be an additional magical object in the castle: a conviare to help them find the hiding place of what they sought. Have you ever heard of a conviare, my Count?*"

I nodded. "*You think this is what they want?*"

"*My information,*" and he lingered proudly over it being *his* information, "*is that there are two magical objects hidden in your castle, and that the conviare, which was only casually hidden, would lead them to that which could not be named.*"

Melchior had taken the conviare to the older members of his Order in the priory in the duke's city; from there, he had said, it would be sent to the main house of the Magians. I glanced sideways at the priest without turning my head. Was there something important he had not told me? Did his own Order of the Three Kings intend to find whatever else the Perfected had hidden at Peyrefixade, to use its forbidden magic for their own purposes?

I had intended to visit the Order's principal house very soon anyway, to make the priests a gift for Bruno's soul and to convey his bones to their cemetery. Now that trip was more urgent than ever.

"*Now that I have shown good faith by warning you,*"

my Count," said the prince with what might have been intended as an ingratiating smile, "*let me ask you a favor.*"

It took me a second to recognize what he meant by "favor." It was not an Auccitan word that I recognized, and it did not help that Melchior immediately translated it by another word that I also did not know, but which almost sent me into a fit of highly inappropriate laughter. The closest cognate in the Royal Tongue meant not a generous gesture toward an equal but the sweet embraces with which a maiden might reward a lover for his service.

Ignoring any insulting implications the prince's words might have—or that might slip unintended into the speech of someone who did not know Auccitan well—I answered cautiously, "*What would you like me to do for you, Prince?*"

Now we had come to the real reason he had asked me here. I knew it more by the intensity with which Alfonso's chancellor leaned forward in his chair than by the prince's own sneering drawl. "*I would like you to promise me that you will not—at least not for the next year—marry the duke's daughter.*"

This was so unexpected that I could not immediately answer.

Melchior answered for me. "*I hope you understand, Prince,*" he said smoothly, "*that it is not seemly that we discuss here a marriage that it is not in our power to determine. The duke has granted his daughter the right to choose her own husband, and we can scarcely decide for her. Nor would it be appropriate to speculate coarsely on a young woman's heart.*"

Alfonso abruptly pushed himself up by the arms of his camp chair. He lost his balance, and only his chancellor's hand under his elbow, steadying him, kept him from falling to his princely backside on the hard ground. Alfonso snapped something at the chancellor, wrenching his arm from his grasp as though it had all been the other's fault. "*Are you saying then,*" he demanded, glaring up at me from a crouch, *"that you are already engaged to marry the young duchess?"*

He had lapsed back into Nabarrese, but his meaning was clear. I adopted a lofty expression, as though I had not even noticed him nearly getting a grass stain on the rear of his expensive outfit. *"No more than you are, Prince,"* I said calmly. *"So there is no need to discuss her further."* The thought came unbidden that the prince's choice of vocabulary in asking me for a favor, coupled with his request that I not take a woman to wife, could have an entirely different explanation than the political borders in these mountains. The idea was so funny—especially the picture of how much redder and more sneering the prince would become if he knew what I was thinking— that I had to struggle hard to keep from laughing.

"Let us go instead to the village of Three Cuckoos," I said airily, turning my back on him so he wouldn't see my grin, and picking up my sword belt, *"and talk with the mayor and the inhabitants. Once we've resolved that issue, we can return if you wish to the topic of the heretics— and the question you still haven't answered, why you tried to kill me."*

I mounted without giving him a chance to answer, doing my best to convey assurance that he would immediately agree. My knights had been working with me for months now, and they seized their own horses' bridles and were in the saddle as smoothly as any cavalry I'd ever commanded for the emperor, before Prince Alfonso was fully on his feet again.

I hadn't left him much choice. Our horses stamped impatiently while Alfonso's men hastily brought forward his steed. It was a magnificent golden stallion, with legs so slender they gave an appearance of delicacy, and wide-spaced intelligent eyes. Not at all the horse, I said to myself, suppressing another chuckle, for a piebald gelding like the prince.

But with his face turned away from me as he mounted,

I lost the effect of his pale blue eyes and was able to concentrate again on his dark hair and complexion, and on the shape of his shoulders under his cloak as he settled himself in the saddle. Though he was much younger and slighter than the duke, something about the way he sat his stallion reminded me of Duke Argave. Both of them were southerners, I reminded myself, men whose ancestors had lived here—and doubtless intermarried—for centuries. Only a quarter of my own blood was southern. The rest of me was foreign, foreign to these mountains, to this land of heretics and intrigues, even to Peyrefixade—except that Peyrefixade now was mine.

Melchior was again concentrating on whatever Alfonso and his chancellor were saying to each other, and as I wheeled my horse around to start toward the disputed village, the priest urged his steed into position beside mine. "Alfonso is complaining," he said in a low voice, again slightly amused, "that his chancellor had not warned him you were such a fierce and headstrong man."

"Do you mean he hadn't realized I was a northerner?" I replied, gratified. But something else in the priest's words caught my attention. "I also gather," I added casually, "that Prince Alfonso has always been an enemy to the Order of the Three Kings, refusing to allow your Order to operate in his principality, saying publicly that an order of Magian priests is no better than a covey of heretics."

"How did you know?" asked Melchior in surprise. I didn't answer but gave a knowing smile. Even a scarred count could sometimes see through the attitudes and prejudices of a magic-working priest.

The village of Three Cuckoos toward which we were heading was, as far as I could tell, quite clearly part of the prince's territory—or at least not part of mine. When I came home from the duke's court with the message conveyed by the duke's old mistress, to meet with Alfonso to settle this purported border dispute, Seneschal Guilhem had told me that the villagers there had always had an independent streak. There had been times under the old count, my great-uncle, he informed me, that they had temporarily claimed to lie under his jurisdiction, but only when they had had some disagreement with Alfonso's predecessors. The late countess—or rather, I expected, Lord Thierri—had tried to make them pay her rent, but without any success. I hadn't even bothered to visit there while making the rounds of my lands earlier in the spring. The village was however located in a potentially crucial position, where a narrow valley coming down from this high, stony plateau widened out enough for fields—and a view toward Peyrefixade. An ideal invasion route from *either* direction.

The village was a several miles' ride from Alfonso's encampment. He kicked his golden stallion forward to ride even with me, and Melchior dropped back. Alfonso looked toward me with a sneer as if to suggest that he too could be headstrong and ferocious if he wanted. I smiled placidly as though not aware of the effect.

"*You did not bring Raymbaud,*" he said as though disappointed.

"*I do not travel with my* bouteillier," I said, using the word from the Royal Tongue because I had no idea of the Auccitan. I was surprised, however, that he even knew my bouteillier's name. Then I realized something. Raymbaud's accent, ever so slightly different from those of the rest of my staff, must be Nabarrese. He must once have worked for Prince Alfonso before deciding the duke— and the counts of Peyrefixade, once he became the duke's spy—would pay better. "*I do not need refined service in the field,*" I added, hoping Alfonso felt the jab.

But at least for the moment his attention was elsewhere. "*You let heretics escape,*" he said abruptly. This, I realized, was something he had been working around to asking me when I cut our discussion short. "*Why?*"

I waited a minute to answer, looking forward between my horse's bobbing ears: wanting both to make sure I had the words right in Auccitan and to make him impatient. *"The Inquisition had not asked my permission to put them to death,"* I said at last. I was certainly not going to tell this young prince I would have faced a hundred enemies single-handed rather than watch someone be burned to death. *"Surely you, Prince, must realize that sometimes one must make a firm gesture to show one's authority."* I was quite proud that I had found the right Auccitan word for "gesture."

Alfonso might not have recognized it himself, but he followed my meaning. *"But you are not in sympathy with them?"*

I was getting used to his accent, and although I was quite sure his word for "sympathy" was not Auccitan, it was close enough to the Royal Tongue for a guess. *"I hate them very much,"* I said, deciding that neither his nor my vocabulary was ready for "despise." *"And if they want to capture my castle, then I shall hate them even more."*

"But is not your priest of the Order of the Three Kings?" Melchior's presence was bothering him, then—and he didn't even know his private conversation was being overheard with magic.

"The Magians hate the heretics as much as we do," I said airily, hoping it was true.

At this point the track turned steeply downward toward the village, requiring us to give full attention to our horses and putting an end to further conversation. We went single file down the narrow and muddy way. From the hillsides around us we could hear the steady calling of the cuckoos that had given the village its name. Once sheltered from the cold wind off the peaks, I found the air growing warm and itched inside my velvet. Smoke drifted up from the huddle of houses before us.

It was clear the villagers had not expected our arrival. So if I had not decided to ride over here, I thought, Three Cuckoos might have remained nothing more than a pretext for our meeting. Several men came running into the village from the fields as we approached; others, bent over as though hoping to avoid detection, darted away. For a moment I saw in an open doorway a face I found strangely familiar, but it was gone before I could identify it. Inbreeding, I thought again. When everyone had similar bone structure, it was easy for an outsider like me to think they all looked alike.

Prince Alfonso, seeing a chance to seize the initiative again, pulled up his stallion in the middle of the cluster of houses and shouted something in Nabarrese. "He's calling for the mayor and the old men," translated Melchior, at my elbow again, "to give testimony about the village's jurisdiction and responsibilities."

This I could have guessed. Having been forced to come here, Alfonso intended to make a good showing of his own authority by having all the elders swear that the counts at Peyrefixade had never exercised justice over this village.

The mayor, an old man with wispy white hair who appeared far more terrified than the simple arrival of his sworn lord should account for, stumbled forward and dropped to his knees. Alfonso did not dismount. With a sneer and a look off over the man's head, he asked him several rapid questions.

The Nabarrese was too fast for me, and I couldn't catch the mayor's words either, but it sounded as though he was earnestly expressing an intent to agree to whatever Alfonso wanted.

What had the prince done here in the past that would make these people so terrified at his mere arrival?

Or, I thought with a sudden chill, was it not Alfonso himself they feared so much as the Inquisition he befriended? Glancing around, I saw many eyes on me, eyes that dropped or disappeared back into a house's shadows as I turned my head. I was used to people staring, but if they thought Alfonso was here at the request of the Inquisition, were they wondering if the scarred count of whom they must have heard, the scarred count who needed to reestablish himself in the Inquisition's eyes as a true son of the Church, was here to force them painfully into confessions, justified or not?

I neither wanted to let Alfonso make a display of his authority nor to terrify innocuous villagers. *"Thank you for your testimony,"* I called out in Auccitan, interrupting the mayor's stammered agreement to something or other. *"I can see, Prince,"* turning to Alfonso, *"that this is a complicated case, one that would take days of questioning to resolve. Let us cut those days short. Out of gratitude for the friendship you have offered me, I hereby yield to you my predecessors' claims and my own to jurisdiction over this village."*

Swinging down from the saddle, I scooped up a stone and held it out toward Alfonso at arm's length. There was a silent pause for about fifteen seconds. Everyone turned to look at the prince. Having no choice, he slowly and grudgingly dismounted and stepped toward me to accept the stone. I deliberately kept myself from smiling as his fingers closed around it.

By holding it toward him from a standing position, rather than kneeling, I had made it clear that this was a resolution of a disagreement between equals, not a situation where one man was forced to subject himself to the other. I might have yielded any claim to lordship over Three Cuckoos—a claim I knew well I could never have sustained anyway—but both Alfonso and I knew I had won.

"Let us return to your encampment, Prince," I said, ignoring his irritation. *"There we can discuss the other issues that still await us."* The mayor, I was interested to see, was so surprised at this sudden end of questioning and so relieved at our imminent departure that he had to support himself against a wall.

Again I took the lead, forcing my horse into a trot until the track became too steep. My knights rode right behind me, leaving Alfonso and his own men rather ignominiously to bring up the rear.

As we came back out onto the plateau, I paused to give my horse a rest from the long climb and turned to look back. Melchior, sitting his horse at my side, spoke without looking at me. "I know you don't want to exercise your authority in someone else's territory," he said in a low, cautious voice. "But if this keeps on, Count, the archbishop really will doubt your dedication to the True Faith. As, I fear . . ."

He let it trail away without finishing the sentence, but his meaning was clear. "*You're* worried about my religious devotion?" I asked sharply. "What are you talking about?"

"Isn't that why you didn't even try to maintain your claim to the village, but got us all away from there so quickly?" he asked, turning toward me now with surprise. "I thought you were afraid that someone in Alfonso's retinue would recognize that man, too, or realize that the mayor's terror was unusually pronounced even for someone with such a prince over him."

Our horses tore at the sharp mountain grass but did not seem to like the flavor. "I saw someone I thought I recognized," I said slowly. "If—" But then the memory snapped into place. "It was one of the heretics I set free."

Melchior nodded. "The whole village must be full of the Perfected. Here, almost out of the prince's territory, very far from any other settlements, they would have thought they were safe from the inquisitors. When a whole troop of armed men suddenly rode up, they must have imagined all too clearly what it meant."

"Especially armed men accompanied by a priest," I agreed. "Heretics are unlikely to make a clear distinction between the vestments of an inquisitor and those of a member of the Order of the Three Kings." I too should have recognized the heretic, I thought, if I had not been so pleased with myself for how I was manipulating the prince.

Melchior looked startled at the implication that he could possibly be mistaken for a member of the Inquisition, but he did not answer at once. At this rate, I thought in irritation, the heretics were going to consider me their friend. I just hoped they didn't pass the news of this friendship on to Prince Alfonso's pet inquisitors the next time they were questioned. "As soon as we're safely home again," I said, "I'm going to send a message to Archbishop Amalric and tell him I've found a nest of heretics. That should make him pleased."

"Perhaps I should alert the superiors of my Order first," said Melchior, looking unhappy. "I haven't told you this, Count, but there is a possibility that some of the Perfected Ones up in these mountains may be working very powerful magic. . . ."

I interrupted him. "What's surprising about that? I thought that magic was always part of heretic lore. Here comes Alfonso."

The prince came up the last rise, sweaty and looking more dissatisfied than ever. I gave him no time to rest his stallion but shook my own horse's reins to lead the way back toward the yellow striped tents.

If I turned the heretics over to the Inquisition, I told myself, the same heretics I had earlier rescued, they would still be burned to death but at least it would not be in my county. The thought was not as reassuring as it should have been.

The sun was high and hot by the time we reached Alfonso's encampment. I unbuckled my sword again and threw myself into a chair, draining the flagon of wine his chancellor handed me, then pushed the hair back from my forehead to let the wind dry my sweat. Doing and saying exactly what I wanted, as though I did not even notice the prince's reaction, had served its purpose in making him sulky, but was tiring work.

"*Let us understand each other, Prince,*" I said in Auccitan, deliberately not giving him an opportunity to finish his wine. "*You would like me as a friend because an enemy at Peyrefixade would be dangerous, might even be an opportunity for the duke to invade your principality. Alternately, an ally there could be a chance for you yourself to plan an invasion of Argave's duchy. . . ."*

Alfonso glared at me and said something to his chancellor. I was starting to feel sorry for the latter. He answered for his prince, hands turned placatingly palms up. *"Prince Alfonso has no intention of invading the duchy of such a stalwart man as Argave, or of depriving a lovely young duchess of her inheritance."* Of course not, I thought. Gaining territory by marriage was always easier than gaining it by conquest. *"But you are quite right that the duke might have unwisely determined to cross the border from your kingdom into ours, by way of Peyrefixade, if the new count at Peyrefixade had been led to believe that Prince Alfonso was his enemy, not his friend. Thus,"* he added pointedly, *"the prince's warning about the heretics, as a demonstration of his goodwill."*

I nodded gravely when the chancellor paused, but did not answer. Alfonso nudged him to go on. *"There is of course one other possibility,"* said the chancellor uneasily. *"The prince wonders— That is— Some have said the duke deliberately chose a man from the north because he would be easily manipulated by whatever the duke told him, lacking local knowledge. My apologies, Count! But others have seen in this a first attempt to expand into our territory by the emperor. . . ."*

The emperor! If these southerners were frightened by the thought of the mighty emperor far off in northern lands, well, my old master would be highly pleased, except that he had probably barely heard of any of these southern counties and duchies. *"In all that does not concern Peyrefixade and my allegiance to the duke who made me count here,"* I said solemnly, *"I am the emperor's sworn man. But I assure you, Prince, that the emperor has no designs on the south—at least, not yet."*

All true. But fear of a rumored emperor had nothing to do with an assassin attacking me in the duke's garden or a mage-fire roaring around my bed. *"You have been evading my question all day, Prince. Someone has tried to kill me, not once but twice. You already know that I will make a good friend. Admit your role in the attempts on my life—or prove you had no part in them by telling me who did—or you shall find me an evil enemy."*

My words sank in to Alfonso. His face, already red, went redder. I had been making him sulky and irritated; now I had made him thoroughly angry. Melchior beside me tried to say something, but I brushed him away.

The prince jumped to his feet and reached a hand behind him. One of his knights slapped the hilt of his sword into it. At my back I could hear the hiss of my own knights drawing their blades, but I remained planted in my chair, unarmed.

Alfonso would suffer enormous damage to his honor by striking down an unresisting man, to say nothing of probably being killed the next instant by my knights. Waiting and watching him from under my brows for the space of two heartbeats, I hoped he would think of this, too.

He might not have, but his chancellor certainly did. He seized the prince by the sword arm and hung on when Alfonso tried to shake him off. The instant the latter took his eyes off me, I leaped to my feet. Before he knew what I was doing, I had my arms around him in a tight bear hug.

And I laughed, a loud, joyous laugh such as the emperor used to give. "By my faith, Prince!" I cried. My heart was pounding too heart to find the Auccitan words; let them interpret the Royal Tongue as best they could. "You are a man of such courage as I have rarely seen!"

All our knights stood with their swords drawn, in readiness for a fight that suddenly seemed unlikely to take place. Alfonso struggled in my embrace, dropping his sword as I squeezed him tighter. But then I pushed him away so he could get a good look at my face, while continuing to hold his shoulders in a grip that would tell him I was a lot stronger than he was. "A man like you I want for my friend, not my enemy," I continued with a grin. "Now that I know you did not plot to assassinate me—and were willing to lay down your life in proving it by the sword—let us drink to our alliance!"

I poured wine into both our flagons, spilling a little as my hand shook, and thrust one at him. "To such a friend as you I am happy to yield a peasant village!" I looked at him over the rim as I drank, watching his reaction. He really was much less pleasant to embrace than I imagined the duke's daughter would be.

He looked more angry than ever but confused as well. His chancellor was babbling furiously in his ear, though I couldn't tell if he was trying to give advice or merely translating what I said into Nabarrese. Time to get away while the confusion lasted.

"I am glad we could have this conversation, Prince," I said heartily, buckling on my sword. "If our two kingdoms ever go to war, it shall not be your principality and my county that begin it. Now that we are friends, I need not fear an invasion through the mountain passes."

He still hadn't answered when I swung up on my horse, wincing from the pain in my ankle, which had started to throb again. I put my heels in my horse's side and started off, back toward Peyrefixade, my knights scrambling to catch up.

2

Not until we were several miles away from Alfonso's encampment, back across the border into my county, did I let my tired horse slacken its pace. A small stand of gnarled oaks stood in the shelter of a ridge, and I slid off into their shade.

At first I simply sat still, head between my knees, trying

to catch my breath. But after a minute I heard someone approaching and glanced up to see Brother Melchior.

He sat down beside me without speaking, although his lips were moving silently. Looking past him, I saw that the knights had also dismounted. They sat in a group a little distance away, talking quietly. "What are they saying?" I asked.

The priest looked surprised at the question, but he obediently turned toward the knights, concentrating with wrinkled forehead. After a minute he said, "They are saying that their Count Sc— That their Count Galoran is a brave man."

This was much better than the alternative, that their Count Scar was a reckless man, likely to start a suicidal fight for no reason at all. I smiled, although judging from Melchior's expression the effect was not as good-humored as I intended. But my breathing was almost under control again. "Well," I said. "I thought the parley went well. I learned several important things."

He cocked his head. "Besides learning where the Perfected fled?"

Should I write to Archbishop Amalric? I wondered. Or would it be better to let the inquisitors do their job, without seeming to interfere or to tell them their own business? "I'm fairly sure now," I said, "that Alfonso was not behind the attempts on my life. I know you traced the one assassin to a cloaked figure with a Nabarrese accent, but that's not enough to implicate the prince himself. Especially since it took three accusations of him being an attempted murderer before he reacted: if he'd really been trying to kill me, he would have been furious the first time I mentioned it."

"Could it have been someone else at his court?" asked Melchior.

I nodded thoughtfully. "I rather had the impression that his chancellor makes most of the decisions that Alfonso thinks he makes himself, and other courtiers may well be pursuing independent policies and plans without bothering the prince with them."

The wind rustled the young oak leaves above us. As the sun moved down the sky, here in the shade I could once again feel the bite of air off the ice. The priest's eyes were dark in the shadows. "What else did you learn?"

No need to mention again the information that the heretics wanted something hidden in Peyrefixade, which he'd heard as clearly as I. "That Alfonso fears the duke intends me for his daughter," I said, looking away. Melchior did not immediately comment, but in a moment I chuckled. "You will note that I left without promising not to marry her. In fact," I added, "I did not promise anything, except not to claim jurisdiction over Three Cuckoos, which I hadn't intended to do anyway."

The priest took a deep breath. "I know that acting as spiritual advisor in a noble court is not the same as contemplating God's will within the walls of the cloister. But there are dangers, to one's soul as well as to one's body, which even among the violence of everyday life may be excessive, which—"

I laughed and rose to my feet, slapping him good-naturedly on the back. "You're going to counsel me, Father," I said, loud enough that the knights could hear me too, "not to perform any more rash deeds that might get me killed with all my sins unconfessed and weighing on my soul. Well, consider the message delivered. Maybe when I'm old and tired I'll take a canon's vestments myself, but not yet."

In spite of my bold words, I felt a prickling between my shoulder blades as we rode on. Prince Alfonso had not found my humiliation of him nearly as amusing as I did. He might not have tried to assassinate me before, but depending on whether his chancellor's good sense prevailed he might decide to try now. And the heretics in the village of Three Cuckoos, knowing I had seen them, might try to find a way to assure that I never wrote any letters to the bishop.

The road we were traveling made great loops down from the plateau on which Alfonso had been camped, and although we had now come some ten miles—which our horses, plodding slowly, certainly wanted us to know—and should see Peyrefixade's far-off tower from the next ridge, we were still not very far away from the plateau in a direct line. The descent would be too steep for horses, but several armed men on foot, who knew these mountains, would be able to get ahead of us and wait in ambush.

Up ahead, the track passed through a narrow defile, overhung with vegetation clinging to the side of the cliff. I pulled up my horse and considered. If I had been sent by the emperor to ambush someone, this is exactly the place I would have chosen.

I might be the fearless Count Scar to my knights, but there was no use getting us all killed to prove it. I motioned to Melchior. "Can your magic tell if there's anyone hiding up ahead there?" I asked.

It took him only a few seconds to realize what I meant. He concentrated for a moment, while the knights waited a dozen yards back. Glancing over at them, I saw them loosening their swords.

The birds around us had begun singing again once we stopped. If there were enemies ahead, they must be keeping very still. "I hear no voices," said Melchior. "If you will but wait a minute, I can tell better with my powders." He reached into his saddlebag and pulled out a little cloth-wrapped bundle, from which he extracted a few grains of a white powder. It did not blow off his palm as he held it up, even when he stirred it with a finger and mumbled over it. Heavy for powder, I thought— perhaps ground from human bones?

That would rather be something for heretics, I told myself firmly. But the magic the Order of the Three Kings practiced owed much to the heretics.

"There are no men within at least half a mile but ourselves," said the priest then. "Beyond that I cannot tell."

"Prince Alfonso's an even bigger fool than I thought," I said loudly, for the knights' benefit. "I would certainly have tried to ambush us on the way home. At least we gave our horses a chance to breathe."

I shook the reins and moved forward. If I didn't have to worry about fighting off Alfonso's men, I could look ahead to supper at Peyrefixade.

My horse trotted through the narrow defile, the sound of hooves echoing loud from the cliffs on either hand. The hanging vegetation swayed in the wind, then suddenly, unbelievably, a hooded figure stood on the track before me.

My horse reared, and I had my sword out in a second. But there was only one man, and I saw no weapon.

"Count Galoran!" he said in a deep voice. "I have a warning for you." His face was invisible in the shadows of his hood, and he stood perfectly still, though my spooked horse's hooves came within a foot of him before I had the animal under control again. It might have been my imagination, but the air seemed to be growing rapidly colder.

The knights rushed up behind me, but I motioned them back. If this was an ambush, it was the most unusual one I had ever seen. But why had Melchior's powders not revealed this man? Unless— Unless this was no fleshly human, but a spirit.

I gritted my teeth and clenched my sword. If he moved toward me, we would see what steel would do against an insubstantial spirit.

"Count Galoran," he said, "you have an enemy at Peyrefixade. Someone in the castle serves not you but another master."

"Someone certainly tried to kill me," I said, not letting down my guard for a second. Could whoever started the mage-fire that killed Bruno have been not the stone masons but someone on the castle staff, someone I saw every day, who was now waiting for a better opportunity?

"And may try again," said the hooded figure. "Watch your back—and, if you leave the castle again, watch who you leave in charge."

I jerked on my horse's reins to take him a step closer. "How do you know this?" I demanded. "And why are you warning me? I don't know if I should believe anything told by a man who hides his identity."

At that he reached up a hand and for a second pushed his hood back so I could see his face. My first reaction was intense relief that he even *had* a face. There was a gravity of presence about him, and his black eyes were intense. He pulled the hood forward again immediately, leaving me with a strange sense of familiarity, even though he was quite clearly not one of Alfonso's men nor one of the heretics from the village of Three Cuckoos.

"I know this," he said quietly, "because I am among those who are making plans to gain control of Peyrefixade. As to why I am telling you: I cannot say myself."

"At least tell me the traitor's name," I said gruffly.

"That," said the figure, "I cannot tell you." And he turned and vanished among the greenery. For a few seconds the hanging vines swayed and there was a crackling of small branches, then all was still again.

I slowly turned to face the others. If he was among those who wanted Peyrefixade, he must be a heretic himself. At this rate I wouldn't need to bother reporting the heretics to the archbishop; my own men would be writing to complain that I was a known friend of the Perfected. I wondered now why I hadn't just run the pestilential heretic dog through on the spot. But I couldn't have attacked an unarmed man, especially one who was trying to warn me.

The knights waited respectfully and with no expression on their faces. But Brother Melchior looked both frightened and distressed.

I let out all my pent-up feelings on him. "What kind of Magian do you call yourself?" I shouted. "Nobody's within half a mile, you tell me. And there's someone concealed not thirty yards away! Can your spells not detect somebody who's hiding in the bushes?"

He started babbling apologies, but I cut him short. "For the rest of the way, you ride in front. Maybe that will give you the incentive you need to make sure there isn't someone *else* waiting in ambush."

We met no more heretics and none of Alfonso's men the rest of the way home. Whoever the heretics had planted in the castle had not taken advantage of my absence to barricade it against me. The horn sounded three times as it always did as I came up the final steep stretch to the gates, but they let me in at once.

I felt a fierce kind of joy as I came through the gates into the grim red castle. Peyrefixade was mine and would remain mine. I had only been count here a few months, but this place was home the way that my brother's castle back in the north had never been.

The knights who had accompanied me were quiet and attentive while we ate, but after supper they slipped off, doubtless to tell everyone else a highly colored version of what had happened. I myself settled down by my new hearth with a keg of beer and set out quite deliberately to get drunk.

But I hadn't gotten very far on this project when Brother Melchior came slowly toward me across the hall. He must have been up in the chapel, praying, I thought, realizing I hadn't seen him in a while. He still clutched a book in his hands.

"I would like to apologize again, Count," he said, "while you are still sober enough to hear me." He managed to look at the same time deferential, self-righteous, and slightly amused. "That spell should have revealed anyone, hidden or not, bushes and rocks or not. There are, however, hints in some of our Order's ancient writings that it is possible for someone well-versed in powerful magic to create a counter-spell, to hide someone's location even from a Magian. Perhaps I should have tried a second divination spell as well, as a check on the first."

So maybe the book in his hand was a book of magic, not of prayers. I shrugged and motioned him to sit beside me. Whoever in the castle wanted me dead might be almost anyone, but not Melchior, because he had saved me from the fire.

"Just be glad the heretic meant us no harm," I said. "I doubt those dogs would spare a priest of the True Church if they were in a murderous mood. You must have heard what he said. What did you think of his warning?"

"If a killer who is one of the Perfected is right here in the castle," he said unhappily, "I must do all I can to find him. But my powers of magical divination will do nothing to reveal the state of a man's soul."

I handed him the mug, and he took a deep draught of beer. "Then we'll have to use other methods," I said grimly. "We could put every man in the castle to the ordeal in turn until one confessed, but it would take a while, and we'd probably get several false confessions along the way." The priest glanced at me nervously, then quickly looked away to refill the mug. I laughed then and slapped him on the shoulder, sloshing the beer. "You really believed me there for a minute, didn't you?"

It occurred to me, through the faint haze that was just starting to slide into my mind, that most counts were probably not so familiar with their spiritual advisors. But with Bruno gone and everyone else here a potential enemy, he was all I had.

He took a deep breath. "It is not right for a priest to reveal the secrets of a man's soul which—"

I took the mug back for another drink. "You think it's the seneschal, don't you?" He looked startled, and I laughed again. "Now you're wondering if your count has divination

powers of his own, is that it? You don't need to tell me
any spiritual doubts that Seneschal Guilhem may have
confessed to you. I've noticed myself that although he
attends chapel service in the mornings with everyone else,
he is always silent and at the back. He seems sick half
the time and is losing weight, as though he'd decided to
give up food. This all sounds like the religion of the
Perfected to me."

"Those who follow its ways," said Melchior quietly, "do
not believe themselves heretics. They think they have
finally discovered God's true purpose."

"Then that makes them all the more dangerous for the
rest of us," I said firmly. "I've also wondered about the
seneschal's devotion to the late countess. He clearly hates
Lord Thierri for having shared her bed; might he hate
me just as much because I replaced her?"

"And we still don't know why or how she died," said
Melchior gloomily. After a brief pause he said, "Might
there not be an assassin in the castle even aside from the
seneschal—someone who pushed her off the wall and is
now plotting against you?"

With no good answer, I only shrugged. "How about
Alfonso's warning that there were *two* magical objects
hidden here in Peyrefixade? One was the conviare I wore
for a while, but might the other be that other telesma,
the one that started the fire? Or," not being able to resist
a final dig, "might another secret heretical object be hidden
from you as thoroughly as the heretic was hidden?"

"I have concentrated my powers on searching for such
an object the last two hours," Melchior said stiffly, "but
have found not the slightest hint of its presence. If there
indeed were two magical objects hidden here when the
Perfected controlled the castle, the second must still be
here, for the fire tile was new and had only been placed
here very recently. It may be so well hidden that I shall
have to recover the conviare from my Order and use it
in the search."

I nodded, took another pull of beer, and lapsed into silence. We sat quietly for several minutes, passing the mug back and forth. I had hoped for forgetfulness but could instead only feel myself growing lugubrious. The sorrow of Bruno's death was as fresh as if he had only just died.

It was now full dark outside, and the only light was the glow from the hearth. Our shadows jerked and flickered across the walls. Though it was late, none of the men had come into the hall to sleep. I wondered vaguely if they had all slipped silently away, leaving the priest and me alone in the castle.

"I ought to send word at once to the archbishop," he said suddenly, breaking the silence. His speech was ever so slightly slurred. "And also the masters of my Order. I ought to tell them where the inquisitors can find a nest of Perfected—and quickly, before they take fright and go elsewhere."

"It sounds as though you're trying to persuade yourself of something you're reluctant to do," I commented, pleased to find my own speech still clear.

"I am," he said miserably. I poked up the fire, and the light played across his face. Looking at him, I thought that here, far from any other priests, he might find that I was all *he* had.

"Don't you agree," I said levelly, "that those who have thrown away their own souls, and whose perfidious preaching may lead others away from God, should be hunted down and put to death before their heresy can infect any more of the faithful?"

"I do," he said, more miserable than ever. "Before God I do. But— Perhaps you can understand this, Count. You said today that you would worry about your soul when you became old and tired. Maybe, when *I'm* old and tired, I shall no longer remember the sight—and the sound and smell—of my grandfather burning to death."

I didn't answer, suddenly too choked up to trust my

voice. Gertrude and Bruno seemed to run together with Melchior's grandfather. It was quite clear that even if everyone in the county but me embraced the religion of the Perfected I could not report them to the Inquisition.

"We should take Bruno's body to its final resting place," I said, finding my voice again. "I don't like to think of him in that village cemetery, with no one praying for him—" I stopped, took another swig of beer, and pushed on. "We'll go in two days and take the seneschal with us, so we can keep an eye on him. The archbishop and the inquisitors can do their own work without any aid from us."

He nodded, not looking at me. Well, I thought, maybe back with the masters of his Order Brother Melchior could come to terms with his incipient sympathy for the heretics, before it became dangerously advanced for someone who was supposed to be leading other souls to God.

The beer wasn't what I needed. I stood up abruptly and went to the door of the hall. "Where is everybody?" I bellowed. "It's time to go to sleep! We have to be up early in the morning for divine service." In the distance I could hear low voices and approaching footsteps. Without waiting for them, I threw myself into bed and drew the curtains.

Chapter Ten ~ Melchior

1

After a good day and a half of riding along constantly on the alert, always probing the way ahead for hidden magic workers (using *two* divination spells each time) or more ordinary villains, it was a relief to round a bend and see the looming bulk of Conaigue blocking out half the southern sky. Almost as soon as we saw the mountain, I felt the faintest touch of magic brushing across us. Whoever was on duty on the watchtower high above had scanned us with his distant sight. I felt relief at having detected him so quickly; it appeared my short but intense review of my books of defensive magic before our departure from Peyrefixade had indeed improved my skills. It had actually been pleasant to immerse myself even so briefly in study, a relief from struggling with the demons of my worries and doubts. But the journey itself had been a strain. It would be good to relax at last during this final stretch of the ride up to the House of the Order, secure that no ambush could have been laid for us under that constant magical watch.

As the man who knew the road, I went at the head of our little party. Count Galoran rode at my shoulder, his soldier's eyes marking every turn and landmark—doubtless he would be able to find the way unescorted another time, should the need arise. Behind came the knights and the pack horses with the baggage. In the midst of them, following a long rein held by the seneschal, plodded a sturdy old mule with Bruno's earth-stained coffin lashed securely across its back. If the seneschal had found anything odd in Count Galoran leaving Bouteillier Raymbaud in command while we were away from Peyrefixade, while ordering him to accompany us, he had given no sign. "I want him under my eye," the count had told me the morning we left. "As for Raymbaud, I'm sure he's spying on me for the duke, but what of it? The fact that he holds the castle for two masters should simply make him the more reliable."

It was fortunate that neither the mule nor any of our horses were skittish or balky beasts. Traveling this steep familiar road with men who were new to it, I was seeing it with fresh eyes for the first time in many years. I had forgotten just how many places one was required to negotiate a path no wider than a man's outstretched arm, strung along the very edge of a steep drop to sharp stones on one hand with an equally steep bank crowding one outward on the other. The count's face would show no emotion when I looked back at such a spot, and the seneschal seemed not even to notice our situation, but there were always rolling eyes and even a few lips moving in prayer among the younger knights behind. The shadows were growing long when we stopped to rest and water the animals for the last time, high in the hills at the little village that sits on a few acres of level ground hard under the shoulder of high Conaigue. When we started up the still steeper road that winds up to the House, hurrying now to avoid being overtaken by twilight, the count was moved to speech.

"By my faith, Brother Melchior, your Order has placed its earthly seat close enough to heaven, at any rate!"

"Our Master wished it so. When he first took up the deep study of magic for the True Faith nearly sixty years ago, he did so as a hermit, placing himself as far as possible from the dwellings of other men."

"So, then, he wanted to purify himself by continual

solitude and frequent prayer, and to seek isolation for his studies?"

"Yes, certainly that. Also, it is not wise to attempt certain magical works for the first time with other persons close at hand, unless they are also versed in the magic arts. There can be—dangers."

"And he lives still, this Master of yours, or so I have heard. Shall I meet him at the House of the Magians?"

"No, he has withdrawn himself from among us these twenty years." I indicated a narrow side track leading off toward a little light far uphill on the left, while our own route swung sharply to the right and zig-zagged steeply to a point far above our heads. "He lives and works now in a small cell by a chapel up there, allowing the Order to send only a single novice to look after him. It is accounted the greatest possible honor to be chosen for the duty of three months' attendance upon the Master, especially a second time."

"You speak with a note of satisfaction," the count said with his quirked smile. "Might I guess that the novice Melchior was one of the twice-chosen in his time, or perhaps even thrice?"

I flushed, hoping it didn't show within my cowl. "I was indeed favored to be called twice, Count. No one goes a third time, however. Our Master's intent in thus withdrawing, having once established the Order of the Three Kings and set it under a proper rule with officers elected by us canons from among our own number, was to wean us gradually from dependence on his presence and leadership, well before it should please God to call him away from all earthly things. He hoped in this way to prevent our being thrown into confusion when his end comes, grievous though the blow will nevertheless be. To allow any of the younger members to become too closely attached to him would defeat his own purpose."

"Your Master sounds wise in more than magic. Many a promising religious house has failed because its founder did not show such foresight. A good commander plans for every possibility, including how order shall be kept among the troops in the event of his own fall." He peered up our track to the next sharp switchback, which seemed to be growing dimmer with every pace the horses made through the twilight. "I only wish he had taken a little more thought for those who might wish to visit when he sited his stronghold."

"Ease of access was not his intention, Count. When we make our final profession as novices, we start at dawn and come up from the village on our knees."

We set poor Bruno's rough coffin up on a bier that had been placed in the chapel off the south transept, with tall candles at head and foot and many more blazing before the altar. In the letter I'd sent ahead, I'd requested that senior canons be assigned to sing the offices for the dead over Bruno from the moment we arrived until the funeral, so two brothers proceeded to the altar and started chanting as soon as we stepped back. I cast a quick glance at the count and saw that he looked satisfied. "When is the burial?" he asked as we went up the side aisle.

"Tomorrow afternoon, as befits a man who had passed the mid-day of life but not yet reached its evening. Under the Rule of our House, we bury babes at dawn, children in the morning, those in the flower of young manhood or maidenhood at noon, older but still quite hale persons during the afternoon, and the aged at dusk."

"And your fellow Magian canons?"

"Ah, brothers are always buried at dawn, Count, having become as babes again."

He laughed his short laugh, then went off behind the novice who had been assigned to guide him to the guesthouse. I remained for a while in the chapel, simply trying to recapture my wavering sense of sureness by being inside those familiar walls once more. Then I sighed and set off to report to Provost Balaam. Stepping from darkness into his candlelit office, I was surprised to discover not only the Provost, but also Abbot Caspar, Prior Belthesar from the duke's city, and most disquietingly, the grim old figure of Brother Endaris, the Spector General of our Order.

"Don't look so amazed, Brother Melchior, and never mind the genuflections," Prior Belthesar said as I made haste to kneel before these major officers, only to have him seize my arm and set me on my feet again. "I have been here most of the week; came up with an escort right after the Sabbath. I wanted our lord abbot and these other masters to have plenty of time to examine your two intriguing finds before you arrived. They had some quite important plans to make, and now that I've had the chance to thoroughly vouch for you, you very much figure in them."

He urged me toward the provost's table. There I saw the ceramic fire telesma and the conviare lying next to their lead caskets. Raising my eyes, I found my gaze locked with the deepset eyes of Brother Endaris, half hidden by the dense gray eyebrows that hung down across them.

I'd had only one real experience with this legendary old figure of our Order, a single course of lectures he had given to my group of novices. Even then, I'd been only one of a group and had managed to be largely successful at keeping his attention off myself. Joke though we might when out of his sight, we'd all been afraid of him then, and I was no less afraid of him now. One of our Master's early companions, having joined the new little Order when already well into his manhood, he was our Order's greatest scholar of battle magic. His true age was unknown, but it had to be at least near that of blind Brother Quercus—or my own grandfather, had he lived. But there was no vagueness in either the eyes nor the manner of Brother Endaris.

His official duty as Spector General of the Order was to inspect that our rule was fully kept, both within the

Mother House and in all its dependencies, and to do so he had mastered difficult and ancient branches of magic that allowed him to pass where he wished unseen, and even enter sealed chambers where people supposed their secrets were quite safe—a power which accounted for the pun of his title. To carry out his duties, he traveled much, still riding out in all weathers. The rest of the time, except when teaching the novices or attending chapter meetings and the offices, he kept to his own spartan cell, busy with the study and praxis of his special fields of magic. As usual, he went straight to the point.

"Brother Melchior, this conviare you've found is the single most important magic object of the Perfected that's come before us in the last generation."

I stared, first at him, then the conviare. "I can't—that is, I can hardly believe it! I probed it as well as I could several times, and never found a hint that it contained truly deep or special powers."

"Not it: the thing it was made to find, and having found, to work together with. And don't blame yourself for not grasping its true significance. Even your old superior Prior Belthesar understood only some of the thing's importance when he examined it down at the duke's city. I, however, had some prior knowledge of it that the rest of you lack. Let's test how well you've retained your studies of the novice's quadrivium. Who was the Magus de Cuza?"

"He—wasn't he the great Perfected Magian who was so deadly? The one who almost destroyed the armies of the present duke's father virtually by himself, just when they were threatening to overtake and destroy the whole host of the Perfected?"

Brother Endaris nodded with a wintery smile. "Full marks. The most terrible battle Magian of that age, perhaps of any. He was always dangerous, but that was his greatest hour. The afternoon of that battle, he stood on a high rock with only three pupils beside him and hurled back the old duke's armies with sendings of whirlwinds and fire and lightning and wraiths with flaming eyes and very real fangs and claws. When a band of horsemen attempted to go around him, he called up a host of the dead out of old stone coffins under the fields they were crossing, skeleton warriors who would kill and kill and never die so long as he continued to channel power into them. The Magus kept these wonders up until his own people had made good their retreat. He consumed himself doing it, however, burning like the wick of a candle within his aureole of magic. When full night finally arrived and the threat of further pursuit was at last ended, he dropped down, withered and senseless, and was carried back by his three pupils to join the Perfected armies' retreat. Some portion of the works he did on that day he produced right there, a wrighting of immediate magic such as had never been seen before or since in this country. But the greater part was accomplished using the stored power of three of his greatest creations, a pair of war telesmas more potent than virtually any others ever wrought, plus a conviare that he fashioned specifically to be linked to them and to channel and direct their power." The old canon shot me a fiery glance, then bent his head over the table until his dark eyes seemed to vanish in their deep sockets. "This conviare."

"By Our Lord! But how did it come to be hidden at Peyrefixade?"

"Ah, well, Peyrefixade was a heretic castle then, and the Magus de Cuza's own seat. He knew that he'd done for himself. He'd long since attained what the heretics call the 'perfected' state in spirit as well as in the art of war magic, and had been eating essentially nothing but bread and a few lentils a day for a very long time. Consider how our Order relaxes all dietary restrictions for a brother when he's actively practicing intensive magic, or think how it spends you just to work divinations for a few hours. Then imagine how it would drain an aged and starved man to do the dread wonders I've described. De Cuza knew he hadn't long, but he had one more great work in him. He directed his pupils and an escort of soldiers to convey him to Peyrefixade as quickly as they could and place him on his high seat in the great hall with the two war telesmas and the conviare before him. Then he ordered them and everyone else out of the castle. No sooner were all of them outside than the gate shut without any hand touching it, and the castle became wrapped in a fog dark as smoke. Huddling before the walls, they heard a sound as of great winds, then creakings and shifting stones, while flames and lightnings leaped between the towers and the very rocks seemed to quake and shift.

"When all this at last ceased and the gate swung wide, they rushed back inside to find the Magus de Cuza stretched on his bed, his flesh so white and bloodless it seemed the bones shone through, with only his eyes alive. Only one war telesma, the less powerful of the pair, lay beside him, and it had been completely emptied of magic. He whispered for his pupils to come forward unaccompanied, swore them to secrecy by the Perfected's strongest oaths, and bade them take it up. Then he explained to them alone that he had hidden the more powerful telesma and the conviare in separate places somewhere within the castle walls. The greater telesma itself lay where even a Magian with skill comparable to theirs would in all likelihood find it only if aided by the conviare. This was both to safeguard the great telesma from their foes and also to safeguard them from it, for he believed that only a Magian who had finally made himself completely perfect according to their heretic understanding could possibly wield either of the battle telesmas linked with the conviare, without bringing destruction upon himself and all near him. The lesser telesma, however, he reckoned any of his three pupils could use if they worked with care, though none had yet attained full perfection. Once any of the three, or if not them then in good time one of their own pupils, had attained a state of sufficient worthiness, that man would be able to use the remaining telesma's linkage with the conviare to recover it, and through it, the great telesma. Each of the three was therefore to keep the secret, with this exception: each of them could communicate it whenever he found among his own pupils one whom he knew would eventually equal or surpass himself, so that the secret would never be lost to the Perfected.

"Having told the three these things, the Magus called for all his servants and people to approach and ordered his great coffin to be brought in and set up beside his bed. He recited the Perfected's heretical confession of faith in full with a strong voice, looked around at them all, and pronounced a heretic blessing upon them. Then he folded his arms, whispered, 'You may bring the lid now,' and died."

"What pride and arrogance!" whispered Abbot Caspar. "To decide the disposition of such important things, and even the moment of his own death, using only his unaided human judgment!"

"So the first of the three pupils thought also. It shocked him that his master, having used those mighty objects to save their people from destruction, should then put them out of reach of anyone else when deadly peril was still at hand, simply because he had decided that none but he was currently worthy to wield them. This one act destroyed that student's faith in the Perfected's greatest man, and it did not take long before his faith in other Perfected doctrines became undermined as well. In the end, he returned from their ranks to the True Faith carrying this account with him, for he no longer felt the least bound by an oath sworn under a false doctrine. When the old duke and his captains raised fresh armies two years later and drove the Perfected out of that region and far to the south, the second pupil also stayed behind. He was by then in love with a local girl from the lesser gentry whose family followed the True Faith, and hoped like many of the Perfected to submerge himself and live peacefully among his neighbors while still cleaving secretly to his own doctrine. It served for a good many years, but the Inquisition took him in the end. Only the last pupil remained faithful both to the Magus de Cuza and his teachings, which he soon began to impart to pupils of his own. When the Perfected were driven from Peyrefixade and the lands round about, he took the lesser battle telesma and fled with his pupils, first down into Nabarra, later to the Perfected's final refuge in the western mountains."

Until that moment I had listened to this amazing story almost as one hears any of the accounts of our iron fathers and grandfathers and their deeds. But with this last statement I threw up my hands in the junior canon's gesture for permission to speak. Receiving Brother Endaris's nod, I stammered: "But that explains the attack upon the count! The third student must finally have revealed the secret to some younger magian. Now the Perfected are trying to recover the great battle telesma from Peyrefixade!"

"Precisely. In fact, I have information that he told at least two of his best pupils the entire story last autumn, just before he died. The Perfected have their attention very much upon Peyrefixade now, and will seek to recover their great lost weapon by any means they can find. That is why we of the Order of the Three Kings intend to send this conviare back to Peyrefixade in the hands of our best young diviner, with the purpose of finding it ourselves first."

It was some moments before I managed to say, "But, Revered Father, surely this is a task for one of the elder brothers, perhaps even yourself. I cannot be the proper man." Turning to Prior Belthesar and Abbot Caspar, I forced myself to add, "In fact, O my fathers and masters, I have lately had reason to doubt I am worthy even for the current position of trust in which you have set me."

Prior Belthesar started to voice one of his hearty reassurances, but bit it off as Abbot Caspar raised his hand. He waved for me to approach. I presented my hands pressed together in the gesture of fealty prescribed in our rule for brothers before the abbot, and he took them between his own and smiled his grave, kind smile. "We expected this doubt and hesitation, younger brother," he declared. "But your work as the count's *capellanus* has fully vindicated the case Prior Belthesar made to the Order for you. Fear not; you shall be well prepared before you go back. Your count plans to remain here not only tomorrow for his man's burial but also through the whole day following, to discuss the first gift he means to make as his family's newest head. During that time, Brother Endaris himself shall instruct you in aspects of concealment and battle magic which you may need, and Brother Quercus in better mastery of the deep and far vision and hearing than you have ever known. The prior must begin his return journey to the duke's city in the morning, but he assures us you have already learned all he has to teach."

I started to speak, but he hushed me. "Oh yes, I know, it is not merely such practical questions of preparedness that trouble you now! You have spiritual and moral concerns, perhaps even concerns as to where your own deepest loyalties may lie, that worry you far more. We intend to address those as well. At dawn, you and I shall walk across to the Chapel of the Cleft, where our reverend Master will be waiting to see and talk with you."

2

"You are troubled at heart," said the Master, motioning me to rise from my knees. "Let us talk of it a little."

I got up slowly from the gravel path. When Abbot and I had entered the little garden of the chapel and seen him, the Master had appeared essentially as I remembered from the last time I had seen him more than seven years before, except that he was even more frail and stooped. But at close quarters I noticed something else; his skin had taken on a translucence, almost a transparency, much like what brother Endaris had described for the Magus de Cuza on his deathbed. Perhaps this happened to all great Magians in the end, when they had virtually consumed themselves in working magic of the highest order.

"You may withdraw, my sons," the Master said to his attendant novice and Abbot Caspar. When they had retreated into the chapel, he turned to me and said, "My old feet have grown a little weary in my morning walk, Brother Melchior, and I am cold. Assist me to that sunny seat at the far end of the garden, and then you can tell me about whatever concerns you."

Once he was seated, I began speaking very hesitantly and with eyes cast down. I had wrestled long with doubts and troubled thoughts through nights of half-sleep, trying with little success to find the words to name them even to myself. Now I spoke disjointedly of my grandfather's death, of the inertia and dread that had held me back from informing the Inquisition as to where a nest of heretics might be found, and even of my doubts about whether I should act against the seneschal despite my fears he was not only at least an incipient heretic but a possible traitor to his master. I spoke as well of how the cool clarity I always knew when working magic had so often dissolved into confusion and uncertainty when I tried to grapple with the deep moral and doctrinal questions that faced me in my role as a priest.

The Master listened in silence with a calm, closed face; only an occasional nod of his head showed he was even attending to my words. When I fell silent at last, he stretched out his hand to bless me, then said, "And do you suppose that I have passed my whole long life quite untouched by doubts, Melchior my son?"

"I—I do not know, my father."

"Then I shall tell you. Sinner that I am, I have many times questioned things we have been told to hold as definitively true, have even asked myself whether I chose the best course in creating the Order within the discipline of the True Faith. I was myself for a time the pupil of a great magus as a youth, and found much to admire in the doctrines of the Perfected and much that raised substantive challenges to accepted precepts. Indeed, my master the magus thought me the most promising of all his pupils and the likeliest to succeed him."

He fell silent, almost as if lost in remembrance. After a few moments I raised my outspread hands for permission to speak. At his nod, I asked, "Then what finally drew you back?"

"Ah, it was the fact that the True Faith does *not* assert that following its precepts and teachings, however faithfully, can alone bring one to perfection while still locked in this body and this life. By contrast, once one has been recognized as a *Parfait* among the Perfected, one is presumed to be a saint on earth and immune to doing any further wrong. There lies the deadliest temptation within their doctrine, particularly for the man who has also schooled himself to wield the powers of a Magian! No person's earthly judgment, however much one may study and pray, can ever be truly perfect. While we remain part of this world we all are prey to the passions of the flesh and the flaws of the spirit to some degree. Are you not sometimes angry, Brother Melchior, even very angry?"

"Of course, my father. But I still have very far to go in becoming a truly worthy member of our Order."

"Hmm. Many would assert that I am the worthiest member of our Order, but I tell you that I am very far from having overcome anger in myself. Or pride, or envy, or doubt, or the hundred other stinging gnats of sin that plague each of us continually. It is an instructive thing to be hailed as saintly when one knows very well that one is not, my son. It makes one realize how necessary is some standard for conduct beyond one's own faulty and frail judgment."

He fell silent again. I recognized this way of his from

my long-ago service as his attendant. He would speak no more until I, the pupil, found the proper question. I strained my thought for several moments, then ventured, "So you returned to the True Faith because it provides such a standard?"

He smiled. "Such was my belief, and to that belief I have always returned in the end. The True Faith never allows me to suppose that I have attained perfection, or become incapable of error. This is a crucial check upon anyone who holds great power in this world, whether power of command over men and lands or magic forces. Especially magic forces. That is why it is so important that the learning and study of magic occur within the Order, where there are others sworn to the same high calling to check pride and excess. None of us is perfect unto himself, and even collectively we can err. But error is much less likely when the action of every Magian is subject to the continual examination of many others who are striving to do right under the same rule. You, as a junior canon, are subject to the review and correction of your superiors. They correct one another. Even my son Abbot Caspar and I myself, who have no earthly superiors within the Order, are nonetheless subject to the constant check of knowing ourselves exemplars to all the brothers under us. We continually examine and reexamine every word and act to test how it accords with the moral precepts and rule we are sworn to uphold, lest we should lead wrongly those who follow us."

"But, my father, Abbot and the others now propose to send me out again to act in a difficult situation quite alone, with only my own judgment to guide me."

"And you fear you may err. But that is quite right. If you did not fear, you would not be sent. What you must also recall is the other support of the True Faith. If you have prepared yourself as well as you are able in both practical and spiritual ways and act based on your conscience, you will have done all that could be hoped for or expected." He held up his hand. "And do not imagine that the promptings of your human goodness are necessarily weakness. I have heard how you helped your count save a band of the Perfected. This was not ill-done by either of you. The more zealous servants of the Inquisition are sometimes far too ready to destroy when their proper mission should be to redeem."

He signaled for me to help him rise; our interview was nearly at an end. "Before you leave, allow me to commend you on how well you have performed in your assignment thus far—despite all these doubts of yours! Your care and zeal, and the excellent magic you have performed in your count's service, have been a credit to our Order. Indeed, you have already fulfilled one of the difficult tasks we set for you by winning Count Galoran's goodwill toward us. I have learned to my amusement that he originally held the notion that *we* might be somehow heretical! But thanks to his association with you, he seems to have come here now with a much more favorable view toward our Order." He smiled. "Now you should go; you have much hard preparation to make in the short time before you begin your return journey. Remember, as his spiritual advisor you are sworn to support your count, to aid and defend him, and you should use all your skills and training as both priest and Magian to do so. In any emergency, unless his cause be manifestly unjust, that is your first duty. But if you have a choice and time to consider, be far more afraid to work destruction than to render mercy."

I spent the rest of that day and the whole of the night, day, and night that succeeded it, in nonstop work, except for Bruno's reburial and attending the Offices. A bitter herbal mixture combined with a potent charm from the Brother Dispenser freed me from any need for food or sleep during the whole of this period. Instead, I spent every available moment of every hour learning and relearning what seemed like more high-order magic than

I had acquired in whole years of previous study. I went round and round among Brother Endaris, blind Brother Quercus, the great library, and the scriptorium for the most part. But there was also a handful of sessions with others to learn specific charms of possible use, even a short visit with Provost Balaam to review the special branch of graphic magic used in sending messages over long distances.

When I finally hauled myself painfully up onto my horse the morning we were to depart, my mind was a disorderly jumble of new knowledge, including some powers and capacities I had only heard rumors of or had never known existed. Moreover, I had only to reach a hand within my cassock to feel the comforting presence of a leather belt carrying an almost unbelievable array of telesmae, phials, powders, and other magically charged objects. Every Magian within the Mother House, it seemed, had devoted all of his work time over the last week to preparing one or another powerful charm or object for my use, if need for it should arise. If I should fail now, it would not be for lack of resources.

"I confess I found both the Mother House of your Order and its officers quite impressive," the count said as our party threaded our way carefully down the mountain. "You Magians seem to lack neither holiness nor devotion to the practical aspects of your art. I gather they kept you rather busy while we were there."

"Yes, Count. I was being schooled in things that will make me more useful in your service."

"So I was told. I must say, I was startled to learn we were to take the conviare back with us, and still more amazed to learn why. In fact, I'm still a little surprised you were not simply given your assignment and told to proceed without anyone's troubling me with an account of the matter."

"The Magus de Cuza's great war telesma is supposed to lie hidden within *your* castle, Count. My Order would not presume to find it and take it from there without your knowledge and permission."

"And very proper of them, too. If all of our future relations are conducted with such mutual respect, your Order will find me almost as good a friend and patron as my great-uncle was in his day."

Once out of the shadow of the mountains, we found ourselves riding in spring sunshine that today felt genuinely warm. I felt clear and bright also, and my distant hearing and vision seemed vastly improved from what I had been able to do riding the same road in the other direction just three days before. Now I could fix my attention upon a speck before a distant cliff and almost effortlessly see it expand in my second vision until I would be looking at a great eagle from what seemed to be only a span beyond his wingtip. Or, in the midst of exchanging some remark with the count, my second ear would be caught and I would find myself overhearing every word of a conversation between two men working in a field behind a hill a mile ahead.

This feeling lasted into the early afternoon. Then, quite suddenly, I found myself swaying in my saddle, hiding yawns and struggling to stay awake. Brother Dispenser's draught and charm had finally worn off, and the powerful weariness that always succeeds any period of magical augmentation of human strength was hard upon me. The count soon noticed. "I'll lead your horse, Brother Melchior; go ahead and sleep in your saddle for a while. We're safe enough for now out in the open like this."

We were in fact riding among broad fields in a wide section of the big valley that leads down toward the pass up to Peyrefixade, and on from there to the duke's city. And my eyes really did feel too heavy to keep open any longer. So, making the count promise to wake me as soon as the terrain changed, I let him lash me loosely to my saddle and fasten a lead rope to my mount's bridle, then fell asleep as soon as I dropped the reins.

I awoke to the sound of shouts, then a distant scream.

For a moment I felt completely befuddled. It seemed as if my vision had somehow been relocated to a position behind our party, which was just passing between two low hills. Then I realized that the count and I were well back along the road behind the knights and baggage mules; the count must have dropped back to avoid getting the long lead rein snagged among the others while he guided the horse bearing my sleeping self. Something confusing was happening among those ahead: a horse reared, a knight clutched at a stick that he was pressing against his leg—suddenly I realized that the "stick" was an arrow! The knights swung their wide shields before them and stared in all directions for the source of the ambush. But the hillsides on either hand seemed empty.

Or rather, they seemed empty until I collected my wits and looked with my newly sharpened second eye. Then I saw the large group of mounted warriors charging down upon the knights, in their midst the Magian working the charm that concealed them. Instantly I pulled forth my grandfather's telesma and sent forth a surge of powerful magic that extinguished the invisibility of the attackers.

As soon as their enemies were revealed, our own knights drew their swords and charged to engage them. As his group joined in battle with our smaller one, the Magian pulled up his horse, then sent a stroke of power toward the count and myself. I parried this with an ease that startled me and sent one back that hit him so hard he fell from his horse, senseless.

"Well struck, Father Melchior, but be ready for more," the count cried, swinging up his own shield and drawing his sword with a hiss. A detachment of attackers had broken away and was riding around the fighting men. Led by a bare-headed man on a fine stallion who appeared vaguely familiar though he was no one I knew, they surrounded the baggage train and began to stampede it up over the hill. I saw the seneschal on his mount trapped among the pack horses. He gesticulated as if in surprise as they went, though he'd presumably known perfectly well what was going to happen.

At a signal from the bare-headed leader, four men of this group wheeled and rode straight for us while the others vanished over the hill with the pack horses. I bent my head to concentrate on another sending of defensive magic, then felt a sudden stabbing pain. One of the oncoming men was an archer, and he'd just sent a shaft straight through the flesh of my upper arm. Count Galoran cursed and forced his horse before mine, swinging his shield to cover me and shouting defiance as he prepared to face four armed men single-handed. Pain seared across my vision like a red band, but I could see our knights were attempting to fight their way in our direction. I could also see there was no chance they would arrive in time.

I used Grandfather's telesma to quench the pain temporarily so I could focus my mind and ran quickly over a battle charm on which Brother Endaris had drilled me to perfection over the previous two days. Then I took a handful of a certain powder from a sack at my belt, jerked the reins with my good hand to bring my horse up even with the count's, and shouted to him to cover his eyes. Hurling the powder toward the oncoming warriors, I screamed out the accompanying incantation and threw up the sleeve of my uninjured arm to shield my own face. There was a great flash, followed by the screams of men and horses.

"Great Heaven, Father Melchior, what have you done?" cried Count Galoran. The horses and men who had been bearing down upon us a moment before were now lurching about in complete confusion. As we watched, one man jerked out his sword and began to lay about him at random, immediately felling one of his companions with a terrible stroke to the head. Just beyond, a horse reared and struck out with its hooves, catching the next horse on its neck so that it crashed into the dust with an awful scream.

Further down the road, both our own knights and the attackers had stopped fighting, dropping weapons and even their reins to clutch at their eyes as their horses jostled.

"They are all—blind, Count," I gasped out, swaying in the saddle as the pain began to return. "Those who were right on top of us and thus looking directly—will have no sight for a day and a night—and will need a week or more to recover fully. Our own men and the ones who were fighting them—will recover in an hour or two."

"And what about that group up there?"

I looked toward where he was pointing and saw several more horsemen on the crest of the hill, all rubbing their eyes. The pain in my arm was growing more and more intense by the moment. Combined with the terrible weariness of doing far too much magic in a short time while deferring needed rest, it made me feel faint and ill. I fought to answer clearly. "They—may already begin to see again—like men who have looked full at the sun— but it will take a few minutes before they can see us well enough—to attack."

"Then we had best be far out of view before that happens," said the count grimly. He reached and swiftly tightened the ropes that still lashed me to my saddle, then caught up the lead from my horse and sent us galloping toward the hill opposite our enemies. As we left the road and hit the broken ground, a terrific flare of pain from my shoulder went through me, so that I fainted dead away and knew nothing more of either men or magic for a long time.

Chapter Eleven ~ Galoran

1

It had been two hours since I had heard any sign of pursuit. At first I thought we had gotten well away after Brother Melchior had blinded those trying to kill us. But just when I pulled up to examine his wounds I had seen distant horsemen silhouetted against the sky, coming over the ridge behind us. My own knights or the heretics? No time to wait and find out.

I urged our tired horses rapidly on, up a narrow, brush-choked gully away from the road, across rocky pasture lands where I kept us below the ridge line, down dry stream beds and along faint boulder-strewn tracks that even the old Master of Melchior's Order might have hesitated to follow in his search for solitude. We seemed finally to have lost our pursuers—as well as ourselves. And all the time the priest lay motionless across his horse's neck, and it crossed my mind to wonder if I was doing all this to save a man already dead.

But he was still breathing, though I didn't like the cold pallor of his skin, when I finally untied him and lowered him to the ground in the shelter of a grassy hollow among the rocks. I wrapped him in the horse blankets, knowing that before dark I had to get that arrow out of his arm. Otherwise by tomorrow the flesh would be starting to turn green, and he would lose the arm even if by some chance he did live.

I always kept a small field kit with me; an old soldier

knows you can never tell when you'll be separated from the baggage train. I found a spring among the rocks and built a fire to heat water, then cut the vestments away from his arm and shoulder while waiting for it to boil. This was going to hurt him like the very devil, but then he was unconscious already.

He had saved my life back there with his magic, and I was going to have to see if soldier skills that had pulled more than one warrior through over the years would also save a priest. If we made it back to Peyrefixade, I thought, buckling a strap tight around his arm above the spot where the arrow protruded, I hoped the archbishop would take our being ambushed and nearly killed by the heretics as sufficient indication that I was not a friend of theirs after all.

The arrow had penetrated deep enough that getting the barbed head out would be no easy matter, but not so deeply that I wanted to push it out the other side. I washed the area well with boiled water, passed the blade of my knife through the flame, and set to work.

It was a long process, and the pain must have reached him even in unconsciousness, for he moaned several times as I dug the barb out of his flesh. The wind rose as darkness approached, and I sang hymns to counter the wind's voice. The priest's blood rushed out, in spite of the strap, when I finally drew the arrow free, but the flow quickly dwindled to a trickle. Probably no severed arteries, then, I thought with grim satisfaction. I washed the area again and wrapped it as well as I could with the bandages from my kit. Even if he lived and saved the arm, he would always have an ugly scar.

Well, at least *his* scar would be hidden by his clothing, I thought, returning to the spring to try to wash some of his blood off me. At this point I had done virtually everything for him I could. The emperor's personal physician had carried poppy juice from the East, but I never had; it was too scarce and too expensive. I did have some powdered willow bark I could brew up into a potion that would help against pain and inflammation, but Melchior would have to be awake to drink it.

I examined his saddlebags, lying where I had thrown them when I pulled the saddle off his horse to get the blanket. He might have something in his own kit of powders that would help, but I was certainly not going to start rummaging around in there. The power of the magic that had blinded those attacking us still staggered me. In spite of an arm across my face and eyes tight shut, I had been dazzled by the white light which had seemed to pass right through bone and flesh.

Melchior also carried the conviare, the same one that had drawn the magical fire to my bed in Peyrefixade. It was sealed in lead marked with potent symbols, which he had assured me would muffle its powers, but I could not help but wonder if it had helped draw the heretics to us.

They *had* to have been heretics, in spite of their horses and swords that had made me momentarily think Prince Alfonso had decided to come after me at last. The Magian who had made them invisible, whom Melchior had felled, was highly unlikely to have been a member of the peaceful Order of the Three Kings, which left only the powerful heretical magic-workers of whom they had been telling me.

When I looked at him again the priest appeared to be resting slightly better, breathing deeply and steadily though with no sign of returning consciousness. The pain and loss of blood, coupled with the exhaustion that had already seized him as we came down from Conaigue, would make him sleep a very long time. But assuming he ever woke he would need food. A check of my own saddlebags revealed only a little bread and cheese, both rather dry, and a wrinkled apple left from the end of last autumn's harvest.

Well, a soldier knows how to live off the land, if not by

hunting—and I had neither bow nor hawk—then certainly by raiding local villages. Far off, lower down the mountain, I could see a spot of yellow glowing in the twilight as someone lit a fire or lantern.

So there was someone else, someone who might have food, within a few miles of here—unless I had spotted the camp of the heretics. Reminded of how far a light may be seen once the sun goes down, I doused the small fire I had built; the minuscule amount of heat it gave would have been swallowed up anyway by the cold mountain wind.

Now I just hoped I would be able to find Melchior again myself without the firelight as a beacon—and that he would still be alive when I returned. I had seen stronger men die from the shock of such a wound, and they hadn't already drained their bodies' strength by working powerful magic.

I went on foot because I didn't want to risk my horse stumbling in the dark, and because a stealthy approach was more likely to be successful. As I started down the mountain toward the distant light, my boots feeling their way on an almost invisible track, I wondered if I might possibly be back in my own county. The borders of my own lands, the duke's, the prince of Nabarra's, and those belonging to the Order of the Three Kings lay close together here, and after my desperate retreat I had no idea where we were. But if the light ahead was from the house of one of my tenants, I ought to be able to get food and help.

It was full night by the time I groped my way to the source of the firelight. The ankle I had strained falling from the damned tree during the duke's Paschal Court had begun to ache again. The moon cast a cold blue light that exaggerated the shadows while doing little to show the way. More than once, the noiseless shape of a hunting owl shot past me, and I heard the faint and quickly cut-off squeak of its prey. As I made out at last the shape of a cottage and outbuildings before me, the light inside went out.

I paused by a stone fence to consider. This was no cottage I recognized. As well as I could see in the moonlight the farmstead appeared fairly prosperous: a solid building of stone, the smell of farm animals, and a plowed field beyond doubtless planted in barley, all silent now except for the constant whisper of the wind. Could I trust whatever man or woman had just doused the light inside? Those who lived here were no tenants of mine, and might well be no one's tenants at all. Would they be just as likely to turn Melchior and me over to the heretics as to help us?

There was a sheepfold, redolent with fresh dung, but no sheep; they must have recently been driven even higher into the mountains for the summer's grazing. Well, I wasn't prepared to butcher a sheep single-handed anyway. And the sheep's absence meant that the strongest members of the household would also be gone, making my raid easier. I climbed the wall cautiously, careful to come down on my sound ankle, and started in search of a chicken coop.

From the cottage there abruptly came a loud barking. I froze, crouching below the wall, knife in my hand. A voice inside spoke in Auccitan. An old man's voice; the dog's bark too had been that of an old dog. The young people and young sheepdogs would all be up on the highest slopes along with the sheep.

I sensed more than saw someone at the doorway. I kept dead still, waiting, as the old man stood listening. The blood pounded in my ears, but I hoped no one could hear it but me. The dog growled as though to justify having barked. After a minute the man said something else, that might have been, *"There's no one here,"* and moved away from the door.

But I waited several more minutes before resuming a stealthy progress around the cottage. I grinned to myself as no further canine challenges came. An old dog slowly loses sensitivity of both hearing and smell; I hoped he had initially been startled into barking by something other than me.

At the back of the house I almost bumped into a low stone structure that turned out to be roofed steps leading down into a root cellar. I regained my balance and groped downward into an enclosed space smelling of dry earth, and discovered by touch the last of the turnips. With three of them in my pouch, I went back up into the moonlight and found the old man's garden patch. It was too early for most of the vegetables, but I located some young lettuces that should be ready; they joined the turnips.

Now for a chicken. I had saved the chicken coop for last, readily identifiable both by the smell and by the occasional sleepy cluck from within. In the flat moonlight I could see it was made of wooden slats, big enough for several birds. The door closed with a simple latch.

I started to reach for the latch, then stopped. Whoever this farmer might be, the duke's tenant or Prince Alfonso's or the Church's, I had no indication that he was sympathetic to the heretics, and he had done nothing to me that deserved such punishment as the loss of a hen. I had been, I thought bitterly, enjoying myself, outwitting an old man and an old dog even though I had had no luck this afternoon outwitting the heretics. A sorry spectacle the Count of Peyrefixade would make if discovered, stealing a chicken like a beggar who has twice been turned away without a scrap and decides to take his own dinner if it won't be freely given.

Well, if I wanted to pay this old man I had better do so before rather than after he set the dog on me. I took a coin from my belt—worth far more than a chicken and a few vegetables, but I didn't have any coppers small enough—and laid it on the chicken coop threshold. Then I carefully unhooked the latch and reached inside.

My hand found warm feathers. A startled flapping

stopped short as I reached in with the other hand and wrung the first chicken's neck.

But I had awakened the other birds. The rooster crowed a challenge, almost deafening at this close range in the quiet night. I shot away, vaulting over the wall with one hand, the other clutching the dead hen. Wild barking broke out in the cottage behind me and lamp light again glowed yellow.

I stumbled in landing but jumped up and ran as fast I could in the dim light away from the cottage. The door banged open, and the dog was after me. Old dog or not, he cleared the wall easily and ran far faster than I could go, barking loudly in the triumphant knowledge that he had been right about an intruder the whole time.

I spun around and landed a solid kick in his chest as he leaped at me. The pain from the ankle shot up my leg, but he tumbled backwards from the impact and took a moment to rise again. I put a few more yards between me and the cottage before he ran snarling at me again, again to meet my boot.

The lantern light had reached the chicken coop, and I heard a surprised shout. The man had found my payment. The shout went promptly still—he was doubtless biting the coin to see if it was genuine. But the old dog took this as a command to return. He had never been a large dog, and he was not at all happy about being kicked twice. But as he retreated toward the cottage he kept up a steady stream of barking, telling me exactly what he would have done to me if he had been five years younger and thirty pounds heavier. I stumbled rapidly away through the night, clutching the spoils of my raid and grinning.

For the first half mile I kept expecting pursuit, but no one followed me. I dropped down to a walk, limping now on my newly strained ankle. As I pressed onward up the mountain I found myself going slower and slower. I thought I had noted the way well in coming down, but the moon was now low in the sky, and all the stones and stunted trees looked different when seen from another angle. Several times I convinced myself that I had lost my way completely and would not find the priest before daylight, if at all. In my exhaustion the rocks between which I threaded my way kept appearing with the shape of the castle of Peyrefixade, until I wasn't sure if I was trying to find where I had left him or trying to find home.

But after what seemed endless hours I heard the stamping of a horse and stumbled into the hollow by the spring. The last of the moonlight made Melchior's face colorless, but his chest still rose and fell steadily. Fighting an almost overwhelming desire for sleep, I wrapped my cloak around me against the chill of the darkest part of the night, relit the fire, and started dressing the chicken by its flickering light.

I was half dozing, sitting with my back against a rock, when I heard his voice. My head jerked, and my eyes flew open to find a faint dawn light cutting through the mists that draped the mountain slopes. The priest's eyes were squeezed shut, and he was mumbling what sounded like a prayer through his teeth.

"Father Melchior," I said quietly, touching his uninjured arm. "Can you hear me?"

He opened his eyes and started to lift his head but fell back weakly. He looked around for a moment, taking in the rocks and the two tethered horses, then focused on me. "The attackers?"

"We outran them—thanks in large part to your magic."

"And your knights?"

I shook my head. "They were *supposed* to be protecting you and me. But the heretics didn't seem particularly interested in them. They were after the two of us, clearly, and they captured the pack horses—took Seneschal Guilhem with them when they went." I spat into the dirt. "I thought if I had him along I could keep an eye on him, and instead he led us straight into ambush."

"Which we might have avoided if I had not been asleep," said Melchior in a small voice.

"You did plenty," I said, pushing myself to my feet. "But here. I've made you some chicken stew, and you should also drink some willow broth."

I had to hold him up, his head and shoulders cradled in my arm, while he drank broth and ate a little meat and turnips. He winced in pain when I shifted him but did not cry out. Fortunately he did not ask where I had procured a chicken.

"Unless the heretics want the war against them to start up again," I said with the most confidence I could muster, "I expect there will be a message from them shortly after we're back in Peyrefixade, telling me the price for ransoming my knights."

Melchior was silent for several minutes after I laid him down again. The sun was fully up now, and in its light I felt hope that in a day or so the priest's wound would have healed enough that I could get him back to Peyrefixade. I rebandaged his arm; the hole out of which I had cut the arrow was ugly and raw, but no flesh had yet begun to turn green.

"We have to get word to my abbot," Melchior said, just as I thought he had fallen asleep again. "Everyone in the castle knew the workmen had found that conviare, and the seneschal must have told the Perfected about it. That's why they were so interested in capturing our luggage—and me."

"But they didn't get it. You saved it as well as saving us."

"That only gives us a short-term advantage. The masters of my Order had thought we had enough time to find the great battle telesma before the Perfected realized we too were looking for it—that's why they sent me back unaided, except by the knowledge they imparted to me while we were there." His voice was tinged with both pain and desperation. "But now that the seneschal has betrayed us, and the pupils of the third student of the old magus have bent their attention to finding the conviare, they will not rest until they find us—and, with the conviare in their hands, enter Peyrefixade."

"They won't get into the castle," I said, trying to reassure myself as well as him. "Peyrefixade could hold out against an army ten times as numerous as the defenders, and I doubt the heretics have many more warriors than those we saw yesterday. The only time the castle's ever been taken was back when the followers of the True Faith captured it from the heretics during the war, and then our side had royal forces from the north to help provide an overwhelming advantage, and the heretics' greatest magus had just died."

"I must get word to my abbot," he insisted again, "before the Perfected warriors find us. I have the strength for only a little magic, and I must notify him before all else." He made an unsuccessful attempt to sit up, then slumped back weakly. "You will have to help me. Bring me my saddlebags."

Not quite sure what he wanted, I brought him his luggage, handling it carefully. I didn't want to set off any powerful spells by mistake. My experiences with the conviare had made me very uneasy.

But the priest made me unpack all his bags and vials of powder and pouches of what might have been bark and could have been bone. My skin shivered to touch them, but I understood his urgency. I didn't like any better than he did the idea of the heretics, maybe made invisible again, quartering these mountains in search of us. Melchior seemed to know a way to warn his abbot of what had happened, and if the two of us were going to make it safely back to Peyrefixade we needed all the help we could get.

At his direction, I spread out a piece of parchment, weighted it at the corners with four rust-colored stones carved intricately with tiny lines and whorls, and finally found the right bag of powder. He had to peer into each one, mumbling, before he decided which to use. One which I opened, thinking it matched his description of what he wanted, he waved away with a wide-eyed look of horror. "No, no, not *that*!" I didn't dare ask what that particular powder would do.

Carefully I sprinkled the gray powder he finally selected onto the piece of parchment. In spite of the constant wind, the powder did not blow around but settled itself in whorled patterns. Would working magic here on the mountain slope alert the heretics to our presence?

Melchior propped himself up, wincing from the pain. "Would any of these other powders help your wound heal?" I ventured to ask. But he only waved me to silence, concentrating on the even distribution of the fine gray powder.

He finally began speaking, words I couldn't quite understand. The incantation seemed to take a long time. His face, which had started to take on a somewhat better color after a helmetful of chicken stew, grew slowly white again.

He finished at last, lying flat, his eyes half shut. "Help me," he said, so softly I could scarcely hear. "Help me up. I must write—"

I lifted him to a sitting position and tried to lift his uninjured arm out over the parchment, but he could not hold it up unassisted. After a moment he closed his eyes and whispered, "You must do it, Count. The graphic magic is prepared and awaits only the writing. Write in the powder. Tell them—"

I waited a minute, but he did not continue. Glancing at his still, pale face I saw that he was no longer conscious. Tiredness made me so lightheaded it was hard to concentrate. I looked at the parchment sprinkled with powder and took a deep breath. How was I supposed to write? And what would I say?

The wind strengthened slightly, and a few grains of gray

powder rose and whirled away. If Melchior's spell had alerted the heretics' Magian, he might already be casting spells of his own to make our magic ineffective. I had better work fast. The thought flitted through my mind that in working magic without all the spiritual training members of the Order of the Three Kings underwent, I might be imperiling my own immortal soul, but I pushed the thought aside. My first responsibility now was to the priest wounded in serving me. With another deep breath I leaned over the parchment and, using my finger, began to write.

"The Perfected know that we have the conviare. They ambushed us and although they did not capture it, Brother Melchior is badly wounded. We are hiding somewhere in the mountains and will try to reach Peyrefixade when we can." I signed it "Galoran" with a flourish—I wasn't going to attempt to recreate my monogram.

As I finished a stronger gust of wind reached us, and all the gray powder rose together in a funnel-shaped cloud. It skittered across the ground and between the rocks, flew upwards, then slowly rained tiny dark grains down on us. A few fell on the parchment but now just lay as ordinary dust, with none of the whorls of a moment ago.

I had no idea if I had succeeded. I scooped the parchment, the rust-colored stones, and all the bags of powder back into Melchior's saddlebags, wrapped my cloak around me, and fell asleep beside him.

Afternoon sun woke me. I rolled over, stiff and aching, checked first to be sure Melchior was still breathing, then sat up to look down the mountainside. There was no sign of Magians from the Order of the Three Kings coming to rescue us, but then there was also no sign of heretic warriors coming to finish us off. I moved my shoulders back and forth, working out the knots, and put a hand on my sword hilt. If the heretics came they would find out that cold steel can be effective even against those who wrongfully imagine they have the approval of God.

I stood up, feeling restless and impatient. My ankle hurt, but I made myself put weight on it. I had no desire to wait here until the heretics showed up—or, even worse, decided that as long as I was out of Peyrefixade this would be the perfect time to assault it. Even that castle might prove vulnerable with a powerful magic-worker at the gates and none inside defending it. I contemplated trying to move Melchior, tied to the saddle again or perhaps in some sort of improvised litter suspended between our horses, but could think of no way of doing so without reopening his wound. Yesterday, with the arrow still in him, he had bled very little; today he could bleed to death long before we reached Peyrefixade.

Although I tried to be quiet, the sound of my pacing must have awakened him, for when I glanced down his eyes were open. I squatted beside him. "Feeling better?" I asked with an effort at cheerfulness.

His lids drooped and lifted again. I could tell he was trying to say that he was but couldn't quite manage it. Agony was printed all over his face; I had seen it too often not to recognize the signs. He might be a priest, but he was as brave against physical pain as any warrior. For a minute his lips moved in prayer, then he spoke at last. "My grandfather's telesma. It should still be inside my cassock, close to my breast."

I found it, trying not to jostle him, and put it into his hand. The white shaft, cut deeply with diagonal lines and carved with the image of the Watercarrier, seemed to burn against my skin.

He moved it slowly until its tip touched the bandage on his upper arm, now dark with crusted blood. He winced but spoke clearly, the words of an incantation coming out one at a time with long pauses in between. I surreptitiously rubbed the palm of my hand on the ground.

Then there was silence while I looked off across the mountain again. The mist was long gone, and I spotted a thread of smoke that must come from the old man's cottage. Melchior spoke at last, and his voice sounded almost normal.

"I fear I have now exhausted all the magic lines I built up so carefully in this telesma. The effort has left me as helpless as a newborn kitten, but without the pain my mind seems clear again."

I brought him water and helped him drink; his limbs flopped as loosely as though there was no bone inside his skin. "I wrote in the powder on the parchment," I told him, "saying that we had been ambushed and needed help but that the conviare was still safe. I couldn't tell your abbot where we were because I don't know myself—will he be able to trace the message back to us?"

"He will not be able to tell from whence the message was sent," Melchior answered quietly, only his lips moving as he spoke. "But there is an ivory tablet always kept in readiness at the abbey, and when a message is sent with the correct spells, the dust on that tablet shapes itself as though an invisible finger wrote. The abbot will then notify the priory of our Order in the duke's city of Ferignan, in the same way."

Although I would have preferred not to have the duke know that I had been ambushed by heretics, losing my baggage, all my knights, and nearly my *capellanus,* having Duke Argave come looking for us would at least mean help was on the way.

"Thank you for assisting me in my spells," Melchior said gravely. "If you followed my instructions strictly, no harm should have come to your body—or your soul." I did not answer, having had no idea I was so transparent.

There was of course always the possibility that my sending of the message had been flawed, that there was some additional incantation that should have been said but hadn't been because I didn't know it and Melchior had fainted, but I didn't mention that. I also didn't mention food, but the priest and I had finished the chicken stew between us, and I had eaten what little else remained in my saddlebags. My desire to face the old man's dog again was markedly low.

Melchior didn't say anything more about the pain in his arm, but I began to wonder if it might indicate a deep infection beginning to spread. And how long would the magical effects of his grandfather's telesma last, before that deep pain broke through into his consciousness again?

But at the moment he appeared to be thinking hard. He couldn't move but he wanted to talk. "What has it been, Count, perhaps twenty-four hours since the warriors attacked?"

"Something like that." I sat beside him, trying to act as though this was a perfectly normal conversation, that we had decided for excellent reasons to be resting here among the long shadows of the rocks, miles from anyone except for one man too aged to go up any more to the high summer pastures with the sheep.

"That they have not found us in that time indicates they may not be looking very thoroughly. Having captured the rest of our party and knowing me wounded, they may feel that you are for now safely out of the way. They may thus be on their way to besiege Peyrefixade."

I tapped my fingers on my sword hilt, not liking this idea any better coming from him than from my own thoughts. Getting home safely to Peyrefixade would be complicated by coming up the hill to find Perfected attackers encamped around it. "But I thought the masters of your Order had decided that the heretics wanted the conviare, that their whole purpose in getting into Peyrefixade—and incidentally killing me—was to use the conviare to search for the great battle telesma their old magus hid there."

"If they have the lesser battle telesma, they may believe that that will be enough. As indeed in skilled hands it may be." Then he added, more loudly than he had spoken yet—almost, I thought, as though trying to persuade himself—"But we must trust in the Lord, Who shall provide for us."

He then fell silent, leaving me to turn over the possibility that after years during which followers of the True Faith had imagined that heresy was made rare if not indeed extinct, outside of one stretch of mountainous territory, the Perfected might rise again, with all the magical strength they had wielded during the great war of two generations ago. And if this time they were led by someone without the overweening pride of the old magus of whom I had learned in the abbey, someone better able to calculate how to defeat the unprepared defenders of the Faith—

"This lesser battle telesma," I said at last. "I understood it was preserved by one of the pupils of the last magus and went with him into hiding. But do you have any idea what happened to the rest of his pupils?"

"According to Brother Endaris, the Spector General of our Order, there were three pupils, only one of whom went into hiding with the remnants of the Perfected at the end of the war. Of the other two, he said that one repented and returned to the True Faith, and one clung to but attempted to hide his Perfected doctrine, living among the faithful until the Inquisition finally uncovered him. I have been thinking over what Brother Endaris told us, his vivid information on the last moments of the life of the great magus, and have concluded that the first pupil, the one who renounced the devil's pernicious doctrines, was Brother Endaris himself."

My first thought was that I had been right all along in my uneasy feeling that the Order of the Three Kings might be a disguised form of heresy. But I ought to have known better. Someone truly repentant should be treated as a lost sheep, welcomed back into the flock. "And the other pupil, the one who would not renounce his beliefs?"

Melchior did not answer at once, and when he did his voice was so low I had to bend toward him to hear. "That man— I believe he was my grandfather."

I glanced toward the priest's saddlebags. His grandfather had taught Melchior the first rudiments of magic, had given him the protective telesma he still carried, and had been burned to death for refusing to renounce his heretical beliefs. Even though the heretics had wounded Melchior, if they came now, reminding him of his grandfather's loyalty to their perverted faith, promising to use their magical arts to restore his wound, would he feel compelled to give them the conviare his grandfather had helped conceal in Peyrefixade?

At once I felt ashamed of the thought. I bustled around our camp for a moment, saying I would try to make him more comfortable, though there was little I could do besides bringing him a drink of water and praying that he did not ask for food.

As I lowered him back down after helping him drink, he suddenly fixed me with his eyes. "They are coming."

I let him down the last few inches faster than I intended and ran to the edge of the stony hollow, my sword already out. "Who is it, Magians of your Order? The duke's men?" I spoke hopefully, but I already knew.

"I can see them with my second eye," he said, sounding weaker, as though this new effort of magic was drawing out what little strength he still had. "Coming from the south. Three of the men who attacked us yesterday."

I could see them now myself, tiny figures several miles away, down in the valley. "They may not even think to look for us here," I said, trying to be encouraging and not feeling at all encouraged. These must have been among those furthest from us when the priest unleashed his terrible light. "Do they have their Magian with them?"

"Not the Magian," said Melchior softly, "nor their leader." The bare-headed man who had directed the knights yesterday had been, I thought, the same man who had appeared so abruptly before me on my way back from meeting Prince Alfonso. He had warned me about a traitor, but then had cheerfully used that traitor for his own purposes. I now regretted bitterly not seizing him and turning him over to the Inquisition.

"Take the conviare, Count, and go," said Melchior weakly. "The life of a wounded priest is not worth the—"

But I cut him off with a rude sound I probably shouldn't have made to my *capellanus*. I hadn't gone to all this effort to keep him alive just to abandon him now.

"If the Magian isn't with them," I said, still trying to sound encouraging, "chances are they will never spot us up here anyway." But the most likely explanation was that the leader and his chief magic-worker were even now laying siege to Peyrefixade, having delegated a few knights to track us down in the meantime. For a horrible moment I wondered if Seneschal Guilhem might try to get the heretics into the castle by passing them off as friends of mine, but Bouteillier Raymbaud would never allow in a strange band of armed men, no matter how convincingly the seneschal vouched for them.

"I think—" Melchior hesitated. "I think they have been equipped with a finding knife by their Magian. I know it."

"And I've been armed with steel," I said shortly. No use then in waiting. An excuse for action at last was welcome. I saddled my horse and pulled on my helmet— still smelling faintly of chicken. Best to meet them far away from Melchior and the conviare.

2

Tracking spell or not, they didn't spot me at once. I circled around, trying to find a way to approach them without being silhouetted against the sky. And then I remembered Melchior following the assassin in the duke's city and realized they must be following the traces of our passage up the mountain. If I didn't stop them, they would be led by the magically enhanced imprint of our horses' hooves straight to where Melchior lay in hiding.

But this also meant I knew the exact route they would

follow. There was one particularly steep slope we had ascended yesterday, with a group of stunted evergreens at the top. I worked around to the spot and pulled my horse up there to wait. If they could ambush us, I could ambush them.

I waited half an hour, listening to the sigh of the wind in the trees above me and wishing I had a bow. All knights agree that a bow is a coward's weapon in war, and all armies march with a contingent of archers anyway. My horse stamped and shook his bridle, but I stilled him with a hand on his neck. After a while I could hear the heretics' approach, the chink of horseshoes on stone, the rattle of harness, and a few exchanged words.

The first rider's head came up over the edge, and I charged.

He was taken totally by surprise. When I rushed at him, screaming the imperial battle cry, he barely had time to swing up his shield before I was on him. He blocked my first stroke and had his sword out by the time I whirled my horse around for a second, but I deflected his own stroke easily and drove in straight and unswerving to the neck.

But as I wrenched my bloody sword out of his body, the other two knights came at me from either side.

They might not have been trained in the emperor's army, but someone had drilled them well in fighting: two men on foot fight back to back, but two mounted men separate to try to trap their enemy between them.

I spun my horse around to dodge one sword while knocking away the other's stroke with my shield. My horse screamed and kicked out as the sword point grazed him. The kick almost jolted me from the saddle, but I heard the dull and satisfying thud of hooves landing against the side of one of the others' horses.

With that rider momentarily out of the fight, I rained blows on the other, but the advantage of surprise was gone now, and he defended himself well, not risking an attack but waiting for his companion to come at me again from the rear.

That is, until I paused for a second to glance backwards. Then his blade flashed out. I just managed to catch the blow on my shield, but it ricocheted from the bosses and sliced into my leg.

For one second I felt nothing at all. Then the cut began to burn like hellfire. My only advantage was that it took him a moment to draw back his bloody sword, during which moment his shield was swung wide. And during that moment my own sword bit deep and true.

And I jerked my blade free just too late to whirl to face the other heretic warrior.

But he stopped short in the middle of aiming steel at me. He cut off his war cry in the middle, his sword raised but the blow not coming. For a second he looked wildly around as though he could not see me. And in that second I charged.

Whatever blindness had seized him passed off almost immediately. He saw me all right, and his eyes widened as he swung his shield, just in time, in front of him. The second blow he deflected as well, but it was not for nothing that I had spent years fighting in the imperial army. In spite of my wounded leg, when I faced only one enemy I was more than a match for him. A tiny miscalculation on his part, an overly enthusiastic swing of his sword, and I had him. In another second he lay on the ground with the other two heretics, his throat gurgling as he died.

My chest rose and fell in great breaths, and I began trembling all over as the battle rage left me. I started to wipe the sweat from my forehead with one sleeve, then realized it was soaked in blood.

I managed to capture one of the three horses, but the other two galloped away riderless down the mountain. I let them go, suddenly too tired to bother. Black spots floated for a moment before my eyes, but I blinked until I could see clearly again. My leg was bleeding hard, and if I lost consciousness now I would die before regaining it. I used a harness strap from the captured horse to make a tourniquet around my leg, managed with gritted teeth to maneuver myself back into the saddle, and turned to ride up the mountain, leading the heretic's steed.

A caw came from the top of the stunted evergreens, and I looked up to see two ravens—drawn by the scent of blood. Just waiting, I thought, for me to be gone. Far up, almost invisible, I could see other great birds beginning slowly to circle and circle.

One of the three heretics lay with his dead face turned toward me and his eyes open, seeming to stare accusingly. Heretics or not, I didn't like to leave any enemy unburied for the carrion-eaters to find. But if I took the time and effort to try to dig a grave in this stony soil I might as well climb in myself.

I did not look back to see the ravens come flapping down from the branches. It had almost been me lying there instead. If it had not been for the third heretic's moment of hesitation, he would have had his sword in me before I could react. Had that, I wondered, been Melchior's magic? The heretics' Magian yesterday had made his warriors invisible, and Melchior, watching the fight with what he called his second eye, might have briefly been able to cast a spell that hid me in the same way. But at what price would that magic-working have come, even a brief second's magic-working, with him already so weak?

As my horse picked his way up the mountain I kept hoping that my leg would grow numb. But the pain only became stronger. Well, I told myself grimly, I had been limping on that leg already—only now the limp would be permanent.

I tried to distract myself by thinking about the dead warriors. They seemed very different from the rather scruffy heretics I had found hiding in the village of Three Cuckoos at the border of Nabarra. Did they perhaps live more openly in that principality, practicing their fighting with the compliance of Prince Alfonso, in spite of all his protestations about his hatred of heretics?

Wondering about the heretics' organization was doing nothing to make me forget the pain. Red lines like giant spiderwebs kept dancing across my vision. Several times I found myself imagining that the young Duchess Arsendis rode before me up the track, smiling over her shoulder and beckoning. I mumbled prayers, probably not what Father Melchior would have counseled, but a soldier's prayer: "Lord, let me live. If I don't live, Lord, let me die quickly. And forgive my sins—I can't remember them all, beyond killing three men just now, but You know them and know how much I need forgiveness."

The evening mists were rising from the valleys as my horse made his way up the final slope toward the sheltered hollow where Melchior lay. I was swaying in the saddle, staying conscious by sheer will, and might have gone right past the place had not the priest's tethered horse heard us and whinnied.

Father Melchior himself lay still and white in the dim light. But his rapid, shallow breathing showed that his magic-working had not finished him yet. I washed myself off with water from the spring, not wanting the ravens to be attracted next by me; probably I should have boiled the water, but I was too weary to care. The gash looked ugly and ragged from what I could see, but I didn't look at it very closely. At least the flow of blood had mostly stopped. I found the last of my bandages, that I had been intending to use on the priest, and bound up the wound. Then I loosened the tourniquet, lay down next to Melchior, my cloak over both of us, and let unconsciousness claim me at last.

Sleep brought solace and forgetfulness, but when I awoke, just before dawn, all the pain was waiting for me. I clenched my jaw to keep from crying out and looked toward Brother Melchior. He slept peacefully. His color had somewhat improved, I tried to persuade myself, thinking that I had done a much better job doctoring him than I had done on me.

I forced myself up, feeling the scabs ripping free at the slightest motion, and found my wounded leg would bear no weight at all. But I managed to hop to the spring for a drink, then belatedly thought to look in the dead heretic's saddlebag for food. All I found was stale bread, but I broke off some and devoured it ravenously, forcing myself to save the rest for Melchior.

My forehead was beaded with sweat and my limbs trembling as I stretched out next to him again on the stony ground. We were both still alive, I told myself determinedly, and we had three horses between us. Now all we had to do was find our way back to Peyrefixade. In Peyrefixade we would be safe.

I slept again, but now evil dreams stalked me. It was not Arsendis who beckoned me now, but heretics with faces like demons who swelled to enormous size, threatening to engulf me when I tried to stare them down. Again and again bloody swords lashed out at me, swords dripping with my own blood, and when I tried to fight back there was no strength in my arms. And then I realized that my opponents were already dead but fighting anyway. At the edge of my dreams was a constant muttering, which, when I briefly woke to roll over and try to pull my cloak closer against the chill, I knew was the wind, but which became a voice as soon as I settled down again, telling me enormously complicated things I was supposed to remember and ponder, but which I did not even understand. Through all my dreams floated the image of Peyrefixade, the red thumb of its great tower thrust against the sky, both repellent and inviting, but always impossibly distant.

At one point I came awake to find Melchior sitting up beside me. "You're not supposed to be moving," I told him, thickly but loudly. "If the infection spreads to your brain you'll go mad and die." He looked at me in concerned pity, and I took the warmth of that look back with me into nightmare.

Later, much later, I awoke with a strange sense of well-being. My muscles all ached and my leg was a dull throb, but I had the sensation of having slept, truly slept without dreams, for a long time. The sun sparkled in the eastern sky, but I realized it must have been at least a day since I had last been fully conscious. For a minute I lay without moving, relishing the almost euphoric sense of peace yet knowing that soon I would have to examine whatever hash the heretics and I between us had made of my leg. Then my nose caught a faint whiff of something familiar. Frying eggs?

I rolled over and tried to focus. On a piece of cloth lay a pile of barley cakes and three sheep's-milk cheeses. Beyond the cloth a small fire burned, and Brother Melchior sat beside it, frying eggs on a hot stone.

This made no sense at all. I pushed myself to a sitting position. He turned and smiled. "There's water beside you in the helmet if you'd like a drink. The eggs are almost ready."

I sat quietly, trying to sort out what had really happened and what had been nightmare. The priest's shoulder was bandaged rather sloppily with a tattered strip of blue cloth, not the bandage I had last tied there. It looked as if he had tried to do it himself one-handed. A glance at my leg showed a similar if much tidier blue bandage.

With eggs and barley cakes in my mouth I slowly began to revive. "We're both alive," I said. Establish the key point first. Good thing my prayers had been answered; I really needed to recall and repent of all my sins if I had any hope of divine mercy. And I had not looked forward to entering Hell where the three heretics I had just killed would be waiting for me.

"I hope you will forgive me, Count," said Melchior, "that I attended to my own needs before yours." Because I had no idea what he was talking about I made an affirmative sound through another mouthful of food. "But I feared that if I did not treat myself first I would not have the strength for the necessary magic to treat you."

"I've been treated with magic?" I looked at my leg in horror. But it really did feel better under the bandage than I had any right to expect.

"Yesterday, when I awoke with just about enough strength to crawl to my saddlebags, I determined I would be able to work one small spell, and that that spell must be the one to activate a strengthening draught for me. I believe I may have fainted on the spot from the effort of working that spell, but with the draught inside me I found my powers slowly returning. That is when I took out the powders that act against infection. I used them on my own arm, and then began the much more wearying work of practicing healing magic on another."

"And what does this powder against infection do?" I had finished the eggs and started on the cheese. He still hadn't said where the food had come from.

"It fights, of course, against the decay of flesh in a living man."

I thought this over, while resolutely pushing the last of the barley cakes toward him. Only then did I admit to myself what I had feared most of all, living but losing the leg, so that Count Scar would also become the one-legged count. "If the emperor knew of your Order's powers, he would have a Magian accompany all his armies."

"It would not be that simple. To heal another, even one person, may temporarily take all a man's strength." Although he was sitting up, I noted that he still appeared extremely tired, and he had been eating much more slowly than I. "The aftermath of a battle would exhaust all a Magian's powers long before he had advanced far down the ranks of the wounded. That is why, Count, I had to delay in treating you, even fearing that delay might be fatal, until I was at least somewhat recovered myself."

"Maybe if the emperor had a whole brigade of Magians—" I mused.

"There is the danger, of course," and for a moment he gave me what might have been a look of amusement, "that the emperor would not like it if 'his' brigade of Magians started healing the wounded on both sides."

Remembering the dead heretics, I wondered if Melchior would have felt compelled to try his magical arts on *them*. I would have to ask him to shrive me for their deaths. "I guess all your magic works to heal or to defend rather than bring active harm," I suggested, "and while the damnable Perfected may study battle magic, the Magians of the Order of the Three Kings learn at most how to distract an enemy or ward off a blow."

"Oh, no, Count," he said, looking very serious. "We *learn* all of magic, even if we do not practice the most terrible sorts unless it is absolutely necessary. I know the same spells to overthrow and destroy as the Perfected do. My own knowledge of these terrible matters is so far only theoretical, beyond the bits of magic I worked the other day and the brief sending that clouded the eyes of your last opponent. I do not have anything like the skill and ability of the great old magus who once commanded the Perfected in your castle. He gloried in using such powers, while I always pray that I shall be spared their necessity, but my training is the same as his."

We both fell silent a moment. Small birds, not ravens, darted among the rocks, singing in the morning sun. "I gather that this is one of the Perfected's horses?" he asked then. Since he had clearly been watching my battle with his "second eye" he must have known I had killed at least two heretics, and when I returned alive he would have known that I had also overcome the third, even if he had fainted right after dazzling the fellow. "There was a tunic in the saddlebag which I ripped up to make us bandages."

"And did you create magical food out of his bag as well? All I found in it was the remains of a loaf."

He smiled and shook his head. "Magic cannot *create*. The food I bought from a sheep farmer a little way down the mountain. I saw his smoke early this morning, and since you appeared to be resting peacefully I took a chance by leaving you and riding down there—tricky, riding with only one hand! While I was out I also performed the incantations that would hide our tracks if any more Perfected came after us—or the farmer proved to be an enemy. The dog at the farm was quite fierce, not at all impressed by a priest's vestments, but the old farmer himself proved as good a son of the True Faith as you are likely to find up in these mountains. He was quite happy to sell me eggs, cheese, and barley cakes—I hope you do not mind, Count, that I took the money from your belt pouch. But he seemed very suspicious about me at first and kept asking if I had already tried to buy some chickens the other night! Poor old man; living alone all summer long may allow his fancies to take more solid form than they otherwise would."

I decided to tell him the story of my chicken raid another time. "Thank you, Father Melchior," I said, leaning back and enjoying the warmth of the sun. "By my calculations you've saved my life at least three times since we buried Bruno. It looks as if the heretics won't find us now, so as soon as we've both recovered a little more strength, we can ride home to Peyrefixade. Maybe by then some of the knights will also have made their way back, and we can plan how to ransom the rest and get started on finding that great telesma your Order wants so badly."

It was two more days before we both felt strong enough to start toward home. I let the priest handle the purchase of additional food. My leg was healing now without infection, but the heretic's sword had severed muscle. Would Arsendis ever be interested, I wondered, in a cripple? The answer kept coming back negative no matter how I phrased it. The name of Count Scar actually sounded rather appealing when compared to Count Stumblefoot.

It took a day of riding just to find a road we recognized again, and it was late in the second day when we reached the bottom of Peyrefixade's mountain and looked up to see the watchfires of besiegers camped all around it.

My heart sank. What I had feared then was true: the heretics had come straight from ambushing us to the castle. "Well, Father Melchior," I said grimly, "it looks like we won't be home to good food and a hot bath as soon as we hoped. We'd better head toward the duke's city to see if he'll put us up, and incidentally ask him for some knights to help us attack these heretics from the rear."

But the priest had been staring up the mountain with an absorbed, faraway expression. "Those are not the heretics besieging your castle, Count. Those *are* the duke's knights."

Which could only mean the heretics were already inside.

Chapter Twelve ~ Melchior

1

I had been filled with unease as we rode up the steep track to the tightly shut gates of Peyrefixade in the early light, and it was proving to have been well justified. Count Galoran and the duke had been like two dogs circling each other from the moment we'd entered the siege-camp the night before, and this parley with the occupiers of Peyrefixade was doing nothing to ease the tension between them. Only the slim, handsome man not far from Count Galoran's age who stood looking down upon us from the wall, with two Perfected Magians standing at his side, seemed to be enjoying the situation.

"Ah, Count, I fear circumstances dictate that I must decline to return control of this castle to you at present. But do allow me to congratulate you and your Magian-priest for having managed to survive both the mountain nights and the weapons of the men who were sent after you." Seeing him now, with the duke at our side, I was amazed I had not realized who he had to be, the day he'd appeared before us so unexpectedly as we returned from meeting Prince Alfonso. Much of the duke showed in the sharp curve of his nose and the arc of his black fine brows—and something of the Lady Arsendis's ironic humor in his eye and voice. Once these had been noted, there could be no doubt this was the duke's son Gavain. Glancing sideways, I saw the duke gazing up at his son with a face that showed both fury and deep sorrow.

247

"The devil take you and your congratulations!" Count Galoran roared back. "I again call upon you to yield up my castle, which you have gained only through a stratagem fully worthy of a heretic and a traitor! How dare you appear upon my wall and speak to me with my own clothing on your back!"

"What, do you not think your raiment becomes me, Count?" Even without use of the second eye, it was easy enough to see Gavain's devilish smile as he stretched out one arm to display the fine broad sleeve of Count Galoran's best doublet, pillaged from our stolen baggage along with his good cloak. "The style is a bit drab for my taste, I own, but the fabric and needlework would do credit to any gentleman. Moreover, I have good evidence that it renders me your very mirror. With this upon my back, the hood of your cloak drawn up about my face, and my fellows riding behind in the evening gloom arrayed in the excellent armor and cloaks your captured knights had so graciously 'lent' them, I had no trouble convincing the sentries upon your formidable gates to admit us to this excellent castle. Nevertheless, I shall wear these borrowed plumes no more now that I find we shall have the unexpected pleasure of your company after all. I have no wish to offend so redoubtable a warrior and gentleman unnecessarily."

As a canon and priest, I could never set down precisely what Count Galoran replied. But the duke's son only laughed. "Ah, it is always so pleasant to bandy courtly witticisms with another gentleman! But you must excuse me now; I have business to which I really must attend. There seems to be at least the possibility that I and my companions shall have to remain here for some time under conditions of siege, and I must look to our supplies and defenses."

As Count Galoran and the duke rode just ahead of me down the steep track from the gates of Peyrefixade, I could see the flesh pull tight around the count's scar. "*Their* supplies! *Their* defenses!" he snarled. "The fellow sits inside my castle, eating my food, drinking my wine, wearing my clothes, then laughs at me from my own wall." He turned in the saddle to glare back up the hill. "I don't suppose there's any chance he'd think it another fine joke to have his archers put a few arrows into our backs as we ride down this road exposed like three roaches on a table?"

"Gavain would not do that, not to men who'd approached openly asking for a parley," the duke answered in an angry tone. "He may have been blinded to much that is good and right by these damned heretics, but he's still both a true knight and a gentleman." Despite the duke's fatherly confidence, I confess I kept the regard of my second eye fixed firmly on the battlements until we were safely back inside the duke's siege-camp.

"I tell you, we *must* find a way to dislodge the Perfected from Peyrefixade before they find the old Magus's great battle telesma!" the count bellowed to the council of war gathered under the duke's pavilion a little later, and struck his fist on the table.

"Do you imagine I don't understand that?" Duke Argave roared back. "My father fought in the great crusades against the Perfected alongside your own ancestors; he told me all about the terrible power of their Magians' magical creations. Why do you suppose my family and your own have always been the most generous patrons of the Order of the Three Kings? Why do you think I was so concerned that this castle in particular, the one nearest to their remaining territory up in the western mountains, be put under a strong master with one of the Order's best Magians at his side? Though it appears I may have erred in my choice. You showed poor judgment, Count. First in going from here at all when you knew yourself to be the target of magical attacks by the heretics, and more particularly in keeping in your service a Magian who appears incompetent to defend you from them. Had you been at your proper post within Peyrefixade, as your duty required, we would not now be facing this situation."

"I am your sworn vassal, duke, but I will not stand silent and hear you impeach Father Melchior, who has saved my life many times by his skill and nearly died for his trouble!" Count Galoran was glaring at Argave as no man facing his lord should, and I began to feel afraid of what might happen if this went on, gratifying though it might be that his first words had been in my defense. "As to my abandoning my place and duty, did I not dispatch a messenger well in advance, informing you that I intended to go from Peyrefixade to the House of the Magians to bury my faithful old companion Bruno? If you had reason to fear anything like this mad attack, why did you not warn me against going? Or failing that, why not send a troop of your own knights to guard the borderland roads? You certainly had far better reason than I to know what an audacious devil the heretics' war captain can be. Besides, did I not leave the castle in the care of the man *you* of all people would have thought most reliable?"

The duke started and glared at this, but the count ignored him and spoke on. "And what of your duty to me, your own sworn vassal? When Father Melchior and I lay hidden in the hills, badly wounded and menaced by heretics seeking our lives, I do not recall that any party of your soldiers came looking to aid us. Instead, we were abandoned to make our way back home however we could, arriving here last evening supposing we had reached safety at last only to find my castle in enemy hands, with you and your men camped comfortably in front of it, doing nothing."

"Nothing! Did I not ransom from my own purse all of your men who were being held within: both those captured holding back the heretics while *you* fled like a frightened rat, and also every man of the castle garrison except for— for the bouteillier, and the other two knights they insisted upon keeping as hostages? And you appeared to be fit enough when you rode in last night, except for a sore leg and a dirty cloak. How am I to know that you and your priest did not simply hide up there in the hills until you were certain I and my men had your castle securely encircled, with ample reinforcements on the way, before you showed yourselves?"

"Are you accusing me of cowardice, Duke?" the count shouted, his hand convulsively gripping the hilt of his sword.

Now thoroughly alarmed, I fixed my attention on Prior Belthesar, who stood by as Duke Argave's spiritual counselor just as I was the count's. I spoke into his second ear, "Prior—we must stop this!"

He pressed his lips together and gave a nod. I stepped forward, so did he, and we moved between the quarreling noblemen with hands upraised as the prior intoned, "Peace, my lords, peace. Your quarrel is not with one another. Divisions among us only serve the interests of those we must all oppose."

"Humph—well, I suppose you are right about that," the duke muttered after a tense silence. "It's a standoff for the moment, anyway; they can't get out and we can't get in. This council is adjourned until tonight, after supper. The additional men I've sent for should arrive by then."

I started after Count Galoran, but Prior Belthesar put his hand on my sleeve and told me to come with him. He led me to his own tent, which stood by itself in the meadow a little below the soldiers' camp, and had a novice bring out a pair of seats.

"That was a close thing, but all's safe for the moment," he said, ordering me to sit despite my protest that I should stand before him, and telling the novice to bring wine. "We'll need to keep alert to prevent more such trouble, though. It appears your count can be a dangerous man if pressed, and I know my duke is! And they're both close to the edge now. But enough of them for the moment. Tell me how you are feeling. I was very glad to see you and the count ride in last night; I'd been very worried ever since the duke's search party met me on the road and told me what had happened. You look better today, but still a little pale."

"I feel better, my father. A night on a camp bed under canvas might have seemed a hardship another time, but after what the count and I have been through it felt like luxury. I have a little pain in my shoulder, nothing more. I intend to begin restoring the magic lines of my grandfather's telesma today."

"Yes, I suppose you're up to that," he said after leaning close to look into my eyes. "But be careful not to overdo. You mustn't risk a bout of mage-sickness today; both the Order and your count will have need of you at your best before very long. This situation cannot be allowed to continue without decisive action, and that soon."

"What do you mean, Prior?"

"Several things come to mind, but the great battle telesma must be the chief concern for us of the Order. There is something you do not know yet that figures into this matter. Using such small skill as I do possess at divination, I have determined for certain that the Perfected have the lesser battle telesma inside the castle now, doubtless hoping to use the affinity that exists between the two as a means of locating its more powerful mate. But we, or rather you, hold the conviare that was wrought to unite and direct their power. Have you considered what might happen if the Perfected should succeed in obtaining the great telesma and tried to wield the joined potency of both against us without the mediation of the conviare?"

My hand went to the cross upon my breast when I grasped his meaning. "Why—that could produce a great surge of destructive magic—completely undirected—as bad for them as for us. It could lay waste to—I can't even calculate how far."

"If the destruction did not extend well beyond Ferignan, I for one should be quite surprised," said the prior with a grim nod.

"But surely the Perfected will understand the danger also?"

"Those bold young Magians they have with them may suppose that they can control the telesmas' power without the conviare. Who knows the quality of their training? It would not be the first time that magic-workers among the Perfected have shown over-much audacity, to the sorrow both of themselves and those about them. And there is always the possibility they might in fact succeed, also not an attractive thought."

"But how are we to prevent one of these things happening?"

"I fear that may require both you and your count to run even greater risks than you have faced thus far." He leaned back. "But the time to think of that is not yet. Right now, you had better get to work on your own telesma. But be sure to take some rest as well. You should recoup more of your strength before you essay any more hard magic in your count's service."

I walked about the camp for a little while after leaving the prior, and what I discovered worried me. It was obvious that the duke had carefully scattered the tents he'd given to Count Galoran's ransomed knights among those of his own men. Moreover, none of those tents were placed anywhere close to the one the count and I were sharing. Dispersing the forces sworn to another man among his own is hardly the way a lord treats a trusted vassal! Returning to the tent, I forced myself to put such worries aside for the moment and set to work with my grandfather's telesma. After my recent bout of intense training, the magic lines seemed almost to flow, and in less than an hour I found I had restored more than half of its power. But then a weariness overtook me so that I remembered the prior's words and went to lie down, and immediately dropped into a deep sleep that lasted several hours.

2

Awakening much restored, I immediately went looking for the count. I finally found him at one of the sentry posts, gazing toward his castle where it stood far up the hill. After thanking him formally for coming to my defense before the duke, I recounted what the prior had told me concerning the danger from the great telesma.

"That sounds very bad, Father Melchior," he replied in a flat and distant tone. "But you had better tell it to the duke. He's the only one in a position to do anything."

"Prior Belthesar will tell Duke Argave, I'm sure. My task is to help you and serve your interest."

"Then perhaps you ought to ask your Order for a new assignment. What point is there in serving a count without a castle?"

"We must find a way to recover your castle, that's all."

"And how are we to do that, Father Melchior? In my years on the northern borders, I saw many a larger castle than Peyrefixade but none more impregnable. The duke's son can well afford to have his jest at my expense; he's safe enough."

"The duke has sent for reinforcements, I understand."

"Yes, though I can't see what good they will do. Gavain could hold Peyrefixade with half the men he's got against ten times the number we have out here." He turned his back to the castle and pointed far down the valley road. "But look there, Father Melchior. I've been keeping watch on that cloud of dust for some time. What do you see with your second eye; is it the new troops coming?"

I concentrated. "It—yes, I can see a large party of knights. Many ride horses carrying the duke's livery."

"Ah, well, at least we can set up a proper siege encirclement now —you are not attending to me, Father Melchior; what else do you see? Is Lord Thierri by chance among them?"

I blinked my fleshly eyes and concentrated to be sure

I was in fact seeing clearly with my second ones. But there could be no doubt. "Yes, Count, Lord Thierri rides just behind the duke's captain of the guard. But that is not all. The Lady Arsendis is with them!"

If the count and I had been startled, the duke was amazed, and also far from pleased. We reached the lower edge of camp just as he stepped forth to meet the arriving party and saw his daughter and her handmaiden among them. "Arsendis!—what does this mean? This is a camp of war, no place for you or any lady!"

"I cannot agree, Father. It seems to me I can be nowhere else now." Lord Thierri offered her his hand and she slipped from her horse with easy grace, her bright scarlet cloak billowing. Spotting us, she smiled and said, "Ah, Count Galoran, you see I have come to visit you at last. I only wish I could have seen your castle the first time under somewhat better circumstances."

"And I fear it is not in my power to offer you the hospitality that is appropriate to such a lady," the count said with a stiff bow and a ghastly smile. "Even the tent that shelters my head is mine only by your good father's charity. I can only offer to surrender it at once if he now requires it for you. Excuse me now; I shall attend upon you again when you are settled." He gave another wooden bow, then turned and limped away while the duke glared and the lady gazed after him with a troubled face. I hurried to follow, but he went at such a pace despite his limp that I didn't catch up until he stopped near one of the picket posts well away from the duke's camp. When I spoke his name he rounded on me.

"What does she mean by coming here now, with Thierri riding at her side!?" The unscarred side of his face showed deep anguish, the scarred side looked like a mask from Hell. "Does she seek some kind of amusement at seeing me cast down, dispossessed, overthrown? Even if we do somehow regain Peyrefixade, I see scant indication her father will ever wish to place it in my hands again. Nor is he likely to encourage any further a union between me and his daughter. I had imagined her different from the heartless ladies one sometimes meets with at the emperor's court, women who derive their pleasure from turning hard fellows into soft fools."

"I cannot believe the Lady Arsendis feels any joy at witnessing your plight, Count."

"Let her not speak lightly of it, then. Tell her that, if you see her before I return to camp. I am going to inspect the other pickets."

I watched him limp off, then hurried back to the tents to seek the lady. As soon as she saw me standing before the duke's pavilion, she said, "Ah, Brother Melchior, I had so hoped you would come! Walk with me a little." As she led the way onto the meadow below the camp, I saw a pair of the duke's guardsmen fall in behind us, too far back to hear our words but close enough for protection should any threat to their lord's daughter appear.

"The situation here is full of danger, Brother Melchior. I had not realized how raw were the count's feelings. And I find now that my father is equally inflamed."

"It is true, my lady. They came within an eyelash of fighting each other just this morning." I told her about the travesty of a parley with her brother and how angry it had left both the count and the duke.

"Ah, my dear brother always has known how to place the pin of his words where it will sting the worst. And you men can be such fools!—priests excepted, of course. A phrase ill spoken, a jab to someone's delicate sense of honor, a defeat some fellow feels he cannot brook, and before one can prevent it the swords are out and something irretrievable has been done. When I was rather younger, I did not understand how much delicacy may be required in dealing with men, and provoked more than one fatal incident when merely seeking a little amusement at the expense of one or another of my dimmer suitors. My father and the count are both full of rage, but neither can strike out at the things that really trouble him. Do you see that?"

"I can understand Count Galoran's difficulty well enough," I told her. "From the first moment I met him, all his thoughts and energies have been fixed on making a success of his position as Count of Peyrefixade. To be dispossessed like this, with no evident course of action he can take to put things right, must be terrible."

She nodded her graceful head. "And my father's situation is no better. He is faced with an invading force of the heretics he despises. They have seized a castle dependent upon him, something no duke could tolerate. But their captain is the son—and the brother—neither of us has quite learned to hate despite all that has happened in the past. If Father were able, he would simply settle in for a long siege and wait until their supplies ran low, then offer terms allowing them to depart if they would yield the castle without a fight. That would be the customary strategy when a commander with far superior numbers faces a foe holding an unbreakable castle, but he cannot use it here. Even if we put aside the danger of this great telesma I've now been told of, my father has the Inquisition to worry about."

"The Inquisition!"

"Certainly, the Inquisition." She gazed at the castle high above us, then down along the valley road running toward her father's city. "They have ears almost everywhere, you know, probably even within your Order and certainly in my father's court. He had no alternative but to send word of this incursion to Haulbé, unless he wished to fall under suspicion himself as soon as the report of it reached them anyway. Of course, Father very shrewdly sent that message to my uncle the archbishop rather than directly to the Inquisition."

"But surely he did not think—?"

"Oh no; he did not do it in hopes of any favor. Uncle is very strict about doing *all* of his duty as a bishop. Indeed, he considers my brother dead to the family, and would show no hesitation about destroying him should he have the opportunity. But he is highly jealous of his position as the highest churchman of the region, and on that account is no friend to the Inquisition. He will not inform the chief inquisitor of what has occurred until he has mobilized his own knights and is fully ready to set forth. That will gain us an extra day, perhaps. But when Uncle does march here with his soldiers, you may be sure the Inquisition will ride with him. Once inquisitors are on this spot, the only possible fate for any man who is with the heretics in Peyrefixade will be death by the sword or death by fire. The Inquisition would never allow any of them to escape after such a daring strike into what they have so long claimed as completely secure territory. You may also be sure the Chief Inquisitor will send for Prince Alfonso to rally to their banner at this place with his army, simply on the chance my father might think of daring to defy them. And if the prince joins the siege, he will certainly allow no end other than the destruction of every man of the Perfected within Peyrefixade—and the castle in his own hands, if he can manage it."

Prior Belthesar had hinted there were dangers other than the great telesma; now I understood what he had meant. "But surely your father is right, my lady—you should not be here."

"Ah, but I must. I have to witness whatever happens for myself." Her eyes flashed now with both anger and tears and all her air of amused aristocratic detachment had fled. "The only men I care anything at all about are facing one another here, and I cannot imagine how this can end without the destruction of some or all of them. I see no possibility of Count Galoran's being restored to both possession of his castle and my father's good will, of my father's escaping the awful necessity of making war upon his own son, and of my brother's being allowed to leave here alive, with the hope that he may yet learn to reject the heretic doctrine and return to the family and station that should be his. But if it ends otherwise, what then? Suppose my father decides to cast off Count Galoran and deliver Peyrefixade back into the hands of Lord Thierri? On the other hand, how could I either continue living with my father or wish even to look Count Galoran in the face if the two of them had united to overthrow my own brother and deliver him to the flames? Or supposing those my brother has allied himself with should find this devilish telesma and destroy my father, the count, and so many others; how could I wish to escape? A way must be found to preserve them all, but what can it be, what can it be?"

She turned her back on me suddenly and stood facing down the valley with her shoulders rising and falling for several minutes, too proud to let even a priest see her weep. When she turned again, her accustomed look of amusement at the whole world had been drawn back across her beautiful features like a veil of silk.

"Ah, Father Melchior, please forgive that moment of indisposition and escort me back to camp. My father has called another council to meet after the evening meal. I intend to be at hand to hear whatever is said, but I must rest a little first if I am to make any sense of it."

The count and I were just finishing our soldiers' supper of lentil stew when we heard the sound of running feet, and I felt my throat tighten with apprehension. Then a man loomed up in the firelight and panted out, "Count Galoran, Father Melchior—you both must come—at once!"

"What is it, man?" said the count in surprise "It's not time for the council to assemble yet."

"A man—badly wounded—escaped from the castle. He is with—they took him to the duke. He's asking for you; it is your seneschal!"

We had to push our way through a crowd of curious knights and soldiers to get to the duke's pavilion. They'd wrapped the seneschal in blankets and laid him near the fire. Duke Argave, his captain, Lord Thierri, and the prior were standing over him while the duke's personal physician-surgeon tended his wounds. I saw a flicker of silk within the tent behind them and guessed that Lady Arsendis must be watching and listening from there. The physician stood up, shaking his head, just as the messenger led us through the guards holding the crowd back. "A knife thrust pierced some of his lower viscera. He may last a few more hours, but he'll not see the dawn."

"Father Melchior, Count Galoran, come closer!" Seneschal Guilhem called in a weak voice. His face already looked like that of a cadaver as we knelt by him; only his eyes seemed alive.

"Well, sirrah, I can understand your crying for Father Melchior if you have decided to make a final confession in hope of reclaiming the True Faith before you die," said the count. "But after betraying me to ambush, and then leading my enemies into my castle, what can you have to say to me?"

"I never betrayed you." He reached out a shaking hand and gave a massive key to the count. "I escaped tonight by the postern gate—I had to kill a man to reach it, and was stabbed myself—to warn you."

"Warn me?"

"Of the true traitor. It is Raymbaud, the bouteillier."

"Raymbaud; but that is impossible!" It had been the duke who shouted; Count Galoran and I were too stunned to speak. "Raymbaud served at my court for years before—that is, I already knew him well when I sent him to the countess upon her marriage to Lord Thierri. I was sure that I—that is the countess—could trust him."

I happened to be standing on the count's good side, so I saw his sudden hard smile. "So, Duke Argave, you acknowledge openly that it was Raymbaud who has been your man within Peyrefixade all the time!" he said with his barking laugh.

I saw the duke wince at having betrayed himself, then flash his own dark smile. "Well caught, Count, that he was. He was a good man for a double game."

"For more than a double game—my lord duke," the seneschal rasped. "He was Prince Alfonso's spy in your court—when you chose him to be your spy in the count's. But even the prince did not know what he was in truth. He was an agent of the Perfected!"

For a moment, no one so much as moved. Then Count Galoran threw back his head and gave a laugh like the one he'd let out the time he threw his arms around the startled Prince Alfonso. "If this tale is true, the rogue is as peerless a traitor as Roland was a knight!"

The duke did not look so amused. "Why should we believe any of this?" he demanded, bending low over the seneschal.

"I am a dying man—why would I lie? Even after the enemy were in the castle he continued to play at deception. He never let the rest of the men—the ones you ransomed, Duke—see that he and the two fellows who had been working for him were anything other than prisoners like themselves. Instead he let it seem that—that they had been kept as hostages when—when the others were let go."

"But why should he bother; why not reveal himself now that his own side was in possession?" the count asked him.

"Because of the plan—which I escaped—to warn you—about." The seneschal stopped, gasping with pain yet clearly anxious to continue. The physician hurried to his tent and returned a moment later with a flagon. He crossed to Prior Belthesar, who sprinkled in something and spoke over it, adding magic to medicine. Seneschal Guilhem drained the draught as soon as it was offered, shivered throughout his gaunt frame, then resumed speaking in a far stronger voice. "They knew that you and Father Melchior had escaped the men who'd been sent after you, and that you'd be coming here with the conviare. They want it badly, because while they are quite sure the great telesma is concealed within Peyrefixade, it will be very difficult to recover without the conviare's aid. Their scheme was put into motion as soon as you were seen this morning. Raymbaud was to have appeared here tonight with a minor wound, claiming to have escaped by the postern gate. He knew you'd have welcomed him, Count: congratulated him, given him a place to sleep near your own tent, perhaps even in it. Later, when the camp was asleep, he was going to murder both you and Father Melchior, steal the conviare, and take it back to his friends in Peyrefixade."

Count Galoran bent over the seneschal with a skeptical face. "And how did you come to know all this?"

"Oh, Raymbaud took me from my cell and let me roam free once your loyal men were safely out of the castle. He'd always talked to me, you know: telling me about the Perfected doctrine, countering my doubts, answering my questions. I had been interested even before he came, and I think he still saw me as a likely convert. Besides, he needed me—as an audience. I was the only one who had been there, knowing what he was, to see him playing his game of mirrors the whole time, you see, the only one who could truly appreciate his boasts about how cleverly he'd fooled you all. But tonight I overheard something, listening to his two comrades talking in the courtyard, that he never intended I should know, and that was when I resolved to break with him and warn you. It was *he* who killed the countess, fully intending to do so!"

Now it was Lord Thierri who bent over the dying man, with an expression not of anger or skepticism but terrible eagerness. "How, man!? Speak, tell them how, and lift this awful suspicion from me!"

"In telling it, I must ask your forgiveness, Lord Thierri." The seneschal's face looked gray now; he was clearly sinking again. "Along with having mastered the ways of the courtier and the knight, Raymbaud had learned—learned some magic from his own people while growing up. Not so much as a Magian, but enough to work with certain magical objects Perfected Magians gave him when he began his life in the duke's court, and others that they—they sent to him in secret later, when he was already here. His magical map was only one small element of what he could do. He told me of this during our many talks, after he discovered my interest in his people's doctrine, and my hatred for—for you, Lord Thierri. Yes, I hated you! I thought you a climbing schemer unworthy of our dear countess, whom I had loved from her girlhood. Also, I was convinced you'd challenged the good old count to a race while hunting that day the winter after you and the countess were married, knowing full well he would likely take a fall that would put an end to him, and Raymbaud agreed with me. I wanted to kill you, had even tried to plan ways to do it so no one would know, but without success. Then, one day last autumn, Raymbaud told me he had decided to help.

"He had, he said, recently been sent a magical object which could be used to drive and confuse and frighten anyone who came up onto the battlements at night into fleeing along the walls until he fell to his death. It was supposed to have been yourself who went up from the hall to investigate a strange sound and meet your death, not my beloved lady! When I pretended to come in from the kitchens that awful night after having placed the terrible thing—only to meet Raymbaud hurrying to find me and learn that she had gone out while you remained with the guests—oh, it was terrible! I rushed back outside, trying to reach her in time, but then I heard her scream and met her servant babbling of apparitions, and I knew that she was dead. I almost threw myself from the battlements then and there, but Raymbaud appeared and stopped me. It was an accident, he said; the thing had been set to act upon whomever came upon the wall at that time. He had never imagined that the dear countess would go instead of you, he told me, and only realized the mistake when he came up from the cellars with more wine to find her already gone from the hall. So I blamed myself alone.

"So I began to study and to fast in the Perfected manner—seeking only to purify myself as much as possible so that my prayers for the dear countess should be most efficacious and that I might, perhaps, one day hope to join her in heaven—and longing only for death. I suspected it was Raymbaud who put the fire telesma into the hearth to attack Count Galoran, but he persuaded me it had been someone among the masons. But it was he, just as it was he who—who told my dear countess to go up onto the walls that night!" He paused; his breath was starting to sound labored again. "If I had had a weapon when I heard that, I would—would have gone straight to the great hall—and stabbed him then and there, in the midst of all his friends. As it was, I had to fight the sentry at the postern gate—for his dagger, and was stabbed myself before—before I could kill him. I knew I could never succeed—in killing Raymbaud—with such a wound, so I resolved to use the last of—of my strength to make my way here—and warn you all of his treason. Even though I die, I know you, Count—and you, Duke—shall see that God's justice—is done upon him."

"You see!" cried Lord Thierri, springing up to face the duke. "I always swore I was innocent. This proves it!"

The duke's only answer was a nod and a noise in his throat. Meanwhile, Count Galoran had knelt at the seneschal's side. "My friend, if you have spoken the truth you have indeed remained true to me, and both Father Melchior and I most likely owe you our lives. And I also owe you another debt, for revealing who committed a black crime against my house and family. Have you any final request of me?"

"I have a widowed sister—a good woman—she lives in Ferignan. Send her my things, and the—the balance of my wages. Other than that, I wish—wish only to make my last confession to Father Melchior and receive absolution—if he will hear me."

"Of course I shall hear you," I said, knowing there was little time now. The same magic draught that had temporarily increased his strength would, as it ebbed, carry him away into death far faster than if he had never drunk it. So I followed as they carried the seneschal into the physician's tent. There I heard him out, then pronounced an absolution, reminding him that it would be efficacious only if he were truly repentant in heart when death came. Then I sat with him, holding his gaunt hand while he slipped slowly away from consciousness and life, until a knight came and whispered, "Come, Father, they want you."

Reentering the pavilion, I found the council of war already in progress. As soon as he saw me, Count Galoran declared, "Father Melchior, with luck they have not yet discovered that the seneschal is gone, nor the way he came out. I intend to try and enter Peyrefixade tonight, to recover this great telesma before the Perfected get it. But I'll need your help with the conviare. Are you prepared to go with me?"

"Not so fast, Galoran!" Lord Thierri interrupted. "You are still hampered by your wounds. Besides, the traitor Raymbaud killed my wife and led to my being dispossessed; I should be the one to go. I'll need a Magian, of course, and I'd be happy to have Father Melchior."

As I stared from one to the other, taken aback, the duke spoke in his smoothest voice. "You appear troubled, Brother Melchior. Are you certain you are up to the task? Do you perhaps fear coming to grips with the Perfected?"

"I—I do, my lord Duke. But my concern is not for my life, nor for whether my skill is sufficient."

"What, then?"

"I fear that if I come too close to the Perfected, they may perhaps be able to claim me for themselves."

The duke arched his thin black brows while Count

Galoran and Lord Thierri both looked at me in surprise.
I saw the prior signaling to me with his hand and heard
his second voice start to speak a firm warning inside my
ear, but I knew I had to go on. "My lords, my first tutor
in magic, my own grandfather, had been a Magian of the
Perfected in his youth. He was a good man, a kind man,
and though he died in the flames unrepentant, I loved
him. I am an anointed priest of the True Faith, but I was
a Magian before that, one who began as the pupil of a
Perfected master. I—I have always feared those first roots
of my training could be used to draw me onto their side
if I ever came into close quarters with Perfected Magians."

Count Galoran's face looked grim and the duke's captain
shocked, while Lord Thierri actually took a backward step
away from me. Duke Argave, however, rounded on Prior
Belthesar with furious eyes. "Prior, how can this be? You
yourself vouched for this man when the question of what
Magian to assign the new count was raised! How can I
trust either him or the count now? Perhaps we can send
someone else—Lord Thierri—no, perhaps not him, but
my captain. But even if we do send Galoran, it must be
you who goes with him to employ the conviare, Prior!"

"Perhaps you are right at that, though I am a bit old
for such a hard work of magic," Prior Belthesar told him
with a thoughtful expression—but his second voice was
saying something entirely different within my second ear.

"If I am the one who goes, Duke, I will accept no
companion but Father Melchior," the count said flatly,
and I felt my heart leap. If both the prior and the count
believed that much in me, should I not also believe in
myself?

"Indeed? Then it shall have to be anoth—*what is that*?!"

The duke, his captain, Lord Thierri, and all the knights
whirled to look toward the lower end of the camp.
Confused shouting and the sound of hooves were coming
from that direction, growing louder every instant. Suddenly,
spectral horsemen on skeletal horses appeared galloping

among the tents. As men shouted to each other and clawed for their swords, Prior Belthesar looked calmly in my direction and one more short phrase from him echoed in my second ear, "Now: both of you, go." I stood still for a moment, then obeyed.

The count gave me a startled look when I stepped to his side and gripped his sword arm. "This is only a distraction to draw away their attention, Count Galoran. We are going now."

His eyes widened briefly, then he gave that quirked smile that I had so gradually come to like. "Lead on, Father Melchior."

As we slipped away, I saw the Lady Arsendis briefly appear in the door of her father's tent where she must have been listening the whole time and gaze after us without saying a word to anyone.

Blood showed black in the moonlight on the steps below the narrow postern gate, where the seneschal must have fallen after relocking it. The massive wooden door, wide enough to admit only a single man at a time, loomed dark and solid. Count Galoran weighed the big iron key in his hand. "Well, Father Melchior, this looks like another chance for you to practice your divination," he whispered. "If the Perfected haven't yet discovered that the seneschal's left the castle, then the portcullis behind this door will still be up, and the narrow steep stair that leads up through the wall behind it will be deserted. If they have, then there are probably five men with long knives standing in a line behind this door to greet anyone who might try to pay a visit. Can you tell me which is the case?"

"Yes." My heart was pounding as I reached into my cassock, drew out the phial the Spector General had prepared for me, and took a long draught. But I made myself speak as calmly and quietly as the count. "Now take me under the arms and hold my body up. Do not be startled into letting it fall by what happens next."

I saw the good side of his mouth quirk with interest, then he stepped behind me and seized me around the chest. He was none too soon; almost as soon as I felt his iron arms around my ribs, the sense of their pressure began to seem distant. I had done this thrice under the Spector General's relentless tutelage while we'd been up at the House of the Order, but it had grown neither familiar nor pleasant, and it was not pleasant now. I felt my senses waver, saw my vision grow dim and double. Then, with a sensation almost like shrugging a wet cloak of heavy wool off one's shoulders, I simply slipped out of my own body. The instant I did so, all feeling vanished—except for a terrible sensation of cold, far worse than any cold that I had ever felt within my flesh. I turned and looked back at my physical self slumped in the count's arms, while he gazed at my spectral form with eyes as big as a staring owl's in the moonlight. Then I raised my hand (speech is impossible for the discorporate), turned, and walked straight through the door.

Even if the count's five killers had been standing just inside, my vaporous form would have been completely invisible to them out of the moonlight. But there was no one, and the narrow portcullis was still up. With a push of my ghostly foot, I sent my spectral self floating up the narrow stairs, which spiraled to the right within the wall so that defenders standing above could swing their swords with their right hands, while attackers coming up could only defend themselves with their left. The door to the courtyard at the top had been pushed shut but not locked, and a dead man lay slumped against the inside, a dagger deep in his chest. In my discorporate state, I could not shudder as I slipped through both corpse and solid door for a quick look about the courtyard.

All seemed quiet, except for distant voices from the hall and the occasional pacing of a guard passing along the battlements above. Where moonlight fell the stones of the castle seemed bright as silver, but the door by which my spectral self was floating luckily lay in deep shadow. Even when I brought my ghostly hand up to within an inch of my face, it was virtually invisible. Two men in their living flesh would need to be far more careful, but we should to be able to slip into the courtyard and make our way along the shadowed wall to the nearest passage unseen unless we were very unlucky. Satisfied, I drifted quickly back through the doorway, down the stairs, and out to the count and my fleshly self.

As soon as I shook my head and got my feet back under me, Count Galoran let go and stepped away, looking at me with a very strange expression. "By my faith, Father Melchior, if you were not a priest I'd cross myself! You slip in and out of your body as easily as I change my cloak!"

"Not nearly—so easily—as that, Count," I gasped, shuddering and leaning against the wall until the moon ceased dancing in the sky and I began to feel at home within my own skin once more. "The Spector General of my Order, who only recently taught me the rudiments of that art, might perhaps make such a boast. That is why nothing can be hidden from him. But for such as I, leaving the body is nothing that can be done either easily or for very long without great risk."

"Then I must thank you for assuming it, as you have assumed so many other risks for me. Now, let's both enter Peyrefixade as living, breathing men—at least when we go in!"

He was smiling his crooked smile as he said this, turning the huge key in the postern door. As I reached inside my cassock and felt the cool, smooth shape of the conviare, I found myself smiling back.

Chapter Thirteen ~ Galoran

1

The narrow passage inside the postern gate was silent and empty, lit only by a single high window that allowed a pale gleam of moonlight to penetrate. For a moment I hesitated, then turned the heavy key behind us and dropped it into my belt pouch. The duke and Lord Thierri would realize quickly enough that we had gone, and I didn't want them coming after us, alerting the heretics to our presence though unable to bring enough warriors through the narrow postern to make any difference. If I left the key in the lock on the inside, as it had been the whole time I was lord of Peyrefixade, some heretic might take it, making impossible the quick escape Melchior and I would need if things went as badly as I feared.

"Bless me, Father," I said quietly, thinking that I might not live to see another dawn over the mountains. He murmured the sacred phrases rapidly, and I pushed aside the doubt whether the blessing of a priest touched with heresy would be efficacious.

But with my sword in my hand, ignoring the throbbing in my leg, I felt in spite of everything a rising of my spirits just to be inside Peyrefixade again. I reminded myself grimly that if I thought of this as *my* castle, then the heretics did, too, and there had been heretics here long, long before I even learned of the southern mountains.

Under the portcullis and up the passage we went, the priest's footfalls so silent behind me that he might almost have become discorporate again. I did not turn my head to look. The passage became darker and darker as it burrowed up under the rocks, constantly rising. It had become completely black by the time we reached the stair that spiraled up to the courtyard above. I wished I had thought to bring a torch and considered asking Melchior if the startling array of battle magic he had learned at his Order's house also included the magic of light. But if we didn't want to announce to the defenders that there was an enemy inside the walls, the darker the better.

All the weight of the stones above us seemed to bear down as I felt along the invisible wall and groped for the first step with one foot. "The first tricky part is going to come when we reach the courtyard," I breathed to Melchior. "Even with the man who was supposed to be guarding the postern stair dead, we may be spotted—either by warriors or by Magians."

"I thought that, too," he replied, his voice a faint murmur in the cold night under my castle. "It might be best if we separate."

I nodded although I knew he couldn't see me—or hoped he couldn't. If he hadn't saved my life—and I his—the proximity of a man with the powers he wielded, powers the pit of my stomach felt quite sure God had never meant mortals to have, would have given me the shakes. But he was closer to me now, heretic Magian or not, than my own brother had ever been.

"You look for the hiding place of the great battle telesma," I whispered. "I'm going to try to get to the main gates. At a minimum I'll distract the Magians from noticing you. And if I can get the gates open the duke's army may be able to rush in and capture the castle."

We went slowly and carefully up the spiral stairs, feeling for each step, the stone wall rough to the touch. I had to shift my sword to the other hand as we climbed, not that I would have been able to see to fight anyway. We would come out, I knew, on a small terrace along a wall at the side of the castle—the same terrace from which the countess had fallen. I had been up and down this stairway several times during the spring as I first explored my castle, but the way seemed much longer now than it had then, coming down it carelessly with a torch in one hand and Bruno behind me.

The other reason I didn't like letting the duke's armies in the front gate, even though I knew perfectly well that I had to if I possibly could, was that I wanted to deal with the damned bouteillier myself. He had killed Bruno.

When a faint trace of light showed before us, I had to blink twice to persuade myself it was real. Very cautiously I moved forward, probing with the point of my sword until I found a door, not quite closed, and a dead body slumped against it.

"Can your spells of divination tell if there's anyone outside on the terrace?" I muttered as I heaved the body to one side with hands under its arms—the same way I had held Father Melchior as he became discorporate. "Without leaving your flesh again?" I added without intending to.

For answer he took a few grains of powder from a small bag—he seemed to have an enormous variety of magical objects inside his cassock—and sprinkled them on the blade of a knife. They stirred and glowed silver as he murmured a few words over them, then faded again. "There are at the moment no warriors on the terrace," he whispered then, "and none overlooking it from the tower."

He did not, I noticed, specify whether there were any Magians there. I also remembered that his spells had not revealed the duke's son, when he had appeared before us on our way back from my meeting with Prince Alfonso. But I did not mention this—Melchior must remember the incident perfectly well himself.

"Then we'd best move now," I said, my hand on the edge of the door. But he forestalled me.

"Wait, Count," he murmured, taking something else from his cassock, something long and white that seemed to glow in the dim light from the moonlit terrace outside. "I want you to have this."

I recognized it at once. It was his grandfather's telesma.

He pressed it into my palm, and I felt again the deeply cut lines in the ivory's surface and the same eerie tingle I had felt up on the slopes of the mountain, when I had given it to him to help ease the excruciating pain in his shoulder. I took a sudden step backwards. Out of several things I might have said I muttered, "No use my taking it. No idea how to use such a thing."

"But it is extremely simple, Count," he said, very low and very insistently. "Although I have not yet fully restored its power after draining it up on the mountain, one need practice virtually no magic oneself to utilize the forces stored within it."

"You'll need it," I protested in a whisper.

"But it will be much easier for you to use than, say, the conviare which I also carry." The conviare which had helped channel destroying flames toward me. "This is as you have seen a quenching telesma: it may be used against another's spells, against pain—and against fire."

It was the fire that decided me. The bouteillier knew perfectly well my aversion to fire and had already used magical flames against me once. "But how do I activate the magic within this?"

"In this case"—Melchior took it back and muttered a few quick words I could not catch before again pressing it into my hand—"you need only hold the telesma before you, speak the words, *Hoc est hora,* meaning the time is now, and the inherent spells in the telesma will take over, to quench that which opposes you."

I thrust it into the back of my belt and hefted my sword. "Then let us see, Father Melchior, who may be opposing us."

❖   ❖   ❖

The priest retreated into the shadows as I made my way across the terrace, carefully staying out of direct moonlight. Several doors and passages opened off it, but I headed for the door on the far side that led into the great tower. Remembering the countess, I went nowhere near the parapet at the terrace's edge, even though a look from there might have shown me lights to indicate where in the castle the heretics had their watchmen. Any dizziness at the edge could have meant me down at the bottom of the mountain and Thierri again master of Peyrefixade.

Assuming of course we were able to recapture this castle. My boots seemed loud on the flagstones as I reached the door leading into the tower. It swung open easily and quietly, just as it should—I'd been strict in directing all hinges be kept well oiled.

This terrace connected with the tower several storeys above its base. I stood silently for a moment, waiting and listening, breathing through my mouth and willing my heart to beat more slowly.

And almost jumped out of my skin when a voice spoke above me. "They're lighting their watchfires for the night. It doesn't look as if they're planning an attack now, but I'll keep an eye on them."

The voice, I realized, came from someone on the stairs that circled up inside the tower, calling through a window to someone outside, on the far side of the tower from the little terrace and the postern gate. He was headed up to the top of the tower, to the spot from which I had first heard my servants call me Count Scar on my first morning in Peyrefixade—servants standing on the terrace where Melchior and I had been a moment earlier. If we had come five minutes later, we would have been spotted.

The person outside said something I didn't catch. But as I slowly descended the tower stairs, setting each foot down with great care, I could hear his own steps retreating. The watchman above me went clattering up to the top of the tower with no effort at silence, his way lit by moonlight through the windows. It was a strange sensation to realize that he had no idea I was here—unless he had what Brother Melchior called a second eye, and was only pretending to be unaware of my presence.

But no one challenged me as I reached the bottom of the tower and opened the door there. Beyond lay a roofless passage between two high walls, which magnified the sound of careless footfalls. The man who had been here a moment ago was gone, but as I craned my neck upward, peering toward the top of the tower with my back pressed against its wall, I caught a flicker of light brighter than the moon. The watchman had lit a lantern to keep himself company.

Which meant he might be too dazzled to spot someone moving in the shadows below. Quickly and cautiously I proceeded down the passage, hunched over to avoid both moonlight and watchful eyes. I had been clenching my sword so tightly the hilt was slippery; I paused to wipe my hand on my tunic, listening but still hearing nothing.

On either side, opening from the passage, were store rooms, certainly rifled now by the heretics. The doors stood ajar, but I did no more than glance into the rooms' black interiors. The Perfected had my treasure chest of carefully collected rents, along with my grain reserves, spices, and wine. I would have happily let them have it all if I could just have control of the castle again.

Almost at the end of the open passage a stairway to my right led upward, toward Melchior's private chambers and the chambers which the countess's ladies had doubtless used when she and Thierri ruled Peyrefixade. From those chambers went one of the staircases that eventually reached the chapel. I didn't like to think what profane rites the heretics might be performing there—animal sacrifice, lustful orgies, even human sacrifices for all I knew. Melchior had tried to tell me the Perfected would not do such things, but I was still sure they would. I would have to have him reconsecrate the chapel immediately if we got the heretics out—assuming we both lived.

Past the staircase, the open passageway opened onto the castle's main courtyard. Very slowly I leaned away from the wall against which I was pressed, just enough to see into it. A short distance away stood several of the damned heretics, yawning and talking. Moonlight glittered on helmets and weapons. Yet there weren't very many of them, I tried to encourage myself, not nearly enough to fight off the duke's forces if the walls were breached or the gates opened.

However, if they had even a few seconds' warning, I reminded myself, they would be able to retreat into the central keep, barring the heavy doors of the great hall, and then wait us out nearly as securely as they had when they controlled the whole castle. That is, if they had thought to shift some of the grain supplies from the main storerooms into the storage cellars of the keep.

I shook my head. Gavain had doubtless already thought of this. He was after all a duke's son, brought up on strategy and command even if he had given it all up to seek his soul's damnation in the mountains. And at the moment he might very well be settling himself by my new hearth into my own bed.

None of the warriors in the courtyard had spotted me. And the fact that no alarm had yet been sounded meant that Melchior too had so far eluded discovery—and that no one had realized the postern was now guarded only by a dead man. But it would be folly to try to make my way across the open courtyard with anyone in it.

But this was my castle. Even if the heretics had Raymbaud's magical map and even though I was slinking around like a thief, I knew Peyrefixade better than any heretics who hadn't even been born the last time the castle had been in Perfected hands. I smiled for a second, ducked out of the passageway, took two steps on the flagstones of the courtyard, and was through the door leading to the kitchen stairs before any of the heretics might turn at the movement in the shadows and see me.

But still I waited for a minute, sword ready, just inside the door, in case any of them became suspicious and came to investigate.

When no one appeared, I slipped down the wide steps into the kitchen itself. The room was empty, the fires banked for the night. Yet I stayed instinctively in the shadows as I crossed it, making for the passage on the far side that came out near the main gates. With teeth clenched, I made my lame leg carry its full weight, to keep from stamping with my good leg at each step. The moonlight cast grotesque shapes on the wall from the cooking spits. So far I wasn't doing much to divert the heretics' attention from whatever Melchior might be doing. But a single-handed fight against all the heretic warriors, while doubtless noisy, would be doomed from the beginning.

I froze. Steps sounded before me. It sounded as though someone was coming into the kitchen looking for something to eat.

Holy, pure, perfected people, they call themselves, I thought bitterly, who claim they relinquish the pleasures of the flesh. And yet after a dinner of dry bread and lentils any of them—even the duke's son—must start thinking how good a bite of meat pastry would taste.

And would have a hungry man's irritation added to a heretic's fanaticism when he found me here.

I stepped behind a bank of shelves, listening to his footsteps. He seemed to hesitate for a moment. Had the way of perfection become stronger for him than hunger—or did he suspect my presence? I tried not to breathe, though the pounding of my heart was so loud it seemed he must hear it. But then the steps began moving again.

In an instant I could have tipped the shelves and all their contents over on him. But I stopped with a hand already braced for the push. The clatter of broken crockery would bring all the warriors from the courtyard down into the kitchen, and besides, this was *my* cook's kitchen and equipment.

Instead I reversed my sword, and as he stepped past the end of the shelves, just as he caught sight of me from the corner of his eye and was opening his mouth to shout, I struck him firmly on the temple with the hilt.

He slumped to the floor with a faint moan. I tied him up swiftly with the twine the cook used for trussing roasts, then thrust the end of a flour sack into his mouth. Going up against heretics I wanted God on my side, and the fewer deaths on my soul the better.

I stood up slowly, trying to steady my ragged breathing. The whole incident had taken under a minute. I strained my ears but did not hear anyone else approaching. At that moment I would cheerfully have exchanged this furtive advance through the castle for open battle in the emperor's armies, the horns calling, men and horses screaming, and the stench of blood everywhere.

But fighting on behalf of the emperor would not get my castle back. I dragged the heretic under a table, in the hopes that he would not be spotted in the shadows if someone else became hungry. He breathed shallowly and did not stir.

Then again I advanced through the moonlight and shadows, across the width of the kitchen and along the passage beyond. Here more steps led up to the courtyard, coming out very near the main gates.

At the top of the stairs I paused again, at the door the heretic had left ajar in entering, and tried to knead some of the pain and stiffness out of my leg. In a very few moments I might need it for running. From the darkness of the doorway I could see the moonlit courtyard and the great gatehouse. A single warrior stood before it. His face was dark so I could see no detail, but he appeared to be looking in my direction.

I did not move. If he had a Magian's second eye he had seen me already, but if this was another soldier with no magical powers he might not have spotted me. After a moment, he turned his head away and walked a short distance up the courtyard before returning again to the gates.

"All right," I told myself. "Assume he hasn't seen you." He was several dozen yards from anyone else, the only person between me and the gates. "Now all I have to do is find a way to get past him and get the gates open before all the rest of the warriors get there."

I would have to kill him, I decided. There was no way I could surprise him as I had the man in the kitchens. But if I appeared suddenly when he thought he was safe he might be just slow enough to react that I could have my sword in him before he had a chance to cry out or fight back.

Then came the tricky part. I could throw the bars off the inner gates and have them open in a moment, probably before the rest of the warriors realized what had happened and were able to reach me. Then I would dart through into the gatehouse and wedge the inner gates shut behind me with the bars. That would give me a minute or so safe from the heretics, during which I would raise the portcullis, get the bars off the outer gates, and retreat into the guard room in the gatehouse. There I would blow the horn to tell Duke Argave and his men to advance at once, while I held off the heretics, who would only be able to reach me one at a time—

There was a difficulty with this plan. Unless Duke Argave was very quick, indeed waiting just outside, the heretics would be able to get the outer gates shut again before he got up the hill. In leaving the siege camp so abruptly I'd had no chance to plan strategy with the duke—not that he had seemed particularly willing to listen to any of my strategy anyway. And the security of the guard room would be security only if there was no one already there, something which seemed less and less likely the more I considered it.

I was almost ready to try it anyway when the man near the gates turned in my direction again. I inched backwards, keeping my sword behind the door frame so the moon would not glint on the blade. And for a moment the light fell on his face.

He turned away again after a few seconds, but I needed only a second to recognize those arched eyebrows and straight, slender nose. It was the duke's son, Gavain.

"It wouldn't have worked anyway," I told myself, backing slowly toward the kitchen. I should have expected that the duke's son would be at the gates, at the most crucial spot; I would have been there myself. "Maybe the priest and I shouldn't have split up. Melchior could have used his magical powders and potions against the warriors while I got the gates open, and given the duke enough time to roll out of bed and get his armor on and his rear end up here."

Excellent reasoning though all this was, I knew perfectly well that it was not the real explanation for why I was now retreating back the way I had come. I just didn't want to have to kill Gavain.

In the kitchen the warrior I had knocked unconscious still lay motionless, his breath snorting around the flour sack. It hadn't been much use trying to hide him, I thought, my own passage silent. Even if someone didn't see him they would certainly hear him.

Was it because I couldn't imagine Arsendis ever marrying me if I had killed her brother? That couldn't be it, I told myself wryly, because I already knew I didn't stand a chance with her. Whatever friendliness she might once have felt toward me would have died in seeing me a lamed man turned out of his own castle. Or did I hope to ingratiate myself with Duke Argave? Considering how furious he had been with me ever since I reached the siege camp, it was hard to see him any more unwilling to have me in Peyrefixade than he already was. A great deal of fuss, in fact, could have been avoided if I had run Gavain through the first time I saw him, when he appeared before us so startlingly in the mountain passes to warn me obliquely against the bouteillier. A knight and a gentleman, he wouldn't have liked a traitor, even a traitor who was working for him, any more than I did.

Proceeding cautiously through the kitchen, I realized that the real reason I didn't like to kill Gavain was that, even if Arsendis ended up married to Thierri or to Prince Alfonso, I knew she would be happier knowing her brother was still alive.

Now I needed a new approach to the gates. My thoughts turned with relief from nebulous affairs of the heart to a concrete stratagem for action.

I rapidly turned the plan of the castle over in my mind. This stair would bring me back to the main courtyard, some distance from the gates. I should be able to wait until no heretic warriors were near and get up from the courtyard onto the walkway along the outer wall. Once on the battlements I could proceed along them to the upper gatehouse, with luck not running into any warriors or attracting Gavain's attention. If the door from the battlements into the gatehouse was open, and there was no reason why it shouldn't be, I could get into the guard room before anyone realized I was there. I would then be positioned between the inner and outer gates.

So far, I thought with new energy, this plan had promise. My mind kept on churning as I climbed back up the stairs by which I had originally descended into the kitchen. Having killed or otherwise incapacitated whatever heretic warrior might be in the guard room, I would raise the portcullis, go down and open the outer gates, return immediately to the guard room, lower the portcullis from there to keep the defenders from reaching the gates to shut them again, blow the horn to alert Duke Argave, then—

The door before me, the door leading from the kitchen into the courtyard, was shut. I had left it open when I came through, not wanting the creaking of hinges, however faint, to attract anyone's attention.

Was there someone beyond it? I tried to listen over the roaring of the blood in my ears, but the heavy door would have stifled the sound of another's breathing anyway. This, I thought grimly, would be a good place for Melchior's most devilish spells.

But he was must be far away in another part of the castle, with luck drawing near to the hiding place of the heretics' great telesma. No use waiting any longer. Gripping my sword, I slowly pushed the door open.

And found myself looking straight into Raymbaud's eyes.

2

His sword was in his right hand, but he raised his left to his lips. "Quiet, Count Galoran," he counseled with a grin that showed his teeth. "Do you want all of Gavain's warriors on you at once?" When I neither moved nor answered, he continued, "My little finding telesma told me that *someone* was here in the castle, but I never dared to hope it would be you!"

"I hear you were planning to fake an escape, come to the duke's camp, and kill me in my sleep," I said quietly. "If you're hoping to do so more conveniently here, you shall find a distinct disadvantage: I am awake and ready for you."

I was thinking rapidly as I spoke, my eyes fixed on his moonlit face. That he had tracked me through the castle without alerting the heretic warriors—doubtless having activated his spell when he found the dead man at the postern, as he himself was preparing to descend to Argave's camp and put his assassination plot into action—meant that for some reason he wanted to face alone whoever had entered. And that he still had not raised the alarm meant that he hadn't changed his mind when he discovered the intruder was me.

It seemed a strange decision. I myself was more than willing to postpone having all the heretics rush at me at once, but it was difficult to understand why Raymbaud would prefer single combat. I had matched swords with him in practice more than once and thought that, good as he was, I would be more than equal to him even with a lame leg.

"You don't want Gavain to know you've found me," I said, guessing but speaking with confidence. A quick glance past his shoulder showed no warriors approaching, so he couldn't be stalling while waiting for reinforcements. "So far you've betrayed me, the duke, and Prince Alfonso. Now you're planning to betray the heretics' war leader, to make it all complete. But one thing I don't understand, Raymbaud. Who can you possibly think will reward you for switching allegiance once *again*? If you think it's me, that I'll forgive you if you help me regain Peyrefixade, you're in for a severe disappointment."

I paused for a deep breath—and to listen in case they were creeping up behind me through the kitchen. "You first sent hired killers to try to assassinate me in the duke's court. Even that I might—perhaps—have forgiven. But then you did something for which there can be no recompense. You killed Bruno. If I'm count here again you'll hang. If I'm just a soldier running around a castle at night, you'll die with my sword in your heart."

I had at least shaken some of his oily self-assurance. "No, no, my count," he said, his own eyes darting from side to side. "I'm not hoping for a reward. And it wasn't me who tried to kill you at Argave's court." I snorted but let him continue. "But you'll understand what I want here—you must understand better than anyone. You think of this as your castle, so you'll know why I think of it as *mine*."

"I understand nothing of the sort," I said icily. I hefted my sword slightly. The desire to run the treacherous murderer through at once was nearly stronger than my sense of self-preservation. From the far side of the courtyard I could hear heretic sentinels calling to each other, and the lantern still glinted at the top of the great tower.

"I've been here far longer than you have, Count.

Peyrefixade was mine when Countess Aenor still ruled here. Oh, I may not have administered justice, or kept track of the rents like that fool Guilhem"—for a second his expression was worried and I wondered if he had yet associated the dead sentry at the postern gate with the seneschal's disappearance from Peyrefixade—"but the organization of castle life, the supervision of supplies and the servants, were always in my hands. And my skill with a sword meant that the knights respected me just as much as did the members of the staff."

I was in no mood for reminiscences about his happy days governing in my castle—to the point where he had easily overcome any hesitation my own knights might have felt in opening the gates to a disguised Gavain. "And now the duke's son is here," I said coldly, "and some of the heretic Magians, and you expect me to sympathize because they lord it in Peyrefixade themselves, and no longer give you the respect you feel your years of scheming have earned. Do they perhaps despise you because they know you killed my cousin the countess through your filthy magic? What's your plan—to regain their respect by killing me in single combat?"

His mouth tightened. "Her death was unfortunate but necessary. I knew the duke would remove Thierri once she was gone—he'd had plenty of reports from me in which I was able to persuade the duke of Thierri's *real* character. I thought the castle would be left without a lord for many months, giving me ample opportunity to find the great telesma myself. But I had done no more in my search than complete a detailed map when the duke produced *you*."

"That must have been a *bitter* disappointment," I said, mocking. "Here you'd contrived to make yourself virtual lord of Peyrefixade, hoping the Perfected would reward you with permanent lordship once you found the telesma, and suddenly this northerner appears and you're back with the wine barrels—hah!"

While distracting him with talk, I had surreptitiously been working my knife from my belt with my left hand. Now I pounced forward, the hilt of my sword locked against the hilt of his to hold both blades high above our heads, my knife beside his ear. "Be absolutely still," I hissed, "and you may delay your entry into Hell a few minutes yet."

This was the most dangerous moment. I had no way of stopping his mouth, and if he had shouted he would have died, but I would have died a minute later with heretic steel in my belly.

But terror for his life kept him silent. That and, I thought wryly, knowing me too well. I could not kill in cold blood someone I had thought of until today as a more or less faithful servitor, even though I now knew he had killed Bruno.

"Turn around," I said harshly, "and hand your sword back to me, hilt first—that's right, slow and easy. We're going somewhere a little more private than this courtyard, where we can settle for a certainty the question of who is the true lord of Peyrefixade. You're walking in front."

He started to protest, but I jabbed him with his own sword. "Start walking. You're in front because I don't trust a traitor. If you don't trust me either, well, that will just give you something to turn over in your mind as we go. If we meet anyone, don't suggest by the slightest sign that there's anything wrong. Otherwise, I'll find out how sharp an edge you keep on your sword by just how easily it slides between your ribs."

He turned and started walking, so meekly that I immediately suspected a plot. "Not that way. Along the edge of the courtyard here."

I closed to within a foot of his back, the glint of steel almost entirely masked by his cloak. We were shadowed here from the moon. I let myself limp as we went, both to ease some of the strain on that leg and to make him think I was weaker than I was. On the far side of the courtyard I thought I spotted Gavain again.

Someone hailed us, someone closer. After only a second's hesitation, prompted by the prick of the sword's point against his ribs, Raymbaud called back, "No sign of anything yet!"

"You don't put poison on your blade, do you?" I suggested in his ear. "Because it would be ironic if you died of it yourself."

From the courtyard I directed him down a low passage that wrapped around the central keep and then through a doorway into a narrow open area, between the storerooms and the outer walls. The wall here dropped from waist height straight down a hundred feet. This was one of the oldest parts of the castle and little used. With luck, I could kill the bastard and get away from here before our noise brought the rest of the heretics.

Suddenly, unbelievably, an apparition appeared on top of the great tower. Twice as tall as a man, a skeletal form riding an equally enormous skeletal horse, it sprang from the tower to the battlements, brandishing a sword from which sparks flew. The horse's long white legs took it careening across the castle, not quite touching down, while the death's-head rider leered and swung its hellish sword through solid stone.

I staggered backwards, and all through the castle I could hear men screaming. But this apparition, I reminded myself as I fought not to scream, too, was very like those which had appeared in the duke's camp just before Brother Melchior had hurried me away to the postern gate. I never had found out for sure where those apparitions had come from, but the priest must now be providing distraction—either for me, or for his own search for the great battle telesma.

Raymbaud seemed frozen in horror. "That's nothing to do with us," I growled. "You don't get out of our fight this easily." I prodded him forward, then tossed him his sword, the steel flashing in the shadows. "Defend yourself!" I called, readying my own blade. "And let God judge between us!"

But he let his sword hit the ground, ringing against a stone, rather than trying to catch it, and he made no effort to pick it up. Instead he reached inside his tunic, and I realized just too late what he must be reaching for. This was the man who had already set my bed ablaze with a fire telesma.

The center of the courtyard was suddenly a mass of flames. I froze, so filled with terror that my jaw went slack and the sword started to slip from my hand. "God will judge *you* for your infidel faith," Raymbaud shouted in triumph, "and punish you for your harsh treatment of me! For I am of the Perfected, skilled just enough in the arts you decry to overcome you easily. And I tell you, Count, that it will pain me no more to see you die in the fire, as you infidels want all of us to die, than to watch the death of a beetle."

"Gertrude!" I started to shout, grasping at the empty air. But my sister wasn't here. Neither was Bruno. It was just me and the maniacally laughing bouteillier, protected from me by a wall of fire that was rapidly closing in.

And then I remembered Melchior's grandfather's telesma.

My left hand shot around behind me to find the cool ivory rod still thrust into my belt. What were those words the priest had told me? I held the telesma before me, glowing pink now in the light of flames that were only a few feet away. The activating words were almost the last thing he had said to me—

"*Hoc est hora!*" I screamed, finding the words just in time. The telesma in my hand seemed to jump as the lines of magic Melchior had carefully restored to it poured out again. The fire shot sparks and rose high for a second, then recoiled and drew back like a lion cheated of its prey, before the force of the telesma's quenching spell. And this time there was no conviare around my neck to give the flames extra strength against me.

In a moment, although the whole area was scorched,

the flames were reduced to something little bigger than a campfire between Raymbaud and me. I leaped forward, my sword ready and the emperor's battle cry on my lips.

But he realized just in time that he had failed. Snatching up his own sword he fled with a squawk, through an archway behind him. I was right on his heels.

Along the walls we raced, Raymbaud slowly pulling ahead. Fear gave wings to his feet while the wound in my leg slowed mine. In a second, I thought grimly, we would attract the attention of the heretics, and we would then see if the fine bouteillier Raymbaud cared any more about the glory of overcoming me single-handed, when he could join with half a dozen other warriors to make very sure I was dead.

Then he darted around a corner, and I thought I had lost him. I slowed to a walk, my heart pounding madly, trying to resolve the darkness within the passages and arches on either side into human form. If he wasn't cowering in terror, he must be preparing to surprise me.

New screams suddenly rang out throughout the castle. I staggered backwards as an apparition shot past me, an enormous disembodied head with eyes of fire and teeth of steel, gnashing as it flew. One of the screams was very close.

That was Raymbaud's voice. Teeth clenched, I sprang through the open door of the dark room from which his voice had come. There was a crash as he knocked something over, then he leaped out through the window and was gone down the passage.

At least none of the other heretics would be interfering in our fight, I thought, pounding after him.

He had doubled back in his flight through the castle and was now approaching the terrace next to the great tower where Melchior and I had originally come up from the postern. I almost stumbled on the steps in the passageway, then found my footing again. No sign of the lantern on top of the tower now—either it had gone out in the excitement, or the watchman had fled. All my attention was fixed on Raymbaud, but as we burst out onto the terrace I was abruptly distracted by the sight of a scarlet cloak, its color so brilliant it showed even in moonlight.

Someone else had come up the postern stair.

No face showed in the hood's shadow, but I felt a sudden horror-struck certainty who it must be. Raymbaud, closer, must have come to the same conclusion. He yanked an arm around the slender figure's neck, providing a human shield against me as he put his back to the wall at the terrace's edge.

"Still care to match swords with me, Count?" Raymbaud shouted. A high squeak came from within his hostage's hood as he tightened his grip. "This is *my* castle." His face was white in the moonlight, and sweat ran glistening down his forehead, but he seemed to have thrown off his fear of the apparitions in his fury against me. "I turned the castle over to Gavain's warriors only because they are my allies, and I will demonstrate that I am still the master here by killing the infidel claimant—you!"

What in the name of Almighty God was Arsendis doing here? I stood paralyzed, fifteen yards away, my sword dangling. She always wanted to be at the center of the action—why else would she have come from the ducal court along with the reinforcements for which Argave had sent? I still had the postern key in my pouch, but there must be another one which she had quietly borrowed—perhaps from Lord Thierri, who after all had lived here until recently, or even her own father.

But standing here gaping would do nothing to save her. "Don't try to bluff, Raymbaud!" I shouted, attempting to cover slightly too long a pause by projecting brazen confidence. "I know even you, traitor and heretic that you may be, with the countess's death on your soul, are still too much of a gentleman to kill a helpless woman with your own hands!"

Raymbaud frowned, his head cocked—he must not have expected this reaction. I started a slow advance across the terrace, my sword ready. "Let her go, traitor," I said firmly. "She has no part in our quarrel." High, wordless squeaks, from a throat constricted by the bouteillier's arm, seemed to agree with me. "Harm her and I run you through at once. Let her go and I'll give you one more chance to defend yourself."

His sword clattered at his feet, and for a second I thought he had surrendered. I should have known better. The arm not holding his hostage shot toward me, and in his hand was the fire telesma.

I sprang backwards instinctively, the wound in my leg throbbing painfully as I landed. Flames filled the center of the terrace, their brilliant orange dimming the moon. But Raymbaud's fire held no fears for me now, I told myself firmly. My hand felt again the solid shape of the quenching telesma, made by a heretic who had himself been burned to death but whose arts were now practiced by his grandson in the service of God.

I held it out before me. "*Hoc est hora!*" I cried, and waited for the magic within to extinguish the fires again.

And nothing happened.

I shook the ivory telesma wildly and tried the incantation again. Still nothing. My fingers tightened around it until it seemed it must break. Melchior had told me he had not had a chance to recharge this telesma completely. He had used all the stored magic in it to quench the pain of his arrow wound, and he had not had his full strength back since to finish restoring it. The telesma's power was all now exhausted.

Raymbaud thrust the scarlet-cloaked figure from him, straight into the center of the flames, laughing the laugh of a demon from Hell. "Afraid of a little fire, Count? Not quite so bold now, with your one magical trick not working right?"

This was it. My only way back was an archway behind

me which the flames had not yet reached, though they were already close enough that I could feel their heat.

But the scarlet cloak was already ablaze. The heavy wool would protect the wearer for only a few more seconds. All I could see were the desperate flailings of someone trying to put out flames without knowing how to do so, while convulsed with desperate terror.

This was not Gertrude. This was Arsendis, whom I loved even if she would never have me. Gertrude I had not been able to save though trying had scarred me for life. Arsendis might still have a chance.

Every nerve in my body screamed for me to flee. Instead I ripped off my own cloak and leaped forward, into the heart of the flames.

If this was a preview of Hell, then I can only hope for God's mercy on the final day of Judgment. All the hairs on the back of my hands immediately were singed off. Tongues of fire reached toward me, so hot that I felt that in another moment my eyeballs must melt. I flung my cloak completely over the figure before me to muffle the flames and squeezed my eyes shut. Arsendis seemed heavier than I expected, but with a strength born of desperation I heaved the struggling form over my shoulder. Three long strides and I was out of the heart of the fire, four more, my eyes open again, and I was through the archway.

My bad leg collapsed beneath me, wrenching all the tendons in the ankle. I rolled us both on the floor to smother our burning clothing, and beat out the remaining flames with the tail of my cloak. No time to check how well Arsendis was; at least I could hear guttural moans from inside the cloak. I pushed myself up on my remaining good leg and stumbled back to the terrace.

My sword was still where I had dropped it, and I snatched it up at once. No sign yet of heretic reinforcements. Raymbaud stood staring from behind subsiding flames. With half my hair and beard burned off I must have seemed another ghastly apparition coming at him, walking with a pronounced limp but moving without hesitation through knee-high flames that scorched my boots.

He realized just too late that he was backed against the wall over which the countess had fallen when she died.

"You killed Bruno in trying to kill me," I rasped through a smoke-hoarsened throat. "You were responsible for the death of my cousin, Countess Aenor of Peyrefixade. You have betrayed me, your sworn lord. As rightful Count of Peyrefixade, with the right and authority invested in me by Duke Argave and, through him, by the king, I sentence you to die."

For a horrible second I thought he was going to shoot fire at me a third time. But that telesma too must now all be exhausted. He snatched up his sword and tried to dodge past me.

Bad leg or not, I was too fast for him. He only avoided being immediately spitted by springing backwards again. My next sword stroke he parried, and the next, not getting in any good return strokes while his eyes grew wider and wider.

He was looking somewhere past my shoulder. I was much too old a soldier to fall for a trick like that, even when he started to point with his left hand. A sharp blow which he barely deflected sent him staggering backwards, fetching up against the parapet. He cried out in fear and what might have been a much too tardy plea for mercy.

I sprang after him, all the weight of my body behind the blade. My sword stroke went straight and true into his throat, and the force of my leap carried him, my sword, and nearly me over the edge.

He disappeared with a dying scream, and I crumbled at the base of the wall, listening. After what seemed a very long time I heard the splat of flesh and bone hitting stone below. At the same instant, a skeletal rider shot overhead and, trailing sparks, galloped away through empty air.

So he *had* seen something. Melchior's magic had served me again. Trembling all over, I groped for my knife. My sword was gone, the good Allemannic steel blade I had carried up and down the Empire. At this point, even if I had it, I wasn't sure I could have used it.

The fire too was gone, leaving the stones of the terrace darkened and hot. I tried standing and ended up crawling instead, on hands and knees now painfully sore, back toward the archway.

"Galoran?" That wasn't Arsendis. That was a man's voice—someone extremely familiar, although I could not at the moment place him.

Someone was standing in the archway, someone wearing the burned remains of a scarlet cloak. As he stepped forward, the moonlight hit his face and I finally placed the voice. It was Lord Thierri.

"You aren't Arsendis," I said stupidly and subsided to the flagstones.

"No," he said, approaching and looking at me critically. His red hair had been burned off close to his head. "I saved your life down in the duke's court, and now you've saved mine. You look terrible."

"It was you the whole time," I said slowly, as my brain refused to accept the obvious. "Raymbaud was trying to use you as a hostage. You got caught in his magical fire. But what are you doing here? And why are you wearing the young duchess's cloak?"

"This is *my* cloak," he said with a sudden smile as he realized my mistake. "Perhaps you've seen her wearing a similar one—one I arranged for my tailor to make her as a gift after she admired mine. As to what I'm doing here, when I realized you and that half-heretic priest had disappeared from camp during all the excitement, I had a good guess where you had gone. So I waited until things were calmer and used the key I'd kept when Argave unceremoniously turned me out—never can tell when a quiet entry will come in handy! I didn't trust what the two of you might be doing, and I was proven right when I arrived to see the castle engulfed in flames!"

I rose to my knees and seized him in a bear hug, laughing so loud it should have brought all the heretics down on us at once. He tried to pull back, the same scheming, ineffective Thierri as ever, who now on top of everything doubted my sanity. My legs might be wounded, but there was nothing wrong with my arms. I clung to him even tighter—he was going to be my friend now whether he wanted to be or not.

"My sister died in a fire when I was just a boy, Thierri," I said, my voice still rough with smoke—and certainly not emotion. "I couldn't save her, and my brother didn't even try. Now that I've saved *you*, you'll have to be both brother and sister to me." He looked at me with no idea what I was talking about, but I didn't care. "I don't think I can walk unaided, but Gavain and all his knights may be here in a second. You'll have to defend me, though here against this wall may not be the best place—"

I was interrupted by a great roar that shook the castle, a roar of rending timber and falling stone.

Chapter Fourteen ~ Melchior

1

I stood motionless in the shadows for some moments after the count was out of sight, probing with my second ear for any sound indicating unease either among the guards on the wall or elsewhere in the castle. But there was nothing. Well, if Count Galoran was making for the gates, it made excellent sense for me to go in the opposite direction. If he succeeded in getting the gates down, it would be best to be out of the way of the melee that would doubtless follow when the duke and his men charged in. And if he failed, it would be equally well for me to be hidden where I could devote myself to our only other hope—finding the great telesma, and quickly. Besides, working from a place of concealment I could create diversions that could help the count evade capture. And luckily we had entered not very far from the best such spot.

The count, long a soldier, was doubtless well practiced in the arts of scouting and ambush; he could probably creep about the castle for a long time without being discovered. But my case was different. Now that I was not discorporate, I would need to employ magical aid if I hoped to move more than a few yards without being detected.

Reaching inside my cassock, I felt along the special belt that held all the things I'd brought from the House of the Order, each hung in a carefully memorized sequence.

I felt my box of divination supplies, then a little further
along the sack containing powder of blindness (I still had
more than half left), the conviare, the parchment and dust
for far-writing, powders and devices for causing fire, fog,
light, and the phial containing the potion of discorporation.
My fingers recoiled when they touched the little bag
containing the terrible *pulvis potentissimus,* and I recalled
the terrifying moment when the Count had briefly held
it in his hand on the mountain. Then I felt the thing I
wanted: a small flat packet of parchment that gave slightly
when I pressed it, containing a magical object supplied
by Prior Belthesar.

I drew it forth, broke the prior's wax seal, and shook
out the soft stringy bundle within until I was holding a
fine net of black mesh. I draped this over my shoulders
like an old woman's shawl and fastened it at my throat
with the clasp I found at the bottom of the packet.
Immediately, I felt the lines of magic begin to stream
from the clasp through the cloak of shadows. Kneeling
by the wall, I murmured a prayer for the count's safety
and followed with another: that if possible I be spared
having to use the more terrible sorts of magic now at my
command. Then I rose and started along the wall, toward
the doorway to a passage that would take me to the tower
at the rear corner of the castle, perched where the
mountain fell away.

I hadn't covered three yards when a man with a gleaming
halberd came out of that door, looking straight in my
direction.

My fingers clenched around the powder of blindness,
which I'd vowed to use in any emergency before anything
more deadly. But then the man looked away and walked
across the terrace and along the base of the tower opposite,
calling out somebody's name. Now I knew the cloak of
shadows really worked. Still, I remained quite still until
the guard was out of sight, recalling that its magic could
not render me actually invisible, merely very hard to notice.

A voice answered from the tower, and the guard called up, "No sign of anything from the rear ramparts. How do things look down toward the siege camp?" Without staying to hear the answer, I slipped into the passage and hurried through.

When I emerged into the moonlight again, I was high on the rear ramparts, above the low courtyard behind the keep where the men sometimes practiced swordplay. Sixty feet ahead loomed the squat square bulk of the back tower.

Once there, I paused to probe the silence carefully with my second ear. While not as familiar with the overall plan of Peyrefixade as the count or any of his knights, I knew this particular tower well. It stood at the point on the castle commanding the best view of the road that led toward the House of my Order; indeed, on a clear day one could sometimes even glimpse the peak of great Conaigue itself, far off beyond the rows of hills and mountains. If the tower was now being used as a sentry point by the occupiers, they'd place their watchmen in the topmost chamber, the same room to which I had occasionally slipped away to gaze along that road that led to my Mother House during my months at Peyrefixade.

But there were other rooms lower down that I'd looked into briefly on one occasion—rooms that shouldn't interest enemy sentries, especially at night. My second ear confirmed this. There were three men in the top room, playing at dice on the table near the fire, but the rest of the tower echoed with emptiness. I waited until one of the sentries threw a winning roll and began to rake in the stakes with a clatter of coppers and a laugh, then pushed open the door to the stairs, stepped inside, and closed it after me. A single torch flickering in a bracket above gave me just enough light to creep down two turns of the stair to a lower room.

This place was used only for storage nowadays, but the pictures and messages patiently scratched into the hard stone walls attested to its long service as a prison cell in times past. It would have been pitch dark to any of the sentries if he'd stepped inside. But with the aid of my second eye, I was easily able to make my way among old chests and heaps of rusty mail to the far side of the circular room. Once there, I paused to consider my next move.

Although there'd been precious little exertion about anything I'd done in the castle so far, my heart was pounding. Forcing myself to put aside my feelings of desperate urgency, I devoted a few minutes to prayer and concentration to calm my poor body. It would not do to make any error in what I was about to attempt.

As soon as I felt in command of myself once more, I closed my true eyes (which were virtually useless in such a dark room anyway) and concentrated all my attention upon my second eyes and ears in the way Brother Quercus had schooled me. Slowly a vision of the room I was in appeared inside my mind, as clear as if I were seeing it in broad daylight. Turning my attention to my second ears, I found I could hear a family of mice in their nest deep inside a chest of old wall hangings next to me, and after a little more time, the very sounds of moths chewing at the rotting fabric. Then another sound caught my attention. Sneaking along near a chest in the corner was the thing I sought: a rat.

The problem I faced was simple. I was about to work some major magic in a castle containing at least two Perfected Magians. These men were presumably at least as skilled as myself. I must find a way to occupy their attention so that, with luck, they would not discover me before I had a chance to achieve my objective. Given the haste with which Count Galoran and I had left the duke's camp, there had been no time to formulate any plan or make preparations. But thanks to the foresight of someone at the Mother House, I had the means of creating some excellent distractions with me.

The method would be based on a prank I had seen

played by some of the more unruly novices when I first joined the Order, one in which I had been too hesitant to join—though evidently Prior Belthesar had been less timid in his day, since he'd used exactly this method to create the diversion that had allowed the count and me to get out of the duke's camp. Focusing my attention on the rat's location, I reached into my cassock, took out a phial containing a powder that could briefly paralyze any living creature, and tossed out its contents. A moment later the rat's limp body was in my hand. Working swiftly, I took the smaller of two telesmae from a certain pouch and bound it firmly to the rat's tail with a length of wire. Then I took the finding knife from my divination box, touched it to the telesma, laid the rat on the floor, and waited. In about two minutes the rat jerked, shook himself, clawed at the wire in futile irritation, then scuttled away.

Now for the difficult part. I moved to the far side of the room and lowered myself down behind a big chest until I was seated on the dusty floor with my back braced, where my body would be completely hidden even if a Magian should come to the door with a speculum capable of revealing a man wearing a cloak of shadows. Setting my divination box on the floor, I took out a small tripod. I attached the mistletoe to the finding knife, suspended it from this tripod with a cord, then sprinkled on the copper dust. Once I was sure the blade was swinging perfectly level and free with a good load of powdered copper, I got out the phial of discorporation. With such a recent memory of the process I was about to undergo I had to force myself to drink, but I got the cold poison down. Settling myself against the chest as best I could, I closed my eyes and concentrated all my skill on the single objective of retaining my second vision and hearing through the process of discorporation.

I knew it was working when I felt the cold again, worse this time. Like the cold of death—my death. After a moment I stood up in spectral form and turned to see my poor body, with no strong soldier's arms to hold it, slumped loose against the chest with lolling jaw, looking unpleasantly like a corpse.

But now everything around me seemed to gleam with clarity. I began to feel the task before me might be possible after all. I would, however, need to scout my opposition before I undertook the actual work. Effortlessly, I whisked up the spiral stairs to just outside the guardroom where the enemy watchmen sat arguing over the stakes for the next roll of the dice. Then I sent my spectral self out through the wall and hung next to the tower. The back exercise yard seemed as bright as day, and I had only to concentrate my attention upon any spot to hear whatever sounds might be there. I felt untouchable, invincible— which merely meant that my peril was severe.

Spector General Endaris, through skill and long practice, could sustain himself discorporate for long periods. But if I, a novice at the art, were to forget myself and remain out of my flesh for more than about half an hour, my spectral body would disperse so that it and my selfhood would be lost forever. As to what might happen to a man and his soul if anyone should happen to discover and destroy his helpless body while he was absent from it, that was a thing no book of Magian lore told, though there were dark legends.

The thought recalled me to the urgency of my task. Floating up until I was higher even than the keep, I began to survey the castle for hints of Magian presence. Almost at once, to my shock, I saw a light in the chapel and sensed the presence of magic there. I sent my spectral body gliding swiftly down until it was hovering just outside the window and halted, stunned, as I encountered a veritable spiderweb of magic lines. Projecting my second vision inside, I discovered a hideous profanation. The lesser battle telesma of the Magus de Cuza, which took the form of a breastplate set with twelve square-cut tiles of obsidian, had been laid upon the altar, where it lay vibrating with a gorgeous but frightening magical pattern! And two men in robes were standing with their hands resting upon it—both of them Perfected Magians.

"You were wrong, the great telesma must be hidden elsewhere," one of them said after a minute, in Nabarrese-accented Auccitan, as he took his hands away. "I told you the old Magus would never have concealed it here in his own chamber of worship; that would have been too obvious."

"And you've proved right," said the other in pure Auccitan as he removed his own hands. He had a dark bruise down one side of his face. "But this room has been a consecrated chapel to the infidel faith since our grandfathers lost this castle. There was always the possibility that cursed infidel mage-priest Malkior, or whatever his name is, might have located the great telesma himself during his months here and hidden it in this room."

"And betray not only his lord but his own infidel Order?" The first one laughed. "Well, you certainly hold a poor opinion of the fellow!—and by the way, his name is Melchior, as you well know. I think you are merely holding a grudge over the fact that he was able to knock you off your horse and help the count escape despite your best magic. Besides, our little Raymbaud has proven surprisingly adroit in using the telesmae and other things we provided him. He would have discovered it if that had occurred."

"Even if he had, I wouldn't put it past him to keep the thing a secret and try to turn it to his own advantage. I don't trust that fellow at all."

"Nor does Lord Gavain. But I don't consider Raymbaud such a bad fellow. The problem with you and Lord Gavain is that you didn't grow up in Nabarra, having to practice the arts of deception your whole lives. If you'd passed as a loyal member of Prince Alfonso's own court as Raymbaud and I have, in the very belly of the monster, you'd understand better how a man can play false to all about him and yet still be true at the core."

"Well, I still don't think we can rely on either his soundness or his use of magic. He certainly failed in his attempt to use his first fïre telesma to assassinate the count; the infidel Magian thwarted him there with little difficulty. Of course, you had no better success at that job using those footpads you hired in the duke's city, and came close to having this Melchior catch you standing over a fresh corpse into the bargain. He's the one we should have tried to eliminate."

"Now, now, I won't hear a word against Magian Melchior. His own grandfather was the close friend of our own dear master when both were pupils of the great de Cuza, and he died faithful in the flames. I think he could have potential for us yet—what is it, what's the matter?"

"I have an odd feeling," said the one I'd knocked down. "As if there were magic about."

"Of course there is. The Magus's lesser telesma lies before us upon the unclean infidel altar. You and I have spent the last half hour plucking at the lines of magic radiating from it in hope of waking an echo from its great mate. There are lines of magic in the very air."

"No, I tell you this is something else! We must immediately—"

I did not stay to learn what they must do immediately. A finding spell, doubtless. It would be directed specifically at locating another magic worker, so Count Galoran should be safe from it. And so would I—exactly as long as I remained in a discorporate condition. But the situation had become even more urgent. Now that I was no longer concentrating every ounce of attention on the Magians in the chapel, I could perceive that the sensation of deadly cold, the only sensation within my spectral form, had most definitely increased. The period remaining before I must reenter my forsaken body or be forever lost was growing shorter by the moment.

Still, it had been worth expending a portion of my limited time eavesdropping at the chapel window. I now knew I would have to contend with the powers of two, but only two, Perfected Magians as soon as I reentered my body—for if there were a third in Peyrefixade, he would certainly have been with them to help search for the great telesma. There was also a good side to their having detected some hint of my presence, since they would now temporarily put aside their efforts to find the great telesma while they searched for me. I must use that time to find it myself.

The first order of business was to distract them, which meant I must activate the telesma I had attached to the rat. In the flesh, I could have activated the thing at a distance by speaking the required charm, but in my discorporate condition I would need to be in the presence of the telesma itself. Like a wisp of fog on the night wind, I whirled back across the courtyard to the rear tower and straight through the lower wall into the chamber where my finding knife was hanging from the tripod. I rested one spectral hand upon the tripod and thought the proper words to activate the finding knife. In my discorporate condition, my retained second vision could see not only the fine spray of copper that leaped from its point once it had found the proper direction, but the line of magic this was indicating as well. As soon as I saw it, I glided swiftly along that line, passing straight through walls and empty air until I found my rat slinking along one of the ramparts. Focusing all my attention upon the little telesma, I "touched" it with my spectral hand and thought the command that would waken its stored power. An instant later the hideous form of a skeletal warrior, clad in full mail and wielding a bloody ax, materialized directly above the rat. The creature took one look and fled with a high-pitched scream, while the illusory monster stalked stiffly away along the parapet.

The thing would only retain its apparent substantiality for a few minutes, but as soon as it dispersed, the telesma would produce another horror wherever the rat happened to be at that moment. These random outbursts of magic, along with the confusion and alarm the illusory monsters would cause among the soldiers, would keep the Magians busy for a while. With luck, they would also create some cover for Count Galoran.

Back in the tower room, I faced my poor abandoned body and reached out my spectral fingers to "touch" the conviare that hung at my belt. "Your spectral form is simply an ephemeral thickening of the air, created from your memory of your physical body," Spector General Endaris had said. "But even though your ghost hand could not so much as lift a penny, touching an object with it is still the best way to focus your attention so you can grip it using those powers that actually work better when you're discorporate." By which he'd meant Magian powers.

And he'd been right! The instant my ghostly fingers contacted the conviare, I felt its lines of powerful magic resonating like the strings of a plucked lute. After what seemed hours with no sensation but that deathly cold, it was like a sudden shock. Within seconds, those vibrations had penetrated the whole of my spectral form. It was almost as if I and the conviare had fused.

I felt an incredible sense of exhilaration, as if no feat of magic was beyond me now. Power, the feeling—the certainty—of enormous power, was within my grasp. Not the vast but always elusive power of faith, continually undercut by my own failings and shortcomings or the doubts created by the evil and injustice that were everywhere in the world, but the sure power of magic when one is working it at the highest level.

And then I remembered the face of the Master of our Order and his calm old voice speaking of how the True Faith had never allowed even him to suppose he was or could be perfect. My sanity returned and I offered up a brief but fervent prayer in thanks for deliverance from a terrible temptation. And to think the Magus de Cuza had created this thing and wielded it for years! With his skill, he would have been able to experience something very close to this sensation even in the flesh—no wonder he'd had the pride of Lucifer.

Well, I was no Magus, nor even a senior Magian of my own Order, just plain Brother Melchior. But the conviare would not care about that. I would not have to be entirely perfect, only to do one bit of work perfectly, and it would serve me as efficiently as it had ever served its great and wicked creator.

Keeping one vaporous hand on the conviare, I reached out my other hand and rested one ghostly finger on top of the tripod from which the finding knife was suspended, linking them. As soon as this link was established, the finding knife began to vibrate at the end of its thread. Fixing my second vision on the conviare, I looked deeper and deeper *into* it until I located the two intricate knots centered within its lines of magic which the masters had already identified at the Mother House. Having glimpsed the object itself within the last few minutes, I recognized right away the smaller pattern as the magical signature of the lesser battle telesma. So the other had to represent the great one.

It was unbelievably intricate, the most complex magic pattern I had ever encountered. Under normal circumstances, no responsible Magian would have dreamed of attempting to do anything with such a powerful object without taking at least a week to analyze it first. But I hadn't that luxury. Offering up another quick prayer, I allowed the simulacrum of that pattern to flow directly through my spectral body to the finding knife.

The knife swung at the end of its cord, spun wildly within the tripod, then froze in the air as firmly as if it had stuck in some solid object, pointing at a downward angle. As soon as the knife stopped moving, every speck of copper dust in the mistletoe came streaming down its blade and off its tip into the dark air. The bright flakes hung suspended for a few seconds, tracing a line straight from the knife to a spot intersecting the floor of the room, then sifted slowly down onto the stones.

But the potent line of magic they had indicated was now as clear to my second eye as if it had been traced in fire. Removing my ghost hands from both the conviare and the tripod, I set my spectral form in motion and swiftly followed that line down into the floor and out through the lower wall of the tower to the courtyard, and from there straight down through the flagstones toward a point directly under the great keep itself.

Some sixty feet beneath the emergency storage room below the keep, in a narrow chamber that appeared to have been hewn into the solid rock, I found the great battle telesma of the Magus de Cuza lying on the rotted remains of a satin cushion.

It was a beautiful and sinister object, a squat crown wrought to suggest the form of a crouching scorpion. I had no need to touch it with my spectral hand to perceive the intricate network of lines of magic spun both through and all around it. The intricacy and pure elegance of the pattern at the telesma's center left me stunned with admiration; monster though he had been, the old magus had wrought an object of absolute genius in this creation. It was charged with enormous power too, almost glowing from the slow buildup of latent magic force over the half century it had lain waiting here in the dark. If this thing could be brought to the surface in its present condition, the count and I would have a weapon that could smash anything.

The question was: how? A melted spot on the rocky roof of the chamber showed how the great telesma had descended; presumably the Magus had used mostly the power of the lesser battle telesma, along with a little of its own, to send it down and seal it here. While it clearly contained enough stored power to make the trip if I were to summon it to the surface now through the conviare, it might arrive too drained to use immediately for the purposes I required. And I rather suspected the two Perfected Magians would be disinclined to allow me the hours or days it would take to charge the great telesma with magic once more. But I must find a way, and quickly too; I could feel the cold increasing rapidly now, an indication that the integrity of my spectral form was beginning to fray.

Suddenly the answer came to me—or at least an answer. One I did not like at all. My mind raced, but nothing else seemed likely to work. Unless, of course, Count Galoran had managed to get the gates open within the last few minutes. Swiftly I retraced the line of magic connecting the great telesma to the conviare, sweeping upward through solid rock and then foundation stones into the little rear exercise yard. I heard yells and the sounds of running feet, and hope flared briefly. Then I saw a skeletal apparition with eyes of fire riding above the keep in the empty air and realized there was no sign of any real fighting, no clash of arms or shouts as the duke's men rushed in through opened gates to overwhelm the demoralized, outnumbered defenders and make them prisoners. Evidently, it was all still up to me.

By the time I reached the tower room, everything was beginning to grow blurry to my second vision. Only a few minutes remained to reenter my fleshly body. But as soon as I did this, any decent finding spell aimed at locating the magic-worker within the castle would begin to track me down. Moreover, all the magic movements that had seemed so effortless while I was discorporate meant that my fleshly self was going to awake with a crushing load of physical fatigue, like a man who had run for many miles. I was cold, so cold, but I forced myself to ignore this until I had gone carefully in my mind over the sequence of acts required to perform what I must do, as well as working out what actions I could take in response to each foreseeable move by my opposition. As soon as I had done this, I summoned all my resolution and collapsed back into my own body.

2

My first breath brought searing pain, worse even than
the cold had been. My limbs seemed made of stone, my
head far too heavy to lift, my whole body wracked by the
worst mage-sickness I had ever experienced. Had I
presented myself to the Brother Infirmerian in either the
Mother House or the Priory in such a condition, he would
at once have ordered me to bed for a week. But no one
here was likely to show that kind of concern for my well-
being. Somehow or other I made it to my feet, kicking
over the tripod with its finding knife in the process. I let
it lie; I could return for it later if I should happen to survive.
It took two tries of my clumsy, shaking fingers to work
the conviare off my belt, make the necessary passes over
it, and hang it about my neck. Once it was in place with
my cassock closed over it, I was able to reach out and
tap the great telesma to gain the power necessary to support
my sagging body.

The stairs seemed to spiral to the moon, but I made
the climb somehow, one weary step at a time. A fallen
cup and some dice lay scattered down the steps by the
tower door; apparently one of my apparitions had visited
the guardroom above while I'd been off in spectral form
searching for the great telesma. I had come along the
wall from the right, the shortest route to the main castle,
and the temptation to return the same way was urgent
in my weakness. But this seemed too risky, since the
Magians might well have discovered how we had entered
and be waiting on the terrace, so I stepped out onto the
ramparts and turned the other way.

Within ten paces I saw three men with drawn swords
coming slowly back along the rampart and froze until I
remembered that I was still wearing the cloak of shadows.
Sure enough, the guards walked right past me, staring up
at the tower with nervous eyes. As soon as they disappeared
inside, I resumed my dragging pace along the wall.

Reaching the lookout post at the northeast angle of the wall, I turned to start along the north rampart toward the main part of the castle, praying that I be allowed to reach it without meeting any obstacles beyond my own weariness. But that was not to be. A dozen men in chain mail were coming along the rampart with swords in their hands. At their head was the Perfected Magian with the bruised face, and in his hand he held a speculum. I turned the other way, only to see the second Magian already at the base of the tower I had just left; the three dicing guards had just emerged to join him. He had the lesser telesma upon his chest and a finding knife in his hand. "It appears our friend Melchior has been here recently!" he called across in his Nabarrese accent to his bruised friend.

"Ah, then he must still be very close despite the phantasms he has somehow been creating everywhere *but* here. Couldn't you bring any more men?"

"No, Lord Gavain insisted on keeping the rest at the front; he fears an attack may come soon. Melchior did not enter alone; a man has been found lying bound and gagged in the kitchen, and Raymbaud is missing entirely." My spirits lifted as I heard this; evidently Count Galoran was still free, and busy creating helpful diversions. Had any more men come with the Magians, the chance of succeeding in my plan would have been far poorer.

"That's bad. If the castle has been penetrated by warriors, too, we have to find this infidel Magian quickly." The bruised fellow twisted the speculum in his hand and sent a shaft of moonlight toward me. I ducked into the little guardroom that stood at one side of the lookout post, but a hint of my form must have been momentarily revealed. "There! He is there, at the watchpost on the corner of the wall!"

I had wanted to meet them; it was necessary for my plan. But it was the wrong Magian who was closest to me at the present moment. Perhaps I could confuse them briefly, and tempt the man I wanted to come nearer.

Reaching into my cassock, I pulled out the little sack
containing the second telesma of apparitions and flung
it out onto the stone floor of the lookout post. A pair of
bat-winged demons eight feet high appeared with hideous
howls and began to stalk along the ramparts toward the
two groups of Perfected. "Hah, look!" called the Nabarrese
Magian to his friend. "You are deceived. It is only more
of his apparitions."

"I am not so sure," the bruised one yelled back. "We
had better go forward and—ooof!" Ill as I felt, I had to
smile at the expression my second eye revealed on his
face as the demon on his rampart reached out and knocked
him down. The telesma I had attached to the rat could
generate only illusions, but this one's productions were
capable of assuming a brief substantiality. The soldiers
behind the fallen Magian began to edge back along the
wall, except for one young fellow who lunged forward
with his sword. The demon caught the blade in its hard
hand and snapped it like a stick, started to reach out for
the man himself—then vanished in a blaze of fire. Casting
my second vision the other way, I saw its counterpart also
flare up into nothingness. On the breast of the Nabarrese
Magian, the dark obsidian tiles of the lesser telesma glowed
for a moment longer, then went black again. But my ruse
had caused the fellow to move closer to me.

"He's here, I tell you, and now we're going to take him!"
shouted the now twice-bruised Magian, scrambling to his
feet and waving to his warriors to follow. But the Nabarrese
one called, "Wait, let me talk to him. Magian Melchior, I
know you are near us now. And I know you are watching
us with your second vision even though you are not where
we can see you. Listen to me."

My body felt worse now than it had that winter seven
years ago when a bad coughing sickness had swept the
whole of the southern mountains, prostrating much of
the population and carrying off many of the aged and
infirm, including a number of the senior brothers, and

my arrow wound had begun to throb again. But my mind felt quite clear. I did not want to hear this man's words: dreaded them, in fact. But the longer I could keep them talking, the closer I could draw them, the more likely it was that I could succeed in the only plan that seemed likely to work. Summoning all my resolution, I took a phial in each hand, walked out into the open, took a few steps along the parapet in his direction, and slipped the cloak of shadows from my shoulders. "Speak if you like, but don't come too near," I rasped in a voice that scarcely sounded like mine even in my own ears. "We of the Order take an oath not to use magic to attack the unoffending, but force is allowed if our lives or those we are sworn to protect are threatened. What do you want?"

"You; I want you!" He took several steps toward me, smiling as if he had just caught sight of a long-absent friend. "Why should you resist us in this way? We are your brother Magians! You are a Magian of great skill and talent, as my friend there"—gesturing toward the bruised fellow with the angry face—"knows to his cost. Why should a man of your powers place yourself at the service of noble fools, whose only power flows from the fact that they have persuaded even greater fools to serve them with their swords? And why should you obey those apostate Magians who have presumed to name their infidel Order for the Three Kings, and use its hierarchy to keep younger and more talented men subject to themselves? Why serve anyone else, when you are already master of great powers of your own, including powers that require no assistance from knights or soldiers? Are you not better than your count or your duke? Come join us, and we shall take you to our own Maguses, who will show you how to gain still greater powers and teach you how to perfect yourself, until in the end you will not need to bow to the judgment of any other man."

"I have pledged myself to the Order and the True Faith,

and sworn to serve Count Galoran!" I cried, as much to myself as to him.

"Pledges made in your youth, in fear and in sadness; how can they bind you now?" He advanced another few steps, shaking his head as if distressed with my obstinate refusal to see the obvious. "Did not this infidel creed that miscalls itself the 'true' faith consign your own grandfather to the flames before your very eyes, merely because he would not bend his neck and bow before it? Our own late Master was your grandfather's intimate friend in youth, when they were both pupils of the great Magus who once held this very castle, and he spoke often of him. Your grandfather was a Magian of marvelous skill, yet never a prideful man, never otherwise than kind and forthcoming to everyone he dealt with. You yourself knew and learned from him when young; you know this. Your own grasp of magic is founded on Perfected teachings, his teachings. Do you know why the working of magic is so difficult for even the senior members of your Order? Why a few simple sendings weary them to the point of death, whereas our own greatest Maguses, men like the Magus de Cuza, could fight entire armies to a standstill unaided? It is because they wrestle continually against themselves, always undercutting their own power in an attempt to be *humble*, as if men were the weakest and least of created beings instead of the greatest!"

"Now you transgress even against your own doctrine," I shouted. "I did indeed learn much from my grandfather, so I know that the Perfected also acknowledge that we are all sinful and fallen."

"Yes, yes, of course we do." He was still smiling, still advancing, as was his sore-faced friend—though that fellow was not smiling. "But unlike what is taught by your Order's doleful creed, we know we can rise while still in this world! When have you felt strongest, most at peace? Was it when you were groveling in false prayers in which you named yourself lower than the dust from which we all come?

Was it not rather when you were working magic as true magic should be worked, freely, raising yourself for at least a little while to a level only slightly lower than the angels? And why should you labor in the service of some scarred and twisted cripple from the northern edge of the world? Come join us, and we will show you what magic can be when worked by free men among people who revere Magians rather than fear them, serve them rather than suppress them!"

Weak as I was with mage-sickness, tired in mind and body from having wrought far too much magic in far too brief a time, his words were almost an incantation in themselves. Of course he was in part only trying to distract me, to keep my mind occupied while he and his companion worked their way close enough to attempt whatever they were planning. But I felt convinced that he was also sincere, that if I were to cast aside my defenses and agree to join them I would be welcomed. I was praying as I listened, seeking a way to keep faith against his blandishments, and watching myself in the old fear that somehow the very roots of my own magic might suddenly be used to turn me to his side. For a moment it almost seemed that I was weakening, feeling myself beginning to give way.

Suddenly the vision of another face swam briefly between my eyes and the Magian, the scarred obstinate face of a man who might be beaten but would never yield—Count Galoran's face. He had trusted me even against his own instincts, and I must keep faith with him, whatever else I might do.

The Perfected Magians and soldiers were close enough now. With a jerk that made my shoulder flare in agony, I threw my left sleeve across my face and flung out the powder of blindness with my right, hearing the bruised Magian's warning yell to his men as the great flash shown all about me.

When I lowered my sleeve, most of the soldiers were staggering aimlessly or clutching at the ramparts with groping hands. Two fell shrieking into the exercise yard when they stepped off into empty air—I prayed they would not be badly hurt. But both Magians and three of the soldiers who were with the bruised one had shielded their eyes in time. He and they were running along the walkway toward me now, the men with swords at the ready. "Stay back!" I yelled. But the bruised Magian answered me with a potent magic stroke, which I deflected only by drawing more power up from the great telesma. The swordsmen were ignoring my warning, too; they were almost on top of me, their blades already upraised. It was too late to evade them with the cloak of shadows, too late for anything—except the one thing I had most hoped to avoid using, the phial in my other hand. Shutting both my physical eyes and my second vision to what must happen now, I threw the awful *pulvis potentissimus*.

When I looked, which I had to do despite myself, it seemed as if four of my apparitions had joined me on the rampart—but it was the Magian and his men, the flesh rapidly melting from their faces and bodies. The soldiers' swords dropped clattering from the their hands, already skeletal, while their dying bodies collapsed against the crenellations or crumpled to the walkway. The bruised Magian, somehow supporting his dissolving form with magic, managed two more paces toward me, shrieking a curse and trying to muster one more magic stroke. But then his staring eyes melted out of their sockets and flowed down his cheeks. An instant later, his face itself fell off, revealing his hollow-eyed skull, and he collapsed lifeless across my feet.

"Melchior!" Blinking away tears of horror and pity, I turned, slowly and painfully to face the other Magian. His hand was stretched out toward me, and the obsidian tiles of the lesser telesma were glowing upon his breast. "I had hoped to win you to us, but I cannot let this pass," he declared. "You must die."

Magic leaped from his fingers with his last word—and

I had him, though not by actually touching the telesma as I had originally thought I would have to do. He had launched his stroke straight at my face, and I saw his eyes grow wide with the realization of his mistake when it bent in midair and went instead to my breast.

But only for an instant. The conviare seemed to leap against my chest as it seized and channeled the power flowing from the lesser battle telesma, then sent it forth again in a white-hot stream straight down the line of magic that still linked it to the greater. In the exercise yard below, cobbles split and flew, then the rock itself melted and vanished like ice touched with a piece of molten iron. I could see the mouth of the Nabarrese Magian work as he screamed incantations, vainly trying to shut off that flow of power. But he was far too late; nothing now could break the lesser telesma's link with the conviare that had been fashioned to command it.

Within seconds, the lines of magic that he and the other Perfected Magian had doubtless spent numberless hours laying into the lesser telesma had been drained and sent down to melt a shaft through the solid rock beneath the keep of Peyrefixade. Then the beam of power flickered and went out. I looked down to see the front of my cassock burnt completely away, exposing the still-glowing conviare. When I raised my eyes, a lurid new light was shining up through the narrow shaft that had been burned down through the rock below. There was a sudden rush of stale wind, then a blaze of fire, and the great battle telesma of the Magus de Cuza soared up, under the open sky again for the first time in half a hundred years, and settled itself upon my tonsured head.

I felt a little push, as if I had been jostled slightly in a crowd, and looked over to see the Nabarrese Magian just lowering his hand. He had tried a magic stroke using his own unaided power—and the great telesma had absorbed it as the sea takes in a raindrop. When he saw me look his way, he composed his face, expecting an annihilating

stroke in return. But I simply waved him into the guard
tower and turned to go my way. I was too weary for needless
fighting, and too sickened by what I had done to the other
Magian and the soldiers to want to harm anyone again.
My legs seemed as heavy as blocks of stone, and I felt far
too weary to stoop and retrieve the cloak of shadows as I
began to walk along the wall. I had no further need of it
now, anyway.

When I got to the watchpost at the northeast corner
of the wall, my foot kicked the apparition telesma and a
dozen horrors leaped into existence. I bound two of them
to walk with me and sent the rest flying or leaping toward
every corner of the castle. No one else appeared to oppose
me as I made my slow way along the north rampart, past
the blinded warriors, and through the long passageway
to the main courtyard.

But there was someone there. He whirled to face me
with sword in hand, staring with a grim, sardonic face at
the monsters beside me and the terrible thing that crowned
my head. Lord Gavain.

"So, you and the count have won, it appears," he rasped.
"We are beaten with the very thing we had hoped to recover
for ourselves. Will you at least grant me the boon of a
clean death, rather than the flames of the Inquisition?"

I was almost beyond feeling anything, yet I felt the
stirring of something like joy at his words, for they meant
the count had neither been killed or taken. "I have killed
too many already this night; I will not kill you, my lord,"
I told him with thick lips and tongue. "Both for your sister
and father's sakes, and because it would break my sworn
oath to kill only in just defense. Take what men you can
still muster into the upper part of the keep and prepare
to make what terms you can with your father and the
count. This place and the lower keep will shortly be
indefensible."

He made as if to turn and go, then suddenly whirled
and swung his sword toward me. One of my hideous

companions caught the blade on a scaly arm, shattering it. Lord Gavain stood still for a moment to see if I would now oblige him with death, then bowed, turned, and walked away without deigning to hurry. Armed men appeared in the doorway to the great hall, but he waved them back inside. More men could now be seen upon the watchpost above the main gate. Lord Gavain called them down and sent them into the keep also, then bowed to me once more and walked calmly inside to join his men just as if he were going in to have his dinner.

Having seen directly into the conviare while discorporate, I now had no need to pronounce incantations to focus it or send forth the power of the great telesma that it channeled; my thoughts alone were enough. Weariness was sitting on my shoulders like a thousand-pound weight, and my body remained standing only with the aid of magic. Slowly, I walked over to the big covered well and sat down on its edge like a man of ninety.

Only one task remained to be done. At my signal, one of my apparitional companions soared to the top of the gate on his dark wings and sounded the horn three times. As the last echoes were still dying away, I extended my right hand toward the main gate and pointed one finger of my left toward the oaken door of the great hall, then thought a single brief command through the conviare. A great bubble of magic force appeared, whirling before me like a star come down to earth, then separated into two parts, one much larger than the other. An instant later the larger one went blazing across the courtyard to my right and struck the main gates with a sound like thunder and a flash brighter than a dozen suns, while the smaller vanished in the opposite direction.

When my sight returned after many seconds, I found myself gazing down the moonlit road to the valley through a great breach in the walls. Of portcullis, gates, guardposts, even the gatehouse itself, there remained no trace at all. I turned my weary head and saw that the oaken door to the great keep was also no more, obliterated by a hole in the wall a quarter the breadth of the hall within. Since I saw no bodies, Lord Gavain had presumably taken all his men to the upper storeys as I'd advised. Leaning my weary body against one of the supports for the well's windlass, I let myself slump at last and waited for the duke and his men— and my confessor, the prior, whose ear and absolution I so desperately needed now. If the Lord willed, I would neither faint nor die before they arrived.

Chapter Fifteen ~ Galoran

1

At first I thought he was dead. Melchior lay slumped across the well in the center of the courtyard. He was crowned with some sort of artifact made to suggest a crouching scorpion, which would have been ridiculous had it not glowed with its own terrible light. Where once the great gates of Peyrefixade had stood was nothing but ruin, from which smoke and dust still rose into the moonlit sky.

Thierri helped me hobble across the courtyard to him. Looking at the priest's motionless form I felt my loss as keenly as if it had been Bruno again. He had become not just my *capellanus*, or even the man who had repeatedly saved my life through his magic, but also my friend.

But as I approached his eyelids fluttered and his lips began to move. I had to go down on my knees and bend close to hear, and when I did I felt the same tingling that I had from his grandfather's telesma, except a hundred, a thousand times stronger. It was only then that I realized what the object on his head must be and knew that he had succeeded in finding the heretics' great battle telesma.

"Please, Count, take it off me," he gasped. "I must apologize for having destroyed so much of your castle. I have sinned deeply in shedding human blood, and I do not know what else the telesma might now do if I were to . . ."

His voice trailed off. I took a deep breath, glanced at

319

Thierri, who had taken several startled steps back, and
reached for the telesma. It seemed to weigh a hundred
pounds as I slowly lifted it, the forces within it buzzing
all up and down my arms. Melchior cried out as I took it
from his head, gestured wildly, then fell back limply. I
set it carefully on the flagstones, staring at it with awe.
The power within it seemed to be seething and stirring,
like a wild animal anxious to escape, heretic power imbued
with the evil mind of the old great Magus who had
commanded and concealed it.

Amid the rubble that had been the gatehouse there
suddenly appeared armed men. I reached desperately for
where my sword no longer was, then saw that it was Duke
Argave and his knights.

He crossed the courtyard in long strides, his cape tossed
back, then stopped. He looked from Melchior to me, at
the glowing scorpion shape of the battle telesma, and
around him at the ruined walls and empty courtyard. For
a long moment he said nothing, and his face, pale in the
moonlight, seemed as I watched to grow older and more
lined.

"Well, Count Galoran," he said at last, in what was clearly
meant to be his ordinary good humor but did not ring
true, "I would say that the two of you looked terrible,
but then your opposition must be even worse off, for I
do not see them at all! I should never have doubted you,
though I must say that if you'd told me you two were
going to retake the castle by yourselves, I would scarcely
have credited it." He seemed then to notice Thierri for
the first time. "Oh, I see you are here too, Lord Thierri.
What happened to your cloak? I missed you a short while
ago; if you were in at the end, observing, perhaps you
can tell me what happened, as these two heroes seem
little fit for speech."

Thierri squirmed, but the duke turned back to me. "We
found this as we were coming up the mountain, Count,
after we heard your horn blast and the roar of the walls

coming down. That must have been a feat like Samson's! At any rate, I would like to return it to you."

I peered at him, uncomprehending, then realized he had two swords at his belt. One he drew and presented to me, hilt first. It was the sword I had received from the emperor's hands, which I had last seen going over the wall in the body of the bouteillier.

"There doesn't seem to be any doubt that the traitor Raymbaud is now dead," the duke said dryly. "Is there any doubt about any of the other defenders?"

As I took back my sword with trembling fingers, Melchior roused himself enough to lift his head. "Most of the heretics are trapped on the upper floors of the keep, my lord, including their leader, Gavain. But there may well be a few others still loose in the castle."

"In the keep . . ." said the duke slowly. Others were hurrying up now, Prior Belthesar among them. He took one horrified look at the telesma, spoke a rapid series of words that seemed to lessen its evil glow, then bent over Melchior, murmuring either prayers or more incantations.

But I was watching Argave. All the years that had seemed to descend on him a minute before were gone as he straightened his back, his eyes flashing. "All right, then!" he snapped to the knights who had begun to gather around us. "Start an immediate search of the castle! Anyone you find, disarm and bring here."

"Excuse me, sire," I said with a slow smile. "This is, I believe, *my* castle, and my knights certainly know it better than yours."

He turned in surprise, then laughed and slapped me on the back. "Quite right, Count. You give the commands here. Once we're sure we've rounded up all the loose heretic scum," and as he spoke his expression began to darken again, "we can decide how to get the main force out of what's left of the keep." And he went off himself with the first expedition.

For the next hour knights scoured the castle, finding

and capturing half a dozen heretic warriors who had not made it into the keep with the rest, and gathering up the remains of the dead. I was impressed at what Brother Melchior must have done—I had killed but one man, while the priest evidently had killed a number, and quite horribly. Prior Belthesar insisted that Melchior be put to bed at once, and I sent the two off with several knights to guard them, making very sure the great battle telesma went along.

Arsendis was not among those now swarming through my castle. The duke, I gathered, had left her in the siege camp below, with half a dozen knights as guard. I wondered with mild curiosity if they were supposed to protect her from enemies or to prevent her from coming to join us in Peyrefixade.

I leaned, half dozing, against the windlass on top of the covered well, pushing back exhaustion at intervals to issue more commands or to hear reports. I would send a message to the Convent of the Holy Family in the morning, I decided, to tell my Great-aunt Richildis what I had learned of my cousin's death: certainly not an accident, but the result of the combination of the bouteillier wanting Peyrefixade empty and the seneschal wanting Lord Thierri dead. Since Seneschal Guilhem was dead now, too, I didn't want to implicate him in this, but I kept losing my concentration as I tried to determine how to explain all this delicately to the abbess. All that kept me awake was the throbbing of my leg and the stinging of the new burns on my face and hands. The moon was setting when Duke Argave came back.

"The castle is free of heretics now, Count," he said, "except for those in the keep." His expression was grim, and he seemed to be waiting for me to say something. When I did not immediately answer, he added, speaking carefully as though not wanting to give anything away, "The archbishop will doubtless arrive in the next three or four days. When he comes—" for a second Argave seemed to hesitate, then continued smoothly "—he will have the Inquisition with him."

Peyrefixade was my castle, and through the fog of pain and exhaustion I realized that the duke was confirming this. But if I did nothing about a nest of heretics still holed up in the central keep, heretics who included the duke's son, then Argave would be compelled to lead the attack himself.

"I am not," I said as clearly as I could, "going to allow the Inquisition to set up stakes in my courtyard at which to burn heretics to death. Let's see if we can talk to them."

The duke's men set up camp chairs in front of the keep and lit flambeaux on either side. Argave, with a powerful hand under my elbow, helped me from the well to a chair.

I looked through the gaping hole in the wall into what had once been my great hall and thought gloomily that I would need an army of masons to repair the damage Melchior and the Magus's battle telesma had done. Maybe the Order of the Three Kings, or my aunt, the abbess of the Holy Family, would be willing to lease or buy a piece of property from me for enough to pay for all that stonework.

But no use thinking about masonry until the castle was firmly in my hands again. I made myself sit up straight, cleared my throat, and shouted. My voice echoed around the courtyard. "Gavain, heretic and dog! You have one chance to parley for your life and those of your men. This is it."

There was a long pause during which I was afraid he would not answer. But then I heard his voice, a veneer of banter lying over the intense strain beneath. "You don't want to have to destroy the rest of your castle, is that it, Count? So you're trying to lure us out with soft words, instead?"

I couldn't see him, but he must be standing by one of the arrow slits on the second storey, from which one could command most of the courtyard. I realized with an itchy feeling that sitting here, torch-lit, the duke and I made excellent targets. Men who thought of themselves as already dead might well decide to take some of us with them to Hell. I glanced at Argave, but his face was expressionless as stone.

"You're not thinking this through, Gavain," I replied, trying to force my own brain to function. "You've lost. Raymbaud, who was supposed to infiltrate our plans and relay them all to you, is dead. We have the great telesma the Perfected have spent the last forty years hoping to recover. You may be safe from us for the moment, but only for the moment. Either we can bring down the keep— and you in it—with the same forces we already used to destroy the gates, or we can wait a few days and starve you out. You can't have more than a minimum of food and water up there with you; the keep's storerooms under the great hall are no longer accessible to you."

"You spoke of a parley, Count," came Gavain's voice out of the dark arrow slit. "But this sounds like boasting."

"Only making sure you understand your situation." I took a deep breath. "Now I'd like to tell you about mine."

"You have your problems, too, Count?" Gavain jeered. "Then I must offer my *sincere* condolences."

The duke at my elbow gave an angry mutter, but I refused to let myself be drawn. "As you have pointed out yourself, I have no desire to finish the destruction of my own castle, so the quick way to get you out of it is closed. And so, I'm afraid, is the slow way. Your damned Perfected beliefs probably make you think that dying in my keep of hunger and thirst would propel you straight into Heaven, but it won't be that simple. The Inquisition is on the way. In a few days, when you're too weak to offer resistance, we'll burrow through the stone you used to block the stairs inside the keep, or put the scaling ladders against the outside and pluck you out like apples from a tree. The inquisitors will give you a final chance to return to the True Faith, but most of you will be burned to death right here."

"I'm still waiting, Count, for you to tell me something I don't already know." The underlying strain in Gavain's voice was becoming stronger than the mocking note he was desperately trying to maintain.

"Then listen to this." There was still smoke in my lungs, and I had to stop and cough for a minute. The castle was perfectly still around me. "I have no intention of letting the inquisitors in to judge you. They may be upholders of the True Faith, but as long as I am Count of Peyrefixade I am the only one here who will pass sentences of life and death. If I sentence you to death myself, I either have to use the terrible destructive forces of magic to kill you immediately—which you cannot deny I have the ability to do—or else starve you out, by which time the inquisitors will be here, impossible to ignore as I value my own salvation. You leave me no alternative, Gavain. I sentence you to life."

Duke Argave jerked in his chair but did not speak. I heard indrawn breaths all around the courtyard but no word was spoken. Gavain waited thirty seconds before answering himself. "Life is given by God, Count. It is not something to which one man can sentence another."

I was suddenly sick of him and all his men, his supercilious tone, their pestilential beliefs, and especially their presence in my castle. "Then let me put it this way," I said roughly, "if you can't understand anything except in the plainest language. Get out. Right now, all of you, get out of my castle. You can even take your horses. I don't care where you go or what you do when you get there, as long as it's very far from Peyrefixade. Starting from right now you have seventy-two hours. No one will impede you, no one will pursue you. After seventy-two hours, you'd better be far away from here, because then the amnesty ends and Prince Alfonso and the Inquisition arrive."

As I spoke I realized I should probably have cleared this with the duke. I could declare an amnesty in my own county, but a lot of these mountains were under the duke's authority, not mine. But looking at him from the corner of my eye I did not think he would object.

"One condition," said Gavain.

"One condition!" I exploded. "I give you a chance to get out of here with your God-forsaken skin still attached to your God-forsaken rear end and you speak to me of conditions?!"

"I misspoke," he said, and for once he sounded deadly serious. "My men trust me, and if I come to an agreement on their behalf I have to be absolutely sure I am not leading them into destruction."

I nodded reluctantly; a good leader has to think of his men first. "If you're wondering if you can trust me, I give you my word before God that no harm shall come to you from me for seventy-two hours —a word I would not break even when given to a heretic." And I had already saved several heretics from the stake once; I hoped he remembered that, because I wasn't going to remind everyone on my own side about it.

"And I give you my word as well," rasped out the duke, so abruptly it made me jump.

Still Gavain did not agree. "That infidel Magian priest," he said at last. "Melchior. I have to talk to him."

On this point he would not budge. Telling him that Brother Melchior was too ill with mage-sickness to speak to anyone only made him more stubborn. When at last I agreed that Melchior would be brought out, we met heated objection from Prior Belthesar. I left the duke to deal with the prior, leaning my head on my hand and closing my eyes. Finally, over the prior's continuing protests, my knights brought Melchior down from his chambers and out into the courtyard.

Melchior had the battle telesma clutched to his chest. He managed to lift his head and smile at me groggily as the knights set down his litter.

"This is a disgraceful way to treat a priest devoted to

God's service," the prior said to me, low and angry, "one who nearly lost his life in serving you as well."

"How about the heretics' Magians?" asked the duke, with the hint of a sardonic smile. "Are they standing by serving Lord Gavain, in spite of their wounds suffered tonight?"

The prior looked surprised. "Did I not tell you? There are no other Magians in the castle but Melchior and myself. One of theirs is dead, and although there are traces that can be discerned in the lines of magic of the presence of another, that one has been gone from this castle for at least as long as you have been in it—and he took my shadow cloak with him."

"If you'd mentioned this earlier, Prior," said the duke with another half-smile, "the last hour would have been far easier, not wondering every minute if I should expect a blast of magic from the keep to knock me senseless. But I thought if Count Galoran can brazen it out, then I can, too."

I ignored them and turned back toward the keep. "Father Melchior is here, Gavain," I shouted. "I hope you aren't planning to add any *more* conditions to getting out of my keep—for example, that you get to take my treasure with you. The longer you delay, the closer the Inquisition will be on your tail."

I kept wishing I could see the duke's son, that he was not just a disembodied voice floating down from the keep. "Melchior!" he called. "You warned me in good faith to bring my men up here to save ourselves, and did not kill me when you could have. You may have rejected the way of Perfection for the infidel path that calls itself the 'True' Faith, but I believe I may still trust you."

"Though not trust me?" the duke rumbled. But he had not spoken loud enough for his words to carry, and he sat back again when I put a hand on his arm.

I could see in the torchlight Melchior struggling to sit up. He managed on the second try, the prior supporting him. "You may trust Count Galoran," he gasped. "Please,

Gavain, take your men and go. Otherwise I shall have to use the hideous magic of the battle telesma to destroy the keep, and I don't want to kill anyone else."

He had not spoken very loudly, but in the predawn stillness, with the moon down and the air chill, his voice echoed around the courtyard. "That's all I can say," he added, though I was not sure if he addressed Gavain or me, and collapsed back down. His eyes were shut and face gray as the prior had him whisked away again.

There was another long pause, during which I again had to fight off sleep. I had almost concluded that Gavain had decided not to trust me after all when there was sudden movement in the gaping hole that had once been the lower wall of my keep. The heretics were coming out.

The first came slowly and cautiously, swords ready, prepared either to fight or to race back inside. I gave a few quick commands, and my knights and many of the duke's hurried to form two lines, on either side of the direct path between the keep and the stables, then between the stables and the rubble of the gatehouse. There they leaned on their swords, thirty feet back on either hand from the column of heretics.

Watching them hurry into the stables and then out with their horses, I thought that they didn't look like practicers of demon worship and child sacrifice. They looked like frightened soldiers, a little embarrassed to be retreating but overwhelmingly glad to be escaping with their lives.

"Make sure there aren't any stragglers left with foolishly brave or suicidal notions," I told the duke, "and send the prisoners we captured off with the rest." I got Thierri to help me rise and hobble, and went off to a storeroom to fall at last into sleep.

2

Light had penetrated the storeroom window when I felt a hand on my shoulder. I rolled over on a pile of dusty wall-hangings, every part of my body in pain. It was the duke.

He squatted beside me, looking furious. At this point I scarcely cared how I might have offended my sworn lord, as long as the heretics were gone. I rubbed the grit from my eyes, coughed, and struggled to a sitting position.

But it was not me with whom he was furious. "We've got a problem," he growled. "Gavain won't leave."

I ran a hand over my close-scorched hair. "They were all leaving," I said, resisting the temptation to flop back down again and sleep for about three days. "He accepted the amnesty."

"And the rest are gone," said Argave, "skipping pretty nimbly down the road, too. But their war-leader"—I noted he had never referred to Gavain as "my son"—"has reblocked the stair in the keep and won't come out."

I looked at the duke from the corner of my eye. He appeared furious enough to put the scaling ladders up himself and go in single-handed to slay the one heretic left, son or no son, without even waiting for the Inquisition. "Did he happen to mention why?"

"He won't deign to talk to me," said Argave, frowning even more heavily. "My men and yours kept a close count of the heretics going out, and then they noticed that Gavain hadn't been among them. When they went to check the keep, they found him holed up again."

"I think I know why he's still there," I said, looking with mild interest at the wound a heretic's sword had put in my leg, up in the mountains. This was the leg I had wrenched last night, tearing the developing scar tissue away from the wound. It ached worse than ever this morning.

If things had worked out only slightly differently, it would have been I who failed, I who promised his men victory and found only humiliating defeat. If we had not regained Peyrefixade, I would have had to slink back north to my brother's castle, or try to catch up with the emperor to see if he might want an old campaigner in his entourage. Gavain had nowhere to slink.

But I didn't say this. "The heretics believe they can make their own salvation," I said instead, "that if they willingly cast off the comforts of the flesh then God will always reward them. Gavain could not recapture the battle telesma that the self-styled Perfected wanted to use to spread their despicable beliefs across the kingdom. But he thinks he can still make amends and purify his soul by dying."

Argave made a desperate attempt at sardonic humor. "I was going to take him apart with my bare hands. But if that's what he wants so badly perhaps I should reconsider."

I rubbed my eyes again, thinking hard. "That's no good, Argave," I said, choosing my words carefully. Gavain, I thought, would not have had a very good look at me last night, at some distance from him and lit only by flickering flambeaux. "I'd be happy to help you tear that trickster apart limb by limb, except that it would just incite the heretics to attack Peyrefixade again. Have someone saddle his horse and have it ready, and see if you can find me any decent clothing."

The duke scowled but went. Half an hour later I was washed and shaved and dressed in my own clothes again, the very clothes that Gavain had worn to impersonate me, which he had left in a chest in the undamaged part of the great hall. I sat amidst hangings my predecessor the countess had rejected, eating hot pancakes rolled with honey in the middle, cooked by my own cook, once again master of his kitchen. Feeling much better than I had any right to feel, I said to the duke and to Lord Thierri, "All right. Let's see if we can get me out into the courtyard without making it obvious I can't walk unaided."

The three of us linked arms, and I did my best, in spite of shooting pain, to put the weight on my bad leg as we went out across the courtyard. Gavain's horse was saddled and waiting—if I could just persuade him to emerge. The guards at the remains of the gate blew the horn, and I was fairly sure I saw a flicker of motion on an upper storey of the keep as I settled majestically into a camp chair.

"I hear you're in still in there, Gavain," I called. There was no answer, but I had not expected any, or not yet. "We had an agreement which I thought you'd accepted. All heretics out of my castle, in return for seventy-two hours during which nobody touches you. But those hours are disappearing fast."

There was still no reply, and I began to wonder if I was wasting my time. For a moment I was distracted by a commotion at the ruins of the gate and glanced over to see that a group of riders had arrived. It couldn't be the archbishop already! But then I turned back toward the keep, smiling inwardly. It looked instead as though the Lady Arsendis on her swift palfrey had eluded her guards and beaten them by a hair up to the castle.

Now I just hoped she had the sense to stay quiet. "All right, Gavain," I continued, shouting up toward my invisible audience, "I can see you're enjoying mocking me one more time. Planning to stay there until the Inquisition is actually within the gates, then tweak their noses and escape, is that it?"

I knew perfectly well that wasn't it, but I couldn't very well accuse him of intending to starve himself until his inevitable death arrived—not if I wanted him out alive.

"Don't you think my uncle the archbishop could use a little nose-tweaking?" a voice suddenly rang out from the keep.

I motioned to my knights, who had begun to murmur angrily. "As a son of the True Faith I can't possibly agree," I said sternly. But inwardly I was gleeful; if he was willing to answer me at all, this just might work. "I have a different proposition, Gavain, one on which we might be able to come to an understanding as knights and gentlemen, even if we cannot agree on religion."

"Are you planning to buy me off, Count?" he asked

with a mocking laugh. "Because if so, let me remind you that I captured your treasure chest and have it up here with me."

Better and better. So all my rent receipts hadn't been blown up along with much of the hall. I might be able to afford the masons yet without having to mortgage half my county. "Not at all," I said, making myself speak still more sternly. "And this is no matter for joking. Because I am challenging you to a fight to the death."

He clearly wondered whether to believe me. "I thought you would have gotten your fill of fights to the death yesterday," he said, but the bantering tone was unconvincing.

"Listen to my terms," I said loudly, ignoring the reactions of everyone around me, who had not expected this any more than Gavain had. "You and I in single combat, here in this courtyard, this morning, now." I twisted in the chair so that I could unsheath my sword smoothly. The Allemannic steel was nicked from its tumble down the mountainside; I made a mental note to have it sharpened this afternoon if I was still alive. But he wouldn't see the nicks from up in the keep, only the morning light flashing on the blade.

"Come now, wouldn't you like a chance to avenge yourself and your dead men on me? And I'd much prefer to kill you on my own terms than to wait for approval from the archbishop! If you win, you leave unmolested. I swear to you that no one but me shall harm you, and that I shall not back down from this fight. But if you yourself wish to back down and take advantage of my amnesty instead, well, that's all right, too." When he did not answer at once, I added, "Why hesitate, Gavain? You know my word is good."

I could almost hear his thoughts. If he could defeat and kill me, he could return to the heretics as a hero. If I defeated him, his death would be much faster than it would be at the hands of the Inquisition. I myself did not believe that a few days of fasting and self-purification could make up for a lifetime of sin, but even if I did, even if I did not know I had to rely on the completely undeserved mercy of God, I would never hesitate to take death in battle over death at the stake.

"How about your priest Melchior?" he called down. "Are you going to have him officiate at our fight?"

"Stop stalling, Gavain," I called back. "He's far too ill to leave his room again and far too much a man of God to take part in a duel. He told you to trust me. If you don't believe him now, why did you believe him last night?"

Still Gavain wouldn't agree. After another long pause he said, mocking once more, "This offer has appealing possibilities, but I'm afraid it's quite impossible. Your Magian priest shattered my sword last night. I am unable to fight you."

"A good sword will be provided you," I replied and turned to motion to one of the knights. But Duke Argave was ahead of me. He stalked forward, jaw clenched, unsheathing his own sword. The sun glinted on his emerald ring as he laid the sword before the ruined keep. For a moment I was afraid he would say something, but he turned, wordless, and stalked back to stand behind me again.

Then at last I could see Gavain's face, pressed into the arrow slit and glaring down. "Everybody else stay back!" he suddenly shouted, sounding as furious as his father. "This is just you and me, Galoran. As soon as everybody's out of the way I'm coming down."

Everyone backed off at my signal. It took several minutes for him to unblock the keep stairway and descend. But then he emerged, bright in chain mail, his helmet cradled in one arm and his shield slung over the other. He snatched up and sheathed his father's sword, then advanced to stand a few paces before me. "So slow in arming yourself, Galoran?" he said, mocking once more, though his eyes were taking in my burns and bruises. "Getting cold feet now that I've accepted your challenge?"

"I don't need armor," I said slowly, "for what I intend to do." And I heaved myself up by the arms of the chair, took one step, and pitched forward.

He pushed me with a toe until I rolled over and sat up. "What kind of trick is this?" he demanded in a low voice, half uneasy and half furious. He glanced behind him to see that my men had stationed themselves in front of the hole in the keep wall; there would be no retreating back there now.

"No trick," I said. "But you have stained my honor, Gavain." I just hoped the word "honor" still had resonances for him. "The only way I can recover it is to fight you and, I hope, kill you. Raymbaud would have told you I'm handy with a sword even when badly wounded. If you help me up I can hop. Once I have my balance you'd better defend yourself!"

He set down his helmet and pulled me to my one good foot with a jerk. For a moment we stood only inches apart, glaring into each other's eyes, his black and uptilted at the corners—just like his sister's. He still supported me with a hand at the elbow. The watching knights, thirty feet away, could have been in another county. "All a trick," he growled. "Your only purpose was to get me out of the keep. Now, if you but raise one hand, all your knights attack me at once."

"Put it to the test," I said, managing to stay upright this time even when he let go of my arm. "Run me through right now. I swore to you that I would not withdraw from this fight—or make it less than fair by having anyone but me try to kill you."

"Fair!" he snapped. "Dear God, Galoran, is it supposed to be fair for me to kill someone who can't even defend himself?"

"If it makes you feel better," I said, drawing my sword, "I'll take the first stroke at *you*."

He stepped back easily out of range but drew his own blade. "This," he said between his teeth, "is going to be the strangest fight—"

"Gavain!" a woman's voice suddenly rang out across the courtyard. "Don't hurt him!"

The heretic war-leader's sword suddenly darted out, and with one sharp blow he knocked my own blade from my hand. A blister had come up on the palm; I hadn't been able to hold the hilt very tightly anyway.

I staggered and closed my eyes for a second, then, when nothing happened, opened them again.

Gavain was laughing, his lips pulled back from his teeth in silent but apparently genuine mirth. "You tried to speak to me of your honor, Galoran," he said, "and yet you'll spend the rest of your life knowing you owe that life to a woman."

I let out all my breath at once.

"I haven't really seen my dear sister Arsendis for years, but that particular note in her voice hasn't changed since she was a little girl. It's the voice of someone who *really* knows what she wants. It's much too late ever to make it up to my father, but I still hope someday Arsendis and I might be friends again—and it would never happen if I had killed you."

"Then what are you going to do?" I asked when he did not seem about to do anything, instead standing with the point of his blade uncomfortably near my throat and my own sword under his foot.

"Take the amnesty you so *generously* offer," he answered at last, and now his voice was bitter.

I breathed an inward prayer of thanks and wondered if Gavain too was giving thanks to God—even if he and the rest of the heretics had completely misconstrued God's message. "You haven't lost," I said, speaking low and fast, hoping he was listening. "I know I told you last night that you had, but I just wanted to get your men out of my keep. In over forty years, no one had taken Peyrefixade, whether by assault, by siege, or by stratagem. You captured it, and you can sweeten your memories of Melchior and me capturing it from you by recalling that you took it

from me in the first place." I paused to make sure I had
his attention. "And though we now have the battle telesma,
we are *not* going to use it against you."

He had been looking off across the mountains, but at
this he turned sharply back toward me, eyebrows raised.
This, I thought, was probably something else I should
have first raised with the duke. For that matter, I should
have brought it up with the Magians, but for at least one
Magian—I knew what he'd say. "It's Melchior's—the priest
you seem to trust more than me. He doesn't want it to
be used again to kill—either followers of the True Faith
or even heretics—and neither does his Order. It will be
hidden again, somewhere you'll *never* find it this time,
but you need not fear to see the scorpion crown coming
to blast your mountain settlements." I smiled for the first
time in what seemed an extremely long time. "You will
live to fight again, Gavain."

He laughed then, still with an edge of bitterness but
only an edge. "Then don't let yourself get too soft, Count,
dancing attendance at court and doing whatever my father's
whim demands. You're a younger son, aren't you? Well,
you should have plenty of experience being the obedient
and dutiful son, rather than emulating Lucifer, God's
rebellious older son. Practice your swordsmanship against
my coming!" He snatched up his helmet and was off,
running across the courtyard. I signaled frantically, making
sure no one would try to stop him. He swung up onto his
stallion, then for just a moment he paused, halfway over
the rubble at the castle entrance. Then he saluted his
sister with their father's sword and was gone.

The duke's physician-surgeon declared I had done new
damage to my leg and ordered me straight into bed. Duke
Argave had his servants carry me into what was left of
my great hall and place me on my own great bed. There
he left me with my knights about me, and took himself,
his own knights, and his daughter back down to the siege

camp. Only then could I be sure at last that he really intended to leave Peyrefixade in my hands. Gavain had doubtless been sleeping in my sheets, but at this point I didn't care. I was smiling as sleep claimed me.

When I awoke again in late afternoon I was pleased to discover that the knights and servants had already begun the job of cleaning up the devastation. But several were waiting when I opened my eyes to ask me something trivial, and I realized I was going to have to give the household orders myself for a while, since I now had neither a bouteillier nor a seneschal. The cook, in spite of his despair over the state of his storerooms and kitchen, somehow rallied to produce a simple but hearty stew. As evening came on, some of the servants improvised a kind of curtain stitched from the wornout hangings the countess had rejected and strung it across the gaping hole where the doors had been. The place might be half in ruins, but I was count in my own castle once more.

As I sat in the windowseat gnawing a slightly stale loaf the next morning, Prior Belthesar swept into the hall and made a very minimal obeisance. "Brother Melchior requests me to say he would like to speak to you, Count," he declared, looking as if he would have preferred not to have Melchior disturbed at all. "But make sure you do not tire him! He has serious mage-sickness and needs to build up his strength so that we can take him back to our Mother House, where the Brother Infirmerian can tend to him properly. He's being very stubborn about going, so please do not encourage his obstinacy!"

I called for the burliest of my knights, and by hooking one arm over his shoulder managed, without doing any further injury to my leg, to hop to the chamber where Melchior was being attended by the prior's servants. He looked even worse than I probably did, ashen-faced, with dark bags under his eyes and a weird, faint translucence to his skin. But he smiled as the knight helped me onto a stool at his bedside.

"I heard what you did with Gavain," he told me in a weak voice. "It was both brave and wise."

"Brave, perhaps. I don't know about wise. Foolhardy maybe."

"No, wise. The True Faith teaches that we do not have the unaided strength to win the greatest prizes. We attain them by facing that which opposes us even though we know we are far weaker."

"Still acting as my spiritual advisor, Father Melchior?"

"I would certainly like to, if you still wish to have me after I've destroyed the castle that was your treasure and pride."

"Of course I want you back!" I caught a glimpse of Prior Belthesar frowning from the door. "But *only* when you are fully recovered. And my castle is not all destroyed, as you can see from the fact that you are lying here in your own bed! But for now you must go back to your Order and recover your strength. We'll be all right here; I presume even that scruffy priest from the village can sing a valid office in the chapel. Besides, I'm too immobile and the men will be far too busy for much sinning!"

"I can recover here, Count—" I cut him off as I saw the prior frown again and shake his head.

"No, no, Father Melchior, I won't hear of it." He started to protest again, but I had an unanswerable argument. "Think of the great battle telesma. I want that devilish thing out of this castle as soon as possible! You don't think I'll trust the other Magians to get it safely stowed within the House of the Three Kings unless you are with them, do you? A good war-captain wants each soldier under his command to be where he can function best, you know. You say your task is to serve me; well then, these are your orders. Just you make sure you get your tonsured head back here again right away as soon as you're well! You're the only *capellanus* I want at Peyrefixade."

A smile slowly spread over Melchior's weary face, and he murmured, "Yes sir, Captain." At the door, the prior smiled, too. I squeezed Melchior on the arm, asked him for his blessing, and left the room leaning on my knight. I hoped he recovered and returned to us soon. Peyrefixade needed him.

Arsendis and I stood at the top of the great tower two days later, looking out across the mountains. Higher peaks, still touched with snow, frowned down on Peyrefixade, but the valleys below us were verdant. The shadows rose and dipped over the slopes as clouds raced across the sky high above. Six months ago, I had been sitting in my brother's castle as bitter winter closed in, with nothing of my own and no future. Now early summer breezes played around my own castle, and, even if the beautiful woman beside me might ultimately decline to marry a man both scarred and crippled, at the moment she seemed happy to be with me.

"I have been eager to ask you this, Count," the duke's daughter said, glancing at me sideways from dark eyes. "How did you know when you challenged my brother, and went to meet him though too weak to fight, that he would not kill you?"

"I didn't."

My words hung for a moment while she turned to stare at me. "You went to meet him thinking he might slay you on the spot?"

"There was always that possibility. I could have died unshriven in my own courtyard." I had a crutch now and was getting better at maneuvering. With luck I would be able to walk again in a week or two, although a slight limp would be permanent. I now turned to lean my back and elbows against the parapet. "I did however hope that his youthful training and knightly courtesy would be too strong for him to kill a defenseless man, even his enemy—and I was right. Sometimes one has to take desperate risks to get what one wants, which means that sometimes one fails."

"I think Father was very pleased," she said after a minute, "though he refuses to say so. It's harder to say what Uncle's opinion will be, when he arrives with the Inquisition to learn that his nephew is safe but a whole coven of heretics have been allowed to escape."

"I assume that's why your father is in such a hurry to leave," I said, "so that he may intercept the archbishop in his own ducal court and explain the situation to him at greater leisure."

She nodded. "We depart within the half hour. But tell me, Count, if it is not too secret: what will happen to the battle telesma?"

"It's not really secret," I said with a smile, "though I'd recommend you not discuss it with your brother if you happen to see him again. It's leaving today, too, secured under powerful spells in a leaden casket, to travel to the House of the Three Kings. The Magians will lock it away there and guard it, lest anyone else be tempted to use its awesome powers. The archbishop might want to commandeer it for the church hierarchy, but it will be hard for him to do so if it's already gone, and it would be even harder for him to argue that the best place for it wasn't among the Magians. It will travel heavily guarded, but the telesma itself, accompanied by two priests of the Order, should be able to guard itself."

Arsendis seemed about to speak but instead just looked again out toward the highest mountains. Down in the courtyard, I heard a horn blowing and knew that the duke was assembling his men for departure. She turned with a swirl of her scarlet cloak to go, but then paused at the top of the stairs, smiling back over her shoulder. "The view from your castle is most pleasing, Count. Thank you for showing it to me at last. I can well understand how you—or anyone—would enjoy the prospect of living here permanently."

ABOUT THE AUTHORS

C. Dale Brittain and Robert A. Bouchard have both been writing stories since they were six years old. True love bloomed on their first date when they told each other about the fantasy tales each was working on. For over twenty-five years they have read and commented on everything the other wrote, from fiction to scholarly articles to their doctoral dissertations—both are academics, Dale a medieval historian and Robert a molecular geneticist. When Dale came up with the ideas and characters that turned into *A Bad Spell in Yurt*, it was Robert who encouraged her and provided feedback and story-conferences as she polished what became her first published novel. *Count Scar*, however, is the first book they have actually written jointly. "People tell us if our marriage can survive a project like this," they comment, "it can last through anything!"

You can write to the authors c/o Baen Books, or at their e-mail address, Bouchard@bright.net.

Paksenarrion, a simple sheepfarmer's daughter, yearns for a life of adventure and glory, such as the heroes in songs and story. At age seventeen she runs away from home to join a mercenary company, and begins her epic life . . .

ELIZABETH MOON

THE DEED OF PAKSENARRION

"This is the first work of high heroic fantasy I've seen, that has taken the work of Tolkien, assimilated it totally and deeply and absolutely, and produced something altogether new and yet incontestably based on the master. . . . This is the real thing. Worldbuilding in the grand tradition, background thought out to the last detail, by someone who knows absolutely whereof she speaks. . . . Her military knowledge is impressive, her picture of life in a mercenary company most convincing."—**Judith Tarr**

About the author: Elizabeth Moon joined the U.S. Marine Corps in 1968 and completed both Officers Candidate School and Basic School, reaching the rank of 1st Lieutenant during active duty. Her background in military training and discipline imbue The Deed of Paksenarrion with a gritty realism that is all too rare in most current fantasy.

"I thoroughly enjoyed *Deed of Paksenarrion*. A most engrossing highly readable work."

—**Anne McCaffrey**

"For once the promises are borne out. *Sheepfarmer's Daughter* is an advance in realism. . . . I can only say that I eagerly await whatever Elizabeth Moon chooses to write next."

—Taras Wolansky, *Lan's Lantern*

* * * * *

Volume One: Sheepfarmer's Daughter—Paks is trained as a mercenary, blooded, and introduced to the life of a soldier . . . and to the followers of Gird, the soldier's god.

Volume Two: Divided Allegiance—Paks leaves the Duke's company to follow the path of Gird alone—and on her lonely quests encounters the other sentient races of her world.

Volume Three: Oath of Gold—Paks the warrior must learn to live with Paks the human. She undertakes a holy quest for a lost elven prince that brings the gods' wrath down on her and tests her very limits.

* * * * *

These books are available at your local bookstore, or you can fill out the coupon and return it to Baen Books, at the address below.

To Read About
Great Characters Having
Incredible Adventures
You Should Try 👉 👉 👉

BAEN

IF YOU LIKE . . .	YOU SHOULD TRY . . .
Anne McCaffrey . . .	Elizabeth Moon
	Mercedes Lackey
	Margaret Ball
Marion Zimmer Bradley . . .	Mercedes Lackey
	Holly Lisle
Mercedes Lackey . . .	Holly Lisle
	Josepha Sherman
	Ellen Guon
	Mark Shepherd
J.R.R. Tolkien . . .	Elizabeth Moon
David Drake . . .	David Weber
	S.M. Stirling
Robert A. Heinlein . . .	Jerry Pournelle
	Lois McMaster Bujold